"He drew some t
they were depos........, ... began to
illuminate them from his own. The red
glare of the torches flashed fearfully on the
massive walls of the Pyramid, throwing part
of their enormous masses into deep shadow,
as they rose in solemn and sublime dignity
around, and seemed frowning upon the
presumptuous mortals who had dared to
invade their recesses, whilst the deep pit
beneath their feet seemed to yawn wide to
engulf them in its abyss.

"Edric's heart beat thick: it throbbed till he
even fancied its pulsations audible; and a
strange, mysterious thrilling of anxiety,
mingled with a wild, undefinable delight,
ran through his frame. A few short hours,
and his wishes would be gratified, or set at
rest for ever…"

—from *The Mummy*
by Jane Webb Loudon

Ancient Egyptian Supernatural Tales

Edited & Introduced
by Jonathan E. Lewis

STARK
HOUSE

Stark House Press • Eureka California

ANCIENT EGYPTIAN SUPERNATURAL TALES

Published by Stark House Press
1315 H Street
Eureka, CA 95501, USA
griffinskye3@sbcglobal.net
www.starkhousepress.com

ISBN: 1-944520-05-8
ISBN-13: 978-1-944520-05-2

Book design by Mark Shepard, shepgraphics.com
Cover illustration and design by JT Lindroos, jtlindroos.carbonmade.com

First Stark House Press Edition: July 2016

FIRST EDITION

Table of Contents

Introduction

At first glance, New Haven, a small urban center not far from where I was born, may not seem like the logical place to begin an anthology of ancient Egyptian supernatural tales. After all, the city where Yale University is located is geographically a world away from the land of the pharaohs. Even so, the distant Egyptian past casts long shadows over the Connecticut port city, something brought further to light at an exhibit I attended several years ago at the Peabody Museum. Entitled "Echoes of Egypt," the temporary exhibition was an enduring reminder of how strong the American fascination with ancient Egypt continues to be. Furthermore, a short drive just north of Yale's campus will take a visitor to the Grove Street Cemetery, which was the first chartered burial ground in the United States. It is there that ancient Egypt's indelible imprint on the New England imagination is most keenly felt, for standing at the Grove Street entrance is a brownstone gateway, or pylon, built in the Egyptian Revival style. Designed by Henry Austin, a prominent New Haven architect, and completed in 1845, the gate entrance looks like an Egyptian temple. Adding to the mystical allure of the place is the phrase taken from Corinthians, "The Dead Shall Be Raised." Standard words one might expect to find in a cemetery.

Yet, understood within the context of nineteenth-century New England's fascination with ancient Egypt, the gateway and its invocation of resurrection take on a larger meaning. Indeed, much like the pylon in New Haven, literature itself has served as a portal for a reading public intrigued by the ancient Egyptian past and its mysteries. After all, it was an author from Massachusetts, Louisa May Alcott, who wrote, "Lost in the Pyramids, or the Mummy's Curse" (1869) one of the earliest mummy curse stories ever put to paper. Edgar Allan Poe, while not a New Englander, also did his part to invoke the specter of ancient Egypt in American letters. Poe's satirical tale, "Some Words With a Mummy" (1845), which appears in this anthology, is one of the most widely reprinted mummy stories and rightly so, for it remains as trenchant and poignant today as it must have been nearly two hundred years ago.

Across the pond, British and Irish authors also penned numerous novels and short stories in which ancient Egyptian themes played dominant roles. Among them are Jane Webb Loudon's *The Mummy* (1827); G.A. Henty's children's book, *The Cat of Bubastes* (1888); and Bram Stoker's *The Jewel of Seven Stars* (1903). Writers such as Algernon Blackwood, Arthur Conan

Doyle, H. Rider Haggard, and Sax Rohmer, names familiar to fans of mystery and supernatural fiction, all wrote stories that are essential reading for anyone interested in the development of the ancient Egyptian supernatural tale. Works by each of the aforementioned authors, with the exception of Henty, appear in this collection.

Twentieth-century American pulp fiction writers also found much to value in ancient Egypt and often incorporated mummies, curses, and antiquity museums into their stories. One such writer, a teenager by the name of Thomas Lanier Williams wrote an extraordinarily vivid account of Queen Nitocris for *Weird Tales*. Entitled "The Vengeance of Nitocris" (1928), that story, reprinted in this anthology, was Williams's only contribution to the famed pulp magazine. That young author, however, would go on to enormous critical and public acclaim as a playwright under the name Tennessee Williams.

Another author who wrote an ancient Egyptian themed story for *Weird Tales* was the prolific pulp writer E. Hoffmann Price, an author perhaps best known for his work in postwar science fiction. His "Tarbis of the Lake," (1934), a Gothic tale set in France which has been reprinted only once before, appears in this collection for a new generation to appreciate. Similarly, I have also included Frank Belknap Long's sublimely weird, "The Dog-Eared God" (1926) and John Murray Reynolds's haunting, "The Soul of Ra-Moses" (1940). While neither story is objectively of a particularly high literary quality, both remain representative of the types of ancient Egyptian supernatural stories to appear in the pages of *Weird Tales* and other pulps.

Reading through these tales, as well as others that I have chosen to include in this anthology, one begins to notice that there are several important themes that appear in many of them, so much so that I contend that the ancient Egyptian supernatural tale should be considered a proper subgenre of proto-weird and weird fiction and appreciated as an equally important subgenre as the vampire tale or the ghost story.

It is my contention that the tropes that have come to define the ancient Egyptian supernatural tale subgenre are best understood in terms of tension, a literary effect that propels the short story forward to a climatic conclusion. Understood in dialectical terms, these include, but are not limited to the following: (1) fascination with the past/fear of disturbing it; (2) superstition/rationality; (3) persistence of the ancient past/the emergence of the modern world; (4) time/timelessness; (5) the human as a biological, flesh and blood being/the human spirit; (6) the quest for knowledge/the fear of acquiring too much knowledge; (7) ancient Egypt as a specific time and place/ancient Egypt as transcending the laws and limitations of time and space; and (8) mysticism/science.

Aside from these aforementioned thematic elements, one may also consider

the ancient Egyptian supernatural tale to reflect the ongoing tension between the pre-modern and the modern, and as an overall reflection of modernity's cultural and political uncertainties. All of the stories included in this anthology were originally published between the late 1820s and the 1940s, a
period of time in which the traditional political institutions of Europe dissi-
pated and were replaced with new, often even more terrifying ones. Likewise,
this period in the United States and Great Britain witnessed the gradual decline of the agricultural sector and small towns, and the emergence of large,
industrial centers. Scientific discoveries, often appearing at a rapid rate, dis-
placed prior superstitious beliefs. Modern medicine and the social sciences
sought to explain human biology and social relations in rational, scientific
terms. Furthermore, the emergence of archaeology and history as academic
disciplines taught in modern universities led scholars to understand the past
in objective, rational terms. It is against this backdrop that one can best appreciate the ancient Egyptian supernatural tale as an act of literary rebellion,
a subversive take on the supposed march of human progress to a glorious, rational future. Indeed, the notion of the distant, mysterious past rudely intruding upon the modern world is a hallmark of the ancient Egyptian supernatural tale.

It should be noted, however, that many of the authors of the stories included
here were writing for the general reading public and as such, their stories are
works of popular fiction with characters who demonstrate high degrees of
agency in their actions. Indeed, protagonists in the ancient Egyptian supernatural tale subgenre tend to make bad decisions, ones that often lead directly
to tragic outcomes, but they do so out of free will. Sometimes love propels
them into danger and at other times, a zealous quest for knowledge leads them
astray. Desires and passions overwhelm the characters, propelling them forward at lightning speed to realms, both geographic and psychological, in
which they must confront forces beyond their control. As such, the ancient
Egyptian supernatural tale can be considered as both character and plot
driven stories, with protagonists making constrained choices in extraordinary
situations. The protagonists in ancient Egyptian supernatural tales aren't
cursed in the way in which characters bitten by vampires or werewolves are
cursed. Their flaws are all too human, so much so that many of the stories in
this anthology can properly be considered tragedies, in the classical sense, as
well as horror stories.

Choosing to include stories in any collection inevitably means leaving
some very good stories out. That's just an unfortunate fact when editing an
anthology such as this and shouldn't be construed to mean that there aren't
other great stories well worth reading. For those interested individuals, I have
included a "Notes for Further Reading" at the end of this work as well as a

brief list of secondary literature that I found immensely useful in helping me appreciate the cultural context in which these stories were written.

Before we turn to the stories themselves, I'd like to address two matters. First, while I believe that it's extraordinarily important to consider the themes and moral issues raised in each of the stories, it's also fundamental that a reader approach the stories assembled here as they were meant to be read, namely as fun, escapist fiction designed to thrill and to entertain. Second, and more importantly, is that I could not have completed this anthology alone. Editing and writing is often a solitary process and it helps to know that there are people who appreciate the work necessary to complete a multi-author project such as this.

Special thanks goes to my mother, Judith Lewis, for always believing in me and in my writing abilities. I'll never forget when we saw the Rosetta Stone together at the British Museum in London, and I know how proud she is that I was able to finish this work. Thanks also go to my father, Stephen Lewis, who runs the Mystery*File blog, for proofreading my work and for helping me acquire some of the books I needed to complete this project. Mike Ashley, editor of many great anthologies, was invaluable in helping me track down copyright claims. He took a lot of time out of his schedule to reply to my frequent inquiries and to correspond with me via email. Thanks also go to S.T. Joshi, Jerad Walters, and Bill Pronzini whose anthology, *Mummy!* (1980), further inspired my decision to pursue this project. My thanks also go out to Bud Webster and Bob Weinberg, two men who have contributed immensely to the preservation of weird fiction. Finally, thanks to Greg Shepard and Stark House Press for supporting my project from the start.

It is my hope that these stories collected here will inspire a new generation to appreciate the mysteries and wonders of ancient Egypt, much as I did as an adolescent and continue to do as an adult. Likewise, I hope that after reading this volume, readers will readily acknowledge that the ancient Egyptian supernatural tale, while not nearly as famous or dare I say, infamous, as the vampire or zombie story, is an equally important subgenre of weird fiction well worth serious consideration by fans and scholars alike.

So, without further ado, let us journey together through a literary portal, and make our way down the Nile, through the dusty streets of Cairo, deep into the pyramids, and into the mysterious ancient Egyptian past.

Jonathan E. Lewis
Connecticut / Los Angeles 2015

Part I: The Genre's Origins

The Mummy
by Jane Webb Loudon

The first entry in this anthology is an excerpt from Jane Webb Loudon's 1827 Gothic novel, The Mummy: A Tale of the Twenty-Second Century. *Arguably the first mummy novel ever penned in the English language, Loudon's lengthy work blends political allegory with supernatural elements into an early and highly imaginative work of fantastic fiction. Written while she was still a teenager, this work demonstrates a precocious mind at work.*

Unlike most of the stories collected in this volume, the excerpt presented here, Volume I, Chapter IX is set chronologically in a science fiction future. Two characters travel from England to Egypt where they utilize an advanced technological device to revive the mummy Cheops from the dead. Although not overly long, this particular chapter contains numerous tropes that would show up time and again in ancient Egyptian supernatural tales written by Englishmen and Americans alike: the timelessness of the pyramids, the notion of "supernatural dread," and the idea that it was an act of sacrilege to disturb the dead. Although not nearly as well known as Mary Shelley's Frankenstein *(1818) or Bram Stoker's* Dracula *(1897), Loudon's proto-weird novel is, in many ways, the closest thing to a founding myth for the mummy horror story. With that in mind, it is well past time to excavate her important contribution to the development of the ancient Egyptian supernatural tale for a new generation of readers.*

Chapter IX

No event of any importance occurred to our travellers in the course of their aerial voyage. They were too well provided with all kinds of necessaries to have any occasion to rest by the way, and in an incredibly short space of time they were hovering over Egypt. Different, however, oh! how different from the Egypt of the nineteenth century, was the fertile country which now lay like a map beneath their feet. Improvement had turned her gigantic steps towards its once deserted plains; Commerce had waved her magic wand; and towns and cities, manufactories and canals, spread in all directions. No more did the Nile overflow its banks: a thousand channels were cut to receive its waters. No longer did the moving sands of the Desert rise in mighty waves, threat-

ening to overwhelm the wayworn traveller: macadamized turnpike roads supplied their place, over which postchaises, with anti-attritioned wheels, bowled
at the rate of fifteen miles an hour. Steamboats glided down the canals, and
furnaces raised their smoky heads amidst groves of palm trees; whilst iron rail-
ways intersected orange groves, and plantations of dates and pomegranates
might be seen bordering excavations intended for coal pits. Colonies of English and Americans peopled the country, and produced a population that
swarmed like bees over the land, and surpassed in numbers even the wondrous throngs of the ancient Mizraim race; whilst industry and science
changed desolation into plenty, and had converted barren plains into fertile
kingdoms.

Amidst all these revolutions, however, the Pyramids still raised their gigantic forms, towering to the sky; unchanged, unchangeable, grand, simple,
and immovable, fit symbols of that majestic nature they were intended to represent, and seeming to look down with contempt upon the ephemeral structures with which they were surrounded; as though they would have said, had
utterance been permitted to them– "Avaunt, ye nothings of the day! Respect
our dignity and sink into your original obscurity; for, know that we alone are
monarchs of the plains." Indestructible, however, as they had proved themselves, even their granite sides had not been able entirely to resist the erod-
ing influence of the smoke with which they were now surrounded, and a slight
crumbling announced the first outward symptom of decay. Still, however,
though blackened and disfigured, they shone stupendous monuments of former greatness; and Edric and his tutor gazed upon them with an awe that for
some moments deprived them of utterance.

The doctor, however, who was too fond of reasoning ever long to remain
willingly silent, after surveying them a few minutes, broke forth as follows:
– "What noble piles! What majesty and grandeur they display in their for-
mation, and yet what dignified simplicity! Can the imagination of man conceive any thing more sublime than the thought that they have stood thus,
frowning in awful magnificence, perhaps since the very creation of the world,
without equals, without even competitors, – mocking the feeble efforts of man
to divine their origin, and seeing generation after generation pass away, whilst
they still remain immutable, and involved in the same deep and unfath-
omable mystery as at first."

"It is very strange," observed Edric, "that, in this age of speculation and discovery, no thing certain should be known concerning them."

"It is," returned the doctor: "but the thick mysterious veil that has rested
upon them for so many ages, seems not intended to be removed by mortal
hands. They remind one of the sublime inscription upon the temple of the
goddess Isis, at Sais:– 'I am whatever was, whatever is, and whatever shall be;

but no mortal has, as yet, presumed to raise the veil that covers me.'"

"Your quotation is apt, doctor," resumed Edric, "for both relate to Nature. Indeed, Nature appears to be the deity which the ancient Egyptians worshipped, under all the various forms in which she presents herself; and their strange and animal deities were but reverenced as her symbols. It was Nature which they worshipped as Isis; it was Nature that was typified in the Pyramids: and the good taste of the Egyptians made them prefer the simple, the majestic, and the sublime, in those works which they destined to last for ages. Formerly, from the immensity of their population, and high state of their civilization, labour was so divided, and consequently so lightened, that multitudes were enabled to exist exempt from toil. These persons, devoting themselves to study, became *initiati*; and either enrolled themselves amongst the priesthood, or passed their lives in making themselves masters of the most abstract sciences. The consequences were natural: they followed up the ramifications of creation to their original source; they penetrated into the most profound secrets of Nature, and traced all her wonders in her works: aware, however, of the taste of the vulgar for any thing above their comprehension, and of the natural craving of the human mind for mystery, they wrapped the discoveries they had made in a deep impenetrable veil, and concealed awful and sublime significations under the meanest and most disgusting images."

"You are right," said the doctor, "in your observations upon the religion of the ancient

Egyptians; but it does not appear to me that the Pyramids were erected by them."

"What! I suppose you draw your conclusions from the want of hieroglyphics in their principal chambers; and, from what Herodotus says of their having been erected by a shepherd, you think they were the work of the Pallic race."

"No; though I allow much may be said in favour of that hypothesis, particularly as Herodotus says the kings under whom they were erected, ordered all the Egyptian temples to be closed, which we know the shepherd or Pallic sovereigns did; but I cannot imagine that an ignorant, Goth-like race of shepherds, men accustomed to live in tents or in the open air, and possessing no talents but for war, were capable of constructing such immense piles. No, no, the Pyramids required gigantic conceptions, highly cultivated minds, and unwearied perseverance; all qualities quite incompatible with a warlike wandering race. I do not think the Palli were capable of imagining such structures, much less of constructing them. I think they were the work of evil spirits."

"Evil spirits!" exclaimed Edric.

"Yes," returned the doctor. "We are told that the evil spirits, after their expulsion from Paradise, were under the command of the Sultan, or Soliman Giam ben Giam, as he is called by Arabic writers, but who is supposed to have been the same as Cheops; and I think that he employed them in this vast work."

"I do not know by what analysis etymologists can draw the name of Cheops from that of Giam ben Giam: but, supposing the fact to be correct, that they designated the same person, I think it only proves more strongly my hypothesis; for the Palli came from Mount Caucasus where the evil spirits were said to have been enchained, and if Cheops was a Pallic king, it is possible the Egyptians might poetically call their conquerors evil spirits."

"That is a good idea, Edric; though I do not think it by any means certain that Cheops was a Pallic king. However, we shall soon be able to see his tomb, and judge for ourselves; for we have now approached near enough to the Pyramids to descend. Foh! what a smoke and what a noise! It is enough to rouse the mummies from their slumbers before their appointed time, and without the aid of galvanism. Have you opened the valves, Edric? Oh yes! I perceive we are getting lower; we will not lose a moment before we visit the Pyramid. But what a crowd of brutes are assembled to witness our arrival! they stare as though they had never seen a balloon before. Egypt is certainly a fine country, but the inhabitants are a century behind us in civilization."

An immense crowd had gathered together to witness the descent of our travellers, and they did indeed stand staring, lost in stupid astonishment at the strange sight that presented itself; for though the Egyptian people had occasionally seen balloons, they had never before beheld one made of Indian rubber. The odd figure of the doctor, too, amused them exceedingly, as he sat wrapt up in the most dignified manner in an asbestos cloak, his bob-wig pushed a little on one side from the heat of the weather and the warmth of his argument; his round, red, oily face attempting to look solemn, and his little fat, punchy figure trying to assume an air of majesty. The Egyptians were amazingly struck with this apparition, and being, like most colonists, somewhat conceited and not very ceremonious in their manners, they looked at him a few minutes in silence, and then burst into immoderate fits of laughter.

The doctor was exceedingly indignant at this rude reception, and rising, shook his fist at them in anger; a manoeuvre that only redoubled the mirth of the unpolished Egyptians, whose peals of laughter now became so tremendous, that they actually shook the skies, and occasioned a most unpleasant vibration in the balloon. Edric, who was almost as much annoyed as the doctor, had yet sufficient self-command to continue calmly making preparations for his descent; and without taking the least notice of the crowd below, he screwed the top upon the propelling vapour-bottle; he let the inflammable air escape from the balloon, which rapidly collapsed as they approached the earth,

and throwing out their patent spring grappling irons, they caught one of the
lower stones of the Great Pyramid, and in a few moments the car in which our
travellers were sitting, was safely moored at a convenient distance from the
earth for them to alight. Edric now unloosed the descending ladder, and rev-
erentially assisted the doctor, who was encumbered with his long cloak, to
reach terra firma in safety, – amidst the bustle and exclamations of the crowd,
who thronged round them expressing their wonder and astonishment audibly, in broad English.

"Where the deuce did this spring from?" cried one; "the car would load a
waggon!"

"And what is gone with the balloon?" said another; "it is clean vanished!"

"Well, I never saw such a thing in all my life before!" exclaimed a third; "I
think they must be come from the moon."

"Hush! hush," cried an old gentleman bustling amongst them, who seemed
as one having authority. "What's the matter? what's the matter?"

"We are strangers, Sir," said Earle, advancing and addressing him: "we
come here to see the wonders of your country, and we wish to explore the Pyramids – but the reception we have met with –"

"Say no more – say no more!" interrupted the worthy justice, for such he
was. "Get about your business, you rapscallions, or I'll read the riot act! Here,
Gregory, call out the *posse comitatus*, and set a guard of constables to keep
watch over these gentlemen's balloon, whilst they go to explore the Pyramids.
Eh! but where is the balloon? I don't see it. I hope neither of the gentlemen
has put it in his pocket!" laughing at his own wit.

"No, Sir," returned Edric, smiling, "though it is a feat which might easily
be accomplished, for that is our balloon," pointing to the caoutchouc bottle,
now shrunk to its original dimensions.

"Very strange, that!" said the Justice; "Very curious, very curious indeed!
Well, gentlemen, if you wish to proceed immediately, you'll want a guide of
course. These cottages at the foot of the Pyramids are all inhabited by guides,
who get their living by showing the sights. They are sad rogues, most of them,
but I can recommend you to one who is a very honest man. Here, Samuel,"
continued he, knocking against a small door, "Samuel, I say!"

Samuel made his appearance, in the guise of a tall, raw-boned, stupid-look-
ing fellow, with a pair of immensely broad stooping shoulders, which looked
as though he could have relieved Atlas occasionally of his burthen, without
much trouble to himself. Coming forth from his hut in an awkward shambling
pace, he scratched his head, and demanded what his honour pleased to want.

"You must show these gentlemen the Pyramids," said the Justice.

"Ay, that I will with pleasure!" returned Samuel; "I've got my living by
showing them these fifty years, man and boy; and I know every crink and

cranny of them, though I'm old now and somewhat lame. So walk this way, gentlemen."

"We are very much obliged to you, Sir," said the doctor, bowing to the Justice; who was in fact one of those good-natured, busy, bustling men, who are always better pleased to transact any other person's business than their own; and are never so happy as when a new arrival gives them an opportunity of showing off their consequence. Indeed, there is a pleasure in showing wonders to a stranger, that only those who have little else to occupy their minds can properly estimate: a man of this kind feels his self-love gratified by the superiority his local knowledge gives him over a stranger; and, as it is, perhaps, the only chance he ever can have of showing superiority, they must be unreasonable who blame him for making the most of it. Justice Freemantle was accordingly exceedingly delighted with travellers who seemed disposed to submit implicitly to his dictation; and he returned a most gracious reply to the doctor's thanks.

"Don't mention it! don't mention it, my dear Sir!" said he; "I am never so happy as when I can make myself useful. Is there any thing else I can do for you? You may command me, I assure you; and you may depend upon it, no injury shall be done to your luggage, whilst you are away."

"What a very civil, obliging, good-natured old gentleman!" said the doctor, as they walked towards the entrance of the Pyramids; "I declare he almost reconciles me to the country, though, I own, I thought at first the people were the greatest brutes I had ever met with."

"Which Pyramid does your honour wish to see?" asked the guide.

"That which contains the tomb of Cheops, man!" cried the doctor solemnly; who, encumbered with his long cloak, and loaded with his walking-stick and galvanic battery, had some difficulty in getting on.

"Won't your honour let me carry that pole and that box?" said the man; "you'd get on a surprising deal better, if you would."

"Avaunt, wretch?" exclaimed the doctor, "nor offer to touch with thy profane fingers the immortal instruments of science."

The man stared, but fell back, and the whole party walked on in perfect silence.

In the meantime, Edric had advanced before his companions, completely lost in meditation. A crowd of conflicting thoughts rushed through his mind; and now, when he found himself at the very goal of his wishes, the daring nature of the purpose he had so long entertained, seemed to strike him for the first time, and he trembled at the consequences that might attend the completion of his desires. With his arms folded on his breast, he stood gazing on the Pyramids, whilst his ideas wandered uncontrolled through the boundless regions of space: "And what am I," thought he, "weak, feeble worm that I am!

who dare seek to penetrate into the awful secrets of my creator? Why should I wish to restore animation to a body now resting in the quiet of the tomb? What right have I to renew the struggles, the pains, the cares, and the anxieties of mortal life? How can I tell the fearful effects that may be produced by the gratification of my unearthly longing? May I not revive a creature whose wickedness may involve mankind in misery? And what if my experiment should fail, and if the moment when I expect my rash wishes to be accomplished, the hand of Almighty vengeance should strike me to the earth, and heap molten fire on my brain to punish my presumption!"

The sound of human voices, as the doctor and the guide approached, grated harshly on the nerves of Edric, already overstrained by the awful nature of the thoughts in which he had been indulging, and he turned away involuntarily, to escape the interruption he dreaded, quite forgetting for the moment from whom the sounds most probably proceeded.

"Lord have mercy on us!" said the guide; "I declare that gentleman looks as if he were beside himself? and see there! if he hasn't walked right by the entrance to the Pyramid without seeing it! Sir! Sir!" halloed he.

Excessively annoyed, but recalled to his recollection by these shouts, Edric returned.

"These Pyramids are wonderful piles," said the doctor, as he stumbled forward to meet him." I really had no adequate conception of the enormity of their size. They did not even look half so large at a distance as they do now."

"Immense masses seldom do," replied Edric; compelling himself with difficulty to speak.

"True," returned the doctor "the simplicity and uniformity of their figures deceive the eyes, and it is only when we approach them that we feel their stupendous magnitude and our own insignificance!"

"They give an amazing idea of the grandeur of the ancient kings of Egypt," said Edric, without exactly knowing what he was saying. "Their palaces must have been superb, if they had such mausoleums."

"How absurdly you reason, Edric!" replied the doctor peevishly; for, being annoyed with his burthens and his cloak, he was not in a humour to hear contradiction. "I thought we had settled that question before. In the first place, I think it very doubtful whether the Egyptians had any thing to do with the building of these monuments; and if they had, I believe they were meant for temples, not mausoleums; and in the next place, even if they were intended for tombs, their greatness affords no argument for the splendour of the surrounding palaces; as the Egyptians were celebrated for the superiority of their burying-places, and for the immense sums they expended upon them. Indeed, you know, ancient writers say they went so far as to call the houses of the living only inns, whilst they considered tombs as everlasting habitations;– a circumstance, by the way, that strongly corroborates my hypothesis, at least as far as their opinions go; as it seems to imply that both soul and body were designed to remain there."

They had now entered the Pyramid, and were proceeding with infinite difficulty along a low, dark, narrow passage: "Observe, Edric," said the doctor, "how the difficulty and obscurity of these winding passages confirm my opinion: you know, the religion of the ancient Egyptians, like that of the ancient Hindoos, was one of penances and personal privations; and, granting that to be the case, what can be more simple, than that the passages the *initiati* had to traverse before they reached the adytum, should be painful and difficult of access. Besides this, as you know, the bones of a bull, no doubt those of the god Apis were found in a sarcophagus in the second Pyramid, it seems probable that it was sacred to his worship: and its vicinity to the Nile, which was indispensable to the temples of Apis, as when it was time for him to die, he was drowned in its waters, confirms the fact. Indeed, I am only surprised that any human being, possessing a grain of common sense, can entertain a single doubt upon the subject."

"How do you account for the tomb we are about to visit being placed in the Pyramid, if you think they were only designed for temples?' asked Edric.

"The question is futile," said the doctor. "A strange fancy prevailed in former times, that burying the dead in consecrated places, particularly in temples intended for divine worship, would scare away the evil spirits, and the practice actually prevailed in England even as lately as the nineteenth or twentieth century. Indeed, it was not till after the country had been almost depopulated by the dreadfully infectious disease which prevailed about two hundred years ago, that a law was passed to prevent the interment of the dead in London, and that those previously buried in and near the churches there, were exhumed and placed in cemeteries beyond the walls."

Edric did not reply, for in fact his ideas were so absorbed by the solemn object before him, that it was painful for him to speak, and the doctor's ill-timed reasoning created such an irritation of his nerves, that he found it required the utmost exertion of his self-command to endure it patiently. The passage they were traversing, now became higher and wider, shelving off occasionally into chambers or recesses on each side, till they approached a kind of vestibule, in the centre of which, yawned a deep, dark, gloomy-looking cavity, like a well.

"We must descend that shaft," said the guide, "and that will lead us to the tomb of King Cheops; but as the road is dark, and rather dangerous, we had better, each of us, take a torch."

As he spoke, he drew some torches from a niche where they were deposited, and began to illuminate them from his own. The red glare of the

torches flashed fearfully on the massive walls of the Pyramid, throwing part
of their enormous masses into deep shadow, as they rose in solemn and sublime dignity around, and seemed frowning upon the presumptuous mortals
who had dared to invade their recesses, whilst the deep pit beneath their feet
seemed to yawn wide to engulf them in its abyss. Edric's heart beat thick: it
throbbed till he even fancied its pulsations audible; and a strange, mysterious thrilling of anxiety, mingled with a wild, undefinable delight, ran through
his frame. A few short hours, and his wishes would be gratified, or set at rest
for ever. The doctor and the guide had already begun to descend, and their
figures seemed changed and unearthly as the gleams of the torches fell upon
them. Edric gazed for a moment, and then followed with feelings worked up
almost to frenzy by the over-excitement of his nerves; whilst the hollow
sounds that re-echoed from the walls, as they struck against them in their descent, thrilled through his whole frame.

No one spoke; and after proceeding for some time along the narrow path,
or rather ledge, formed on the sides of the cavity, which gradually shelved
downwards, the guide suddenly stopped, and touching a secret spring, a solid
block of granite slowly detached itself from the wall, and, rising majestically
like the portcullis of an ancient fortress showed the entrance to a dark and
dreary cave. The guide advanced, followed by our travellers, into a gloomy
vaulted apartment, where long vistas of ponderous arches stretched on every
side, till their termination was lost in darkness, and gave a feeling of immensity and obscurity to the scene.

"I will wait here, said the guide; "and here, if you please, you had better leave
your torches. That avenue will lead you to the tomb."

The travellers obeyed; and the guide, placing himself in a recess in the wall,
extinguished all the torches except one, which he shrouded so as to leave the
travellers in total darkness. Nothing could be now more terrific than their situation: immured in the recesses of the tomb, involved in darkness, and their
bosoms throbbing with hopes that they scarcely dared avow even to themselves; with faltering steps they proceeded slowly along the path the guide had
pointed out, shuddering even at the hollow echo of their own footsteps,
which alone broke the solemn silence that reigned throughout these fearful
regions of terror and the tomb.

Suddenly, a vivid light flashed upon them, and, as they advanced, they
found it proceeded from torches placed in the hands of two colossal figures,
who, placed in a sitting posture, seemed guarding an enormous portal, surmounted by the image of a fox, the constant guardian of an Egyptian tomb.
The immense dimensions and air of grandeur and repose about these colossi
had something in it very imposing; and our travellers felt a sensation of awe
creep over them as they gazed upon their calm unmoved features so strikingly

emblematic of that immutable nature which they were doubtless placed there to typify.

It was with feelings of indescribable solemnity, that the doctor and Edric passed through this majestic portal, and found themselves in an apartment gloomily illumined by the light shed faintly from an inner chamber, through ponderous brazen gates beautifully wrought. The light thus feebly emitted, showed that the room in which they stood, was dedicated to Typhon, the evil spirit, as his fierce and savage types covered the walls; and images of his symbols, the crocodile and the dragon, placed beneath the shadow of the brazen gates, and dimly seen by the imperfect light, seemed starting into life, and grimly to forbid the farther advance of the intruders. Our travellers shuddered, and opening with trembling hand the ponderous gates, they entered *the tomb of Cheops.*

In the centre of the chamber, stood a superb, highly ornamented sarcophagus of alabaster, beautifully wrought: over this hung a lamp of wondrous workmanship, supplied by a potent mixture, so as to burn for ages unconsumed; thus awfully lighting up with perpetual flame the solemn mansions of the dead, and typifying life eternal even in the silent tomb. Around the room, on marble benches, were arranged mummies simply dried, apparently those of slaves; and close to the sarcophagus was placed one contained in a case, which the doctor approached to examine. This was supposed to be that of Sores, the confidant and prime-minister of Cheops. The chest that enclosed the body was splendidly ornamented with embossed gilt leather, whilst the parts not otherwise covered were stained with red and green curiously blended, and of a vivid brightness.

The mighty Phtah, the Jupiter of the Egyptians, spread its widely extended wings over the head, grasping in his monstrous claws a ring, the emblem of eternity; whilst below, the vulture-form of Rhea proclaimed the deceased a votary of that powerful deity; and on the sides were innumerable hieroglyphics. The doctor removed the lid, and shuddered as the crimson tinge of the everlasting lamp fell upon the hideous and distorted features thus suddenly exhibited to view. This sepulchral light, indeed, added unspeakable horror to the scene, and its peculiar glare threw such a wild and demoniac expression on the dark lines and ghastly lineaments of the mummies, that even the doctor felt his spirits depressed, and a supernatural dread creep over his mind as he gazed upon them.

In the mean time, Edric had stood gazing upon the sarcophagus of Cheops, the sides of which were beautifully sculptured with groups of figures, which, from the peculiar light thrown upon them, seemed to possess all the force and reality of life. On one side was represented an armed and youthful warrior bearing off in his arms a beautiful female, on whom he gazed with the most passionate fondness. He was pursued by a crowd of people and soldiers, who seemed rending the air with vehement exclamations against his violence, and endeavouring in vain to arrest his progress; whilst in the background appeared an old man, who was tearing his hair and wringing his hands in ineffectual rage against the ravisher.

The other side presented the same old man wrestling with the youthful warrior, who had just overpowered and stabbed him; the helpless victim raising his withered hands and failing eyes to Heaven as he fell, as though to implore vengeance upon his murderer, whilst the crimson current was fast ebbing from his bosom, The dying look and agony of the old man were forcibly depicted, whilst upon the features of the youthful warrior glowed the fury of a demon.

The sarcophagus was supported by the lion emblem of royalty, the symbol of the solar god Horus; and above it sat the majestic hawk of Osiris, gazing upwards, and unmindful of the subtle crocodile of Typhon, that, crouching under its feet, was just about to seize its breast in its enormous jaws. Neither of the travellers had as yet spoken, for it seemed like sacrilege to disturb the awful stillness that prevailed even by a whisper. Indeed, the solemn aspect of the chamber thrilled through every nerve, and they moved slowly, gliding along with noiseless steps as though they feared prematurely to break the slumbers of the mighty dead it contained. They gazed, however, with deep but undefinable interest upon the sculptured mysteries of the tomb of Cheops, vainly endeavouring to decipher their meaning; whilst, as they found their efforts useless, a secret voice seemed to whisper in their bosoms—"And shall finite creatures like these, who cannot even explain the signification of objects presented before their eyes, presume to dive into the mysteries of their Creator's will? Learn wisdom by this omen, nor seek again to explore secrets above your comprehension! Retire whilst it is yet time; soon it will be too late!"

Edric started at his own thoughts as the fearful warning, "soon it will be too late," rang in his ears; and a fearful presentiment of evil weighed heavily upon his soul. He turned to look upon the doctor, but he had already seized the lid of the sarcophagus, and, with a daring hand, removed it from its place, displaying in the fearful light the royal form that lay beneath. For a moment, both Edric and the doctor paused, not daring to survey it; and when they did, they both uttered an involuntary cry of astonishment, as the striking features of the mummy met their eyes, for both instantly recognized the sculptured warrior in his traits. Yes, it was indeed the same, but the fierce expression of fiery and ungoverned passions depicted upon the countenance of the marble figure, had settled down to a calm, vindictive, and concentrated hatred upon that of its mummy prototype in the tomb.

Awful, indeed, was the gloom that sat upon that brow, and bitter the sardonic smile that curled those haughty lips. All was perfect as though life still animated the form before them, and it had only reclined there to seek a short repose. The dark eyebrows, the thick raven hair which hung upon the forehead, and the snow-white teeth seen through the half open lips, forbade the idea of death; whilst the fiend-like expression of the features made Edric shudder, as he recollected the purpose that brought him to the tomb, and he trembled at the thought of awakening such a fearful being from the torpor of the grave to all the renewed energies of life.

"Let us go," whispered the doctor to his pupil, in a low, deep. and unearthly tone, fearfully different from his usually cheerful voice, Edric started at the sound, for it seemed the last sad warning of his better genius, before it abandoned him for ever. The die however, was cast and it was too late to recede. Edric felt worked up to frenzy by the over-wrought feelings of the moment. He seized the machine, and resolutely advanced towards the sarcophagus, whilst the doctor gazed upon him with a horror that deprived him of either speech or motion.

Innumerable folds of red and white linen disposed alternately, swathed the gigantic limbs of the royal mummy; and upon his breast lay a piece of metal, shining like silver, and stamped with the figure of a winged globe. Edric attempted to remove this but recoiled with horror, when he found it bend beneath his fingers with an unnatural softness; whilst, as the flickering light of the lamp fell upon the face of the mummy, he fancied its stern features relaxed into a ghastly laugh of scornful mockery. Worked up to desperation, he applied the wires of the battery and put the apparatus in motion, whilst a demoniac laugh of derision appeared to ring in his ears and the surrounding mummies seemed starting from their places and dancing in unearthly merriment. Thunder now roared in tremendous peals through the Pyramids, shaking their enormous masses to the foundation, and vivid flashes of light darted round in quick succession. Edric stood aghast amidst this fearful convulsion of nature. A horrid creeping seemed to run though every vein, every nerve feeling as though drawn from its extremity, and wrapped in icy chillness round his heart. Still, he stood immoveable, and gazing intently on the mummy, whose eyes had opened with the shock, and were now fixed on those of Erdic, shining with supernatural lustre. In vain Edric attempted to rouse himself;—in vain to turn away from that withering glance. The mummy's eyes still pursued him with their ghastly brightness; they seemed to possess the fabled fascination of those of the rattle-snake, and though he shrank from their gaze, they still glared horribly upon him. Edric's senses swam, yet he could not move from the spot; he remained fixed, chained, and immoveable, his eyes still rivetted upon those of the mummy, and every thought absorbed in horror. Another fearful peal of thunder now rolled in lengthened vibrations above his head, and the Mummy rose slowly, his eyes still fixed upon those of Edric, from his marble tomb. The thunder pealed louder and louder. Yells and groans seemed mingled with its roar;— the sepulchral lamp flared with re-doubled fierceness, flashing its rays around in quick succession, and with vivid brightness; whilst by its horrid and uncertain glare, Edric saw the Mummy stretch out its withered hand as though to seize him. He saw it rise gradually—he heard the dry, bony fingers rattle as it drew them forth—he felt its tremendous grip—human nature could bear no more—his senses were rap-idly deserting him; he felt, however, the fixed stedfast eyes of Cheops still glowing upon his failing orbs, as the lamp gave a sudden flash, and then all was darkness! The brazen gates now shut with a fearful clang, and Edric, ut-tering a shriek of horror, fell senseless upon the ground, whilst his shrill cry of anguish rang wildly through the marble vaults, till its re-echoes seemed like the yell of demons joining in fearful mockery.

How long he lay in this state he knew not; but when he re-opened his eyes, for the moment, he fancied all that had passed a dream. As his senses returned he recollected where he was, and shuddered to find himself yet in that place of horrors. All now was dark, except a faint gleam that shone feebly through the half-open gates; these ponderous portals slowly unclosed, and the form of a man, wrapped in a large cloak, and bearing a torch, entered, peering around as it advanced, as though half afraid to proceed. Edric's feelings were too highly wrought to bear any fresh horrors and he shrieked in agony, as the figure approached. The sound of his voice subdued the terrors of the intruder, and the doctor, for it was he, shouted with joy, as be rushed forward to em-brace him.

"Edric! Edric! thank God he is alive!" exclaimed he. "Edric! my beloved Edric! for God's sake, let us leave this den of horrors! come, come!"

Reassured by his tutor's voice, Edric arose, and taking one hasty, shudder-ing glance around as the light gleamed on the sarcophagus he hurried out of the tomb. Neither he nor the doctor spoke as they passed through the vestibule, where the colossal figures still sat in awful majesty; indeed, as their torches were extinguished, their gigantic forms looked still more terrific than before, from the wavering and in distinct light thrown upon them. Edric shuddered as he looked, and hurried on with hasty strides to the place where they had left the guide, whom they found kneeling in a corner, hiding his face in his hands, and roaring out, "O Lord, defend us! Heaven have mercy upon us! Lord have mercy upon us! Heaven have mercy upon us!"

"He has been in that state for more than an hour," said the doctor mourn-fully; "for, after I came to myself, I tried to rouse him, but all to no purpose."

"Then you also fainted?" said Edric with difficulty compelling himself to speak.

"Why," resumed the doctor with some hesitation, "I don't know that you can exactly call it fainting; but the fact was, when I saw you touch the plate upon the mummy's breast, and start back, looking so horribly frightened, I – I thought I had better call for assistance; so as I ran for that purpose, somehow or other I fell down, and lay insensible I don't know how long. When I came to myself, I tried to rouse the guide, and when I found I could not, I came to seek you; but now that we are both recovered, I really don't know what is to become of us; for this fellow will never be able to show us the way out, and I'm sure I don't know the road."

"Let us try to find it, at any rate," said Edward faintly.

"Oh, for God's sake, take me too!" screamed the guide. "If you have any mercy, don't leave me in this fearful place."

"Take the light then, and lead the way," said Edric. The guide obeyed, shaking in every limb, and every now and then casting a terrified look behind, whilst the quivering flame of the torch betrayed the unsteadiness of the trembling hands that bore it. In this manner they proceeded starting at every sound, and frightened even at their own shadows, without daring to stop till they reached the plain.

"Thank God!" cried the doctor, the moment they stepped out of the Pyramid; looking around him, gasping for breath, and inhaling the fresh air with rapture.

"Thank God!" reiterated Edric and the guide, as they walked rapidly towards the place where they had left their balloon. When arrived there, however, they looked for it in vain; and fancying themselves under the influence of a delusion, they rubbed their eyes, and again looked, but without success.

"Dear me, it is very strange!" said the doctor; "this is certainly the place, and yet, where can it be?"

"Where, indeed!" repeated Edric; "horrors and unaccountable incidents environ us at every step; I am not naturally timid, yet–"

"Ah!" screamed the doctor, as he tumbled over a man lying with his face upon the ground; "Oh!" groaned he, as Edric and the guide with difficulty raised him; "would to Heaven I were safe at home again in my own comfortable little study, indulging in pleasing anticipations of that, which I find is any thing in the world but pleasing in reality."

Some Words With a Mummy

by Edgar Allan Poe

First published in the American Whig Review, *Edgar Allan Poe's "Some Words With a Mummy" (1845) is the sole tale in this anthology in which a re-vivified mummy actually speaks – and boy, does this mummy have a lot on his mind! Upon first reading, one might take this tale as being nothing more than lighthearted escapism. Indeed, Poe's story is rife with humor and wit. If you, as a reader, dig a little deeper, you'll soon find that beneath the immediate surface lies a trenchant criticism of American society and politics in the era in which Poe lived and wrote.*

The famed American author's foray into the ancient Egyptian supernatural involves the unwrapping of a mummy, a quasi-scientific ceremony in nineteenth-century high society in which people would gather around to remove mummies from their coffins and unwrap them all in the name of expanding human knowledge.

In Poe's story, much like in many tales that followed, men find a way to rean-imate a dead mummy. What distinguishes "Some Words with a Mummy" is that in this instance, the mummy not only speaks, but pontificates upon the differences between ancient Egypt and nineteenth-century New England. It's an altogether quick read, but it contains tremendous cultural and literary depth.

The symposium of the preceding evening had been a little too much for my nerves. I had a wretched headache, and was desperately drowsy. Instead of going out therefore to spend the evening as I had proposed, it occurred to me that I could not do a wiser thing than just eat a mouthful of supper and go immediately to bed.

A *light* supper of course. I am exceedingly fond of Welsh rabbit. More than a pound at once, however, may not at all times be advisable. Still, there can be no material objection to two. And really between two and three, there is merely a single unit of difference. I ventured, perhaps, upon four. My wife will have it five;—but, clearly, she has confounded two very distinct affairs. The abstract number, five, I am willing to admit; but, concretely, it has reference to bottles of Brown Stout, without which, in the way of condiment,

Welsh rabbit is to be eschewed.

Having thus concluded a frugal meal, and donned my night-cap, with the serene hope of enjoying it till noon the next day, I placed my head upon the pillow, and, through the aid of a capital conscience, fell into a profound slumber forthwith.

But when were the hopes of humanity fulfilled? I could not have completed my third snore when there came a furious ringing at the street-door bell, and then an impatient thumping at the knocker, which awakened me at once. In a minute afterward, and while I was still rubbing my eyes, my wife thrust in my face a note, from my old friend, Doctor Ponnonner. It ran thus:

"Come to me, by all means, my dear good friend, as soon as you receive this. Come and help us to rejoice. At last, by long persevering diplomacy, I have gained the assent of the Directors of the City Museum, to my examination of the mummy—you know the one I mean. I have permission to unswathe it and open it, if desirable. A few friends only will be present—you, of course. The mummy is now at my house, and we shall begin to unroll it at eleven to-night.

Yours, ever,
PONNONNER.

By the time I had reached the "Ponnonner," it struck me that I was as wide awake as a man need be. I leaped out of bed in an ecstacy, overthrowing all in my way; dressed myself with a rapidity truly marvellous; and set off, at the top of my speed, for the doctor's.

There I found a very eager company assembled. They had been awaiting me with much impatience; the mummy was extended upon the dining-table; and the moment I entered its examination was commenced.

It was one of a pair brought, several years previously, by Captain Arthur Sabretash, a cousin of Ponnonner's from a tomb near Eleithias, in the Lybian mountains, a considerable distance above Thebes on the Nile. The grottoes at this point, although less magnificent than the Theban sepulchres, are of higher interest, on account of affording more numerous illustrations of the private life of the Egyptians. The chamber from which our specimen was taken, was said to be very rich in such illustrations; the walls being completely covered with fresco paintings and bas-reliefs, while statues, vases, and mosaic work of rich patterns, indicated the vast wealth of the deceased.

The treasure had been deposited in the Museum precisely in the same condition in which Captain Sabretash had found it—that is to say, the coffin had not been disturbed. For eight years it had thus stood, subject only externally to public inspection. We had now, therefore, the complete mummy at our disposal; and to those who are aware how very rarely the unransacked antique reaches our shores, it will be evident, at once that we had great reason to congratulate ourselves upon our good fortune.

Approaching the table, I saw on it a large box, or case, nearly seven feet long, and perhaps three feet wide, by two feet and a half deep. It was oblong—not coffin-shaped. The material was at first supposed to be the wood of the sycamore (*platanus*), but, upon cutting into it, we found it to be pasteboard, or, more properly, *papier mâché*, composed of papyrus. It was thickly ornamented with paintings, representing funeral scenes, and other mournful subjects—interspersed among which, in every variety of position, were certain series of hieroglyphical characters, intended, no doubt, for the name of the departed. By good luck, Mr. Gliddon formed one of our party; and he had no difficulty in translating the letters, which were simply phonetic, and represented the word "*Allamistakeo.*"

We had some difficulty in getting this case open without injury; but having at length accomplished the task, we came to a second, coffin-shaped, and very considerably less in size than the exterior one, but resembling it precisely in every other respect. The interval between the two was filled with resin, which had, in some degree, defaced the colors of the interior box.

Upon opening this latter (which we did quite easily), we arrived at a third case, also coffin-shaped, and varying from the second one in no particular, except in that of its material, which was cedar, and still emitted the peculiar and highly aromatic odor of that wood. Between the second and the third case there was no interval—the one fitting accurately within the other.

Removing the third case, we discovered and took out the body itself. We had expected to find it, as usual, enveloped in frequent rolls, or bandages, of linen; but, in place of these, we found a sort of sheath, made of papyrus, and coated with a layer of plaster, thickly gilt and painted. The paintings represented subjects connected with the various supposed duties of the soul, and its presentation to different divinities, with numerous identical human figures, intended, very probably, as portraits of the persons embalmed. Extending from head to foot was a columnar, or perpendicular, inscription, in phonetic hieroglyphics, giving again his name and titles, and the names and titles of his relations.

Around the neck thus ensheathed, was a collar of cylindrical glass beads, diverse in color, and so arranged as to form images of deities, of the scarabaeus, etc., with the winged globe. Around the small of the waist was a similar collar or belt.

Stripping off the papyrus, we found the flesh in excellent preservation, with no perceptible odor. The color was reddish. The skin was hard, smooth, and glossy. The teeth and hair were in good condition. The eyes (it seemed) had been removed, and glass ones substituted, which were very beautiful and wonderfully life-like, with the exception of somewhat too determined a stare. The fingers and the nails were brilliantly gilded.

Mr. Gliddon was of opinion, from the redness of the epidermis, that the embalmment had been effected altogether by asphaltum; but, on scraping the surface with a steel instrument, and throwing into the fire some of the powder thus obtained, the flavor of camphor and other sweet-scented gums became apparent.

We searched the corpse very carefully for the usual openings through which the entrails are extracted, but, to our surprise, we could discover none. No member of the party was at that period aware that entire or unopened mummies are not infrequently met. The brain it was customary to withdraw through the nose; the intestines through an incision in the side; the body was then shaved, washed, and salted; then laid aside for several weeks, when the operation of embalming, properly so called, began.

As no trace of an opening could be found, Doctor Ponnonner was preparing his instruments for dissection, when I observed that it was then past two o'clock. Hereupon it was agreed to postpone the internal examination until the next evening; and we were about to separate for the present, when someone suggested an experiment or two with the voltaic pile.

The application of electricity to a mummy three or four thousand years old at the least, was an idea, if not very sage, still sufficiently original, and we all caught it at once. About one-tenth in earnest and nine-tenths in jest, we arranged a battery in the doctor's study, and conveyed thither the Egyptian.

It was only after much trouble that we succeeded in laying bare some portions of the temporal muscle which appeared of less stony rigidity than other parts of the frame, but which, as we had anticipated, of course, gave no indication of galvanic susceptibility when brought in contact with the wire. This, the first trial, indeed, seemed decisive, and, with a hearty laugh at our own absurdity, we were bidding each other good night, when my eyes, happening to fall upon those of the mummy, were there immediately riveted in amazement. My brief glance, in fact, had sufficed to assure me that the orbs which we had all supposed to be glass, and which were originally noticeable for a certain wild stare, were now so far covered by the lids, that only a small portion of the *tunica albuginea* remained visible.

With a shout I called attention to the fact, and it became immediately obvious to all.

I cannot say that I was *alarmed* at the phenomenon, because "alarmed" is, in my case, not exactly the word. It is possible, however, that, but for the

Brown Stout, I might have been a little nervous. As for the rest of the company, they really made no attempt at concealing the downright fright which possessed them. Doctor Ponnonner was a man to be pitied. Mr. Gliddon, by some peculiar process, rendered himself invisible. Mr. Silk Buckingham, I fancy, will scarcely be so bold as to deny that he made his way, upon all fours, under the table.

After the first shock of astonishment, however, we resolved, as a matter of course, upon further experiment forthwith. Our operations were now directed against the great toe of the right foot. We made an incision over the outside of the exterior *os sesamoideum pollicis pedis*, and thus got at the root of the abductor muscle. Readjusting the battery, we now applied the fluid to the bisected nerves—when, with a movement of exceeding life-likeness, the mummy first drew up its right knee so as to bring it nearly in contact with the abdomen, and then, straightening the limb with inconceivable force, bestowed a kick upon Doctor Ponnonner, which had the effect of discharging that gentleman, like an arrow from a catapult, through a window into the street below.

We rushed out en masse to bring in the mangled remains of the victim, but had the happiness to meet him upon the staircase, coming up in an unaccountable hurry, brimful of the most ardent philosophy, and more than ever impressed with the necessity of prosecuting our experiment with vigor and with zeal.

It was by his advice, accordingly, that we made, upon the spot, a profound incision into the tip of the subject's nose, while the doctor himself, laying violent hands upon it, pulled it into vehement contact with the wire.

Morally and physically—figuratively and literally—was the effect electric. In the first place, the corpse opened its eyes and winked very rapidly for several minutes, as does Mr. Barnes in the pantomime, in the second place, it sneezed; in the third, it sat upon end; in the fourth, it shook its fist in Doctor Ponnonner's face; in the fifth, turning to Messieurs Gliddon and Buckingham, it addressed them, in very capital Egyptian, thus:

"I must say, gentlemen, that I am as much surprised as I am mortified at your behavior. Of Doctor Ponnonner nothing better was to be expected. He is a poor little fat fool who knows no better. I pity and forgive him. But you, Mr. Gliddon—and you, Silk—who have travelled and resided in Egypt until one might imagine you to the manner born—you, I say who have been so much among us that you speak Egyptian fully as well, I think, as you write your mother tongue—you, whom I have always been led to regard as the firm friend of the mummies—I really did anticipate more gentlemanly conduct from *you*. What am I to think of your standing quietly by and seeing me thus unhandsomely used? What am I to suppose by your permitting Tom, Dick, and Harry to strip me of my coffins, and my clothes, in this wretchedly cold climate? In what light (to come to the point) am I to regard your aiding and abetting that miserable little villain, Doctor Ponnonner, in pulling me by the nose?"

It will be taken for granted, no doubt, that upon hearing this speech under the circumstances, we all either made for the door, or fell into violent hysterics, or went off in a general swoon. One of these three things was, I say, to be expected. Indeed each and all of these lines of conduct might have been very plausibly pursued. And, upon my word, I am at a loss to know how or why it was that we pursued neither the one nor the other. But, perhaps, the true reason is to be sought in the spirit of the age, which proceeds by the rule of contraries altogether, and is now usually admitted as the solution of everything in the way of paradox and impossibility. Or, perhaps, after all, it was only the mummy's exceedingly natural and matter-of-course air that divested his words of the terrible. However this may be, the facts are clear, and no member of our party betrayed any very particular trepidation, or seemed to consider that any thing had gone very especially wrong.

For my part I was convinced it was all right, and merely stepped aside, out of the range of the Egyptian's fist. Doctor Ponnonner thrust his hands into his breeches' pockets, looked hard at the mummy, and grew excessively red in the face. Mr. Glidden stroked his whiskers and drew up the collar of his shirt. Mr. Buckingham hung down his head, and put his right thumb into the left corner of his mouth.

The Egyptian regarded him with a severe countenance for some minutes and at length, with a sneer, said:

"Why don't you speak, Mr. Buckingham? Did you hear what I asked you, or not? *Do* take your thumb out of your mouth!"

Mr. Buckingham, hereupon, gave a slight start, took his right thumb out of the left corner of his mouth, and, by way of indemnification inserted his left thumb in the right corner of the aperture above-mentioned.

Not being able to get an answer from Mr. B., the figure turned peevishly to Mr. Glidden, and, in a peremptory tone, demanded in general terms what we all meant.

Mr. Glidden replied at great length, in phonetics; and but for the deficiency of American printing-offices in hieroglyphical type, it would afford me much pleasure to record here, in the original, the whole of his very excellent speech.

I may as well take this occasion to remark, that all the subsequent conversation in which the mummy took a part, was carried on in primitive Egyptian, through the medium (so far as concerned myself and other untravelled members of the company)—through the medium, I say, of Messieurs Gliddon and Buckingham, as interpreters. These gentlemen spoke the mother tongue of the mummy with inimitable fluency and grace; but I could not help observing that (owing, no doubt, to the introduction of images entirely modern, and, of course, entirely novel to the stranger) the two travellers were reduced, occasionally, to the employment of sensible forms for the purpose of conveying a particular meaning. Mr. Gliddon, at one period, for example, could not make the Egyptian comprehend the term "politics," until he sketched upon the wall, with a bit of charcoal a little carbuncle-nosed gentleman, out at elbows, standing upon a stump, with his left leg drawn back, right arm thrown forward, with his fist shut, the eyes rolled up toward Heaven, and the mouth open at an angle of ninety degrees. Just in the same way Mr. Buckingham failed to convey the absolutely modern idea "wig," until (at Doctor Ponnonner's suggestion) he grew very pale in the face, and consented to take off his own.

It will be readily understood that Mr. Gliddon's discourse turned chiefly upon the vast benefits accruing to science from the unrolling and disembowelling of mummies; apologizing, upon this score, for any disturbance that might have been occasioned *him*, in particular, the individual mummy called Allamistakeo; and concluding with a mere hint (for it could scarcely be considered more) that, as these little matters were now explained, it might be as well to proceed with the investigation intended. Here Doctor Ponnonner made ready his instruments.

In regard to the latter suggestions of the orator, it appears that Allamistakeo had certain scruples of conscience, the nature of which I did not distinctly learn; but he expressed himself satisfied with the apologies tendered, and, getting down from the table, shook hands with the company all round.

When this ceremony was at an end, we immediately busied ourselves in repairing the damages which our subject had sustained from the scalpel. We sewed up the wound in his temple, bandaged his foot, and applied a square inch of black plaster to the tip of his nose.

It was now observed that the Count (this was the title, it seems, of Allamistakeo) had a slight fit of shivering—no doubt from the cold. The Doctor immediately repaired to his wardrobe, and soon returned with a black dress coat, made in Jennings' best manner, a pair of sky-blue plaid pantaloons with straps, a pink gingham chemise, a flapped vest of brocade, a white sack overcoat, a walking cane with a hook, a hat with no brim, patent-leather boots, straw-colored kid gloves, an eye-glass, a pair of whiskers, and a waterfall cravat. Owing to the disparity of size between the Count and the doctor (the proportion being as two to one), there was some little difficulty in adjusting these habiliments upon the person of the Egyptian; but when all was arranged, he might have been said to be dressed. Mr. Gliddon, therefore, gave him his arm, and led him to a comfortable chair by the fire, while the Doctor rang the bell upon the spot and ordered a supply of cigars and wine.

The conversation soon grew animated. Much curiosity was, of course, expressed in regard to the somewhat remarkable fact of Allamistakeo's still remaining alive.

"I should have thought," observed Mr. Buckingham, "that it is high time you were dead."

"Why," replied the Count, very much astonished, "I am little more than seven hundred years old! My father lived a thousand, and was by no means in his dotage when he died."

Here ensued a brisk series of questions and computations, by means of which it became evident that the antiquity of the mummy had been grossly misjudged. It had been five thousand and fifty years and some months since he had been consigned to the catacombs at Eleithias.

"But my remark," resumed Mr. Buckingham, "had no reference to your age at the period of interment (I am willing to grant, in fact, that you are still a young man), and my illusion was to the immensity of time during which, by your own showing, you must have been done up in asphaltum."

"In what?" said the Count.

"In asphaltum," persisted Mr. B.

"Ah, yes; I have some faint notion of what you mean; it might be made to answer, no doubt—but in my time we employed scarcely anything else than the bichloride of mercury."

"But what we are especially at a loss to understand," said Doctor Ponnonner, "is how it happens that, having been dead and buried in Egypt five thousand years ago, you are here today all alive and looking so delightfully well."

"Had I been, as you say, *dead*," replied the Count, "it is more than probable that dead, I should still be; for I perceive you are yet in the infancy of galvanism, and cannot accomplish with it what was a common thing among us in the old days. But the fact is, I fell into catalepsy, and it was considered by my best friends that I was either dead or should be; they accordingly embalmed me at once—I presume you are aware of the chief principle of the embalming process?"

"Why not altogether."

"Why, I perceive—a deplorable condition of ignorance! Well I cannot enter into details just now: but it is necessary to explain that to embalm (properly speaking), in Egypt, was to arrest indefinitely *all* the animal functions subjected to the process. I use the word 'animal' in its widest sense, as including the physical not more than the moral and *vital* being. I repeat that the leading principle of embalmment consisted, with us, in the immediately arresting, and holding in perpetual *abeyance*, *all* the animal functions subjected to the process. To be brief, in whatever condition the individual was, at the period of embalmment, in that condition he remained. Now, as it is my good fortune to be of the blood of the Scarabaeus, I was embalmed alive, as you see me at present."

"The blood of the Scarabaeus!" exclaimed Doctor Ponnonner.

"Yes. The Scarabaeus was the *insignium* or the 'arms,' of a very distinguished and very rare patrician family. To be 'of the blood of the Scarabaeus,' is merely to be one of that family of which the Scarabaeus is the *insignium*. I speak figuratively."

"But what has this to do with you being alive?"

"Why, it is the general custom in Egypt to deprive a corpse, before embalmment, of its bowels and brains; the race of the Scarabaei alone did not coincide with the custom. Had I not been a Scarabeus, therefore, I should have been without bowels and brains; and without either it is inconvenient to live."

"I perceive that," said Mr. Buckingham, "and I presume that all the *entire* mummies that come to hand are of the race of Scarabaei."

"Beyond doubt."

"I thought," said Mr. Gliddon, very meekly, "that the Scarabaeus was one of the Egyptian gods."

"One of the Egyptian *what?*" exclaimed the mummy, starting to its feet.

"Gods!" repeated the traveller.

"Mr. Gliddon, I really am astonished to hear you talk in this style," said the Count, resuming his chair. "No nation upon the face of the earth has ever acknowledged more than one *god*. The Scarabaeus, the Ibis, etc., were with us (as similar creatures have been with others) the symbols, or media, through which we offered worship to the Creator too august to be more directly approached."

There was here a pause. At length the colloquy was renewed by Doctor Ponnonner.

"It is not improbable, then, from what you have explained," said he, "that among the catacombs near the Nile there may exist other mummies of the Scarabaeus tribe, in a condition of vitality?"

"There can be no question of it," replied the Count; "all the Scarabaei embalmed accidentally while alive, are alive now. Even some of those *purposely* so embalmed, may have been overlooked by their executors, and still remain in the tomb."

"Will you be kind enough to explain," I said, "what you mean by 'purposely so embalmed'?"

"With great pleasure!" answered the mummy, after surveying me leisurely through his eye-glass—for it was the first time I had ventured to address him a direct question.

"With great pleasure," he said. "The usual duration of man's life, in my time, was about eight hundred years. Few men died, unless by most extraordinary accident, before the age of six hundred; few lived longer than a decade of centuries; but eight were considered the natural term. After the discovery of the embalming principle, as I have already described it to you, it occurred to our philosophers that a laudable curiosity might be gratified, and, at the same time, the interests of science much advanced, by living this natural term in installments. In the case of history, indeed, experience demonstrated that something of this kind was indispensable. An historian, for example, having attained the age of five hundred, would write a book with great labor and then get himself carefully embalmed; leaving instructions to his executors pro tem., that they should cause him to be revivified after the lapse of a certain period—say five or six hundred years. Resuming existence at the expiration of this time, he would invariably find his great work converted into a species of hap-hazard notebook—that is to say, into a kind of literary arena for the conflicting guesses, riddles, and personal squabbles of whole herds of exasperated commentators. These guesses, etc., which passed under the name of annotations, or emendations, were found so completely to have enveloped, distorted, and overwhelmed the text, that the author had to go about with a lantern to discover his own book. When discovered, it was never worth the trouble of the search. After rewriting it throughout, it was regarded as the bounden duty of the historian to set himself to work immediately in correcting, from his own private knowledge and experience, the traditions of the day concerning the epoch at which he had originally lived. Now this process of rescription and personal rectification, pursued by various individual sages from time to time, had the effect of preventing our history from degenerating into absolute fable."

"I beg your pardon," said Doctor Ponnonner at this point, laying his hand gently upon the arm of the Egyptian—"I beg your pardon, sir, but may I presume to interrupt you for one moment?"

"By all means, *sir*," replied the Count, drawing up.

"I merely wished to ask you a question," said the Doctor. "You mentioned the historian's personal correction of *traditions* respecting his own epoch. Pray, sir, upon an average what proportion of these kabbala were usually found to be right?"

"The kabbala, as you properly term them, sir, were generally discovered to be precisely on a par with the facts recorded in the un-re-written histories themselves;—that is to say, not one individual iota of either was ever known, under any circumstances, to be not totally and radically wrong."

"But since it is quite clear," resumed the Doctor, "that at least five thousand years have elapsed since your entombment, I take it for granted that your histories at that period, if not your traditions were sufficiently explicit on that one topic of universal interest, the Creation, which took place, as I presume you are aware, only about ten centuries before."

"Sir!" said the Count Allamistakeo.

The Doctor repeated his remarks, but it was only after much additional explanation that the foreigner could be made to comprehend them. The latter at length said, hesitatingly:

"The ideas you have suggested are to me, I confess, utterly novel. During my time I never knew any one to entertain so singular a fancy as that the universe (or this world if you will have it so) ever had a beginning at all. I remember once, and once only, hearing something remotely hinted, by a man of many speculations, concerning the origin *of the human race*; and by this individual, the very word *Adam* (or Red Earth), which you make use of, was employed. He employed it, however, in a generical sense, with reference to the spontaneous germination from rank soil (just as a thousand of the lower genera of creatures are germinated)—the spontaneous germination, I say, of five vast hordes of men, simultaneously upspringing in five distinct and nearly equal divisions of the globe."

Here, in general, the company shrugged their shoulders, and one or two of us touched our foreheads with a very significant air. Mr. Silk Buckingham, first glancing slightly at the occiput and then at the sinciput of Allamistakeo, thus:

"The long duration of human life in your time, together with the occasional practice of passing it, as you have explained, in installments, must have had, indeed, a strong tendency to the general development and conglomeration of knowledge. I presume, therefore, that we are to attribute the marked inferiority of the old Egyptians in all particulars of science, when compared with the moderns, and more especially with the Yankees, altogether to the superior solidity of the Egyptian skull."

"I confess again," replied the Count, with much suavity, "that I am somewhat at a loss to comprehend you; pray, to what particulars of science do you allude?"

Here our whole party, joining voices, detailed, at great length, the assumptions of phrenology and the marvels of animal magnetism.

Having heard us to an end, the Count proceeded to relate a few anecdotes, which rendered it evident that prototypes of Gall and Spurzheim had flourished and faded in Egypt so long ago as to have been nearly forgotten, and that the manoeuvres of Mesmer were really very contemptible tricks when put in collation with the positive miracles of the Theban *savans*, who created lice and a great many other similar things.

I here asked the Count if his people were able to calculate eclipses. He smiled rather contemptuously, and said they were.

This put me a little out, but I began to make other inquiries in regard to his astronomical knowledge, when a member of the company, who had never as yet opened his mouth, whispered in my ear, that for information on this head, I had better consult Ptolemy (whoever Ptolemy is), as well as one Plutarch *de facie lunae*.

I then questioned the mummy about burning-glasses and lenses, and, in general, about the manufacture of glass; but I had not made an end of my queries before the silent member again touched me quietly on the elbow, and begged me for God's sake to take a peep at Diodorus Siculus. As for the Count, he merely asked me, in the way of reply, if we moderns possessed any such microscopes as would enable us to cut cameos in the style of the Egyptians. While I was thinking how I should answer this question, little Doctor Ponnonner committed himself in a very extraordinary way.

"Look at our architecture!" he exclaimed, greatly to the indignation of both the travellers, who pinched him black and blue to no purpose.

"Look," he cried with enthusiasm, "at the Bowling-Green Fountain in New York! or if this be too vast a contemplation, regard for a moment the Capitol at Washington, D. C.!"—and the good little medical man went on to detail very minutely, the proportions of the fabric to which he referred. He explained that the portico alone was adorned with no less than four and twenty columns, five feet in diameter, and ten feet apart.

The Count said that he regretted not being able to remember, just at that moment, the precise dimensions of any one of the principal buildings of the city of Aznac, whose foundations were laid in the night of Time, but the ruins of which were still standing, at the epoch of his entombment, in a vast plain of sand to the westward of Thebes. He recollected, however, (talking of the porticoes,) that one affixed to an inferior palace in a kind of suburb called Carnac, consisted of a hundred and forty-four columns, thirty-seven feet in circumference, and twenty-five feet apart. The approach to this portico, from the Nile, was through an avenue two miles long, composed of sphynxes, statues, and obelisks, twenty, sixty, and a hundred feet in height. The palace itself (as well as he could remember) was, in one direction, two miles long, and might have been altogether about seven in circuit. Its walls were richly painted all over, within and without, with hieroglyphics. He would not pretend to *assert* that even fifty or sixty of the Doctor's Capitols might have been built within these walls, but he was by no means sure that two or three hundred of them might not have been squeezed in with some trouble. That palace at Carnac was an insignificant little building after all. He (the Count), however, could not conscientiously refuse to admit the ingenuity, magnificence, and superiority of the fountain at the Bowling Green, as described by the Doctor. Nothing like it, he was forced to allow, had ever been seen in Egypt or elsewhere.

I here asked the Count what he had to say to our railroads.

"Nothing," he replied, "in particular." They were rather slight, rather ill-conceived, and clumsily put together. They could not be compared, of course, with the vast, level, direct, iron-grooved causeways upon which the Egyptians conveyed entire temples and solid obelisks of a hundred and fifty feet in altitude.

I spoke of our gigantic mechanical forces.

He agreed that we knew something in that way, but inquired how I should have gone to work in getting up the imposts on the lintels of even the little palace at Carnac.

This question I concluded not to hear, and demanded if he had any idea of Artesian wells; but he simply raised his eyebrows; while Mr. Gliddon winked at me very hard and said, in a low tone, that one had been recently discovered by the engineers employed to bore for water in the Great Oasis.

I then mentioned our steel; but the foreigner elevated his nose, and asked me if our steel could have executed the sharp carved work seen on the obelisks, and which was wrought altogether by edge-tools of copper.

This disconcerted us so greatly that we thought it advisable to vary the attack to metaphysics. We sent for a copy of a book called the "Dial," and read out of it a chapter or two about something that is not very clear, but which the Bostonians call the Great Movement of Progress.

The Count merely said that Great Movements were awfully common things in his day, and as for Progress, it was at one time quite a nuisance, but it never progressed.

We then spoke of the great beauty and importance of democracy, and were at much trouble in impressing the Count with a due sense of the advantages we enjoyed in living where there was suffrage *ad libitum*, and no king.

He listened with marked interest, and in fact seemed not a little amused. When we had done, he said that, a great while ago, there had occurred something of a very similar sort. Thirteen Egyptian provinces determined all at once to be free, and to set a magnificent example to the rest of mankind. They assembled their wise men, and concocted the most ingenious constitution it is possible to conceive. For a while they managed remarkably well; only their habit of bragging was prodigious. The thing ended, however, in the consolidation of the thirteen states, with some fifteen or twenty others, in the most odious and insupportable despotism that was ever heard of upon the face of the Earth.

I asked what was the name of the usurping tyrant.

As well as the Count could recollect, it was *Mob*.

Not knowing what to say to this, I raised my voice, and deplored the Egyptian ignorance of steam.

The Count looked at me with much astonishment, but made no answer. The silent gentleman, however, gave me a violent nudge in the ribs with his elbows—told me I had sufficiently exposed myself for once—and demanded if I was really such a fool as not to know that the modern steam engine is derived from the invention of Hero, through Solomon de Caus.

We were now in imminent danger of being discomfited; but, as good luck would have it, Doctor Ponnonner, having rallied, returned to our rescue, and inquired if the people of Egypt would seriously pretend to rival the moderns in the all-important particular of dress.

The Count, at this, glanced downward to the straps of his pantaloons, and then taking hold of the end of one of his coat tails, held it up close to his eyes for some minutes. Letting it fall, at last, his mouth extended itself very gradually from ear to ear; but I do not remember that he said any thing in the way of reply.

Hereupon we recovered our spirits, and the Doctor, approaching the mummy with great dignity, desired it to say candidly, upon its honor as a gentleman, if the Egyptians had comprehended, at any period, the manufacture of either Ponnonner's lozenges or Brandreth's pills.

We looked, with profound anxiety, for an answer—but in vain. It was not forthcoming. The Egyptian blushed and hung down his head. Never was triumph more consummate; never was defeat borne with so ill a grace. Indeed, I could not endure the spectacle of the poor mummy's mortification. I reached my hat, bowed to him stiffly, and took leave.

Upon getting home I found it past four o'clock, and went immediately to bed. It is now 10 A.M. I have been up since seven, penning these memoranda for the benefit of my family and of mankind. The former I shall behold no more. My wife is a shrew. The truth is, I am heartily sick of this life and of the nineteenth century in general. I am convinced that everything is going wrong. Besides, I am anxious to know who will be President in 2045. As soon, therefore, as I shave and swallow a cup of coffee, I shall just step over to Ponnonner's and get embalmed for a couple of hundred years.

Lost in a Pyramid,
or the Mummy's Curse
by Louisa May Alcott

Originally published in 1869, Louisa May Alcott's "Lost in a Pyramid, or the Mummy's Curse" is perhaps the first American short story written by a well-known author to juxtapose a love story with a mummy-themed supernatural tale. The curse within the story, in which a deceased Egyptian sorceress exacts revenge upon those who disturbed her tomb, is a particularly cruel one.

Like other stories that involve an unwrapping of a mummy or the archaeological excavation of a tomb, "Lost in a Pyramid, or the Mummy's Curse" is a tale in which a mysterious past violently intrudes upon the genteel present. Part morality tale, part study of how Nature can overwhelm man, this chilling story can be considered both part of the New England literary tradition and a direct precursor to the weird fiction genre that came fully alive in pulp magazines decades later.

Early in the story, one of the characters tells another that she likes "weird tales." Well, this one is eerie, no doubt about it! Alcott's work is a labyrinthine story within a story that takes the reader deep into the darkness of the Cheops pyramid and back again into the light. Similarly, it allows the reader to soar vicariously into the heights of love and affection and then plummet back down into the pit of despair. Although rather economical in length, this tale by the author of Little Women *(1880) still packs a formidable psychological punch. Indeed, this particular Alcott story, which even many of the author's admirers might not be aware of, remains a significant contribution to the burgeoning subgenre of Egyptian tales of the macabre and the supernatural.*

———🔲———

I

"And what are these, Paul?" asked Evelyn, opening a tarnished gold box and examining its contents curiously.

"Seeds of some unknown Egyptian plant," replied Forsyth, with a sudden shadow on his dark face, as he looked down at the three scarlet grains lying in the white hand lifted to him.

"Where did you get them?" asked the girl.

"That is a weird story, which will only haunt you if I tell it," said Forsyth, with an absent expression that strongly excited the girl's curiosity.

"Please tell it, I like weird tales, and they never trouble me. Ah, do tell it; your stories are always so interesting," she cried, looking up with such a pretty blending of entreaty and command in her charming face, that refusal was impossible.

"You'll be sorry for it, and so shall I, perhaps; I warn you beforehand, that harm is foretold to the possessor of those mysterious seeds," said Forsyth, smiling, even while he knit his black brows, and regarded the blooming creature before him with a fond yet foreboding glance.

"Tell on, I'm not afraid of these pretty atoms," she answered, with an imperious nod.

"To hear is to obey. Let me read the facts, and then I will begin," returned Forsyth, pacing to and fro with the far-off look of one who turns the pages of the past.

Evelyn watched him a moment, and then returned to her work, or play, rather, for the task seemed well suited to the vivacious little creature, half-child, half-woman.

"While in Egypt," commenced Forsyth, slowly, "I went one day with my guide and Professor Niles, to explore the Cheops. Niles had a mania for antiquities of all sorts, and forgot time, danger and fatigue in the ardor of his pursuit. We rummaged up and down the narrow passages, half choked with dust and close air; reading inscriptions on the walls, stumbling over shattered mummy-cases, or coming face to face with some shriveled specimen perched like a hobgoblin on the little shelves where the dead used to be stowed away for ages. I was desperately tired after a few hours of it, and begged the professor to return. But he was bent on exploring certain places, and would not desist. We had but one guide, so I was forced to stay; but Jumal, my man, seeing how weary I was, proposed to us to rest in one of the larger passages, while he went to procure another guide for Niles. We consented, and assuring us that we were perfectly safe, if we did not quit the spot, Jumal left us, promising to return speedily. The professor sat down to take notes of his researches, and stretching myself on the soft sand, I fell asleep.

"I was roused by that indescribable thrill which instinctively warns us of danger, and springing up, I found myself alone. One torch burned faintly where Jumal had struck it, but Niles and the other light were gone. A dreadful sense of loneliness oppressed me for a moment; then I collected myself and looked well about me. A bit of paper was pinned to my hat, which lay near me, and on it, in the professor's writing were these words:

"'I've gone back a little to refresh my memory on certain points. Don't follow me till Jumal comes. I can find my way back to you, for I have a clue. Sleep well, and dream gloriously of the Pharaohs. N N.'

"I laughed at first over the old enthusiast, then felt anxious then restless, and finally resolved to follow him, for I discovered a strong cord fastened to a fallen stone, and knew that this was the clue he spoke of. Leaving a line for Jumal, I took my torch and retraced my steps, following the cord along the winding ways. I often shouted, but received no reply, and pressed on, hoping at each turn to see the old man poring over some musty relic of antiquity. Suddenly the cord ended, and lowering my torch, I saw that the footsteps had gone on.

"'Rash fellow, he'll lose himself, to a certainty,' I thought, really alarmed now.

"As I paused, a faint call reached me, and I answered it, waited, shouted again, and a still fainter echo replied.

"Niles was evidently going on, misled by the reverberations of the low passages. No time was to be lost, and, forgetting myself, I stuck my torch in the deep sand to guide me back to the clue, and ran down the straight path before me, whooping like a madman as I went. I did not mean to lose sight of the light, but in my eagerness to find Niles I turned from the main passage, and, guided by his voice, hastened on. His torch soon gladdened my eyes, and the clutch of his trembling hands told me what agony he had suffered.

"'Let us get out of this horrible place at once,' he said, wiping the great drops off his forehead.

"'Come, we're not far from the clue. I can soon reach it, and then we are safe'; but as I spoke, a chill passed over me, for a perfect labyrinth of narrow paths lay before us.

"Trying to guide myself by such land-marks as I had observed in my hasty passage, I followed the tracks in the sand till I fancied we must be near my light. No glimmer appeared, however, and kneeling down to examine the footprints nearer, I discovered, to my dismay, that I had been following the wrong ones, for among those marked by a deep boot-heel, were prints of bare feet; we had had no guide there, and Jumal wore sandals.

"Rising, I confronted Niles, with the one despairing word, 'Lost!' as I pointed from the treacherous sand to the fast-waning light.

"I thought the old man would be overwhelmed but, to my surprise, he grew quite calm and steady, thought a moment, and then went on, saying, quietly:

"'Other men have passed here before us; let us follow their steps, for, if I do not greatly err, they lead toward great passages, where one's way is easily found.'

"On we went, bravely, till a misstep threw the professor violently to the ground with a broken leg, and nearly extinguished the torch. It was a horrible predicament, and I gave up all hope as I sat beside the poor fellow, who lay exhausted with fatigue, remorse and pain, for I would not leave him.

"'Paul,' he said suddenly, 'if you will not go on, there is one more effort we can make. I remember hearing that a party lost as we are, saved themselves by building a fire. The smoke penetrated further than sound or light, and the guide's quick wit understood the unusual mist; he followed it, and rescued the party. Make a fire and trust to Jumal.'

"'A fire without wood?' I began; but he pointed to a shelf behind me, which had escaped me in the gloom; and on it I saw a slender mummy-case. I understood him, for these dry cases, which lie about in hundreds, are freely used as firewood. Reaching up, I pulled it down, believing it to be empty, but as it fell, it burst open, and out rolled a mummy. Accustomed as I was to such sights, it startled me a little, for danger had unstrung my nerves. Laying the little brown chrysalis aside, I smashed the case, lit the pile with my torch, and soon a light cloud of smoke drifted down the three passages which diverged from the cell-like place where we had paused.

"While busied with the fire, Niles, forgetful of pain and peril, had dragged the mummy nearer, and was examining it with the interest of a man whose ruling passion was strong even in death.

"'Come and help me unroll this. I have always longed to be the first to see and secure the curious treasures put away among the folds of these uncanny winding-sheets. This is a woman, and we may find something rare and precious here,' he said, beginning to unfold the outer coverings, from which a strange aromatic odor came.

"Reluctantly I obeyed, for to me there was something sacred in the bones of this unknown woman. But to beguile the time and amuse the poor fellow, I lent a hand, wondering as I worked, if this dark, ugly thing had ever been a lovely, soft-eyed Egyptian girl.

"From the fibrous folds of the wrappings dropped precious gums and spices, which half intoxicated us with their potent breath, antique coins, and a curious jewel or two, which Niles eagerly examined.

"All the bandages but one were cut off at last, and a small head laid bare, round which still hung great plaits of what had once been luxuriant hair. The shriveled hands were folded on the breast, and clasped in them lay that gold box."

"Ah!" cried Evelyn, dropping it from her rosy palm with a shudder.

"Nay; don't reject the poor little mummy's treasure. I never have quite forgiven myself for stealing it, or for burning her," said Forsyth, painting rapidly, as if the recollection of that experience lent energy to his hand.

"Burning her! Oh, Paul, what do you mean?" asked the girl, sitting up with a face full of excitement.

"I'll tell you. While busied with Madame la Momie, our fire had burned low, for the dry case went like tinder. A faint, far-off sound made our hearts leap, and Niles cried out: 'Pile on the wood; Jumal is tracking us; don't let the smoke fail now or we are lost!'

"'There is no more wood; the case was very small, and is all gone,' I answered, tearing off such of my garments as would burn readily, and piling them upon the embers.

"Niles did the same, but the light fabrics were quickly consumed, and made no smoke.

"'Burn that!' commanded the professor, pointing to the mummy.

"I hesitated a moment. Again came the faint echo of a horn. Life was dear to me. A few dry bones might save us, and I obeyed him in silence.

"A dull blaze sprung up, and a heavy smoke rose from the burning mummy, rolling in volumes through the low passages, and threatening to suffocate us with its fragrant mist. My brain grew dizzy, the light danced before my eyes, strange phantoms seemed to people the air, and, in the act of asking Niles why he gasped and looked so pale, I lost consciousness."

Evelyn drew a long breath, and put away the scented toys from her lap as if their odor oppressed her.

Forsyth's swarthy face was all aglow with the excitement of his story, and his black eyes glittered as he added, with a quick laugh:

"That's all; Jumal found and got us out, and we both forswore pyramids for the rest of our days."

"But the box: how came you to keep it?" asked Evelyn, eyeing it askance as it lay gleaming in a streak of sunshine.

"Oh, I brought it away as a souvenir, and Niles kept the other trinkets."

"But you said harm was foretold to the possessor of those scarlet seeds," persisted the girl, whose fancy was excited by the tale, and who fancied all was not told.

"Among his spoils, Niles found a bit of parchment, which he deciphered, and this inscription said that the mummy we had so ungallantly burned was that of a famous sorceress who bequeathed her curse to whoever should disturb her rest. Of course I don't believe that curse has anything to do with it, but it's a fact that Niles never prospered from that day. He says it's because he has never recovered from the fall and fright and I dare say it is so; but I sometimes wonder if I am to share the curse, for I've a vein of superstition in me, and that poor little mummy haunts my dreams still."

A long silence followed these words. Paul painted mechanically and Evelyn lay regarding him with a thoughtful face. But gloomy fancies were as foreign to her nature as shadows are to noonday, and presently she laughed a cheery laugh, saying as she took up the box again:

"Why don't you plant them, and see what wondrous flower they will bear?"

"I doubt if they would bear anything after lying in a mummy's hand for centuries," replied Forsyth, gravely.

"Let me plant them and try. You know wheat has sprouted and grown that was taken from a mummy's coffin; why should not these pretty seeds? I should so like to watch them grow; may I, Paul?"

"No, I'd rather leave that experiment untried. I have a queer feeling about the matter, and don't want to meddle myself or let anyone I love meddle with these seeds. They may be some horrible poison, or possess some evil power, for the sorceress evidently valued them, since she clutched them fast even in her tomb."

"Now, you are foolishly superstitious, and I laugh at you. Be generous; give me one seed, just to learn if it will grow. See I'll pay for it," and Evelyn, who now stood beside him, dropped a kiss on his forehead as she made her request, with the most engaging air.

But Forsyth would not yield. He smiled and returned the embrace with lover-like warmth, then flung the seeds into the fire, and gave her back the golden box, saying, tenderly:

"My darling, I'll fill it with diamonds or bonbons, if you please, but I will not let you play with that witch's spells. You've enough of your own, so forget the 'pretty seeds' and see what a Light of the Harem I've made of you."

Evelyn frowned, and smiled, and presently the lovers were out in the spring sunshine reveling in their own happy hopes, untroubled by one foreboding fear.

II

"I have a little surprise for you, love," said Forsyth, as he greeted his cousin three months later on the morning of his wedding day.

"And I have one for you," she answered, smiling faintly.

"How pale you are, and how thin you grow! All this bridal bustle is too much for you, Evelyn," he said, with fond anxiety, as he watched the strange pallor of her face, and pressed the wasted little hand in his.

"I am so tired," she said, and leaned her head wearily on her lover's breast. "Neither sleep, food, nor air gives me strength, and a curious mist seems to cloud my mind at times. Mamma says it is the heat, but I shiver even in the sun, while at night I burn with fever. Paul, dear, I'm glad you are going to take me away to lead a quiet, happy life with you, but I'm afraid it will be a very short one."

"My fanciful little wife! You are tired and nervous with all this worry, but a few weeks of rest in the country will give us back our blooming Eve again. Have you no curiosity to learn my surprise?" he asked, to change her thoughts.

The vacant look stealing over the girl's face gave place to one of interest, but as she listened it seemed to require an effort to fix her mind on her lover's words.

"You remember the day we rummaged in the old cabinet?"

"Yes," and a smile touched her lips for a moment.

"And how you wanted to plant those queer red seeds I stole from the mummy?"

"I remember," and her eyes kindled with sudden fire.

"Well, I tossed them into the fire, as I thought, and gave you the box. But when I went back to cover up my picture, and found one of those seeds on the rug, a sudden fancy to gratify your whim led me to send it to Niles and ask him to plant and report on its progress. Today I hear from him for the first time, and he reports that the seed has grown marvelously, has budded, and that he intends to take the first flower, if it blooms in time, to a meeting of famous scientific men, after which he will send me its true name and the plant itself. From his description, it must be very curious, and I'm impatient to see it."

"You need not wait; I can show you the flower in its bloom," and Evelyn beckoned with the *mechanté* smile so long a stranger to her lips.

Much amazed, Forsyth followed her to her own little boudoir, and there, standing in the sunshine, was the unknown plant. Almost rank in their luxuriance were the vivid green leaves on the slender purple stems, and rising from the midst, one ghostly-white flower, shaped like the head of a hooded snake, with scarlet stamens like forked tongues, and on the petals glittered spots like dew.

"A strange, uncanny flower! Has it any odor?" asked Forsyth, bending to examine it, and forgetting, in his interest, to ask how it came there.

"None, and that disappoints me, I am so fond of perfumes," answered the girl, caressing the green leaves which trembled at her touch, while the purple stems deepened their tint.

"Now tell me about it," said Forsyth, after standing silent for several minutes.

"I had been before you, and secured one of the seeds, for two fell on the rug. I planted it under a glass in the richest soil I could find, watered it faithfully, and was amazed at the rapidity with which it grew when once it appeared above the earth. I told no-one, for I meant to surprise you with it; but this bud has been so long in blooming, I have had to wait. It is a good omen that it blossoms today, and as it is nearly white, I mean to wear it, for I've learned to love it, having been my pet for so long."

"I would not wear it, for, in spite of its innocent color, it is an evil-looking plant, with its adder's tongue and unnatural dew. Wait till Niles tells us what it is, then pet it if it is harmless.

"Perhaps my sorceress cherished it for some symbolic beauty–those old Egyptians were full of fancies. It was very sly of you to turn the tables on me in this way. But I forgive you, since in a few hours, I shall chain this mysterious hand forever. How cold it is! Come out into the garden and get some warmth and color for tonight, my love."

But when night came, no-one could reproach the girl with her pallor, for she glowed like a pomegranate-flower, her eyes were full of fire, her lips scarlet, and all her old vivacity seemed to have returned. A more brilliant bride never blushed under a misty veil, and when her lover saw her, he was absolutely startled by the almost unearthly beauty which transformed the pale, languid creature of the morning into this radiant woman.

They were married, and if love, many blessings, and all good gifts lavishly showered upon them could make them happy, then this young pair were truly blest. But even in the rapture of the moment that made her his, Forsyth observed how icy cold was the little hand he held, how feverish the deep color on the soft cheek he kissed, and what a strange fire burned in the tender eyes that looked so wistfully at him.

Blithe and beautiful as a spirit, the smiling bride played her part in all the festivities of that long evening, and when at last light, life and color began to fade, the loving eyes that watched her thought it but the natural weariness of the hour. As the last guest departed, Forsyth was met by a servant, who gave him a letter marked "Haste." Tearing it open, he read these lines, from a friend of the professor's:

"DEAR SIR – Poor Niles died suddenly two days ago, while at the Scientific Club, and his last words were: 'Tell Paul Forsyth to beware of the Mummy's Curse, for this fatal flower has killed me.' The circumstances of his death were so peculiar, that I add them as a sequel to this message. For several months, as he told us, he had been watching an unknown plant, and that evening he brought us the flower to examine. Other matters of interest absorbed us till a late hour, and the plant was forgotten. The professor wore it in his buttonhole–a strange white, serpent-headed blossom, with pale glittering spots, which slowly changed to a glittering scarlet, till the leaves looked as if sprinkled with blood. It was observed that instead of the pallor and feebleness which had recently come over him, that the professor was unusually animated, and seemed in an almost unnatural state of high spirits. Near the close of the meeting, in the midst of a lively discussion, he suddenly dropped, as if smitten with apoplexy. He was conveyed home insensible, and after one lucid interval, in which he gave me the message I have recorded above, he died in great agony, raving of mummies, pyramids, serpents, and some fatal curse which had fallen upon him.

"After his death, livid scarlet spots, like those on the flower, appeared upon his skin, and he shriveled like a withered leaf. At my desire, the mysterious plant was examined, and pronounced by the best authority one of the most deadly poisons known to the Egyptian sorceresses. The plant slowly absorbs the vitality of whoever cultivates it, and the blossom, worn for two or three hours, produces either madness or death."

Down dropped the paper from Forsyth's hand; he read no further, but hurried back into the room where he had left his young wife. As if worn out with fatigue, she had thrown herself upon a couch, and lay there motionless, her face half-hidden by the light folds of the veil, which had blown over it.

"Evelyn, my dearest! Wake up and answer me. Did you wear that strange flower today?" whispered Forsyth, putting the misty screen away.

There was no need for her to answer, for there, gleaming spectrally on her bosom, was the evil blossom, its white petals spotted now with flecks of scarlet, vivid as drops of newly spilt blood.

But the unhappy bridegroom scarcely saw it, for the face above it appalled him by its utter vacancy. Drawn and pallid, as if with some wasting malady, the young face, so lovely an hour ago, lay before him aged and blighted by the baleful influence of the plant which had drunk up her life. No recognition in the eyes, no word upon the lips, no motion of the hand—only the faint breath, the fluttering pulse, and wide-opened eyes, betrayed that she was alive.

Alas for the young wife! The superstitious fear at which she had smiled had proved true: the curse that had bided its time for ages was fulfilled at last, and her own hand wrecked her happiness for ever. Death in life was her doom, and for years Forsyth secluded himself to tend with pathetic devotion the pale ghost, who never, by word or look, could thank him for the love that outlived even such a fate as this.

Lot No. 249

by Arthur Conan Doyle

Sir Arthur Conan Doyle's "Lot No. 249" is part mystery, part supernatural morality tale, with a medical student as a protagonist. Originally published in 1892, it is the perhaps the first short story in which a villain resurrects an Egyptian mummy from the dead and then uses said mummy as an instrument of revenge and terror. Set at Oxford University, this story written by the creator of Sherlock Holmes not only delves deep into the mysterious and the weird, it also delivers a striking portrait of English university student life at a certain time and in a certain place.

Unlike in Louisa May Alcott's "Lost in a Pyramid, or The Mummy's Curse," there is no curse in this story. Instead, Lot 249, as the mummy is known, is predominantly an instrument of human evil, rather than an independent actor in its own right. The story therefore is as much a work of crime fiction and a portrait of human villainy as it is a supernatural tale.

Still, one can equally consider "Lot No. 249" to be an early work of modern horror fiction. Indeed, Doyle's story about a violent mummy was skillfully adapted for the big screen as one feature story in the anthology film, Tales From The Darkside: The Movie *(1990). In this film, actor Steve Buscemi portrays the owner of Lot 249. While set in the modern era, this segment in the portmanteau horror film is overall quite faithful to both the text and the spirit of Doyle's story. All told, Doyle's story remains one of the most important ancient Egyptian supernatural tales ever written.*

Of the dealings of Edward Bellingham with William Monkhouse Lee, and of the cause of the great terror of Abercrombie Smith, it may be that no absolute and final judgment will ever be delivered. It is true that we have the full and clear narrative of Smith himself, and such corroboration as he could look for from Thomas Styles the servant, from the Reverend Plumptree Peterson, Fellow of Old's, and from such other people as chanced to gain some passing glance at this or that incident in a singular chain of events. Yet, in the main, the story must rest upon Smith alone, and the most will think that it is more likely that one brain, however outwardly sane, has some subtle warp in its texture, some strange flaw in its workings, than that the path of Nature has been overstepped in open day in so famed a centre of learning and light as the University of Oxford. Yet when we think how narrow and how devious this path of Nature is, how dimly we can trace it, for all our lamps of science, and how from the darkness which girds it round great and terrible possibilities loom ever shadowly upwards, it is a bold and confident man who will put a limit to the strange bypaths into which the human spirit may wander.

In a certain wing of what we will call Old College in Oxford there is a corner turret of an exceeding great age. The heavy arch which spans the open door has bent downwards in the centre under the weight of its years, and the grey, lichen-blotched blocks of stone are bound and knitted together with withes and strands of ivy, as though the old mother had set herself to brace them up against wind and weather. From the door a stone stair curves upward spirally, passing two landings, and terminating in a third one, its steps all shapeless and hollowed by the tread of so many generations of the seekers after knowledge. Life has flowed like water down this winding stair, and, waterlike, has left these smooth-worn grooves behind it. From the long-gowned, pedantic scholars of Plantagenet days down to the young bloods of a later age, how full and strong has been that tide of young, English life. And what was left now of all those hopes, those strivings, those fiery energies, save here and there in some old-world churchyard a few scratches upon a stone, and perchance a handful of dust in a mouldering coffin? Yet here were the silent stair and the grey, old wall, with bend and saltire and many another heraldic device still to be read upon its surface, like grotesque shadows thrown back from the days that had passed.

In the month of May, in the year 1884, three young men occupied the sets of rooms which opened on to the separate landings of the old stair. Each set consisted simply of a sitting-room and of a bedroom, while the two corresponding rooms upon the ground-floor were used, the one as a coal-cellar, and the other as the living-room of the servant, or scout, Thomas Styles, whose duty it was to wait upon the three men above him. To right and to left was a line of lecture-rooms and of offices, so that the dwellers in the old turret enjoyed a certain seclusion, which made the chambers popular among the more studious undergraduates. Such were the three who occupied them now – Abercrombie Smith above, Edward Bellingham beneath him, and William Monkhouse Lee upon the lowest storey.

It was ten o'clock on a bright, spring night, and Abercrombie Smith lay back in his arm-chair, his feet upon the fender, and his briar-root pipe between his lips. In a similar chair, and equally at his ease, there lounged on the other side of the fireplace his old school friend Jephro Hastie. Both men were in flannels, for they had spent their evening upon the river, but apart from their dress no one could look at their hard-cut, alert faces without seeing that they were open-air men—men whose minds and tastes turned naturally to all that was manly and robust. Hastie, indeed, was stroke of his college boat, and Smith was an even better oar, but a coming examination had already cast its shadow over him and held him to his work, save for a few hours a week which health demanded. A litter of medical books upon the table, with scattered bones, models, and anatomical plates, pointed to the extent as well as the nature of his studies, while a couple of single-sticks and a set of boxing-gloves above the mantelpiece hinted at the means by which, with Hastie's help, he might take his exercise in its most compressed and least-distant form. They knew each other very well – so well that they could sit now in that soothing silence which is the very highest development of companionship.

"Have some whisky," said Abercrombie Smith at last between two cloud-bursts. "Scotch in the jug and Irish in the bottle."

"No, thanks. I'm in for the sculls. I don't liquor when I'm training. How about you?"

"I'm reading hard. I think it best to leave it alone."

Hastie nodded, and they relapsed into a contented silence.

"By the way, Smith," asked Hastie, presently, "have you made the acquaintance of either of the fellows on your stair yet?"

"Just a nod when we pass. Nothing more."

"Hum! I should be inclined to let it stand at that. I know something of them both. Not much, but as much as I want. I don't think I should take them to my bosom if I were you. Not that there's much amiss with Monkhouse Lee."

"Meaning the thin one?"

"Precisely. He is a gentlemanly little fellow. I don't think there is any vice in him. But then you can't know him without knowing Bellingham."

"Meaning the fat one?"

"Yes, the fat one. And he's a man whom I, for one, would rather not know."

Abercrombie Smith raised his eyebrows and glanced across at his companion.

"What's up, then?" he asked. "Drink? Cards? Cad? You used not to be censorious."

"Ah! you evidently don't know the man, or you wouldn't ask. There's something damnable about him – something reptilian. My gorge always rises at him. I should put him down as a man with secret vices – an evil liver. He's no fool, though. They say that he is one of the best men in his line that they have ever had in the college."

"Medicine or classics?"

"Eastern languages. He's a demon at them. Chillingworth met him somewhere above the second cataract last long, and he told me that he just prattled to the Arabs as if he had been born and nursed and weaned among them.

He talked Coptic to the Copts, and Hebrew to the Jews, and Arabic to the Bedouins, and they were all ready to kiss the hem of his frock-coat. There are some old hermit Johnnies up in those parts who sit on rocks and scowl and spit at the casual stranger. Well, when they saw this chap Bellingham, before he had said five words they just lay down on their bellies and wriggled. Chillingworth said that he never saw anything like it. Bellingham seemed to take it as his right, too, and strutted about among them and talked down to them like a Dutch uncle. Pretty good for an undergrad. of Old's, wasn't it?"

"Why do you say you can't know Lee without knowing Bellingham?"

"Because Bellingham is engaged to his sister Eveline. Such a bright little girl, Smith! I know the whole family well. It's disgusting to see that brute with her. A toad and a dove, that's what they always remind me of."

Abercrombie Smith grinned and knocked his ashes out against the side of the grate.

"You show every card in your hand, old chap," said he. "What a prejudiced, green-eyed, evil-thinking old man it is! You have really nothing against the fellow except that."

"Well, I've known her ever since she was as long as that cherry-wood pipe, and I don't like to see her taking risks. And it is a risk. He looks beastly. And he has a beastly temper, a venomous temper. You remember his row with Long Norton?"

"No; you always forget that I am a freshman."

"Ah, it was last winter. Of course. Well, you know the towpath along by the river. There were several fellows going along it, Bellingham in front, when they came on an old market-woman coming the other way. It had been raining – you know what those fields are like when it has rained – and the path ran between the river and a great puddle that was nearly as broad. Well, what does this swine do but keep the path, and push the old girl into the mud, where she and her marketings came to terrible grief. It was a blackguard thing to do, and Long Norton, who is as gentle a fellow as ever stepped, told him what he thought of it. One word led to another, and it ended in Norton laying his stick across the fellow's shoulders. There was the deuce of a fuss about it, and it's a treat to see the way in which Bellingham looks at Norton when they meet now. By Jove, Smith, it's nearly eleven o'clock!"

"No hurry. Light your pipe again."

"Not I. I'm supposed to be in training. Here I've been sitting gossiping when I ought to have been safely tucked up. I'll borrow your skull, if you can share it. Williams has had mine for a month. I'll take the little bones of your ear, too, if you are sure you won't need them. Thanks very much. Never mind a bag, I can carry them very well under my arm. Good night, my son, and take my tip as to your neighbour."

When Hastie, bearing his anatomical plunder, had clattered off down the winding stair, Abercrombie Smith hurled his pipe into the wastepaper basket, and drawing his chair nearer to the lamp, plunged into a formidable, green-covered volume, adorned with great, coloured maps of that strange, internal kingdom of which we are the hapless and helpless monarchs. Though a freshman at Oxford, the student was not so in medicine, for he had worked for four years at Glasgow and at Berlin, and this coming examination would place him finally as a member of his profession. With his firm mouth, broad forehead, and clear-cut, somewhat hard-featured face, he was a man who, if he had no brilliant talent, was yet so dogged, so patient, and so strong that he might in the end overtop a more showy genius. A man who can hold his own among Scotchmen and North Germans is not a man to be easily set back. Smith had left a name at Glasgow and at Berlin, and he was bent now upon doing as much at Oxford, if hard work and devotion could accomplish it.

He had sat reading for about an hour, and the hands of the noisy carriage clock upon the side-table were rapidly closing together upon the twelve, when a sudden sound fell upon the student's ear–a sharp, rather shrill sound, like the hissing intake of a man's breath who gasps under some strong emotion. Smith laid down his book and slanted his ear to listen. There was no one on either side or above him, so that the interruption came certainly from the neighbour beneath–the same neighbour of whom Hastie had given so unsavoury an account. Smith knew him only as a flabby, pale-faced man of silent and studious habits, a man whose lamp threw a golden bar from the old turret even after he had extinguished his own. This community in lateness had formed a certain silent bond between them. It was soothing to Smith when the hours stole on towards dawning to feel that there was another so close who set as small a value upon his sleep as he did. Even now, as his thoughts turned towards him, Smith's feelings were kindly. Hastie was a good fellow, but he was rough, strong-fibred, with no imagination or sympathy. He could not tolerate departures from what he looked upon as the model type of manliness. If a man could not be measured by a public-school standard, then he was beyond the pale with Hastie. Like so many who are themselves robust, he was apt to confuse the constitution with the character, to ascribe to want of principle what was really a want of circulation. Smith, with his stronger mind, knew his friend's habit, and made allowance for it now as his thoughts turned towards the man beneath him.

There was no return of the singular sound, and Smith was about to turn to his work once more, when suddenly there broke out in the silence of the night a hoarse cry, a positive scream – the call of a man who is moved and shaken beyond all control. Smith sprang out of his chair and dropped his book. He was a man of fairly firm fibre, but there was something in this sudden, uncontrollable shriek of horror which chilled his blood and pringled in his skin. Coming in such a place and at such an hour, it brought a thousand fantastic possibilities into his head. Should he rush down, or was it better to wait? He had all the national hatred of making a scene, and he knew so little of his neighbour that he would not lightly intrude upon his affairs. For a moment he stood in doubt and even as he balanced the matter there was a quick rattle of footsteps upon the stairs, and young Monkhouse Lee, half-dressed and as white as ashes, burst into his room.

"Come down!" he gasped. "Bellingham's ill."

Abercrombie Smith followed him closely downstairs into the sitting-room which was beneath his own, and intent as he was upon the matter in hand, he could not but take an amazed glance around him as he crossed the threshold. It was such a chamber as he had never seen before–a museum rather than a study. Walls and ceiling were thickly covered with a thousand strange relics from Egypt and the East. Tall, angular figures bearing burdens or weapons stalked in an uncouth frieze round the apartments. Above were bull-headed, stork-headed, cat-headed, owl-headed statues, with viper-crowned, almond-eyed monarchs and strange, beetle-like deities cut out of the blue Egyptian lapis lazuli. Horus and Isis and Osiris peeped down from every niche and shelf, while across the ceiling a true son of Old Nile, a great, hanging-jawed crocodile, was slung in a double noose.

In the centre of this singular chamber was a large, square table, littered with papers, bottles, and the dried leaves of some graceful, palm-like plant. These varied objects had all been heaped together in order to make room for a mummy case, which had been conveyed from the wall, as was evident from the gap there, and laid across the front of the table. The mummy itself, a horrid, black, withered thing, like a charred head on a gnarled bush, was lying half out of the case, with its claw-like hand and bony forearm resting upon the table. Propped up against the sarcophagus was an old, yellow scroll of papyrus, and in front of it, in a wooden armchair, sat the owner of the room, his head thrown back, his widely opened eyes directed in a horrified stare to the crocodile above him, and his blue, thick lips puffing loudly with every expiration.

"My God! he's dying!" cried Monkhouse Lee, distractedly.

He was a slim, handsome young fellow, olive-skinned and dark-eyed, of a Spanish rather than of an English type, with a Celtic intensity of manner which contrasted with the Saxon phlegm of Abercrombie Smith.

"Only a faint, I think," said the medical student. "Just give me a hand with him. You take his feet. Now on to the sofa. Can you kick all those little wooden devils off? What a litter it is! Now he will be all right if we undo his collar and give him some water. What has he been up to at all?"

"I don't know. I heard him cry out. I ran up. I know him pretty well, you know. It is very good of you to come down."

"His heart is going like a pair of castanets," said Smith, laying his hand on the breast of the unconscious man. "He seems to me to be frightened all to pieces. Chuck the water over him! What a face he has got on him!"

It was indeed a strange and most repellent face, for colour and outline were equally unnatural. It was white, not with the ordinary pallor of fear, but with an absolutely bloodless white, like the under side of a sole. He was very fat, but gave the impression of having at some time been considerably fatter, for his skin hung loosely in creases and folds, and was shot with a meshwork of wrinkles. Short, stubbly brown hair bristled up from his scalp, with a pair of thick, wrinkled ears protruding at the sides. His light-grey eyes were still open, the pupils dilated and the balls projecting in a fixed and horrid stare. It seemed to Smith as he looked down upon him that he had never seen Nature's danger signals flying so plainly upon a man's countenance, and his thoughts turned more seriously to the warning which Hastie had given him an hour before.

"What the deuce can have frightened him so?" he asked.

"It's the mummy."

"The mummy? How, then?"

"I don't know. It's beastly and morbid. I wish he would drop it. It's the second fright he has given me. It was the same last winter. I found him just like this, with that horrid thing in front of him."

"What does he want with the mummy, then?"

"Oh, he's a crank, you know. It's his hobby. He knows more about these things than any man in England. But I wish he wouldn't! Ah, he's beginning to come to."

A faint tinge of colour had begun to steal back into Bellingham's ghastly cheeks, and his eyelids shivered like a sail after a calm. He clasped and unclasped his hands, drew a long, thin breath between his teeth, and suddenly jerking up his head, threw a glance of recognition around him. As his eyes fell upon the mummy, he sprang off the sofa, seized the roll of papyrus, thrust it into a drawer, turned the key, and staggered back on to the sofa.

"What's up?" he asked. "What do you chaps want?"

"You've been shrieking out and making no end of a fuss," said Monkhouse Lee. "If our neighbour here from above hadn't come down, I'm sure I don't know what I should have done with you."

"Ah, it's Abercrombie Smith," said Bellingham, glancing up at him. "How very good of you to come in! What a fool I am! Oh, my God, what a fool I am!"

He sank his head on to his hands, and burst into peal after peal of hysterical laughter.

"Look here! Drop it!" cried Smith, shaking him roughly by the shoulder.

"Your nerves are all in a jangle. You must drop these little midnight games with mummies, or you'll be going off your chump. You're all on wires now."

"I wonder," said Bellingham, "whether you would be as cool as I am if you had seen —"

"What then?"

"Oh, nothing. I meant that I wonder if you could sit up at night with a mummy without trying your nerves. I have no doubt that you are quite right. I dare say that I have been taking it out of myself too much lately. But I am all right now. Please don't go, though. Just wait for a few minutes until I am quite myself."

"The room is very close," remarked Lee, throwing open the window and letting in the cool night air.

"It's balsamic resin," said Bellingham. He lifted up one of the dried palmate leaves from the table and frizzled it over the chimney of the lamp. It broke away into heavy smoke wreaths, and a pungent, biting odour filled the chamber. "It's the sacred plant—the plant of the priests," he remarked. "Do you know anything of Eastern languages, Smith?"

"Nothing at all. Not a word."

The answer seemed to lift a weight from the Egyptologist's mind.

"By the way," he continued, "how long was it from the time that you ran down, until I came to my senses?"

"Not long. Some four or five minutes."

"I thought it could not be very long," said he, drawing a long breath. "But what a strange thing unconsciousness is! There is no measurement to it. I could not tell from my own sensations if it were seconds or weeks. Now that gentleman on the table was packed up in the days of the eleventh dynasty, some forty centuries ago, and yet if he could find his tongue, he would tell us that this lapse of time has been but a closing of the eyes and a reopening of them. He is a singularly fine mummy, Smith."

Smith stepped over to the table and looked down with a professional eye at the black and twisted form in front of him. The features, though horribly discoloured, were perfect, and two little nut-like eyes still lurked in the depths of the black, hollow sockets. The blotched skin was drawn tightly from bone to bone, and a tangled wrap of black, coarse hair fell over the ears. Two thin teeth, like those of a rat, overlay the shrivelled lower lip. In its crouching position, with bent joints and craned head, there was a suggestion of energy about the horrid thing which made Smith's gorge rise. The gaunt ribs, with their parchment-like covering, were exposed, and the sunken, leaden-hued abdomen, with the long slit where the embalmer had left his mark; but the lower limbs were wrapped round with coarse, yellow bandages. A number of little clove-like pieces of myrrh and of cassia were sprinkled over the body, and lay scattered on the inside of the case.

"I don't know his name," said Bellingham, passing his hand over the shrivelled head. "You see the outer sarcophagus with the inscriptions is missing. Lot 249 is all the title he has now. You see it printed on his case. That was his number in the auction at which I picked him up."

"He has been a very pretty sort of fellow in his day," remarked Abercrombie Smith.

"He has been a giant. His mummy is six feet seven in length, and that would be a giant over there, for they were never a very robust race. Feel these great, knotted bones, too. He would be a nasty fellow to tackle."

"Perhaps these very hands helped to build the stones into the pyramids," suggested Monkhouse Lee, looking down with disgust in his eyes at the crooked, unclean talons.

"No fear. This fellow has been pickled in natron, and looked after in the most approved style. They did not serve hodsmen in that fashion. Salt or bitumen was enough for them. It has been calculated that this sort of thing cost about seven hundred and thirty pounds in our money. Our friend was a noble at the least. What do you make of that small inscription near his feet, Smith?"

"I told you that I know no Eastern tongue."

"Ah, so you did. It is the name of the embalmer, I take it. A very conscientious worker he must have been. I wonder how many modern works will survive four thousand years?"

He kept on speaking lightly and rapidly, but it was evident to Abercrombie Smith that he was still palpitating with fear. His hands shook, his lower lip trembled, and look where he would, his eye always came sliding round to his gruesome companion. Through all his fear, however, there was a suspicion of triumph in his tone and manner. His eyes shone, and his footstep, as he paced the room, was brisk and jaunty. He gave the impression of a man who has gone through an ordeal, the marks of which he still bears upon him, but which has helped him to his end.

"You're not going yet?" he cried, as Smith rose from the sofa.

At the prospect of solitude, his fears seemed to crowd back upon him, and he stretched out a hand to detain him.

"Yes, I must go. I have my work to do. You are all right now. I think that with your nervous system you should take up some less morbid study."

"Oh, I am not nervous as a rule; and I have unwrapped mummies before."

"You fainted last time," observed Monkhouse Lee.

"Ah, yes, so I did. Well, I must have a nerve tonic or a course of electricity. You are not going, Lee?"

"I'll do whatever you wish, Ned."

"Then I'll come down with you and have a shakedown on your sofa. Good night, Smith. I am so sorry to have disturbed you with my foolishness."

They shook hands, and as the medical student stumbled up the spiral and irregular stair he heard a key turn in a door, and the steps of his two new acquaintances as they descended to the lower floor.

In this strange way began the acquaintance between Edward Bellingham and Abercrombie Smith, an acquaintance which the latter, at least, had no desire to push further. Bellingham, however, appeared to have taken a fancy to his rough-spoken neighbour, and made his advances in such a way that he could hardly be repulsed without absolute brutality. Twice he called to thank Smith for his assistance, and many times afterwards he looked in with books, papers and such other civilities as two bachelor neighbours can offer each other. He was, as Smith soon found, a man of wide reading, with catholic tastes and an extraordinary memory. His manner, too, was so pleasing and suave that one came, after a time, to overlook his repellent appearance. For a jaded and wearied man he was no unpleasant companion, and Smith found himself, after a time, looking forward to his visits, and even returning them.

Clever as he undoubtedly was, however, the medical student seemed to detect a dash of insanity in the man. He broke out at times into a high, inflated style of talk which was in contrast with the simplicity of his life.

"It is a wonderful thing," he cried, "to feel that one can command powers of good and of evil–a ministering angel or a demon of vengeance." And again, of Monkhouse Lee, he said – "Lee is a good fellow, an honest fellow, but he is without strength or ambition. He would not make a fit partner for a man with a great enterprise. He would not make a fit partner for me."

At such hints and innuendoes stolid Smith, puffing solemnly at his pipe, would simply raise his eyebrows and shake his head, with little interjections of medical wisdom as to earlier hours and fresher air.

One habit Bellingham had developed of late which Smith knew to be a frequent herald of a weakening mind. He appeared to be for ever talking to himself. At late hours of the night, when there could be no visitor with him, Smith could still hear his voice beneath him in a low, muffled monologue, sunk almost to a whisper, and yet very audible in the silence. This solitary babbling annoyed and distracted the student, so that he spoke more than once to his neighbour about it. Bellingham, however, flushed up at the charge, and denied curtly that he had uttered a sound; indeed, he showed more annoyance over the matter than the occasion seemed to demand.

Had Abercrombie Smith had any doubt as to his own ears he had not to go far to find corroboration. Tom Styles, the little wrinkled man-servant who had attended to the wants of the lodgers in the turret for a longer time than any man's memory could carry him, was sorely put to it over the same matter.

"If you please, sir," said he, as he tidied down the top chamber one morning, "do you think Mr. Bellingham is all right, sir?"

"All right, Styles?"

"Yes, sir. Right in the head, sir."

"Why should he not be, then?"

"Well, I don't know, sir. His habits has changed of late. He's not the same man he used to be, though I make free to say that he was never quite one of my gentlemen, like Mr. Hastie or yourself, sir. He's took to talkin' to himself something awful. I wonder it don't disturb you. I don't know what to make of him, sir."

"I don't know what business it is of yours, Styles."

"Well, I takes an interest, Mr. Smith. It may be forward of me, but I can't help it. I feel sometimes as if I was mother and father to my young gentlemen. It all falls on me when things go wrong and the relations come. But Mr. Bellingham, sir. I want to know what it is that walks about his room sometimes when he's out and when the door's locked on the outside."

"Eh? you're talking nonsense, Styles."

"Maybe so, sir; but I heard it more'n once with my own ears."

"Rubbish, Styles."

"Very good, sir. You'll ring the bell if you want me."

Abercrombie Smith gave little heed to the gossip of the old man-servant, but a small incident occurred a few days later which left an unpleasant effect upon his mind, and brought the words of Styles forcibly to his memory.

Bellingham had come up to see him late one night, and was entertaining him with an interesting account of the rock tombs of Beni Hassan in Upper Egypt, when Smith, whose hearing was remarkably acute, distinctly heard the sound of a door opening on the landing below.

"There's some fellow gone in or out of your room," he remarked.

Bellingham sprang up and stood helpless for a moment, with the expression of a man who is half-incredulous and half-afraid.

"I surely locked it. I am almost positive that I locked it," he stammered. "No one could have opened it."

"Why, I hear someone coming up the steps now," said Smith.

Bellingham rushed out through the door, slammed it loudly behind him, and hurried down the stairs. About half-way down Smith heard him stop, and thought he caught the sound of whispering. A moment later the door beneath him shut, a key creaked in a lock, and Bellingham, with beads of moisture upon his pale face, ascended the stairs once more, and re-entered the room.

"It's all right," he said, throwing himself down in a chair. "It was that fool of a dog. He had pushed the door open. I don't know how I came to forget to lock it."

"I didn't know you kept a dog," said Smith, looking very thoughtfully at the disturbed face of his companion.

"Yes, I haven't had him long. I must get rid of him. He's a great nuisance."

"He must be, if you find it so hard to shut him up. I should have thought that shutting the door would have been enough, without locking it."

"I want to prevent old Styles from letting him out. He's of some value, you know, and it would be awkward to lose him."

"I am a bit of a dog-fancier myself," said Smith, still gazing hard at his companion from the corner of his eyes. "Perhaps you'll let me have a look at it."

"Certainly. But I am afraid it cannot be to-night; I have an appointment. Is that clock right? Then I am a quarter of an hour late already. You'll excuse me, I am sure."

He picked up his cap and hurried from the room. In spite of his appointment, Smith heard him re-enter his own chamber and lock his door upon the inside.

This interview left a disagreeable impression upon the medical student's mind. Bellingham had lied to him, and lied so clumsily that it looked as if he had desperate reasons for concealing the truth. Smith knew that his neighbour had no dog. He knew, also, that the step which he had heard upon the stairs was not the step of an animal. But if it were not, then what could it be? There was old Style's statement about the something which used to pace the room at times when the owner was absent. Could it be a woman? Smith rather inclined to the view. If so, it would mean disgrace and expulsion to Bellingham if it were discovered by the authorities, so that his anxiety and falsehoods might be accounted for. And yet it was inconceivable that an undergraduate could keep a woman in his rooms without being instantly detected. Be the explanation what it might, there was something ugly about it, and Smith determined, as he turned to his books, to discourage all further attempts at intimacy on the part of his soft-spoken and ill-favoured neighbour.

But his work was destined to interruption that night. He had hardly caught up the broken threads when a firm, heavy footfall came three steps at a time from below, and Hastie, in blazer and flannels, burst into the room.

"Still at it!" said he, plumping down into his wonted arm-chair. "What a chap you are to stew! I believe an earthquake might come and knock Oxford into a cocked hat, and you would sit perfectly placid with your books among the ruins. However, I won't bore you long. Three whiffs of baccy, and I am off."

"What's the news, then?" asked Smith, cramming a plug of bird's-eye into his briar with his forefinger.

"Nothing very much. Wilson made seventy for the freshmen against the eleven. They say that they will play him instead of Buddicomb, for Buddi-comb is clean off colour. He used to be able to bowl a little, but it's nothing but half-volleys and long hops now."

"Medium right," suggested Smith, with the intense gravity which comes upon a 'varsity man when he speaks of athletics.

"Inclining to fast, with a work from leg. Comes with the arm about three inches or so. He used to be nasty on a wet wicket. Oh, by the way, have you heard about Long Norton?"

"What's that?"

"He's been attacked."

"Attacked?"

"Yes, just as he was turning out of the High Street, and within a hundred yards of the gate of Old's."

"But who —"

"Ah, that's the rub! If you said 'what,' you would be more grammatical. Norton swears that it was not human, and, indeed, from the scratches on his throat, I should be inclined to agree with him."

"What, then? Have we come down to spooks?"

Abercrombie Smith puffed his scientific contempt.

"Well, no; I don't think that is quite the idea, either. I am inclined to think that if any showman has lost a great ape lately, and the brute is in these parts, a jury would find a true bill against it. Norton passes that way every night, you know, about the same hour. There's a tree that hangs low over the path – the big elm from Rainy's garden. Norton thinks the thing dropped on him out of the tree. Anyhow, he was nearly strangled by two arms, which, he says, were as strong and as thin as steel bands. He saw nothing; only those beastly arms that tightened and tightened on him. He yelled his head nearly off, and a couple of chaps came running, and the thing went over the wall like a cat. He never got a fair sight of it the whole time. It gave Norton a shake up, I can tell you. I tell him it has been as good as a change at the seaside for him."

"A garrotter, most likely," said Smith.

"Very possibly. Norton says not; but we don't mind what he says. The gar-rotter had long nails, and was pretty smart at swinging himself over walls. By the way, your beautiful neighbour would be pleased if he heard about it. He had a grudge against Norton, and he's not a man, from what I know of him, to forget his little debts. But hallo, old chap, what have you got in your nod-dle?"

"Nothing," Smith answered, curtly.

He had started in his chair, and the look had flashed over his face which comes upon a man who is struck suddenly by some unpleasant idea.

"You looked as if something I had said had taken you on the raw. By the way, you have made the acquaintance of Master B. since I looked in last, have you not? Young Monkhouse Lee told me something to that effect."

"Yes; I know him slightly. He has been up here once or twice."

"Well, you're big enough and ugly enough to take care of yourself. He's not what I should call exactly a healthy sort of Johnny, though, no doubt, he's very clever, and all that. But you'll soon find out for yourself. Lee is all right; he's a very decent little fellow. Well, so long, old chap! I row Mullins for the Vice-Chancellor's pot on Wednesday week, so mind you come down, in case I don't see you before."

Bovine Smith laid down his pipe and turned stolidly to his books once more. But with all the will in the world, he found it very hard to keep his mind upon his work. It would slip away to brood upon the man beneath him, and upon the little mystery which hung round his chambers. Then his thoughts turned to this singular attack of which Hastie had spoken, and to the grudge which Bellingham was said to owe to the object of it. The two ideas would persist in rising together in his mind, as though there were some close and intimate connection between them. And yet the suspicion was so dim and vague that it could not be put down in words.

"Confound the chap!" cried Smith, as he shied his book on pathology across the room. "He has spoiled my night's reading, and that's reason enough, if there were no other, why I should steer clear of him in the future."

For ten days the medical student confined himself so closely to his studies that he neither saw nor heard anything of either of the men beneath him. At the hours when Bellingham had been accustomed to visit him, he took care to sport his oak, and though he more than once heard a knocking at his outer door, he resolutely refused to answer it. One afternoon, however, he was descending the stairs when, just as he was passing it, Bellingham's door flew open, and young Monkhouse Lee came out with his eyes sparkling and a dark flush of anger upon his olive cheeks. Close at his heels followed Bellingham, his fat, unhealthy face all quivering with malignant passion.

"You fool!" he hissed. "You'll be sorry."

"Very likely," cried the other. "Mind what I say. It's off! I won't hear of it!"

"You've promised, anyhow."

"Oh, I'll keep that! I won't speak. But I'd rather little Eva was in her grave. Once for all, it's off. She'll do what I say. We don't want to see you again."

So much Smith could not avoid hearing, but he hurried on, for he had no wish to be involved in their dispute. There had been a serious breach between them, that was clear enough, and Lee was going to cause the engagement with his sister to be broken off. Smith thought of Hastie's comparison of the toad and the dove, and was glad to think that the matter was at an end. Bellingham's face when he was in a passion was not pleasant to look upon. He was not a man to whom an innocent girl could be trusted for life. As he walked, Smith wondered languidly what could have caused the quarrel, and what the promise might be which Bellingham had been so anxious that Monkhouse Lee should keep.

It was the day of the sculling match between Hastie and Mullins, and a stream of men were making their way down to the banks of the Isis. A May sun was shining brightly, and the yellow path was barred with the black shadows of tall elm trees. On either side the grey colleges lay back from the road, the hoary old mothers of minds looking out from their high, mullioned windows at the tide of young life which swept so merrily past them. Black-clad tutors, prim officials, pale, reading men, brown-faced, straw-hatted young athletes in white sweaters or many-coloured blazers, all were hurrying towards the blue, winding river which curves through the Oxford meadows.

Abercrombie Smith, with the intuition of an old oarsman, chose his position at the point where he knew that the struggle, if there were a struggle, would come. Far off he heard the hum which announced the start, the gathering roar of the approach, the thunder of running feet, and the shouts of the men in the boats beneath him. A spray of half-clad, deep-breathing runners shot past him, and craning over their shoulders, he saw Hastie pulling a steady thirty-six, while his opponent, with a jerky forty, was a good boat's length behind him. Smith gave a cheer for his friend, and pulling out his watch, was starting off again for his chambers, when he felt a touch upon his shoulder, and found that young Monkhouse Lee was beside him.

"I saw you there," he said, in a timid, deprecating way. "I wanted to speak to you, if you could spare me a half-hour. This cottage is mine. I share it with Harrington of King's. Come in and have a cup of tea."

"I must be back presently," said Smith. "I am hard on the grind at present. But I'll come in for a few minutes with pleasure. I wouldn't have come out only Hastie is a friend of mine."

"So he is of mine. Hasn't he a beautiful style? Mullins wasn't in it. But come into the cottage. It's a little den of a place, but it is pleasant to work in during the summer months."

It was a small, square, white building, with green doors and shutters, and a rustic trellis-work porch, standing back some fifty yards from the river's bank. Inside, the main room was roughly fitted up as a study – deal table, unpainted shelves with books, and a few cheap oleographs upon the wall. A kettle sang upon a spirit-stove, and there were tea things upon a tray on the table.

"Try that chair and have a cigarette," said Lee. "Let me pour you out a cup of tea. It's so good of you to come in, for I know that your time is a good deal taken up. I wanted to say to you that, if I were you, I should change my rooms at once."

"Eh?"

Smith sat staring at a lighted match in one hand and his unlit cigarette in the other.

"Yes; it must seem very extraordinary, and the worst of it is that I cannot give my reasons, for I am under a solemn promise – a very solemn promise. But I may go so far as to say that I don't think Bellingham is a very safe man to live near. I intend to camp out here as much as I can for a time."

"Not safe! What do you mean?"

"Ah, that's what I mustn't say. But do take my advice and move your rooms. We had a grand row to-day. You must have heard us, for you came down the stairs."

"I saw that you had fallen out."

"He's a horrible chap, Smith. That is the only word for him. I have had doubts about him ever since that night when he fainted – you remember, when you came down. I taxed him to-day, and he told me things that made my hair rise, and wanted me to stand in with him. I'm not straight-laced, but I am a clergyman's son, you know, and I think there are some things which are quite beyond the pale. I only thank God that I found him out before it was too late, for he was to have married into my family."

"This is all very fine, Lee," said Abercrombie Smith curtly. "But either you are saying a great deal too much or a great deal too little."

"I give you a warning."

"If there is real reason for warning, no promise can bind you. If I see a rascal about to blow a place up with dynamite no pledge will stand in my way of preventing him."

"Ah, but I cannot prevent him, and I can do nothing but warn you."

"Without saying what you warn me against."

"Against Bellingham."

"But that is childish. Why should I fear him, or any man?"

"I can't tell you. I can only entreat you to change your rooms. You are in danger where you are. I don't even say that Bellingham would wish to injure you. But it might happen, for he is a dangerous neighbour just now."

"Perhaps I know more than you think," said Smith, looking keenly at the young man's boyish, earnest face. "Suppose I tell you that someone else shares Bellingham's rooms."

Monkhouse Lee sprang from his chair in uncontrollable excitement.

"You know, then?" he gasped.

"A woman."

Lee dropped back again with a groan.

"My lips are sealed," he said. "I must not speak."

"Well, anyhow," said Smith, rising, "it is not likely that I should allow myself to be frightened out of rooms which suit me very nicely. It would be a little too feeble for me to move out all my goods and chattels because you say that Bellingham might in some unexplained way do me an injury. I think that I'll just take my chance, and stay where I am, and as I see that it's nearly five o'clock, I must ask you to excuse me."

He bade the young student adieu in a few curt words, and made his way homeward through the sweet spring evening, feeling half-ruffled, half-amused, as any other strong, unimaginative man might who has been menaced by a vague and shadowy danger.

There was one little indulgence which Abercrombie Smith always allowed himself, however closely his work might press upon him. Twice a week, on the Tuesday and the Friday, it was his invariable custom to walk over to Farlingford, the residence of Doctor Plumptree Peterson, situated about a mile and a half out of Oxford. Peterson had been a close friend of Smith's elder brother, Francis, and as he was a bachelor, fairly well-to-do, with a good cellar and a better library, his house was a pleasant goal for a man who was in need of a brisk walk. Twice a week, then, the medical student would swing out there along the dark country roads and spend a pleasant hour in Peterson's comfortable study, discussing, over a glass of old port, the gossip of the varsity or the latest developments of medicine or of surgery.

On the day which followed his interview with Monkhouse Lee, Smith shut up his books at a quarter past eight, the hour when he usually started for his friend's house. As he was leaving his room, however, his eyes chanced to fall upon one of the books which Bellingham had lent him, and his conscience pricked him for not having returned it. However repellent the man might be, he should not be treated with discourtesy. Taking the book, he walked downstairs and knocked at his neighbour's door. There was no answer; but on turning the handle he found that it was unlocked. Pleased at the thought of avoiding an interview, he stepped inside, and placed the book with his card upon the table.

The lamp was turned half down, but Smith could see the details of the room plainly enough. It was all much as he had seen it before – the frieze, the animal-headed gods, the hanging crocodile, and the table littered over with papers and dried leaves. The mummy case stood upright against the wall, but the mummy itself was missing. There was no sign of any second occupant of the room, and he felt as he withdrew that he had probably done Bellingham an injustice. Had he a guilty secret to preserve, he would hardly leave his door open so that all the world might enter.

The spiral stair was as black as pitch, and Smith was slowly making his way down its irregular steps, when he was suddenly conscious that something had passed him in the darkness. There was a faint sound, a whiff of air, a light brushing past his elbow, but so slight that he could scarcely be certain of it. He stopped and listened, but the wind was rustling among the ivy outside, and he could hear nothing else.

"Is that you, Styles?" he shouted.

There was no answer, and all was still behind him. It must have been a sudden gust of air, for there were crannies and cracks in the old turret. And yet he could almost have sworn that he heard a footfall by his very side. He had emerged into the quadrangle, still turning the matter over in his head, when a man came running swiftly across the smooth-cropped lawn.

"Is that you, Smith?"

"Hullo, Hastie!"

"For God's sake come at once! Young Lee is drowned! Here's Harrington of King's with the news. The doctor is out. You'll do, but come along at once. There may be life in him."

"Have you brandy?"

"No."

"I'll bring some. There's a flask on my table."

Smith bounded up the stairs, taking three at a time, seized the flask, and was rushing down with it, when, as he passed Bellingham's room, his eyes fell upon something which left him gasping and staring upon the landing.

The door, which he had closed behind him, was now open, and right in front of him, with the lamp-light shining upon it, was the mummy case. Three minutes ago it had been empty. He could swear to that. Now it framed the lank body of its horrible occupant, who stood, grim and stark, with his black, shrivelled face towards the door. The form was lifeless and inert, but it seemed to Smith as he gazed that there still lingered a lurid spark of vitality, some faint sign of consciousness in the little eyes which lurked in the depths of the hollow sockets. So astounded and shaken was he that he had forgotten his errand, and was still staring at the lean, sunken figure when the voice of his friend below recalled him to himself.

"Come on, Smith!" he shouted. "It's life and death, you know. Hurry up! Now, then," he added, as the medical student reappeared, "let us do a sprint. It is well under a mile, and we should do it in five minutes. A human life is better worth running for than a pot."

Neck and neck they dashed through the darkness, and did not pull up until panting and spent, they had reached the little cottage by the river. Young Lee, limp and dripping like a broken water-plant, was stretched upon the sofa, the green scum of the river upon his black hair, and a fringe of white foam upon his leaden-hued lips. Beside him knelt his fellow-student, Harrington, endeavouring to chafe some warmth back into his rigid limbs.

"I think there's life in him," said Smith, with his hand to the lad's side. "Put your watch glass to his lips. Yes, there's dimming on it. You take one arm, Hastie. Now work it as I do, and we'll soon pull him round."

For ten minutes they worked in silence, inflating and depressing the chest of the unconscious man. At the end of that time a shiver ran through his body, his lips trembled, and he opened his eyes. The three students burst out into an irrepressible cheer.

"Wake up, old chap. You've frightened us quite enough."

"Have some brandy. Take a sip from the flask."

"He's all right now," said his companion Harrington. "Heavens, what a fright I got! I was reading here, and he had gone out for a stroll as far as the river, when I heard a scream and a splash. Out I ran, and by the time I could find him and fish him out, all life seemed to have gone. Then Simpson couldn't get a doctor, for he has a game-leg, and I had to run, and I don't know what I'd have done without you fellows. That's right, old chap. Sit up."

Monkhouse Lee had raised himself on his hands, and looked wildly about him.

"What's up?" he asked. "I've been in the water. Ah, yes; I remember."

A look of fear came into his eyes, and he sank his face into his hands.

"How did you fall in?"

"I didn't fall in."

"How then?"

"I was thrown in. I was standing by the bank, and something from behind picked me up like a feather and hurled me in. I heard nothing, and I saw nothing. But I know what it was, for all that."

"And so do I," whispered Smith.

Lee looked up with a quick glance of surprise.

"You've learned, then?" he said. "You remember the advice I gave you?"

"Yes, and I begin to think that I shall take it."

"I don't know what the deuce you fellows are talking about," said Hastie, "but I think, if I were you, Harrington, I should get Lee to bed at once. It will be time enough to discuss the why and the wherefore when he is a little stronger. I think, Smith, you and I can leave him alone now. I am walking back to college; if you are coming in that direction, we can have a chat."

But it was little chat that they had upon their homeward path. Smith's mind was too full of the incidents of the evening, the absence of the mummy from his neighbour's rooms, the step that passed him on the stair, the reappearance – the extraordinary, inexplicable reappearance of the grisly thing – and then this attack upon Lee, corresponding so closely to the previous outrage upon another man against whom Bellingham bore a grudge. All this settled in his thoughts, together with the many little incidents which had previously turned him against his neighbour, and the singular circumstances under which he

was first called in to him. What had been a dim suspicion, a vague, fantastic
conjecture, had suddenly taken form, and stood out in his mind as a grim fact,
a thing not to be denied. And yet, how monstrous it was! how unheard of! how
entirely beyond all bounds of human experience. An impartial judge, or
even the friend who walked by his side, would simply tell him that his eyes
had deceived him, that the mummy had been there all the time, that young
Lee had tumbled into the river as any other man tumbles into a river, and the
blue pill was the best thing for a disordered liver. He felt that he would have
said as much if the positions had been reversed. And yet he could swear that
Bellingham was a murderer at heart, and that he wielded a weapon such as no
man had ever used in all the grim history of crime.

Hastie had branched off to his rooms with a few crisp and emphatic comments upon his friend's unsociability, and Abercrombie Smith crossed the
quadrangle to his corner turret with a strong feeling of repulsion for his
chambers and their associations. He would take Lee's advice, and move his
quarters as soon as possible, for how could a man study when his ear was ever
straining for every murmur or footstep in the room below? He observed, as
he crossed over the lawn, that the light was still shining in Bellingham's window, and as he passed up the staircase the door opened, and the man himself
looked out at him. With his fat, evil face he was like some bloated spider fresh
from the weaving of his poisonous web.

"Good evening," said he. "Won't you come in?"

"No," cried Smith fiercely.

"No? You are as busy as ever? I wanted to ask you about Lee. I was sorry to
hear that there was a rumour that something was amiss with him."

His features were grave, but there was the gleam of a hidden laugh in his eyes
as he spoke. Smith saw it, and he could have knocked him down for it.

"You'll be sorrier still to hear that Monkhouse Lee is doing very well, and
is out of all danger," he answered. "Your hellish tricks have not come off this
time. Oh, you needn't try to brazen it out. I know all about it."

Bellingham took a step back from the angry student, and half-closed the
door as if to protect himself.

"You are mad," he said. "What do you mean? Do you assert that I had anything to do with Lee's accident?"

"Yes," thundered Smith. "You and that bag of bones behind you; you
worked it between you. I tell you what it is, Master B., they have given up
burning folk like you, but we still keep a hangman, and, by George! if any man
in this college meets his death while you are here, I'll have you up, and if you
don't swing for it, it won't be my fault. You'll find that your filthy Egyptian
tricks won't answer in England."

"You're a raving lunatic," said Bellingham.

"All right. You just remember what I say, for you'll find that I'll be better than my word."

The door slammed, and Smith went fuming up to his chamber, where he locked the door upon the inside, and spent half the night in smoking his old briar and brooding over the strange events of the evening.

Next morning Abercrombie Smith heard nothing of his neighbour, but Harrington called upon him in the afternoon to say that Lee was almost himself again. All day Smith stuck fast to his work, but in the evening he determined to pay the visit to his friend Doctor Peterson upon which he had started the night before. A good walk and a friendly chat would be welcome to his jangled nerves.

Bellingham's door was shut as he passed, but glancing back when he was some distance from the turret, he saw his neighbour's head at the window outlined against the lamp-light, his face pressed apparently against the glass as he gazed out into the darkness. It was a blessing to be away from all contact with him, if but for a few hours, and Smith stepped out briskly, and breathed the soft spring air into his lungs. The half-moon lay in the west between two Gothic pinnacles, and threw upon the silvered street a dark tracery from the stonework above. There was a brisk breeze, and light, fleecy clouds drifted swiftly across the sky. Old's was on the very border of the town, and in five minutes Smith found himself beyond the houses and between the hedges of a May-scented, Oxfordshire lane.

It was a lonely and little-frequented road which led to his friend's house. Early as it was, Smith did not meet a single soul upon his way. He walked briskly along until he came to the avenue gate, which opened into the long, gravel drive leading up to Farlingford. In front of him he could see the cosy, red light of the windows glimmering through the foliage. He stood with his hand upon the iron latch of the swinging gate, and he glanced back at the road along which he had come. Something was coming swiftly down it.

It moved in the shadow of the hedge, silently and furtively, a dark, crouching figure, dimly visible against the black background. Even as he gazed back at it, it had lessened its distance by twenty paces, and was fast closing upon him. Out of the darkness he had a glimpse of a scraggy neck, and of two eyes that will ever haunt him in his dreams. He turned, and with a cry of terror he ran for his life up the avenue. There were the red lights, the signals of safety, almost within a stone's-throw of him. He was a famous runner, but never had he run as he ran that night.

The heavy gate had swung into place behind him but he heard it dash open again before his pursuer. As he rushed madly and wildly through the night, he could hear a swift, dry patter behind him, and could see, as he threw back a glance, that this horror was bounding like a tiger at his heels, with blazing eyes and one stringy arm out-thrown. Thank God, the door was ajar. He could see the thin bar of light which shot from the lamp in the hall. Nearer yet sounded the clatter from behind. He heard a hoarse gurgling at his very shoulder. With a shriek he flung himself against the door, slammed and bolted it behind him, and sank half-fainting on to the hall chair.

"My goodness, Smith, what's the matter?" asked Peterson, appearing at the door of his study.

"Give me some brandy."

Peterson disappeared, and came rushing out again with a glass and a decanter.

"You need it," he said, as his visitor drank off what he poured out for him. "Why, man, you are as white as a cheese."

Smith laid down his glass, rose up, and took a deep breath.

"I am my own man again now," said he. "I was never so unmanned before. But, with your leave, Peterson, I will sleep here to-night, for I don't think I could face that road again except by daylight. It's weak, I know, but I can't help it."

Peterson looked at his visitor with a very questioning eye.

"Of course you shall sleep here if you wish. I'll tell Mrs. Burney to make up the spare bed. Where are you off to now?"

"Come up with me to the window that overlooks the door. I want you to see what I have seen."

They went up to the window of the upper hall whence they could look down upon the approach to the house. The drive and the fields on either side lay quiet and still, bathed in the peaceful moonlight.

"Well, really, Smith," remarked Peterson, "it is well that I know you to be an abstemious man. What in the world can have frightened you?"

"I'll tell you presently. But where can it have gone? Ah, now, look, look! See the curve of the road just beyond your gate."

"Yes, I see; you needn't pinch my arm off. I saw someone pass. I should say a man, rather thin, apparently, and tall, very tall. But what of him? And what of yourself? You are still shaking like an aspen leaf."

"I have been within hand-grip of the devil, that's all. But come down to your study, and I shall tell you the whole story."

He did so. Under the cheery lamp-light with a glass of wine on the table beside him, and the portly form and florid face of his friend in front, he narrated, in their order, all the events, great and small, which had formed so singular a chain, from the night on which he had found Bellingham fainting in front of the mummy case until this horrid experience of an hour ago.

"There now," he said as he concluded, "that's the whole, black business. It is monstrous and incredible, but it is true."

Doctor Plumptree Peterson sat for some time in silence with a very puzzled expression upon his face.

"I never heard of such a thing in my life, never!" he said at last. "You have told me the facts. Now tell me your inferences."

"You can draw your own."

"But I should like to hear yours. You have thought over the matter, and I have not."

"Well, it must be a little vague in detail, but the main points seem to me to be clear enough. This fellow Bellingham, in his Eastern studies, has got hold of some infernal secret by which a mummy–or possibly only this particular mummy – can be temporarily brought to life. He was trying this disgusting business on the night when he fainted. No doubt the sight of the creature moving had shaken his nerve, even though he had expected it. You remember that almost the first words he said were to call out upon himself as a fool. Well, he got more hardened afterwards, and carried the matter through without fainting. The vitality which he could put into it was evidently only a passing thing, for I have seen it continually in its case as dead as this table. He has some elaborate process, I fancy, by which he brings the thing to pass. Having done it, he naturally bethought him that he might use the creature as an agent. It has intelligence and it has strength. For some purpose he took Lee into his confidence; but Lee, like a decent Christian, would have nothing to do with such a business. Then they had a row, and Lee vowed that he would tell his sister of Bellingham's true character. Bellingham's game was to prevent him, and he nearly managed it, by setting this creature of his on his track. He had already tried its powers upon another man – Norton – towards whom he had a grudge. It is the merest chance that he has not two murders upon his soul. Then, when I taxed him with the matter, he had the strongest reasons for wishing to get me out of the way before I could convey my knowledge to anyone else. He got his chance when I went out, for he knew my habits and where I was bound for. I have had a narrow shave, Peterson, and it is mere luck that you didn't find me on your doorstep in the morning. I'm not a nervous man as a rule, and I never thought to have the fear of death put upon me as it was tonight."

"My dear boy, you take the matter too seriously," said his companion. "Your nerves are out of order with your work, and you make too much of it. How could such a thing as this stride about the streets of Oxford, even at night, without being seen?"

"It has been seen. There is quite a scare in the town about an escaped ape, as they imagine the creature to be. It is the talk of the place."

"Well, it's a striking chain of events. And yet, my dear fellow, you must allow that each incident in itself is capable of a more natural explanation?"

"What! even my adventure of tonight?"

"Certainly. You come out with your nerves all unstrung, and your head full of this theory of yours. Some gaunt, half-famished tramp steals after you, and seeing you run, is emboldened to pursue you. Your fears and imagination do the rest."

"It won't do, Peterson; it won't do."

"And again, in the instance of your finding the mummy case empty, and then a few moments later with an occupant, you know that it was lamp-light, that the lamp was half turned down, and that you had no special reason to look hard at the case. It is quite possible that you may have overlooked the creature in the first instance."

"No, no; it is out of the question."

"And then Lee may have fallen into the river, and Norton been garrotted. It is certainly a formidable indictment that you have against Bellingham; but if you were to place it before a police magistrate, he would simply laugh in your face."

"I know he would. That is why I mean to take the matter into my own hands."

"Eh?"

"Yes; I feel that a public duty rests upon me, and besides, I must do it for my own safety, unless I choose to allow myself to be hunted by this beast out of the college, and that would be a little too feeble. I have quite made up my mind what I shall do. And first of all, may I use your paper and pens for an hour?"

"Most certainly. You will find all that you want upon that side-table."

Abercrombie Smith sat down before a sheet of foolscap, and for an hour, and then for a second hour his pen travelled swiftly over it. Page after page was finished and tossed aside while his friend leaned back in his armchair, looking across at him with patient curiosity. At last, with an exclamation of satisfaction, Smith sprang to his feet, gathered his papers up into order, and laid the last one upon Peterson's desk.

"Kindly sign this as a witness," he said.

"A witness? Of what?"

"Of my signature, and of the date. The date is the most important. Why, Peterson, my life might hang upon it."

"My dear Smith, you are talking wildly. Let me beg you to go to bed."

"On the contrary, I never spoke so deliberately in my life. And I will promise to go to bed the moment you have signed it."

"But what is it?"

"It is a statement of all that I have been telling you to-night. I wish you to witness it."

"Certainly," said Peterson, signing his name under that of his companion. "There you are! But what is the idea?"

"You will kindly retain it, and produce it in case I am arrested."

"Arrested? For what?"

"For murder. It is quite on the cards. I wish to be ready for every event. There is only one course open to me, and I am determined to take it."

"For Heaven's sake, don't do anything rash!"

"Believe me, it would be far more rash to adopt any other course. I hope that we won't need to bother you, but it will ease my mind to know that you have this statement of my motives. And now I am ready to take your advice and to go to roost, for I want to be at my best in the morning."

Abercrombie Smith was not an entirely pleasant man to have as an enemy. Slow and easy-tempered, he was formidable when driven to action. He brought to every purpose in life the same deliberate resoluteness which had distinguished him as a scientific student. He had laid his studies aside for a day, but he intended that the day should not be wasted. Not a word did he say to his host as to his plans, but by nine o'clock he was well on his way to Oxford.

In the High Street he stopped at Clifford's, the gun-maker's, and bought a heavy revolver, with a box of central-fire cartridges. Six of them he slipped into the chambers, and half-cocking the weapon, placed it in the pocket of his coat. He then made his way to Hastie's rooms, where the big oarsman was lounging over his breakfast, with the *Sporting Times* propped up against the coffee-pot.

"Hullo! What's up?" he asked. "Have some coffee?"

"No, thank you. I want you to come with me, Hastie, and do what I ask you."

"Certainly, my boy."

"And bring a heavy stick with you."

"Hullo!" Hastie stared. "Here's a hunting crop that would fell an ox."

"One other thing. You have a box of amputating knives. Give me the longest of them."

"There you are. You seem to be fairly on the war trail. Anything else?"

"No; that will do." Smith placed the knife inside his coat, and led the way to the quadrangle. "We are neither of us chickens, Hastie," said he. "I think I can do this job alone, but I take you as a precaution. I am going to have a little talk with Bellingham. If I have only him to deal with, I won't, of course, need you. If I shout, however, up you come, and lam out with your whip as hard as you can lick. Do you understand?"

"All right. I'll come if I hear you bellow."

"Stay here, then. I may be a little time, but don't budge until I come down."

"I'm a fixture."

Smith ascended the stairs, opened Bellingham's door and stepped in. Bellingham was seated behind his table, writing. Beside him, among his litter of strange possessions, towered the mummy case, with its sale number 249 still stuck upon its front, and its hideous occupant stiff and stark within it. Smith looked very deliberately round him, closed the door, and then, stepping across to the fireplace, struck a match and set the fire alight. Bellingham sat staring, with amazement and rage upon his bloated face.

"Well, really now, you make yourself at home," he gasped.

Smith sat himself deliberately down, placing his watch upon the table, drew out his pistol, cocked it, and laid it in his lap. Then he took the long amputating knife from his bosom, and threw it down in front of Bellingham.

"Now, then," said he, "just get to work and cut up that mummy."

"Oh, is that it?" said Bellingham with a sneer.

"Yes, that is it. They tell me that the law can't touch you. But I have a law that will set matters straight. If in five minutes you have not set to work, I swear by the God who made me that I will put a bullet through your brain!"

"You would murder me?"

Bellingham had half-risen, and his face was the colour of putty.

"Yes."

"And for what?"

"To stop your mischief. One minute has gone."

"But what have I done?"

"I know and you know."

"This is mere bullying."

"Two minutes are gone."

"But you must give reasons. You are a madman—a dangerous madman. Why should I destroy my own property? It is a valuable mummy."

"You must cut it up, and you must burn it."

"I will do no such thing."

"Four minutes are gone."

Smith took up the pistol and he looked towards Bellingham with an inexorable face. As the second-hand stole round, he raised his hand, and the finger twitched upon the trigger.

"There! there! I'll do it!" screamed Bellingham.

In frantic haste he caught up the knife and hacked at the figure of the mummy, ever glancing round to see the eye and the weapon of his terrible visitor bent upon him. The creature crackled and snapped under every stab of the keen blade. A thick, yellow dust rose up from it. Spices and dried essences rained down upon the floor. Suddenly, with a rending crack, its backbone snapped asunder, and it fell, a brown heap of sprawling limbs, upon the floor.

"Now into the fire!" said Smith.

The flames leaped and roared as the dried and tinder-like debris was piled upon it. The little room was like the stoke-hole of a steamer and the sweat ran down the faces of the two men; but still the one stooped and worked, while the other sat watching him with a set face. A thick, fat smoke oozed out from the fire, and a heavy smell of burned resin and singed hair filled the air. In a quarter of an hour a few charred and brittle sticks were all that was left of Lot No. 249.

"Perhaps that will satisfy you," snarled Bellingham, with hate and fear in his little grey eyes as he glanced back at his tormentor.

"No; I must make a clean sweep of all your materials. We must have no more devil's tricks. In with all these leaves! They may have something to do with it."

"And what now?" asked Bellingham, when the leaves also had been added to the blaze.

"Now the roll of papyrus which you had on the table that night. It is in that drawer, I think."

"No, no," shouted Bellingham. "Don't burn that! Why, man, you don't know what you do. It is unique; it contains wisdom which is nowhere else to be found."

"Out with it!"

"But look here, Smith, you can't really mean it. I'll share the knowledge with you. I'll teach you all that is in it. Or, stay, let me only copy it before you burn it!"

Smith stepped forward and turned the key in the drawer. Taking out the yellow, curled roll of paper, he threw it into the fire, and pressed it down with his heel. Bellingham screamed, and grabbed at it; but Smith pushed him back and stood over it until it was reduced to a formless, grey ash.

"Now, Master B.," said he, "I think I have pretty well drawn your teeth. You'll hear from me again, if you return to your old tricks. And now good morning, for I must go back to my studies."

And such is the narrative of Abercrombie Smith as to the singular events which occurred in Old College, Oxford, in the spring of '84. As Bellingham left the university immediately afterwards, and was last heard of in the Sudan, there is no one who can contradict his statement. But the wisdom of men is small, and the ways of Nature are strange, and who shall put a bound to the dark things which may be found by those who seek for them?

The Jewel of Seven Stars
by Bram Stoker

Although he is rightly best known for writing Dracula *(1897), the most infamous vampire tale ever put to paper, Bram Stoker also wrote an ancient Egyptian supernatural themed novel worth reading. Originally published in 1903,* The Jewel of Seven Stars *tells the story of how the ancient Egyptian past haunts the lives of Abel Trelawny, an Egyptologist, his daughter, Margaret, and their household. Part detective story, part supernatural tale, Stoker's novel doesn't have quite the same resonance as Sir Arthur Conan Doyle's "Lot No. 249," a story also included in this anthology. Nevertheless, it remains a significant milestone in the development of the ancient Egyptian supernatural tale. It is also one of the more readable novels in that particular subgenre.*

In this excerpt, the book's ninth chapter entitled "The Need of Knowledge," the story makes a noticeable transition from an Edwardian detective novel to a modern horror story. After some ancient Egyptian lamps, presumed stolen, magically reappear in the living area of Margaret Trelawny, the assembled characters have to consider the fact that such things just don't happen in a purely rational universe. Adding to the mystery is the fact that Abel Trelawny is paralyzed by an unexplained ailment. In the chapter presented here, the work's protagonist-narrator, a barrister named Malcolm Ross, recounts how the characters begin to consider a supernatural explanation for the strange events they have been witness to.

---□---

Chapter IX

The Need of Knowledge

Mr. Corbeck seemed to go almost off his head at the recovery of the lamps. He took them up one by one and looked them all over tenderly, as though they were things that he loved. In his delight and excitement he breathed so hard that it seemed almost like a cat purring. Sergeant Daw said quietly, his voice breaking the silence like a discord in a melody:

"Are you quite sure those lamps are the ones you had, and that were stolen?"

His answer was in an indignant tone: "Sure! Of course I'm sure. There isn't another set of lamps like these in the world!"

"So far as you know!" The Detective's words were smooth enough, but his manner was so exasperating that I was sure he had some motive in it; so I waited in silence. He went on:

"Of course there may be some in the British Museum; or Mr. Trelawny may have had these already. There's nothing new under the sun, you know, Mr. Corbeck; not even in Egypt. These may be the originals, and yours may have been the copies. Are there any points by which you can identify these as yours?"

Mr. Corbeck was really angry by this time. He forgot his reserve; and in his indignation poured forth a torrent of almost incoherent, but enlightening, broken sentences:

"Identify! Copies of them! British Museum! Rot! Perhaps they keep a set in Scotland Yard for teaching idiot policemen Egyptology! Do I know them? When I have carried them about my body, in the desert, for three months; and lay awake night after night to watch them! When I have looked them over with a magnifying-glass, hour after hour, till my eyes ached; till every tiny blotch, and chip, and dinge became as familiar to me as his chart to a captain; as familiar as they doubtless have been all the time to every thick-headed areaprowler within the bounds of mortality. See here, young man, look at these!" He ranged the lamps in a row on the top of the cabinet. "Did you ever see a set of lamps of these shapes—of any one of these shapes? Look at these dominant figures on them! Did you ever see so complete a set—even in Scotland Yard; even in Bow Street? Look! one on each, the seven forms of Hathor. Look at that figure of the Ka of a Princess of the Two Egypts, standing between Ra and Osiris in the Boat of the Dead, with the Eye of Sleep, supported on legs, bending before her; and Harmochis rising in the north. Will you find that in the British Museum—or Bow Street? Or perhaps your studies in the Gizeh Museum, or the Fitzwilliam, or Paris, or Leyden, or Berlin, have shown you that the episode is common in hieroglyphics; and that this is only a copy. Perhaps you can tell me what that figure of Ptah-Seker-Ausar holding the Tet wrapped in the Sceptre of Papyrus means? Did you ever see it before; even in the British Museum, or Gizeh, or Scotland Yard?"

He broke off suddenly; and then went on in quite a different way:

"Look here! it seems to me that the thick-headed idiot is myself! I beg your pardon, old fellow, for my rudeness. I quite lost my temper at the suggestion that I do not know these lamps. You don't mind, do you?" The Detective answered heartily:

"Lord, sir, not I. I like to see folks angry when I am dealing with them, whether they are on my side or the other. It is when people are angry that you learn the truth from them. I keep cool; that is my trade! Do you know, you have told me more about those lamps in the past two minutes than when you filled me up with details of how to identify them."

Mr. Corbeck grunted; he was not pleased at having given himself away. All at once he turned to me and said in his natural way:

"Now tell me how you got them back?" I was so surprised that I said without thinking:

"We didn't get them back!" The traveller laughed openly.

"What on earth do you mean?" he asked. "You didn't get them back! Why, there they are before your eyes! We found you looking at them when we came in." By this time I had recovered my surprise and had my wits about me.

"Why, that's just it," I said. "We had only come across them, by accident, that very moment!"

Mr. Corbeck drew back and looked hard at Miss Trelawny and myself; turning his eyes from one to the other as he asked:

"Do you mean to tell me that no one brought them here; that you found them in that drawer? That, so to speak, no one at all brought them back?"

"I suppose someone must have brought them here; they couldn't have come of their own accord. But who it was, or when, or how, neither of us knows. We shall have to make inquiry, and see if any of the servants know anything of it."

We all stood silent for several seconds. It seemed a long time. The first to speak was the Detective, who said in an unconscious way:

"Well, I'm damned! I beg your pardon, miss!" Then his mouth shut like a steel trap.

We called up the servants, one by one, and asked them if they knew anything of some articles placed in a drawer in the boudoir; but none of them could throw any light on the circumstance. We did not tell them what the articles were; or let them see them.

Mr. Corbeck packed the lamps in cotton wool, and placed them in a tin box. This, I may mention incidentally, was then brought up to the detectives' room, where one of the men stood guard over them with a revolver the whole night. Next day we got a small safe into the house, and placed them in it. There were two different keys. One of them I kept myself; the other I placed in my drawer in the Safe Deposit vault. We were all determined that the lamps should not be lost again.

About an hour after we had found the lamps, Doctor Winchester arrived. He had a large parcel with him, which, when unwrapped, proved to be the mummy of a cat. With Miss Trelawny's permission he placed this in the boudoir; and Silvio was brought close to it. To the surprise of us all, however, except perhaps Doctor Winchester, he did not manifest the least annoyance; he took no notice of it whatever. He stood on the table close beside it, purring loudly. Then, following out his plan, the Doctor brought him into Mr. Trelawny's room, we all following. Doctor Winchester was excited; Miss Trelawny anxious. I was more than interested myself, for I began to have a glimmering of the Doctor's idea. The Detective was calmly and coldly superior; but Mr. Corbeck, who was an enthusiast, was full of eager curiosity.

The moment Doctor Winchester got into the room, Silvio began to mew and wriggle; and jumping out of his arms, ran over to the cat mummy and began to scratch angrily at it. Miss Trelawny had some difficulty in taking him away; but so soon as he was out of the room he became quiet. When she came back there was a clamour of comments:

"I thought so!" from the Doctor.

"What can it mean?" from Miss Trelawny.

"That's a very strange thing!" from Mr. Corbeck.

"Odd! but it doesn't prove anything!" from the Detective.

"I suspend my judgment!" from myself, thinking it advisable to say something.

Then by common consent we dropped the theme—for the present.

In my room that evening I was making some notes of what had happened, when there came a low tap on the door. In obedience to my summons Sergeant Daw came in, carefully closing the door behind him.

"Well, Sergeant," said I, "sit down. What is it?"

"I wanted to speak to you, sir, about those lamps." I nodded and waited: he went on: "You know that that room where they were found opens directly into the room where Miss Trelawny slept last night?"

"Yes."

"During the night a window somewhere in that part of the house was opened, and shut again. I heard it, and took a look round; but I could see no sign of anything."

"Yes, I know that!" I said; "I heard a window moved myself."

"Does nothing strike you as strange about it, sir?"

"Strange!" I said; "Strange! why it's all the most bewildering, maddening thing I have ever encountered. It is all so strange that one seems to wonder, and simply waits for what will happen next. But what do you mean by strange?"

The Detective paused, as if choosing his words to begin; and then said deliberately:

"You see, I am not one who believes in magic and such things. I am for facts all the time; and I always find in the long-run that there is a reason and a cause for everything. This new gentleman says these things were stolen out of his room in the hotel. The lamps, I take it from some things he has said, really belong to Mr. Trelawny. His daughter, the lady of the house, having left the room she usually occupies, sleeps that night on the ground floor. A window is heard to open and shut during the night. When we, who have been during the day trying to find a clue to the robbery, come to the house, we find the stolen goods in a room close to where she slept, and opening out of it!"

He stopped. I felt that same sense of pain and apprehension, which I had experienced when he had spoken to me before, creeping, or rather rushing, over me again. I had to face the matter out, however. My relations with her, and the feeling toward her which I now knew full well meant a very deep love and devotion, demanded so much. I said as calmly as I could, for I knew the keen eyes of the skilful investigator were on me:

"And the inference?"

He answered with the cool audacity of conviction:

"The inference to me is that there was no robbery at all. The goods were taken by someone to this house, where they were received through a window on the ground floor. They were placed in the cabinet, ready to be discovered when the proper time should come!"

Somehow I felt relieved; the assumption was too monstrous. I did not want, however, my relief to be apparent, so I answered as gravely as I could:

"And who do you suppose brought them to the house?"

"I keep my mind open as to that. Possibly Mr. Corbeck himself; the matter might be too risky to trust to a third party."

"Then the natural extension of your inference is that Mr. Corbeck is a liar and a fraud; and that he is in conspiracy with Miss Trelawny to deceive someone or other about those lamps."

"Those are harsh words, Mr. Ross. They're so plain-spoken that they bring a man up standing, and make new doubts for him. But I have to go where my reason points. It may be that there is another party than Miss Trelawny in it. Indeed, if it hadn't been for the other matter that set me thinking and bred doubts of its own about her, I wouldn't dream of mixing her up in this. But I'm safe on Corbeck. Whoever else is in it, he is! The things couldn't have been taken without his connivance—if what he says is true. If it isn't—well! he is a liar anyhow. I would think it a bad job to have him stay in the house with so many valuables, only that it will give me and my mate a chance of watching him. We'll keep a pretty good look-out, too, I tell you. He's up in my room now, guarding those lamps; but Johnny Wright is there too. I go on before he comes off; so there won't be much chance of another housebreaking. Of course, Mr. Ross, all this, too, is between you and me."

"Quite so! You may depend on my silence!" I said; and he went away to keep a close eye on the Egyptologist.

It seemed as though all my painful experiences were to go in pairs, and that the sequence of the previous day was to be repeated; for before long I had another private visit from Doctor Winchester who had now paid his nightly visit to his patient and was on his way home. He took the seat which I proffered and began at once:

"This is a strange affair altogether. Miss Trelawny has just been telling me about the stolen lamps, and of the finding of them in the Napoleon cabinet. It would seem to be another complication of the mystery; and yet, do you know, it is a relief to me. I have exhausted all human and natural possibilities of the case, and am beginning to fall back on superhuman and supernatural possibilities. Here are such strange things that, if I am not going mad, I think we must have a solution before long. I wonder if I might ask some questions and some help from Mr. Corbeck, without making further complications and embarrassing us. He seems to know an amazing amount regarding Egypt and all relating to it. Perhaps he wouldn't mind translating a little bit of hieroglyphic. It is child's play to him. What do you think?"

When I had thought the matter over a few seconds I spoke. We wanted all the help we could get. For myself, I had perfect confidence in both men; and any comparing notes, or mutual assistance, might bring good results. Such could hardly bring evil.

"By all means I should ask him. He seems an extraordinarily learned man in Egyptology; and he seems to me a good fellow as well as an enthusiast. By the way, it will be necessary to be a little guarded as to whom you speak regarding any information which he may give you."

"Of course!" he answered. "Indeed I should not dream of saying anything to anybody, excepting yourself. We have to remember that when Mr. Trelawny recovers he may not like to think that we have been chattering unduly over his affairs."

"Look here!" I said, "why not stay for a while: and I shall ask him to come and have a pipe with us. We can then talk over things."

He acquiesced: so I went to the room where Mr. Corbeck was, and brought him back with me. I thought the detectives were pleased at his going. On the way to my room he said:

"I don't half like leaving those things there, with only those men to guard them. They're a deal sight too precious to be left to the police!"

From which it would appear that suspicion was not confined to Sergeant Daw.

Mr. Corbeck and Doctor Winchester, after a quick glance at each other, became at once on most friendly terms. The traveller professed his willingness to be of any assistance which he could, provided, he added, that it was anything about which he was free to speak. This was not very promising; but Doctor Winchester began at once:

"I want you, if you will, to translate some hieroglyphic for me."

"Certainly, with the greatest pleasure, so far as I can. For I may tell you that hieroglyphic writing is not quite mastered yet; though we are getting at it! We are getting at it! What is the inscription?"

"There are two," he answered. "One of them I shall bring here."

He went out, and returned in a minute with the mummy cat which he had that evening introduced to Silvio. The scholar took it; and, after a short examination, said:

"There is nothing especial in this. It is an appeal to Bast, the Lady of Bubastis, to give her good bread and milk in the Elysian Fields. There may be more inside; and if you will care to unroll it, I will do my best. I do not think, however, that there is anything special. From the method of wrapping I should say it is from the Delta; and of a late period, when such mummy work was common and cheap. What is the other inscription you wish me to see?"

"The inscription on the mummy cat in Mr. Trelawny's room."

Mr. Corbeck's face fell. "No!" he said, "I cannot do that! I am, for the present at all events, practically bound to secrecy regarding any of the things in Mr. Trelawny's room."

Doctor Winchester's comment and my own were made at the same moment. I said only the one word "Checkmate!" from which I think he may have gathered that I guessed more of his idea and purpose than perhaps I had intentionally conveyed to him. He murmured:

"Practically bound to secrecy?"

Mr. Corbeck at once took up the challenge conveyed:

"Do not misunderstand me! I am not bound by any definite pledge of secrecy; but I am bound in honour to respect Mr. Trelawny's confidence, given to me, I may tell you, in a very large measure. Regarding many of the objects in his room he has a definite purpose in view; and it would not be either right or becoming for me, his trusted friend and confidant, to forestall that purpose. Mr. Trelawny, you may know—or rather you do not know or you would not have so construed my remark—is a scholar, a very great scholar. He has worked for years toward a certain end. For this he has spared no labour, no expense, no personal danger or self-denial. He is on the line of a result which will place him amongst the foremost discoverers or investigators of his age. And now, just at the time when any hour might bring him success, he is stricken down!"

He stopped, seemingly overcome with emotion. After a time he recovered himself and went on:

"Again, do not misunderstand me as to another point. I have said that Mr.

Trelawny has made much confidence with me; but I do not mean to lead you to believe that I know all his plans, or his aims or objects. I know the period which he has been studying; and the definite historical individual whose life he has been investigating, and whose records he has been following up one by one with infinite patience. But beyond this I know nothing. That he has some aim or object in the completion of this knowledge I am convinced. What it is I may guess; but I must say nothing. Please to remember, gentlemen, that I have voluntarily accepted the position of recipient of a partial confidence. I have respected that; and I must ask any of my friends to do the same."

He spoke with great dignity; and he grew, moment by moment, in the respect and esteem of both Doctor Winchester and myself. We understood that he had not done speaking; so we waited in silence till he continued:

"I have spoken this much, although I know well that even such a hint as either of you might gather from my words might jeopardise the success of his work. But I am convinced that you both wish to help him—and his daughter," he said this looking me fairly between the eyes, "to the best of your power, honestly and unselfishly. He is so stricken down, and the manner of it is so mysterious that I cannot but think that it is in some way a result of his own work. That he calculated on some set-back is manifest to us all. God knows! I am willing to do what I can, and to use any knowledge I have in his behalf. I arrived in England full of exultation at the thought that I had fulfilled the mission with which he had trusted me. I had got what he said were the last objects of his search; and I felt assured that he would now be able to begin the experiment of which he had often hinted to me. It is too dreadful that at just such a time such a calamity should have fallen on him. Doctor Winchester, you are a physician; and, if your face does not belie you, you are a clever and a bold one. Is there no way which you can devise to wake this man from his unnatural stupor?"

There was a pause; then the answer came slowly and deliberately:

"There is no ordinary remedy that I know of. There might possibly be some extraordinary one. But there would be no use in trying to find it, except on one condition."

"And that?"

"Knowledge! I am completely ignorant of Egyptian matters, language, writing, history, secrets, medicines, poisons, occult powers—all that go to make up the mystery of that mysterious land. This disease, or condition, or whatever it may be called, from which Mr. Trelawny is suffering, is in some way connected with Egypt. I have had a suspicion of this from the first; and later it grew into a certainty, though without proof. What you have said tonight confirms my conjecture, and makes me believe that a proof is to be had. I do not think that you quite know all that has gone on in this house since the night of the attack—of the finding of Mr. Trelawny's body. Now I propose that we confide in you. If Mr. Ross agrees, I shall ask him to tell you. He is more skilled than I am in putting facts before other people. He can speak by his brief; and in this case he has the best of all briefs, the experience of his own eyes and ears, and the evidence that he has himself taken on the spot from participators in, or spectators of, what has happened. When you know all, you will, I hope, be in a position to judge as to whether you can best help Mr. Trelawny, and further his secret wishes, by your silence or your speech."

I nodded approval. Mr. Corbeck jumped up, and in his impulsive way held out a hand to each.

"Done!" he said. "I acknowledge the honour of your confidence; and on my part I pledge myself that if I find my duty to Mr. Trelawny's wishes will, in his own interest, allow my lips to open on his affairs, I shall speak so freely as I may."

Accordingly I began, and told him, as exactly as I could, everything that had happened from the moment of my waking at the knocking on the door in Jermyn Street. The only reservations I made were as to my own feeling toward Miss Trelawny and the matters of small import to the main subject which followed it; and my conversations with Sergeant Daw, which were in themselves private, and which would have demanded discretionary silence in any case. As I spoke, Mr. Corbeck followed with breathless interest. Sometimes he would stand up and pace about the room in uncontrollable excitement; and then recover himself suddenly, and sit down again. Sometimes he would be about to speak, but would, with an effort, restrain himself. I think the narration helped me to make up my own mind; for even as I talked, things seemed to appear in a clearer light. Things big and little, in relation of their importance to the case, fell into proper perspective. The story up to date became coherent, except as to its cause, which seemed a greater mystery than ever. This is the merit of entire, or collected, narrative. Isolated facts, doubts, suspicions, conjectures, give way to a homogeneity which is convincing.

That Mr. Corbeck was convinced was evident. He did not go through any process of explanation or limitation, but spoke right out at once to the point, and fearlessly like a man:

"That settles me! There is in activity some Force that needs special care. If we all go on working in the dark we shall get in one another's way, and by hampering each other, undo the good that any or each of us, working in different directions, might do. It seems to me that the first thing we have to accomplish is to get Mr. Trelawny waked out of that unnatural sleep. That he can be waked is apparent from the way the Nurse has recovered; though what additional harm may have been done to him in the time he has been lying in that room I suppose no one can tell. We must chance that, however. He *has* lain there, and whatever the effect might be, it is there now; and we have, and shall have, to deal with it as a fact. A day more or less won't hurt in the long-run. It is late now; and we shall probably have tomorrow a task before us that will require our energies afresh. You, Doctor, will want to get to your sleep; for I suppose you have other work as well as this to do tomorrow. As for you, Mr. Ross, I understand that you are to have a spell of watching in the sick-room tonight. I shall get you a book which will help to pass the time for you. I shall go and look for it in the library. I know where it was when I was here last; and I don't suppose Mr. Trelawny has used it since. He knew long ago all that was in it which was or might be of interest to him. But it will be necessary, or at least helpful, to understand other things which I shall tell you later. You will be able to tell Doctor Winchester all that would aid him. For I take it that our work will branch out pretty soon. We shall each have our own end to hold up; and it will take each of us all our time and understanding to get through his own tasks. It will not be necessary for you to read the whole book. All that will interest you … with regard to our matter I mean of course, for the whole book is interesting as a record of travel in a country then quite unknown—is the preface, and two or three chapters which I shall mark for you."

He shook hands warmly with Doctor Winchester who had stood up to go.

Whilst he was away I sat lonely, thinking. As I thought, the world around me seemed to be illimitably great. The only little spot in which I was interested seemed like a tiny speck in the midst of a wilderness. Without and around it were darkness and unknown danger, pressing in from every side. And the central figure in our little oasis was one of sweetness and beauty. A figure one could love; could work for; could die for…!

Mr. Corbeck came back in a very short time with the book; he had found it at once in the spot where he had seen it three years before. Having placed in it several slips of paper, marking the places where I was to read, he put it into my hands, saying:

"That is what started Mr. Trelawny; what started me when I read it; and which will, I have no doubt, be to you an interesting beginning to a special study—whatever the end may be. If, indeed, any of us here may ever see the end."

At the door he paused and said:

"I want to take back one thing. That Detective is a good fellow. What you have told me of him puts him in a new light. The best proof of it is that I can go quietly to sleep tonight, and leave the lamps in his care!"

When he had gone I took the book with me, put on my respirator, and went to my spell of duty in the sick-room!

Part II: The Weird

The Vengeance of Nitocris
by Tennessee Williams

In 1928, well before he became one of America's most esteemed playwrights, Thomas Lanier (Tennessee) Williams penned a story for Weird Tales. *Published when he was merely sixteen years old, "The Vengeance of Nitocris" shows a formidable imagination at work. This historical revenge story, in which an empress avenges her brother's death, may not be as weird as it is psychologically unnerving. This is true in both its vivid language and its macabre plot.*

The story's depiction of mob violence, slave labor, and vengeance remind the reader that politics can really be a blood sport. Indeed, ancient Egypt, now most associated with mummies and mysticism, was part of human history and, as such, had political dynamics like any other society before or since.

Williams's story, which was reprinted in the first issue of the science fiction magazine Gamma, *is also notable for its rather anti-clerical tone. Whether this was deliberate on the young author's part is debatable, but a close reading suggests that he was well aware of how earthly political power and religious authority might clash with violent and cataclysmic results.*

Most importantly, "The Vengeance of Nitocris" remains significant for its depiction of a strong-willed female protagonist. Although Nitocris is described as being "famously beautiful," it soon becomes apparent that our beautiful empress is no damsel in distress waiting to be rescued by a swashbuckling male. With a sadistic and villainous streak a mile wide, she is both the tale's heroine and villainess, something to consider in light of Williams's future female characters in his plays. Ultimately, Williams's sole contribution to Weird Tales *is not particularly supernatural, but it is most memorable for its depiction of a woman determined at all cost to avenge her brother. In that regard, this story, though set in the distant past, is truly a timeless one.*

Hushed were the streets of many peopled Thebes. Those few who passed through them moved with the shadowy fleetness of bats near dawn, and bent their faces from the sky as if fearful of seeing what in their fancies might be hovering there. Weird, high-noted incantations of a wailing sound were audible through the barred doors. On corners groups of naked and bleeding priests cast themselves repeatedly and with loud cries upon the rough stones of the walks. Even dogs and cats and oxen seemed impressed by some strange menace and foreboding and cowered and slunk dejectedly. All Thebes was in dread. And indeed there was cause for their dread and for their wails of lamentation. A terrible sacrilege had been committed. In all the annals of Egypt none more monstrous was recorded.

Five days had the altar fires of the god of gods, Osiris, been left unburning. Even for one moment to allow darkness upon the altars of the god was considered by the priests to be a great offense against him. Whole years of dearth and famine had been known to result from such an offense. But now the altar fires had been deliberately extinguished, and left extinguished for five days. It was an unspeakable sacrilege.

Hourly there was expectancy of some great calamity to befall. Perhaps within the approaching night a mighty earthquake would shake the city to the ground, or a fire from heaven would sweep upon them, or some monster from the desert, where wild and terrible monsters were said to dwell, would rush upon them and Osiris himself would rise up, as he had done before, and swallow all Egypt in his wrath. Surely some such dread catastrophe would befall them ere the week had passed. Unless—unless the sacrilege were avenged.

But how might it be avenged? That was the question high lords and priests debated. Pharaoh alone had committed the sacrilege. It was he, angered because the bridge, which he had spent five years in constructing so that one day he might cross the Nile in his chariot as he had once boasted that he would do, had been swept away by the rising waters. Raging with anger, he had flogged the priests from the temple. He had barred the temple doors and with his own breath had blown out the sacred candles. He had defiled the hallowed altars with the carcasses of beasts. Even, it was said in low, shocked whispers, in a mock ceremony of worship he had burned the carrion of a hyena, most abhorrent of all beasts to Osiris, upon the holy altar of gold, which even the most high of priests forbore to lay naked hands upon!

Surely, even though he be Pharaoh, ruler of all Egypt and holder of the golden eagle, he could not be permitted to commit such violent sacrileges without punishment from man. The god Osiris was waiting for them to inflict that punishment, and if they failed to do it, upon them would come a scourge from heaven.

Standing before the awed assembly of nobles, the high Kha Semblor made a gesture with his hands. A cry broke from those who watched. Sentence had been delivered. Death had been pronounced as doom for the pharaoh.

The heavy, barred, doors were shoved open. The crowd came out, and within an hour a well-organized mob passed through the streets of Thebes, directed for the palace of the pharaoh. Mob justice was to be done.

Within the resplendent portals of the palace the pharaoh, ruler of all Egypt, watched with tightened brow the orderly but menacing approach of the mob. He divined their intent. But was he not their pharaoh? He could contend with gods, so why should he fear mere dogs of men?

A woman clung to his stiffened arm. She was tall and as majestically handsome as he. A garb of linen, as brilliantly golden as the sun, entwined her body closely, and bands of jet were around her throat and forehead. She was the fair and well-loved Nitocris, sister of the pharaoh.

"Brother, brother!" she cried, "light the fires! Pacify the dogs! They come to kill you."

Only more stern grew the look of the pharaoh. He thrust aside his pleading sister, and beckoned to the attendants.

"Open the doors!"

Startled, trembling, the men obeyed.

The haughty lord of Egypt drew his sword from its sheath. He slashed the air with a stroke that would have severed stone. Out on the steep steps leading between tall, colored pillars to the doors of the palace he stepped. The people saw him. A howl rose from their lips.

"Light the fires!"

The figure of the pharaoh stood inflexible as rock. Superbly tall and muscular, his bare arms and limbs glittering like burnished copper in the light of the brilliant sun, his body erect and tense in his attitude of defiance, he looked indeed a mortal fit almost to challenge gods.

The mob, led by the black-robed priests and nobles who had arrived at the foot of the steps, now fell back before the stunning, magnificent defiance of their giant ruler. They felt like demons who had assailed the heavens and had been abashed and shamed by the mere sight of that which they had assailed. A hush fell over them. Their upraised arms faltered and sank down. A moment more and they would have fallen to their knees.

What happened then seemed nothing less than a miracle. In his triumph and exultation, the pharaoh had been careless of the crumbling edges of the steps. Centuries old, there were sections of these steps which were falling apart. Upon such a section had the gold-sandaled foot of the pharaoh descended, and it was not strong enough to sustain his great weight. With a scuttling sound it broke loose. A gasp came from the mob—the pharaoh was about to fall. He was palpitating, wavering in the air, fighting to retain his balance. He looked as if he were grappling with some monstrous, invisible snake, coiled about his gleaming body. A hoarse cry burst from his lips; his sword fell; and then his body thudded down the steps in a series of wild somersaults, and landed at the foot, sprawled out before the gasping mob. For a moment there was breathless silence. And then came the shout of a priest.

"A sign from the gods!"

That vibrant cry seemed to restore the mob to all of its wolflike rage. They surged forward. The struggling body of the pharaoh was lifted up and torn to pieces by their clawing hands and weapons. Thus was the god Osiris avenged.

A week later another large assembly of persons confronted the brilliant-pillared palace. This time they were there to acknowledge a ruler, not to slay one. The week before they had rended the pharaoh and now they were proclaiming his sister empress. Priests had declared that it was the will of the gods that she should succeed her brother. She was famously beautiful, pious, and wise. The people were not reluctant to accept her.

When she was borne down the steps of the palace in her rich litter after the elaborate ceremony of coronation had been concluded, she responded to the cheers of the multitude with a smile which could not have appeared more amicable and gracious. None might know from that smile upon her beautiful carmined lips that within her heart she was thinking, "These are the people who slew my brother. Ah, god Issus grant me power to avenge his death upon them!"

Not long after the beauteous Nitocris mounted the golden throne of Egypt, rumors were whispered of some vast, mysterious enterprise being conducted in secret. A large number of slaves were observed each dawn to embark upon barges and to be carried down the river to some unknown point, where they labored throughout the day, returning after dark. The slaves were Ethiopians, neither able to speak nor to understand the Egyptian language, and therefore no information could be gotten from them by the curious as to the object of their mysterious daily excursions. The general opinion, though, was that the pious queen was having a great temple constructed to the gods and that when it was finished, enormous public banquets would be held within it before its dedication. She meant it to be a surprise gift to the priests who were ever desirous of some new place of worship and were dissatisfied with their old altars, which they said were defiled.

Throughout the winter the slaves repeated daily their excursions. Traffic of all kinds plying down the river was restricted for several miles to within forty yards of one shore. Any craft seen to disregard that restriction was set upon by a galley of armed men and pursued back into bounds. All that could be learned was that a prodigious temple or hall of some sort was in construction.

It was late in the spring when the excursions of the workmen were finally discontinued. Restrictions upon river traffic were withdrawn. The men who went eagerly to investigate the mysterious construction returned with tales of a magnificent new temple, surrounded by rich green, tropical verdure, situated near the bank of the river. It was temple to the god Osiris. It had been built by the queen probably that she might partly atone for the sacrilege of her brother and deliver him from some of the torture which he undoubtedly suffered. It was to be dedicated within the month by a great banquet. All the nobles and the high priests of Osiris, of which there were a tremendous number, were to be invited.

Never had the delighted priests been more extravagant in their praises of Queen Nitocris. When she passed through the streets in her open litter, bedazzling eyes by the glitter of her golden ornaments, the cries of the people were almost frantic in their exaltation of her.

True to the predictions of the gossipers, before the month had passed the banquet had been formally announced and to all the nobility and the priests of Osiris had been issued invitations to attend.

The day of the dedication, which was to be followed by the night of banqueting, was a gala holiday. At noon the guests of the empress formed a colorful assembly upon the bank of the river. Gayly draped barges floated at their moorings until preparations should be completed for the transportation of the guests to the temple. All anticipated a holiday of great merriment, and the lustful epicureans were warmed by visualizations of the delightful banquet of copious meats, fruits, luscious delicacies and other less innocent indulgences.

When the queen arrived, clamorous shouts rang deafeningly in her ears. She responded with charming smiles and gracious bows. The most discerning observer could not have detected anything but the greatest cordiality and kindliness reflected in her bearing toward those around her. No action, no fleeting expression upon her lovely face could have caused anyone to suspect anything except entire amicability in her feelings or her intentions. The rats, as they followed the Pied Piper of Hamelin through the streets, entranced by the notes of his magical pipe, could not have been less apprehensive of any great danger impending them than were the guests of the empress as they followed her in gaily draped barges, singing and laughing down the sun-glowing waters of the Nile.

The most vivid descriptions of those who had already seen the temple did not prepare the others for the spectacle of beauty and grandeur which it presented. Gasps of delight came from the priests. What a place in which to conduct their ceremonies! They began to feel that the sacrilege of the dead pharaoh was not, after all, to be so greatly regretted, since it was responsible for the building of this glorious new temple.

The columns were massive and painted with the greatest artistry. The temple itself was proportionately large. The center of it was unroofed. Above the entrance were carved the various symbols of the god Osiris, with splendid workmanship. The building was immensely big, and against the background of green foliage it presented a picture of almost breathtaking beauty. Ethiopian attendants stood on each side of the doorway, their shining black bodies ornamented with bands of brilliant gold. On the interior the guests were inspired to even greater wonderment. The walls were hung with magnificent painted tapestries. The altars were more beautifully and elaborately carved than any seen before. Aromatic powders were burning upon them and sending up veils of scented smoke. The sacramental vessels were of the most exquisite and costly metals. Golden coffers and urns were piled high with perfect fruits of all kinds.

Ah, yes—a splendid place for the making of sacrifices, gloated the staring priests.

Ah, yes indeed, agreed the queen Nitocris, smiling with half-crossed eyes, it was a splendid place for sacrifices—especially for the human sacrifice that had been planned. But all who observed that guileful smile interpreted it as gratification over the pleasure which her creation in honor of their god had brought to the priests of Osiris. Not the slightest shadow of portent was upon the hearts of the joyous guests.

The ceremony of dedication occupied the whole of the afternoon. And when it drew to its impressive conclusion, the large assembly, their nostrils quivering from the savory odor of the roasting meats, were fully ready and impatient for the banquet that awaited them. They gazed about them, observing that the whole building composed an unpartitioned amphitheater and wondering where might be the room of the banquet. However, when the concluding processional chant had been completed the queen summoned a number of burly slaves, and by several iron rings attached to its outer edge they lifted up a large slab of the flooring, disclosing to the astonished guests the fact that the scene of the banquet was to be an immense subterranean vault.

Such vaults were decidedly uncommon among the Egyptians. The idea of feasting in one was novel and appealing. Thrilled exclamations came from the eager, excited crowd and they pressed forward to gaze into the depths, now brightly illuminated. They saw a room beneath them almost as vast in size as the amphitheater in which they were standing. It was filled with banquet tables upon which were set the most delectable foods and rich, sparkling wines in an abundance that would satiate the banqueters of Bacchus. Luxurious, thick rugs covered the floors. Among the tables passed nymphlike maidens, and at one end of the room harpists and singers stood, making sublime music.

The air was cool with the dampness of under-earth, and it was made delightfully fragrant by the perfumes of burning spices and the savory odors of the feast. If it had been heaven itself which the crowd of the queen's guests now gazed down upon they would not have considered the vision disappointing. Perhaps even if they had known the hideous menace that lurked in those gay-draped walls beneath them, they would still have found the allurement of the banquet scene difficult to resist.

Decorum and reserve were almost completely forgotten in the swiftness of the guests' descent. The stairs were not wide enough to afford room for all those who rushed upon them, and some tumbled over, landing unhurt upon the thick carpets. The priests themselves forgot their customary dignity and aloofness when they looked upon the beauty of the maiden attendants.

Immediately all of the guests gathered around the banquet tables, and the next hour was occupied in gluttonous feasting. Wine was unlimited, and so was the thirst of the guests. Goblets were refilled as quickly as they were made empty by the capacious mouths of the drinkers. The songs and the laughter, the dancing and the wild frolicking grew less and less restrained until the banquet became a delirious orgy.

The queen alone, seated upon a cushioned dais from which she might overlook the whole room, remained aloof from the general hilarity. Her thick black brows twitched; her luminous black eyes shone strangely between their narrow painted lids. There was something peculiarly feline in the curl of her rich red lips. Now and again her eyes sought the section of wall to her left, where hung gorgeous braided tapestries from the East. But it seemed not the tapestries that she looked upon. Color would mount upon her brow and her slender fingers would dig still tighter into the cushions she reclined upon.

In her mind the queen Nitocris was seeing a ghastly picture. It was the picture of a room of orgy and feasting suddenly converted into a room of terror and horror, human beings one moment drunken and lustful, the next screaming in the seizure of sudden and awful death. If any of those present had been empowered to see also that picture of dire horror, they would have clambered wildly to make their escape. But none was so empowered.

With increasing wildness the banquet continued into the middle of the night. Some of the banqueters, disgustingly gluttonous, still gorged themselves at the greasy tables. Others lay in drunken stupor, or lolled amorously with the slave-girls. But most of them, formed in a great irregular circle, skipped about the room in a barbaric, joy-mad dance, dragging and tripping each other in uncouth merriment and making the hall ring with their ceaseless shouts, laughter, and hoarse song.

When the hour had approached near to midnight, the queen, who had sat like one entranced, arose from the cushioned dais. One last intent survey she gave to the crowded room of banquet. It was a scene which she wished to imprint permanently upon her mind. Much pleasure might she derive in the future by recalling that picture, and then imagining what came afterward—

stark, searing terror rushing in upon barbaric joy!

She stepped down from the dais and walked swiftly to the steps. Her departure made no impression upon the revelers. When she had arrived at the top of the stairs she looked down and observed that no one had marked her exit.

Around the walls of the temple, dim-lit and fantastic-looking at night, with the cool wind from the river sweeping through and bending the flames of the tall candelabra, stalwart guardsmen were standing at their posts, and when the gold cloaked figure of the queen arose from the aperture, they advanced toward her hurriedly. With a motion, she directed them to place the slab of rock in its tight-fitting sockets. With a swift, noiseless hoist and lowering, they obeyed the command. The queen bent down. There was no change in the boisterous sounds from below. Nothing was yet suspected.

Drawing the soft and shimmering folds of her cloak about her with fingers that trembled with eagerness, excitement and the intense emotion which she felt, the queen passed swiftly across the stone floor of the temple toward the open front through which the night wind swept, blowing her cloak in sheenful waves about her tall and graceful figure. The slaves followed after in silent file, well aware of the monstrous deed about to be executed and without reluctance to play their parts.

Down the steps of the palace into the moon-white night, passed the weird procession. Their way led them down an obviously secreted path through thick ranks of murmuring palms which in their low voices seemed to be whispering shocked remonstrances against what was about to be done. But in her stern purpose the queen was not susceptible to any dissuasion from god or man. Vengeance, strongest of passions, made her obdurate as stone.

Out upon a rough and apparently new-constructed stone pier the thin path led. Beneath, the cold, dark waters of the Nile surged silently by. Here the party came to a halt. Upon this stone pier would the object of their awful midnight errand be accomplished.

With a low-spoken word, the queen commanded her followers to hold back. With her own hand she would perform the act of vengeance.

In the foreground of the pier a number of fantastic, wand-like levers extended upward. Toward these the queen advanced, slowly and stiffly as an executioner mounts the steps of the scaffold. When she had come beside them, she grasped one upthrust bar, fiercely, as if it had been the throat of a hated antagonist. Then she lifted her face with a quick intake of breath toward the moon-lightened sky. This was to her a moment of supreme ecstasy. Grasped in her hand was an instrument which could release awful death upon those against whom she wished vengeance. Their lives were as securely in her grasp as was this bar of iron.

Slowly, lusting upon every triumph-filled second of this time of ecstasy, she turned her face down again to the formidable bar in her hand. Deliberately she drew it back to its limit. This was the lever that opened the wall in the banquet vault. It gave entrance to death. Only the other bar now intervened between the banqueters, probably still reveling undisturbed, and the dreadful fate which she had prepared for them. Upon this bar now her jeweled fingers clutched. Savagely this time she pulled it; then with the litheness of a tiger she sprang to the edge of the pier. She leaned over it and stared down into the inky rush of the river. A new sound she heard above the steady flow. It was the sound of waters suddenly diverted into a new channel—an eager, plunging sound. Down to the hall of revelry they were rushing—these savage waters— bringing terror and sudden death.

A cry of triumph, wild and terrible enough to make even the hearts of the brutish slaves turn cold, now broke from the lips of the queen. The pharaoh was avenged.

And even he must have considered his avenging adequate had he been able to witness it.

After the retiring of the queen, the banquet had gone on without interruption of gayety. None noticed her absence. None noticed the silent replacing of the stone in the socket. No premonition of disaster was felt. The musicians, having been informed beforehand of the intended event of the evening, had made their withdrawal before the queen. The slaves, whose lives were of little value to the queen, were as ignorant of what was to happen as were the guests themselves.

Not until the wall opened up, with a loud and startling crunch, did even those most inclined toward suspicion feel the slightest uneasiness. Then it was that a few noticed the slab to have been replaced, shutting them in. This discovery, communicated throughout the hall in a moment, seemed to instill a sudden fear in the hearts of all. Laughter did not cease, but the ring of dancers were distracted from their wild jubilee. They all turned toward the mysteriously opened wall and gazed into its black depths.

A hush fell over them. And then became audible the mounting sound of rushing water. A shriek rose from the throat of a woman. And then terror took possession of all within the room. Panic like the burst of flames flared into their hearts. Of one accord, they rushed upon the stair. And it, being purposely made frail, collapsed before the foremost of the wildly screaming mob had reached its summit. Turbulently they piled over the tables, filling the room with a hideous clamor. But rising above their screams was the shrill roar of the rushing water, and no sound could be more provoking of dread and terror. Somewhere in its circuitous route from the pier to the chamber of its reception it must have met with temporary blockade, for it was several minutes after the sound of it was first detected that the first spray of that death-bringing water leapt into the faces of the doomed occupants of the room.

With the ferocity of a lion springing into the arena of a Roman amphitheater to devour the gladiators set there for its delectation, the black water plunged in. Furiously it surged over the floor of the room, sweeping tables before it and sending its victims, now face to face with their harrowing doom, into a hysteria of terror. In a moment that icy, black water had risen to their knees, although the room was vast. Some fell instantly dead from the shock, or were trampled upon by the desperate rushing of the mob. Tables were clambered upon. Lamps and candles were extinguished. Brilliant light rapidly faded to twilight, and a ghastly dimness fell over the room as only the suspended lanterns remained lit. And what a scene of chaotic and hideous horror might a spectator have beheld! The gorgeous trumpery of banquet invaded by howling waters of death! Gayly dressed merrymakers caught suddenly in the grip of terror! Gasps and screams of the dying amid tumult and thickening dark!

What more horrible vengeance could Queen Nitocris have conceived than this banquet of death? Not Diablo himself could be capable of anything more fiendishly artistic. Here in the temple of Osiris those nobles and priests who had slain the pharaoh in expiation of his sacrilege against Osiris had now met their deaths. And it was in the waters of the Nile, material symbol of the god Osiris, that they had died. It was magnificent in its irony!

I would be content to end this story here if it were but a story. However, it is not merely a story, as you will have discerned before now if you have been a student of the history of Egypt. Queen Nitocris is not a fictitious personage. In the annals of ancient Egypt she is no inconspicuous figure. Principally responsible for her prominence is her monstrous revenge upon the slayers of her brother, the narration of which I have just concluded. Glad would I be to end this story here, for surely anything following must be in the nature of an anticlimax. However, being not a mere storyteller here, but having upon me also the responsibility of a historian, I feel obliged to continue the account to the point where it was left off by Herodotus, the great Greek historian. And therefore I add this postscript, anticlimax though it be.

The morning of the day after the massacre in the temple, the guests of the queen not having made their return, the citizens of Thebes began to glower with dark suspicions. Rumors came to them through divers channels that something of a most extraordinary and calamitous nature had occurred at the scene of the banquet during the night. Some had it that the temple had collapsed upon the revelers and all had been killed. However, this theory was speedily dispelled when a voyager from down the river reported having passed the temple in a perfectly firm condition but declared that he had seen no signs of life about the place—only the brightly canopied boats, drifting at their moorings.

Uneasiness steadily increased throughout the day. Sage persons recalled the great devotion of the queen toward her dead brother, and noted that the guests at the banquet of last night had been composed almost entirely of those who had participated in his slaying.

When in the evening the queen arrived in the city, pale, silent, and obviously nervous, threatening crowds blocked the path of her chariot, demanding roughly an explanation of the disappearance of her guests. Haughtily she ignored them and lashed forward the horses of her chariot, pushing aside the tight mass of people. Well she knew, however, that her life would be doomed as soon as they confirmed their suspicions. She resolved to meet her inevitable death in a way that befitted one of her rank, not at the filthy hands of a mob.

Therefore upon her entrance into the palace she ordered her slaves to fill instantly her boudoir with hot and smoking ashes. When this had been done, she went to the room, entered it, closed the door and locked it securely, and then flung herself down upon a couch in the center of the room. In a short time the scorching heat and the suffocating thick fumes of the smoke overpowered her. Only her beautiful dead body remained for the hands of the mob.

Smith and the Pharaohs
by H. Rider Haggard

Penned by H. Rider Haggard, "Smith and the Pharaohs" (1921) sits at the crossroads between traditional adventure tale and English ghost story. Haggard, the author of King Solomon's Mines *(1885) and* She: A History of Adventure *(1887), has provided us with an unusually eerie tale in which the primary locus of strange happenings is an antiquities museum.*

At first glance, "Smith and the Pharaohs" may appear to be merely a proto-weird story about a man captivated by his love for a long deceased ancient Egyptian woman. Yet, upon closer inspection one sees that it is also a philosophical reflection on the nature of man, a subtle critique of purely materialist understandings of the universe, and a flight of imaginative fancy into the phantasmagoric borderlands between past and present. With its evocation of true love, Haggard's story also has elements of a fairy tale, taking the reader on an unsettling journey into the heart of a lonely man whose object of his affections cannot but elude his romantic grasp.

"Smith and the Pharaohs" also touches upon another important theme found in mummy stories and ancient Egyptian supernatural tales, namely the palpable tension between wanting to understand the past and the fear of disturbing it. The protagonist in this unsettling supernatural tale, a man literally in love with the past, will be forced to reflect on this very question as he stands alone at the threshold where human dreams and earthly reality collide.

I

Scientists, or some scientists — for occasionally one learned person differs from other learned persons — tell us they know all that is worth knowing about man, which statement, of course, includes woman. They trace him from his remotest origin; they show us how his bones changed and his shape modified, also how, under the influence of his needs and passions, his intelligence developed from something very humble. They demonstrate conclusively that there is nothing in man which the dissecting-table will not explain; that his aspirations towards another life have their root in the fear of death, or, say others of them, in that of earthquake or thunder; that his affinities with the past are merely inherited from remote ancestors who lived in that past, perhaps a million years ago; and that everything noble about him is but the fruit of expediency or of a veneer of civilisation, while everything base must be attributed to the instincts of his dominant and primeval nature. Man, in short, is an animal who, like every other animal, is finally subdued by his environment and takes his colour from his surroundings, as cattle do from the red soil of Devon. Such are the facts, they (or some of them) declare; all the rest is rubbish.

At times we are inclined to agree with these sages, especially after it has been our privilege to attend a course of lectures by one of them. Then perhaps something comes within the range of our experience which gives us pause and causes doubts, the old divine doubts, to arise again deep in our hearts, and with them a yet diviner hope.

Perchance when all is said, so we think to ourselves, man is something more than an animal. Perchance he has known the past, the far past, and will know the future, the far, far future. Perchance the dream is true, and he does indeed possess what for convenience is called an immortal soul, that may manifest itself in one shape or another; that may sleep for ages, but, waking or sleeping, still remains itself, indestructible as the matter of the Universe.

An incident in the career of Mr. James Ebenezer Smith might well occasion such reflections, were any acquainted with its details, which until this, its setting forth, was not the case. Mr. Smith is a person who knows when to be silent. Still, undoubtedly it gave cause for thought to one individual — namely, to him to whom it happened. Indeed, James Ebenezer Smith is still thinking over it, thinking very hard indeed.

J. E. Smith was well born and well educated. When he was a good-looking and able young man at college, but before he had taken his degree, trouble came to him, the particulars of which do not matter, and he was thrown penniless, also friendless, upon the rocky bosom of the world. No, not quite friendless, for he had a godfather, a gentleman connected with business whose Christian name was Ebenezer. To him, as a last resource, Smith went, feeling that Ebenezer owed him something in return for the awful appellation wherewith he had been endowed in baptism.

To a certain extent Ebenezer recognised the obligation. He did nothing heroic, but he found his godson a clerkship in a bank of which he was one of the directors — a modest clerkship, no more. Also, when he died a year later, he left him a hundred pounds to be spent upon some souvenir.

Smith, being of a practical turn of mind, instead of adorning himself with memorial jewellery for which he had no use, invested the hundred pounds in an exceedingly promising speculation. As it happened, he was not misinformed, and his talent returned to him multiplied by ten. He repeated the experiment, and, being in a position to know what he was doing, with considerable success. By the time that he was thirty he found himself possessed of a fortune of something over twenty-five thousand pounds. Then (and this shows the wise and practical nature of the man) he stopped speculating and put out his money in such a fashion that it brought him a safe and clear four per cent.

By this time Smith, being an excellent man of business, was well up in the service of his bank — as yet only a clerk, it is true, but one who drew his four hundred pounds a year, with prospects. In short, he was in a position to marry had he wished to do so. As it happened, he did not wish — perhaps because, being very friendless, no lady who attracted him crossed his path; perhaps for other reasons.

Shy and reserved in temperament, he confided only in himself. None, not even his superiors at the bank or the Board of Management, knew how well off he had become. No one visited him at the flat which he was understood to occupy somewhere in the neighbourhood of Putney; he belonged to no club, and possessed not a single intimate. The blow which the world had dealt him in his early days, the harsh repulses and the rough treatment he had then experienced, sank so deep into his sensitive soul that never again did he seek close converse with his kind. In fact, while still young, he fell into a condition of old-bachelorhood of a refined type.

Soon, however, Smith discovered — it was after he had given up speculating — that a man must have something to occupy his mind. He tried philanthropy, but found himself too sensitive for a business which so often resolves itself into rude inquiry as to the affairs of other people. After a struggle, therefore, he compromised with his conscience by setting aside a liberal portion of his income for anonymous distribution among deserving persons and objects.

While still in this vacant frame of mind Smith chanced one day, when the bank was closed, to drift into the British Museum, more to escape the vile weather that prevailed without than for any other reason. Wandering hither and thither at hazard, he found himself in the great gallery devoted to Egyptian stone objects and sculpture. The place bewildered him somewhat, for he knew nothing of Egyptology; indeed, there remained upon his mind only a sense of wonderment not unmixed with awe. It must have been a great people, he thought to himself, that executed these works, and with the thought came a desire to know more about them. Yet he was going away when suddenly his eye fell on the sculptured head of a woman which hung upon the wall.

Smith looked at it once, twice, thrice, and at the third look he fell in love.

Needless to say, he was not aware that such was his condition. He knew only that a change had come over him, and never, never could he forget the face which that carven mask portrayed. Perhaps it was not really beautiful save for its wondrous and mystic smile; perhaps the lips were too thick and the nostrils too broad. Yet to him that face was Beauty itself, beauty which drew him as with a cart-rope, and awoke within him all kinds of wonderful imaginings, some of them so strange and tender that almost they partook of the nature of memories. He stared at the image, and the image smiled back sweetly at him, as doubtless it, or rather its original — for this was but a plaster cast — had smiled at nothingness in some tomb or hiding-hole for over thirty centuries, and as the woman whose likeness it was had once smiled upon the world.

A short, stout gentleman bustled up and, in tones of authority, addressed some workmen who were arranging a base for a neighbouring statue. It occurred to Smith that he must be someone who knew about these objects. Overcoming his natural diffidence with an effort, he raised his hat and asked the gentleman if he could tell him who was the original of the mask.

The official — who, in fact, was a very great man in the Museum — glanced at Smith shrewdly, and, seeing that his interest was genuine, answered:

"I don't know. Nobody knows. She has been given several names, but none of them have authority. Perhaps one day the rest of the statue may be found, and then we shall learn—that is, if it is inscribed. Most likely, however, it has been burnt for lime long ago."

"Then you can't tell me anything about her?" said Smith.

"Well, only a little. To begin with, that's a cast. The original is in the Cairo Museum. Mariette found it, I believe at Karnak, and gave it a name after his fashion. Probably she was a queen—of the eighteenth dynasty, by the work. But you can see her rank for yourself from the broken *uraeus*." (Smith did not stop him to explain that he had not the faintest idea what a *uraeus* might be, seeing that he was utterly unfamiliar with the snake-headed crest of Egyptian royalty.) "You should go to Egypt and study the head for yourself. It is one of the most beautiful things that ever was found. Well, I must be off. Good day."

And he bustled down the long gallery.

Smith found his way upstairs and looked at mummies and other things. Somehow it hurt him to reflect that the owner of yonder sweet, alluring face must have become a mummy long, long before the Christian era. Mummies did not strike him as attractive.

He returned to the statuary and stared at his plaster cast till one of the workmen remarked to his fellow that if he were the gent he'd go and look at "a live 'un" for a change.

Then Smith retired abashed.

On his way home he called at his bookseller's and ordered "all the best works on Egyptology." When, a day or two later, they arrived in a packing-case, together with a bill for thirty-eight pounds, he was somewhat dismayed. Still, he tackled those books like a man, and, being clever and industrious, within three months had a fair working knowledge of the subject, and had even picked up a smattering of hieroglyphics.

In January — that was, at the end of those three months — Smith astonished his Board of Directors by applying for ten weeks' leave, he who had hitherto been content with a fortnight in the year. When questioned he explained that he had been suffering from bronchitis, and was advised to take a change in Egypt.

"A very good idea," said the manager; "but I'm afraid you'll find it expensive. They fleece one in Egypt."

"I know," answered Smith; "but I've saved a little and have only myself to spend it upon."

So Smith went to Egypt and saw the original of the beauteous head and a thousand other fascinating things. Indeed, he did more. Attaching himself to some excavators who were glad of his intelligent assistance, he actually dug for a month in the neighbourhood of ancient Thebes, but without finding anything in particular.

It was not till two years later that he made his great discovery, that which is known as Smith's Tomb. Here it may be explained that the state of his health had become such as to necessitate an annual visit to Egypt, or so his superiors understood.

However, as he asked for no summer holiday, and was always ready to do another man's work or to stop overtime, he found it easy to arrange for these winter excursions.

On this, his third visit to Egypt, Smith obtained from the Director-General of Antiquities at Cairo a licence to dig upon his own account. Being already well known in the country as a skilled Egyptologist, this was granted upon the usual terms — namely, that the Department of Antiquities should have a right to take any of the objects which might be found, or all of them, if it so desired.

Such preliminary matters having been arranged by correspondence, Smith, after a few days spent in the Museum at Cairo, took the night train to Luxor, where he found his head-man, an ex-dragoman named Mahomet, waiting for him and his fellaheen labourers already hired. There were but forty of them, for his was a comparatively small venture. Three hundred pounds was the amount that he had made up his mind to expend, and such a sum does not go far in excavations.

During his visit of the previous year Smith had marked the place where he meant to dig. It was in the cemetery of old Thebes, at the wild spot not far from the temple of Medinet Habu, that is known as the Valley of the Queens. Here, separated from the resting-places of their royal lords by the bold mass of the intervening hill, some of the greatest ladies of Egypt have been laid to rest, and it was their tombs that Smith desired to investigate. As he knew well, some of these must yet remain to be discovered. Who could say? Fortune favours the bold. It might be that he would find the holy grave of that beauteous, unknown Royalty whose face had haunted him for three long years!

For a whole month he dug without the slightest success. The spot that he selected had proved, indeed, to be the mouth of a tomb. After twenty-five days of laborious exploration it was at length cleared out, and he stood in a rude, unfinished cave. The queen for whom it had been designed must have died quite young and been buried elsewhere; or she had chosen herself another sepulchre, or mayhap the rock had proved unsuitable for sculpture.

Smith shrugged his shoulders and moved on, sinking trial pits and trenches here and there, but still finding nothing. Two-thirds of his time and money had been spent when at last the luck turned. One day, towards evening, with some half-dozen of his best men he was returning after a fruitless morning of labour, when something seemed to attract him towards a little *wadi*, or bay, in the hillside that was filled with tumbled rocks and sand. There were scores of such places, and this one looked no more promising than any of the others had proved to be. Yet it attracted him. Thoroughly dispirited, he walked past it twenty paces or more, then turned.

"Where go you, sah?" asked his head-man, Mahomet.

He pointed to the recess in the cliff.

"No good, sah," said Mahomet. "No tomb there. Bed-rock too near top. Too much water run in there; dead queen like keep dry!"

But Smith went on, and the others followed obediently.

He walked down the little slope of sand and boulders and examined the cliff. It was virgin rock; never a tool mark was to be seen. Already the men were going, when the same strange instinct which had drawn him to the spot caused him to take a spade from one of them and begin to shovel away the sand from the face of the cliff — for here, for some unexplained reason, were no boulders or *debris*. Seeing their master, to whom they were attached, at work, they began to work too, and for twenty minutes or more dug on cheerfully enough, just to humour him, since all were sure that here there was no tomb. At length Smith ordered them to desist, for, although now they were six feet down, the rock remained of the same virgin character.

With an exclamation of disgust he threw out a last shovelful of sand. The edge of his spade struck on something that projected. He cleared away a little more sand, and there appeared a rounded ledge which seemed to be a cornice. Calling back the men, he pointed to it, and without a word all of them began to dig again. Five minutes more of work made it clear that it was a cornice, and half an hour later there appeared the top of the doorway of a tomb.

"Old people wall him up," said Mahomet, pointing to the flat stones set in mud for mortar with which the doorway had been closed, and to the undecipherable impress upon the mud of the scarab seals of the officials whose duty it had been to close the last resting-place of the royal dead for ever.

"Perhaps queen all right inside," he went on, receiving no answer to his remark.

"Perhaps," replied Smith, briefly. "Dig, man, dig! Don't waste time in talking."

So they dug on furiously till at length Smith saw something which caused him to groan aloud. There was a hole in the masonry — the tomb had been broken into. Mahomet saw it too, and examined the top of the aperture with his skilled eye.

"Very old thief," he said. "Look, he try build up wall again, but run away before he have time finish." And he pointed to certain flat stones which had been roughly and hurriedly replaced.

"Dig — dig!" said Smith.

Ten minutes more and the aperture was cleared. It was only just big enough to admit the body of a man.

By now the sun was setting. Swiftly, swiftly it seemed to tumble down the sky. One minute it was above the rough crests of the western hills behind them; the next, a great ball of glowing fire, it rested on their topmost ridge. Then it was gone. For an instant a kind of green spark shone where it had been. This too went out, and the sudden Egyptian night was upon them.

The fellaheen muttered among themselves, and one or two of them wandered off on some pretext. The rest threw down their tools and looked at Smith. "Men say they no like stop here. They afraid of ghost! Too many *afreet* live in these tomb. That what they say. Come back finish tomorrow morning when it light. Very foolish people, these common fellaheen," remarked Mahomet, in a superior tone.

"Quite so," replied Smith, who knew well that nothing that he could offer would tempt his men to go on with the opening of a tomb after sunset. "Let them go away. You and I will stop and watch the place till morning."

"Sorry, sah," said Mahomet, "but I not feel quite well inside; think I got fever. I go to camp and lie down and pray under plenty blanket."

"All right, go," said Smith; "but if there is anyone who is not a coward, let him bring me my big coat, something to eat and drink, and the lantern that hangs in my tent. I will meet him there in the valley."

Mahomet, though rather doubtfully, promised that this should be done, and, after begging Smith to accompany them, lest the spirit of whoever slept in the tomb should work him a mischief during the night, they departed quickly enough.

Smith lit his pipe, sat down on the sand, and waited. Half an hour later he heard a sound of singing, and through the darkness, which was dense, saw lights coming up the valley.

"My brave men," he thought to himself, and scrambled up the slope to meet them.

He was right. These were his men, no less than twenty of them, for with a fewer number they did not dare to face the ghosts which they believed haunted the valley after nightfall. Presently the light from the lantern which one of them carried (not Mahomet, whose sickness had increased too suddenly to enable him to come) fell upon the tall form of Smith, who, dressed in his white working clothes, was leaning against a rock. Down went the lantern, and with a howl of terror the brave company turned and fled.

"Sons of cowards!" roared Smith after them, in his most vigorous Arabic. "It is I, your master, not an *afreet*."

They heard, and by degrees crept back again. Then he perceived that in order to account for their number each of them carried some article. Thus one had the bread, another the lantern, another a tin of sardines, another the sardine-opener, another a box of matches, another a bottle of beer, and so on. As even thus there were not enough things to go round, two of them bore his big coat between them, the first holding it by the sleeves and the second by the tail as though it were a stretcher.

"Put them down," said Smith, and they obeyed. "Now," he added, "run for your lives; I thought I heard two *afreets* talking up there just now of what they would do to any followers of the Prophet who mocked their gods, if perchance they should meet them in their holy place at night."

This kindly counsel was accepted with much eagerness. In another minute Smith was alone with the stars and the dying desert wind.

Collecting his goods, or as many of them as he wanted, he thrust them into the pockets of the great-coat and returned to the mouth of the tomb. Here he made his simple meal by the light of the lantern, and afterwards tried to go to sleep. But sleep he could not. Something always woke him. First it was a jackal howling amongst the rocks; next a sand-fly bit him in the ankle so sharply that he thought he must have been stung by a scorpion. Then, notwithstanding his warm coat, the cold got hold of him, for the clothes beneath were wet through with perspiration, and it occurred to him that unless he did something he would probably contract an internal chill or perhaps fever. He rose and walked about.

By now the moon was up, revealing all the sad, wild scene in its every de-tail. The mystery of Egypt entered his soul and oppressed him. How much dead majesty lay in the hill upon which he stood? Were they all really dead, he wondered, or were those fellaheen right? Did their spirits still come forth at night and wander through the land where once they ruled? Of course that was the Egyptian faith according to which the *Ka*, or Double, eternally haunted the place where its earthly counterpart had been laid to rest. When one came to think of it, beneath a mass of unintelligible symbolism there was much in the Egyptian faith which it was hard for a Christian to disbelieve. Sal-vation through a Redeemer, for instance, and the resurrection of the body. Had he, Smith, not already written a treatise upon these points of similarity which he proposed to publish one day, not under his own name? Well, he would not think of them now; the occasion seemed scarcely fitting — they came home too pointedly to one who was engaged in violating a tomb.

His mind, or rather his imagination — of which he had plenty — went off at a tangent. What sights had this place seen thousands of years ago! Once, thousands of years ago, a procession had wound up along the roadway which was doubtless buried beneath the sand whereon he stood towards the dark door of this sepulchre. He could see it as it passed in and out between the rocks. The priests, shaven-headed and robed in leopards' skins, or some of them in pure white, bearing the mystic symbols of their office. The funeral sledge drawn by oxen, and on it the great rectangular case that contained the outer and the inner coffins, and within them the mummy of some departed Majesty; in the Egyptian formula, "the hawk that had spread its wings and flown into the bosom of Osiris," God of Death. Behind, the mourners, rend-ing the air with their lamentations. Then those who bore the funeral furniture and offerings. Then the high officers of State and the first priests of Amen and of the other gods. Then the sister queens, leading by the hand a wondering child or two. Then the sons of Pharaoh, young men carrying the emblems of their rank.

Lastly, walking alone, Pharaoh himself in his ceremonial robes, his apron, his double crown of linen surmounted by the golden snake, his inlaid bracelets and his heavy, tinkling earrings. Pharaoh, his head bowed, his feet travelling wearily, and in his heart — what thoughts? Sorrow, perhaps, for her who had departed. Yet he had other queens and fair women without count. Doubtless she was sweet and beautiful, but sweetness and beauty were not given to her alone. Moreover, was she not wont to cross his will and to question his di-vinity? No, surely it is not only of her that he thinks, her for whom he had pre-pared this splendid tomb with all things needful to unite her with the gods. Surely he thinks also of himself and that other tomb on the farther side of the hill whereat the artists labour day by day — yes, and have laboured these many years; that tomb to which before so very long he too must travel in just this fashion, to seek his place beyond the doors of Death, who lays his equal hand on king and queen and slave.

The vision passed. It was so real that Smith thought he must have been dreaming. Well, he was awake now, and colder than ever. Moreover, the jackals had multiplied. There were a whole pack of them, and not far away. Look! One crossed in the ring of the lamplight, a slinking, yellow beast that smelt the remains of dinner. Or perhaps it smelt himself. Moreover, there were bad characters who haunted these mountains, and he was alone and quite un-armed. Perhaps he ought to put out the light which advertised his where-abouts. It would be wise, and yet in this particular he rejected wisdom. Af-ter all, the light was some company.

Since sleep seemed to be out of the question, he fell back upon poor hu-manity's other anodyne, work, which has the incidental advantage of gener-ating warmth. Seizing a shovel, he began to dig at the doorway of the tomb, whilst the jackals howled louder than ever in astonishment. They were not used to such a sight. For thousands of years, as the old moon above could have told, no man, or at least no solitary man, had dared to rob tombs at such an unnatural hour.

When Smith had been digging for about twenty minutes something tinkled on his shovel with a noise which sounded loud in that silence.

"A stone which may come in handy for the jackals," he thought to himself, shaking the sand slowly off the spade until it appeared. There it was, and not large enough to be of much service. Still, he picked it up, and rubbed it in his hands to clear off the encrusting dirt. When he opened them he saw that it was no stone, but a bronze.

"Osiris," reflected Smith, "buried in front of the tomb to hallow the ground. No, an Isis. No, the head of a statuette, and a jolly good one, too — at any rate, in moonlight. Seems to have been gilded." And, reaching out for the lamp, he held it over the object.

Another minute, and he found himself sitting at the bottom of the hole, lamp in one hand and statuette, or rather head, in the other.

"The Queen of the Mask!" he gasped. "The same — the same! By heav-ens, the very same!"

Oh, he could not be mistaken. There were the identical lips, a little thick and pouted; the identical nostrils, curved and quivering, but a little wide; the iden-tical arched eyebrows and dreamy eyes set somewhat far apart. Above all, there was the identical alluring and mysterious smile. Only on this master-piece of ancient art was set a whole crown of uraei surrounding the entire head. Beneath the crown and pressed back behind the ears was a full-bottomed wig or royal head-dress, of which the ends descended to the breasts. The statuette, that, having been gilt, remained quite perfect and uncorroded, was broken just above the middle, apparently by a single violent blow, for the fracture was very clean.

At once it occurred to Smith that it had been stolen from the tomb by a thief who thought it to be gold; that outside of the tomb doubt had overtaken him and caused him to break it upon a stone or otherwise. The rest was clear. Finding that it was but gold-washed bronze he had thrown away the fragments, rather than be at the pains of carrying them. This was his theory, probably not a correct one, as the sequel seems to show.

Smith's first idea was to recover the other portion. He searched quite a long while, but without success. Neither then nor afterwards could it be found. He reflected that perhaps this lower half had remained in the thief's hand, who, in his vexation, had thrown it far away, leaving the head to lie where it fell. Again Smith examined this head, and more closely. Now he saw that just beneath the breasts was a delicately cut cartouche.

Being by this time a master of hieroglyphics, he read it without trouble. It ran: "Ma-Mee, Great Royal Lady. Beloved of..." Here the cartouche was broken away.

"Ma-Mé, or it might be Ma-Mi," he reflected. "I never heard of a queen called Ma-Mé, or Ma-Mi, or Ma-Mu. She must be quite new to history. I wonder of whom she was beloved? Amen, or Horus, or Isis, probably. Of some god, I have no doubt, at least I hope so!"

He stared at the beautiful portrait in his hand, as once he had stared at the cast on the Museum wall, and the beautiful portrait, emerging from the dust of ages, smiled back at him there in the solemn moonlight as once the cast had smiled from the Museum wall. Only that had been but a cast, whereas this was real. This had slept with the dead from whose features it had been fashioned, the dead who lay, or who had lain, within.

A sudden resolution took hold of Smith. He would explore that tomb, at once and alone. No one should accompany him on this his first visit; it would be a sacrilege that anyone save himself should set foot there until he had looked on what it might contain.

Why should he not enter? His lamp, of what is called the "hurricane" brand, was very good and bright, and would burn for many hours. Moreover, there had been time for the foul air to escape through the hole that they had cleared. Lastly, something seemed to call on him to come and see. He placed the bronze head in his breast-pocket over his heart, and, thrusting the lamp through the hole, looked down. Here there was no difficulty, since sand had drifted in to the level of the bottom of the aperture. Through it he struggled, to find himself upon a bed of sand that only just left him room to push himself along between it and the roof. A little farther on the passage was almost filled with mud.

Mahomet had been right when, from his knowledge of the bed-rock, he said that any tomb made in this place must be flooded. It had been flooded by some ancient rainstorm, and Smith began to fear that he would find it quite filled with soil caked as hard as iron. So, indeed, it was to a certain depth, a result that apparently had been anticipated by those who hollowed it, for this entrance shaft was left quite undecorated. Indeed, as Smith found after- wards, a hole had been dug beneath the doorway to allow the mud to enter after the burial was completed. Only a miscalculation had been made. The natural level of the mud did not quite reach the roof of the tomb, and there- fore still left it open.

After crawling for forty feet or so over this caked mud, Smith suddenly found himself on a rising stair. Then he understood the plan; the tomb itself was on a higher level.

Here began the paintings. Here the Queen Ma-Mee, wearing her crowns and dressed in diaphanous garments, was presented to god after god. Between her figure and those of the divinities the wall was covered with hieroglyphs as fresh today as on that when the artist had limned them. A glance told him that they were extracts from the Book of the Dead. When the thief of bygone ages had broken into the tomb, probably not very long after the interment, the mud over which Smith had just crawled was still wet. This he could tell, since the clay from the rascal's feet remained upon the stairs, and that upon his fingers had stained the paintings on the wall against which he had sup- ported himself; indeed, in one place was an exact impression of his hand, showing its shape and even the lines of the skin.

At the top of the flight of steps ran another passage at a higher level, which the water had never reached, and to right and left were the beginnings of un- finished chambers. It was clear to him that this queen had died young. Her tomb, as she or the king had designed it, was never finished. A few more paces, and the passage enlarged itself into a hall about thirty feet square. The ceiling was decorated with vultures, their wings outspread, the looped Cross of Life hanging from their talons. On one wall her Majesty Ma-Mee stood expectant while Anubis weighed her heart against the feather of truth, and Thoth, the Recorder, wrote down the verdict upon his tablets. All her titles were given to her here, such as — "Great Royal Heiress, Royal Sister, Royal Wife, Royal Mother, Lady of the Two Lands, Palm-branch of Love, Beau- tiful-exceedingly."

Smith read them hurriedly and noted that nowhere could he see the name of the king who had been her husband. It would almost seem as though this had been purposely omitted. On the other walls Ma-Mee, accompanied by her *Ka*, or Double, made offerings to the various gods, or uttered propitiatory speeches to the hideous demons of the underworld, declaring their names to them and forcing them to say: "Pass on. Thou art pure!"

Lastly, on the end wall, triumphant, all her trials done, she, the justified Osiris, or Spirit, was received by the god Osiris, Saviour of Spirits.

All these things Smith noted hurriedly as he swung the lamp to and fro in that hallowed place. Then he saw something else which filled him with dismay. On the floor of the chamber where the coffins had been — for this was the burial chamber — lay a heap of black fragments charred with fire. Instantly he understood. After the thief had done his work he had burned the mummy-cases, and with them the body of the queen. There could be no doubt that this was so, for look! among the ashes lay some calcined human bones, while the roof above was blackened with the smoke and cracked by the heat of the conflagration. There was nothing left for him to find!

Oppressed with the closeness of the atmosphere, he sat down upon a little bench or table cut in the rock that evidently had been meant to receive offerings to the dead. Indeed, on it still lay the scorched remains of some votive flowers. Here, his lamp between his feet, he rested a while, staring at those calcined bones. See, yonder was the lower jaw, and in it some teeth, small, white, regular and but little worn. Yes, she had died young. Then he turned to go, for disappointment and the holiness of the place overcame him; he could endure no more of it that night.

Leaving the burial hall, he walked along the painted passage, the lamp swinging and his eyes fixed upon the floor. He was disheartened, and the paintings could wait till the morrow. He descended the steps and came to the foot of the mud slope. Here suddenly he perceived, projecting from some sand that had drifted down over the mud, what seemed to be the corner of a reed box or basket. To clear away the sand was easy, and — yes, it was a basket, a foot or so in length, such a basket as the old Egyptians used to contain the funeral figures which are called *ushaptis*, or other objects connected with the dead. It looked as though it had been dropped, for it lay upon its side. Smith opened it — not very hopefully, for surely nothing of value would have been abandoned thus.

The first thing that met his eyes was a mummied hand, broken off at the wrist, a woman's little hand, most delicately shaped. It was withered and paper-white, but the contours still remained; the long fingers were perfect, and the almond-shaped nails had been stained with henna, as was the embalmers' fashion. On the hand were two gold rings, and for those rings it had been stolen. Smith looked at it for a long while, and his heart swelled within him, for here was the hand of that royal lady of his dreams.

Indeed, he did more than look; he kissed it, and as his lips touched the holy relic it seemed to him as though a wind, cold but scented, blew upon his brow.

Then, growing fearful of the thoughts that arose within him, he hurried his mind back to the world, or rather to the examination of the basket.

Here he found other objects roughly wrapped in fragments of mummy-cloth that had been torn from the body of the queen. These it is needless to describe, for are they not to be seen in the gold room of the Museum, labelled "Bijouterie de la Reine Ma-Me, XVIIIeme Dynastie. Thebes (Smith's Tomb)"? It may be mentioned, however, that the set was incomplete. For instance, there was but one of the great gold ceremonial ear-rings fashioned like a group of pomegranate blooms, and the most beautiful of the necklaces had been torn in two — half of it was missing.

It was clear to Smith that only a portion of the precious objects which were buried with the mummy had been placed in this basket. Why had these been left where he found them? A little reflection made that clear also. Something had prompted the thief to destroy the desecrated body and its coffin with fire, probably in the hope of hiding his evil handiwork. Then he fled with his spoil. But he had forgotten how fiercely mummies and their trappings can burn. Or perhaps the thing was an accident. He must have had a lamp, and if its flame chanced to touch this bituminous tinder!

At any rate, the smoke overtook the man in that narrow place as he began to climb the slippery slope of clay. In his haste he dropped the basket, and dared not return to search for it. It could wait till the morrow, when the fire would be out and the air pure. Only for this desecrator of the royal dead that morrow never came, as was discovered afterwards.

When at length Smith struggled into the open air the stars were paling before the dawn. An hour later, after the sky was well up, Mahomet (recovered from his sickness) and his myrmidons arrived.

"I have been busy while you slept," said Smith, showing them the mummied hand (but not the rings which he had removed from the shrunk fingers), and the broken bronze, but not the priceless jewellery which was hidden in his pockets.

For the next ten days they dug till the tomb and its approach were quite clear. In the sand, at the head of a flight of steps which led down to the doorway, they found the skeleton of a man, who evidently had been buried there in a hurried fashion. His skull was shattered by the blow of an axe, and the shaven scalp that still clung to it suggested that he might have been a priest.

Mahomet thought, and Smith agreed with him, that this was the person who had violated the tomb. As he was escaping from it the guards of the holy place surprised him after he had covered up the hole by which he had entered and purposed to return. There they executed him without trial and divided up the plunder, thinking that no more was to be found. Or perhaps his confederates killed him.

Such at least were the theories advanced by Mahomet. Whether they were right or wrong none will ever know. For instance, the skeleton may not have been that of the thief, though probability appears to point the other way.

Nothing more was found in the tomb, not even a scarab or a mummy-bead. Smith spent the remainder of his time in photographing the pictures and copying the inscriptions, which for various reasons proved to be of extraordinary interest. Then, having reverently buried the charred bones of the queen in a secret place of the sepulchre, he handed it over to the care of the local Guardian of Antiquities, paid off Mahomet and the fellaheen, and departed for Cairo. With him went the wonderful jewels of which he had breathed no word, and another relic to him yet more precious — the hand of her Majesty Ma-Mee, Palm-branch of Love.

II

Smith was seated in the sanctum of the distinguished Director-General of Antiquities at the new Cairo Museum. It was a very interesting room. Books piled upon the floor; objects from tombs awaiting examination, lying here and there; a hoard of Ptolemaic silver coins, just dug up at Alexandria, standing on a table in the pot that had hidden them for two thousand years; in the corner the mummy of a royal child, aged six or seven, not long ago discovered, with some inscription scrawled upon the wrappings (brought here to be deciphered by the Master), and the withered lotus-bloom, love's last offering, thrust beneath one of the pink retaining bands.

"A touching object," thought Smith to himself. "Really, they might have left the dear little girl in peace."

Smith had a tender heart, but even as he reflected he became aware that some of the jewellery hidden in an inner pocket of his waistcoat (designed for bank-notes) was fretting his skin. He had a tender conscience also.

Just then the Director, a French savant, bustled in, alert, vigorous, full of interest.

"Ah, my dear Mr. Smith!" he said, in his excellent English. "I am indeed glad to see you back again, especially as I understand that you are come rejoicing and bringing your sheaves with you. They tell me you have been extraordinarily successful. What do you say is the name of this queen whose tomb you have found — Ma-Mee? A very unusual name. How do you get the extra vowel? Is it for euphony, eh? Did I not know how good a scholar you are, I should be tempted to believe that you had misread it. Me-Mee, Ma-Mee! That would be pretty in French, would it not? Ma mie — my darling!

Well, I dare say she was somebody's *mie* in her time. But tell me the story."

Smith told him shortly and clearly; also he produced his photographs and copies of inscriptions.

"This is interesting — interesting truly," said the Director, when he had glanced through them. "You must leave them with me to study. Also you will publish them, is it not so? Perhaps one of the Societies would help you with the cost, for it should be done in facsimile. Look at this vignette! Most unusual. Oh, what a pity that scoundrelly priest got off with the jewellery and burnt her Majesty's body!"

"He didn't get off with all of it."

"What, Mr. Smith? Our inspector reported to me that you found nothing."

"I dare say, sir; but your inspector did not know what I found."

"Ah, you are a discreet man! Well, let us see."

Slowly Smith unbuttoned his waistcoat. From its inner pocket and elsewhere about his person he extracted the jewels wrapped in mummy-cloth as he had found them. First he produced a sceptre-head of gold, in the shape of a pomegranate fruit and engraved with the throne name and titles of Ma-Mee.

"What a beautiful object!" said the Director. "Look! the handle was of ivory, and that sacré thief of a priest smashed it out at the socket. It was fresh ivory then; the robbery must have taken place not long after the burial. See, this magnifying-glass shows it. Is that all?"

Smith handed him the surviving half of the marvellous necklace that had been torn in two.

"I have re-threaded it," he muttered, "but every bead is in its place."

"Oh, heavens! How lovely! Note the cutting of those cornelian heads of Hathor and the gold lotus-blooms between — yes, and the enamelled flies beneath. We have nothing like it in the Museum."

So it went on.

"Is that all?" gasped the Director at last, when every object from the basket glittered before them on the table.

"Yes," said Smith. "That is — no. I found a broken statuette hidden in the sand outside the tomb. It is of the queen, but I thought perhaps you would allow me to keep this."

"But certainly, Mr. Smith; it is yours indeed. We are not niggards here. Still, if I might see it ——"

From yet another pocket Smith produced the head. The Director gazed at it, then he spoke with feeling.

"I said just now that you were discreet, Mr. Smith, and I have been reflecting that you are honest. But now I must add that you are very clever. If you had not made me promise that this bronze should be yours before you showed it me — well, it would never have gone into that pocket again. And, in the public interest, won't you release me from the promise?"

"No," said Smith.

"You are perhaps not aware," went on the Director, with a groan, "that this is a portrait of Mariette's unknown queen whom we are thus able to identify. It seems a pity that the two should be separated; a replica we could let you have."

"I am quite aware," said Smith, "and I will be sure to send you a replica, with photographs. Also I promise to leave the original to some museum by will."

The Director clasped the image tenderly, and, holding it to the light, read the broken cartouche beneath the breasts.

"'Ma-Mé, Great Royal Lady. Beloved of ——' Beloved of whom? Well, of Smith, for one. Take it, monsieur, and hide it away at once, lest soon there should be another mummy in this collection, a modern mummy called Smith; and, in the name of Justice, let the museum which inherits it be not the British, but that of Cairo, for this queen belongs to Egypt. By the way, I have been told that you are delicate in the lungs. How is your health now? Our cold winds are very trying. Quite good? Ah, that is excellent! I suppose that you have no more articles that you can show me?"

"I have nothing more except a mummied hand, which I found in the basket with the jewels. The two rings off it lie there. Doubtless it was removed to get at that bracelet. I suppose you will not mind my keeping the hand — —"

"Of the beloved of Smith," interrupted the Director drolly. "No, I suppose not, though for my part I should prefer one that was not quite so old. Still, perhaps you will not mind my seeing it. That pocket of yours still looks a little bulky; I thought that it contained books!"

Smith produced a cigar-box; in it was the hand wrapped in cotton wool.

"Ah," said the Director, "a pretty, well-bred hand. No doubt this Ma-Mee was the real heiress to the throne, as she describes herself. The Pharaoh was somebody of inferior birth, half-brother — she is called 'Royal Sister,' you remember — son of one of the Pharaoh's slave-women, perhaps. Odd that she never mentioned him in the tomb. It looks as though they didn't get on in life, and that she was determined to have done with him in death. Those were the rings upon that hand, were they not?"

He replaced them on the fingers, then took off one, a royal signet in a cartouche, and read the inscription on the other: "'Bes Ank, Ank Bes.' 'Bes the Living, the Living Bes.'

"Your Ma-Mee had some human vanity about her," he added. "Bes, among other things, as you know, was the god of beauty and of the adornments of women. She wore that ring that she might remain beautiful, and that

her dresses might always fit, and her rouge never cake when she was dancing before the gods. Also it fixes her period pretty closely, but then so do other
things. It seems a pity to rob Ma-Mee of her pet ring, does it not? The royal
signet will be enough for us."

With a little bow he gave the hand back to Smith, leaving the Bes ring on
the finger that had worn it for more than three thousand years. At least, Smith
was so sure it was the Bes ring that at the time he did not look at it again.

Then they parted, Smith promising to return upon the morrow, which, owing to events to be described, he did not do.

"Ah!" said the Master to himself, as the door closed behind his visitor. "He's
in a hurry to be gone. He has fear lest I should change my mind about that
ring. Also there is the bronze. Monsieur Smith was *rusé* there. It is worth a
thousand pounds, that bronze. Yet I do not believe he was thinking of the
money. I believe he is in love with that Ma-Mee and wants to keep her picture. *Mon Dieu!* A well-established affection. At least he is what the English
call an odd fish, one whom I could never make out, and of whom no one seems
to know anything. Still, honest, I am sure — quite honest. Why, he might have
kept every one of those jewels and no one have been the wiser. And what
things! What a find! *Ciel!* what a find! There has been nothing like it for years.
Benedictions on the head of Odd-fish Smith!"

Then he collected the precious objects, thrust them into an inner compartment of his safe, which he locked and double-locked, and, as it was
nearly five o'clock, departed from the Museum to his private residence in the
grounds, there to study Smith's copies and photographs, and to tell some
friends of the great things that had happened.

When Smith found himself outside the sacred door, and had presented its
venerable guardian with a baksheesh of five piastres, he walked a few paces
to the right and paused a while to watch some native labourers who were dragging a huge sarcophagus upon an improvised tramway. As they dragged they
sang an echoing rhythmic song, whereof each line ended with an invocation
to Allah.

Just so, reflected Smith, had their forefathers sung when, millenniums
ago, they dragged that very sarcophagus from the quarries to the Nile and
from the Nile to the tomb whence it reappeared today, or when they slid the
casing blocks of the pyramids up the great causeway and smooth slope of sand,
and laid them in their dizzy resting-places. Only then each line of the immemorial chant of toil ended with an invocation to Amen, now transformed
to Allah. The East may change its masters and its gods, but its customs
never change, and if today Allah wore the feathers of Amen one wonders

whether the worshippers would find the difference so very great.

Thus thought Smith as he hurried away from the sarcophagus and those blue-robed, dark-skinned fellaheen, down the long gallery that is filled with a thousand sculptures. For a moment he paused before the wonderful white statue of Queen Amenartas, then, remembering that his time was short, hastened on to a certain room, one of those which opened out of the gallery.

In a corner of this room, upon the wall, amongst many other beautiful objects, stood that head which Mariette had found, whereof in past years the cast had fascinated him in London. Now he knew whose head it was; to him it had been given to find the tomb of her who had sat for that statue. Her very hand was in his pocket — yes, the hand that had touched yonder marble, pointing out its defects to the sculptor, or perhaps swearing that he flattered her. Smith wondered who that sculptor was; surely he must have been a happy man. Also he wondered whether the statuette was also this master's work. He thought so, but he wished to make sure.

Near to the end of the room he stopped and looked about him like a thief. He was alone in the place; not a single student or tourist could be seen, and its guardian was somewhere else. He drew out the box that contained the hand. From the hand he slipped the ring which the Director-General had left there as a gift to himself. He would much have preferred the other with the signet, but how could he say so, especially after the episode of the statuette?

Replacing the hand in his pocket without looking at the ring — for his eyes were watching to see whether he was observed — he set it upon his little finger, which it exactly fitted. (Ma-Mee had worn both of them upon the third finger of her left hand, the Bes ring as a guard to the signet.) He had the fancy to approach the effigy of Ma-Mee wearing a ring which she had worn and that came straight from her finger to his own.

Smith found the head in its accustomed place. Weeks had gone by since he looked upon it, and now, to his eyes, it had grown more beautiful than ever, and its smile was more mystical and living. He drew out the statuette and began to compare them point by point. Oh, no doubt was possible! Both were likenesses of the same woman, though the statuette might have been executed two or three years later than the statue. To him the face of it looked a little older and more spiritual. Perhaps illness, or some premonition of her end had then thrown its shadow on the queen. He compared and compared. He made some rough measurements and sketches in his pocket-book, and set himself to work out a canon of proportions.

So hard and earnestly did he work, so lost was his mind that he never heard the accustomed warning sound which announces that the Museum is about to close. Hidden behind an altar as he was, in his distant, shadowed corner, the guardian of the room never saw him as he cast a last perfunctory glance about the place before departing till the Saturday morning; for the morrow was Friday, the Mohammedan Sabbath, on which the Museum remains shut, and he would not be called upon to attend. So he went. Everybody went. The great doors clanged, were locked and bolted, and, save for a watchman outside, no one was left in all that vast place except Smith in his corner, engaged in sketching and in measurements.

The difficulty of seeing, owing to the increase of shadow, first called his attention to the fact that time was slipping away. He glanced at his watch and saw that it was ten minutes to the hour.

"Soon be time to go," he thought to himself, and resumed his work. How strangely silent the place seemed! Not a footstep to be heard or the sound of a human voice. He looked at his watch again, and saw that it was six o'clock, not five, or so the thing said. But that was impossible, for the Museum shut at five; evidently the desert sand had got into the works. The room in which he stood was that known as Room I, and he had noticed that its Arab custodian often frequented Room K or the gallery outside. He would find him and ask what was the real time.

Passing round the effigy of the wonderful Hathor cow, perhaps the finest example of an ancient sculpture of a beast in the whole world, Smith came to the doorway and looked up and down the gallery. Not a soul to be seen. He ran to Room K, to Room H, and others. Still not a soul to be seen. Then he made his way as fast as he could go to the great entrance. The doors were locked and bolted.

"Watch must be right after all. I'm shut in," he said to himself. "However, there's sure to be someone about somewhere. Probably the *salle des ventes* is still open. Shops don't shut till they are obliged."

Thither he went, to find its door as firmly closed as a door can be. He knocked on it, but a sepulchral echo was the only answer.

"I know," he reflected. "The Director must still be in his room. It will take him a long while to examine all that jewellery and put it away."

So for the room he headed, and, after losing his path twice, found it by help of the sarcophagus that the Arabs had been dragging, which now stood as deserted as it had done in the tomb, a lonesome and impressive object in the gathering shadows. The Director's door was shut, and again his knockings produced nothing but an echo. He started on a tour round the Museum, and, having searched the ground floors, ascended to the upper galleries by the great stairway.

Presently he found himself in that devoted to the royal mummies, and, being tired, rested there a while. Opposite to him, in a glass case in the middle of the gallery, reposed Rameses II. Near to, on shelves in a side case, were Rameses' son, Meneptah, and above, his son, Seti II, while in other cases were the mortal remains of many more of the royalties of Egypt. He looked at the proud face of Rameses and at the little fringe of white locks turned yellow by the embalmer's spices, also at the raised left arm. He remembered how the Director had told him that when they were unrolling this mighty monarch they went away to lunch, and that presently the man who had been left in charge of the body rushed into the room with his hair on end, and said that the dead king had lifted his arm and pointed at him.

Back they went, and there, true enough, was the arm lifted; nor were they ever able to get it quite into its place again. The explanation given was that the warmth of the sun had contracted the withered muscles, a very natural and correct explanation.

Still, Smith wished that he had not recollected the story just at this moment, especially as the arm seemed to move while he contemplated it — a very little, but still to move.

He turned round and gazed at Meneptah, whose hollow eyes stared at him from between the wrappings carelessly thrown across the parchment-like and ashen face. There, probably, lay the countenance that had frowned on Moses. There was the heart which God had hardened. Well, it was hard enough now, for the doctors said he died of ossification of the arteries, and that the vessels of the heart were full of lime!

Smith stood upon a chair and peeped at Seti II above. His weaker countenance was very peaceful, but it seemed to wear an air of reproach. In getting down Smith managed to upset the heavy chair. The noise it made was terrific. He would not have thought it possible that the fall of such an article could produce so much sound. Satisfied with his inspection of these particular kings, who somehow looked quite different now from what they had ever done before—more real and imminent, so to speak — he renewed his search for a living man.

On he went, mummies to his right, mummies to his left, of every style and period, till he began to feel as though he never wished to see another dried remnant of mortality. He peeped into the room where lay the relics of Iouiya and Touiyou, the father and mother of the great Queen Taia. Cloths had been drawn over these, and really they looked worse and more suggestive thus draped than in their frigid and unadorned blackness. He came to the coffins of the priest-kings of the twentieth dynasty, formidable painted coffins with human faces. There seemed to be a vast number of these priest-kings, but perhaps they were better than the gold masks of the great Ptolemaic ladies which glinted at him through the gathering gloom.

Really, he had seen enough of the upper floors. The statues downstairs were better than all these dead, although it was true that, according to the Egyptian faith, every one of those statues was haunted eternally by the *Ka*, or Double, of the person whom it represented. He descended the great stairway. Was it fancy, or did something run across the bottom step in front of him—an animal of some kind, followed by a swift-moving and indefinite shadow? If so, it must have been the Museum cat hunting a Museum mouse. Only then what on earth was that very peculiar and unpleasant shadow?

He called, "Puss! puss! puss!" for he would have been quite glad of its company; but there came no friendly "miau" in response. Perhaps it was only the *Ka* of a cat and the shadow was — oh! never mind what. The Egyptians worshipped cats, and there were plenty of their mummies about on the shelves. But the shadow!

Once he shouted in the hope of attracting attention, for there were no windows to which he could climb. He did not repeat the experiment, for it seemed as though a thousand voices were answering him from every corner and roof of the gigantic edifice.

Well, he must face the thing out. He was shut in a museum, and the question was in what part of it he should camp for the night. Moreover, as it was growing rapidly dark, the problem must be solved at once. He thought with affection of the lavatory, where, before going to see the Director, only that afternoon he had washed his hands with the assistance of a kindly Arab who watched the door and gracefully accepted a piastre. But there was no Arab there now, and the door, like every other in this confounded place, was locked. He marched on to the entrance.

Here, opposite to each other, stood the red sarcophagi of the great Queen Hatshepu and her brother and husband, Thotmes III. He looked at them. Why should not one of these afford him a night's lodging? They were deep and quiet, and would fit the human frame very nicely. For a while Smith wondered which of these monarchs would be the more likely to take offence at such a use of a private sarcophagus, and, acting on general principles, concluded that he would rather throw himself on the mercy of the lady.

Already one of his legs was over the edge of that solemn coffer, and he was squeezing his body beneath the massive lid that was propped above it on blocks of wood, when he remembered a little, naked, withered thing with long hair that he had seen in a side chamber of the tomb of Amenhotep II in the Valley of Kings at Thebes. This caricature of humanity many thought, and he agreed with them, to be the actual body of the mighty Hatshepu as it appeared after the robbers had done with it.

Supposing now, that when he was lying at the bottom of that sarcophagus, sleeping the sleep of the just, this little personage should peep over its edge and ask him what he was doing there! Of course the idea was absurd; he was tired, and his nerves were a little shaken. Still, the fact remained that for centuries the hallowed dust of Queen Hatshepu had slept where he, a modern man, was proposing to sleep.

He scrambled down from the sarcophagus and looked round him in despair. Opposite to the main entrance was the huge central hall of the Museum. Now the cement roof of this hall had, he knew, gone wrong, with the result that very extensive repairs had become necessary. So extensive were they, indeed, that the Director-General had informed him that they would take several years to complete. Therefore this hall was boarded up, only a little doorway being left by which the workmen could enter. Certain statues, of Seti II and others, too large to be moved, were also roughly boarded over, as were some great funeral boats on either side of the entrance. The rest of the place, which might be two hundred feet long with a proportionate breadth, was empty save for the colossi of Amenhotep III and his queen Taia that stood beneath the gallery at its farther end.

It was an appalling place in which to sleep, but better, reflected Smith, than a sarcophagus or those mummy chambers. If, for instance, he could creep behind the deal boards that enclosed one of the funeral boats he would be quite comfortable there. Lifting the curtain, he slipped into the hall, where the gloom of evening had already settled. Only the skylights and the outline of the towering colossi at the far end remained visible. Close to him were the two funeral boats which he had noted when he looked into the hall earlier on that day, standing at the head of a flight of steps which led to the sunken floor of the centre. He groped his way to that on the right. As he expected, the projecting planks were not quite joined at the bow. He crept in between them and the boat and laid himself down.

Presumably, being altogether tired out, Smith did ultimately fall asleep, for how long he never knew. At any rate, it is certain that, if so, he woke up again. He could not tell the time, because his watch was not a repeater, and the place was as black as the pit. He had some matches in his pocket, and might have struck one and even have lit his pipe. To his credit be it said, however, he remembered that he was the sole tenant of one of the most valuable museums in the world, and his responsibilities with reference to fire. So he refrained from striking that match under the keel of a boat which had become very dry in the course of five thousand years.

Smith found himself very wide awake indeed. Never in all his life did he remember being more so, not even in the hour of its great catastrophe, or when his godfather, Ebenezer, after much hesitation, had promised him a clerkship in the bank of which he was a director. His nerves seemed strung tight as harpstrings, and his every sense was painfully acute. Thus he could even smell the odour of mummies that floated down from the upper galleries and the earthy scent of the boat which had been buried for thousands of years in sand at the foot of the pyramid of one of the fifth dynasty kings.

Moreover, he could hear all sorts of strange sounds, faint and far-away sounds which at first he thought must emanate from Cairo without. Soon, however, he grew sure that their origin was more local. Doubtless the cement work and the cases in the galleries were cracking audibly, as is the unpleasant habit of such things at night.

Yet why should these common manifestations be so universal and affect him so strangely? Really, it seemed as though people were stirring all about him. More, he could have sworn that the great funeral boat beneath which he lay had become re-peopled with the crew that once it bore.

He heard them at their business above him. There were trampings and a sound as though something heavy were being laid on the deck, such, for instance, as must have been made when the mummy of Pharaoh was set there for its last journey to the western bank of the Nile. Yes, and now he could have sworn again that the priestly crew were getting out the oars.

Smith began to meditate flight from the neighbourhood of that place when something occurred which determined him to stop where he was.

The huge hall was growing light, but not, as at first he hoped, with the rays of dawn. This light was pale and ghostly, though very penetrating. Also it had a blue tinge, unlike any other he had ever seen. At first it arose in a kind of fan or fountain at the far end of the hall, illuminating the steps there and the two noble colossi which sat above.

But what was this that stood at the head of the steps, radiating glory? By heavens! it was Osiris himself or the image of Osiris, god of the Dead, the Egyptian saviour of the world!

There he stood, in his mummy-cloths, wearing the feathered crown, and holding in his hands, which projected from an opening in the wrappings, the crook and the scourge of power. Was he alive, or was he dead? Smith could not tell, since he never moved, only stood there, splendid and fearful, his calm, benignant face staring into nothingness.

Smith became aware that the darkness between him and the vision of this god was peopled; that a great congregation was gathering, or had gathered there. The blue light began to grow; long tongues of it shot forward, which joined themselves together, illumining all that huge hall.

Now, too, he saw the congregation. Before him, rank upon rank of them, stood the kings and queens of Egypt. As though at a given signal, they bowed themselves to the Osiris, and ere the tinkling of their ornaments had died away, lo! Osiris was gone. But in his place stood another, Isis, the Mother of Mystery, her deep eyes looking forth from beneath the jewelled vulture-cap. Again the congregation bowed, and, lo! she was gone. But in her place stood yet another, a radiant, lovely being, who held in her hand the Sign of

Life, and wore upon her head the symbol of the shining disc — Hathor, Goddess of Love. A third time the congregation bowed, and she, too, was gone;
nor did any other appear in her place.

The Pharaohs and their queens began to move about and speak to each
other; their voices came to his ears in one low, sweet murmur.

In his amaze Smith had forgotten fear. From his hiding-place he watched
them intently. Some of them he knew by their faces. There, for instance, was
the long-necked Khu-en-aten, talking somewhat angrily to the imperial
Rameses II. Smith could understand what he said, for this power seemed to
have been given to him. He was complaining in a high, weak voice that on this,
the one night of the year when they might meet, the gods, or the magic images of the gods who were put up for them to worship, should not include *his*
god, symbolized by the "Aten," or the sun's disc.

"I have heard of your Majesty's god," replied Rameses; "the priests used
to tell me of him, also that he did not last long after your Majesty flew to
heaven. The Fathers of Amen gave you a bad name; they called you 'the
heretic' and hammered out your cartouches. They were quite rare in my time.
Oh, do not let your Majesty be angry! So many of us have been heretics. My
grandson, Seti, there" — and he pointed to a mild, thoughtful-faced man —
"for example. I am told that he really worshipped the god of those Hebrew
slaves whom I used to press to build my cities. Look at that lady with him.
Beautiful, isn't she? Observe her large, violet eyes! Well, she was the one who
did the mischief, a Hebrew herself. At least, they tell me so."

"I will talk with him," answered Khu-en-aten. "It is more than possible that
we may agree on certain points. Meanwhile, let me explain to your Majesty
——"

"Oh, I pray you, not now. There is my wife."

"Your wife?" said Khu-en-aten, drawing himself up. "Which wife? I am
told that your Majesty had many and left a large family; indeed, I see some
hundreds of them here tonight. Now, I—but let me introduce Nefertiti to
your Majesty. I may explain that she was my only wife."

"So I have understood. Your Majesty was rather an invalid, were you not?
Of course, in those circumstances, one prefers the nurse whom one can trust.
Oh, pray, no offence! Nefertari, my love — oh, I beg pardon! — Astnefert —
Nefertari has gone to speak to some of her children — let me introduce you
to your predecessor, the Queen Nefertiti, wife of Amenhotep IV — I mean
Khu-en-aten (he changed his name, you know, because half of it was that of
the father of the gods). She is interested in the question of plural marriage.
Good-bye! I wish to have a word with my grandfather, Rameses I. He was
fond of me as a little boy."

At this moment Smith's interest in that queer conversation died away, for of a sudden he beheld none other than the queen of his dreams, Ma-Mee. Oh! there she stood, without a doubt, only ten times more beautiful than he had ever pictured her. She was tall and somewhat fair-complexioned, with slumbrous, dark eyes, and on her face gleamed the mystic smile he loved. She wore a robe of simple white and a purple-broidered apron, a crown of golden *uraei* with turquoise eyes was set upon her dark hair as in her statue, and on her breast and arms were the very necklace and bracelets that he had taken from her tomb. She appeared to be somewhat moody, or rather thoughtful, for she leaned by herself against a balustrade, watching the throng without much interest.

Presently a Pharaoh, a black-browed, vigorous man with thick lips, drew near.

"I greet your Majesty," he said.

She started, and answered: "Oh, it is you! I make my obeisance to your Majesty," and she curtsied to him, humbly enough, but with a suggestion of mockery in her movements.

"Well, you do not seem to have been very anxious to find me, Ma-Mee, which, considering that we meet so seldom ——"

"I saw that your Majesty was engaged with my sister queens," she interrupted, in a rich, low voice, "and with some other ladies in the gallery there, whose faces I seem to remember, but who I think were not queens. Unless, indeed, you married them after I was drawn away."

"One must talk to one's relations," replied the Pharaoh.

"Quite so. But, you see, I have no relations — at least, none whom I know well. My parents, you will remember, died when I was young, leaving me Egypt's heiress, and they are still vexed at the marriage which I made on the advice of my counsellors. But, is it not annoying? I have lost one of my rings, that which had the god Bes on it. Some dweller on the earth must be wearing it today, and that is why I cannot get it back from him."

"Him! Why 'him'? Hush; the business is about to begin."

"What business, my lord?"

"Oh, the question of the violation of our tombs, I believe."

"Indeed! That is a large subject, and not a very profitable one, I should say. Tell me, who is that?" And she pointed to a lady who had stepped forward, a very splendid person, magnificently arrayed.

"Cleopatra the Greek," he answered, "the last of Egypt's Sovereigns, one of the Ptolemys. You can always know her by that Roman who walks about after her."

"Which?" asked Ma-Mee. "I see several — also other men. She was the wretch who rolled Egypt in the dirt and betrayed her. Oh, if it were not for the law of peace by which we must abide when we meet thus!"

"You mean that she would be torn to shreds, Ma-Mee, and her very soul scattered like the limbs of Osiris? Well, if it were not for that law of peace, so perhaps would many of us, for never have I heard a single king among these hundreds speak altogether well of those who went before or followed after him."

"Especially of those who went before if they happen to have hammered out their cartouches and usurped their monuments," said the queen, dryly, and looking him in the eyes.

At this home-thrust the Pharaoh seemed to wince. Making no answer, he pointed to the royal woman who had mounted the steps at the end of the hall.

Queen Cleopatra lifted her hand and stood thus for a while. Very splendid she was, and Smith, on his hands and knees behind the boarding of the boat, thanked his stars that alone among modern men it had been his lot to look upon her rich and living loveliness. There she shone, she who had changed the fortunes of the world, she who, whatever she did amiss, at least had known how to die.

Silence fell upon that glittering galaxy of kings and queens and upon all the hundreds of their offspring, their women, and their great officers who crowded the double tier of galleries around the hall.

"Royalties of Egypt," she began, in a sweet, clear voice which penetrated to the farthest recesses of the place, "I, Cleopatra, the sixth of that name and the last monarch who ruled over the Upper and the Lower Lands before Egypt became a home of slaves, have a word to say to your Majesties, who, in your mortal days, all of you more worthily filled the throne on which once I sat. I do not speak of Egypt and its fate, or of our sins — whereof mine were not the least — that brought her to the dust. Those sins I and others expiate elsewhere, and of them, from age to age, we hear enough. But on this one night of the year, that of the feast of him whom we call Osiris, but whom other nations have known and know by different names, it is given to us once more to be mortal for an hour, and, though we be but shadows, to renew the loves and hates of our long-perished flesh. Here for an hour we strut in our forgotten pomp; the crowns that were ours still adorn our brows, and once more we seem to listen to our people's praise. Our hopes are the hopes of mortal life, our foes are the foes we feared, our gods grow real again, and our lovers whisper in our ears. Moreover, this joy is given to us — to see each other as we are, to know as the gods know, and therefore to forgive, even where we despise and hate. Now I have done, and I, the youngest of the rulers of ancient Egypt, call upon him who was the first of her kings to take my place."

She bowed, and the audience bowed back to her. Then she descended the steps and was lost in the throng. Where she had been appeared an old man, simply-clad, long-bearded, wise-faced, and wearing on his grey hair no crown save a plain band of gold, from the centre of which rose the snake-headed *uraeus* crest.

"Your Majesties who came after me," said the old man, "I am Menes, the first of the accepted Pharaohs of Egypt, although many of those who went before me were more truly kings than I. Yet as the first who joined the Upper and the Lower Lands, and took the royal style and titles, and ruled as well as I could rule, it is given to me to talk with you for a while this night whereon our spirits are permitted to gather from the uttermost parts of the uttermost worlds and see each other face to face. First, in darkness and in secret, let us speak of the mystery of the gods and of its meanings. Next, in darkness and in secret, let us speak of the mystery of our lives, of whence they come, of where they tarry by the road, and whither they go at last. And afterwards, let us speak of other matters face to face in light and openness, as we were wont to do when we were men. Then hence to Thebes, there to celebrate our yearly festival. Is such your will?"

"Such is our will," they answered.

It seemed to Smith that dense darkness fell upon the place, and with it a silence that was awful. For a time that he could not reckon, that might have been years or might have been moments, he sat there in the utter darkness and the utter silence.

At length the light came again, first as a blue spark, then in upward pouring rays, and lastly pervading all. There stood Menes on the steps, and there in front of him was gathered the same royal throng.

"The mysteries are finished," said the old king. "Now, if any have aught to say, let it be said openly."

A young man dressed in the robes and ornaments of an early dynasty came forward and stood upon the steps between the Pharaoh Menes and all those who had reigned after him. His face seemed familiar to Smith, as was the side lock that hung down behind his right ear in token of his youth. Where had he seen him? Ah, he remembered. Only a few hours ago lying in one of the cases of the Museum, together with the bones of the Pharaoh Unas.

"Your Majesties," he began, "I am the King Metesuphis. The matter that I wish to lay before you is that of the violation of our sepulchres by those men who now live upon the earth. The mortal bodies of many who are gathered here tonight lie in this place to be stared at and mocked by the curious. I myself am one of them, jawless, broken, hideous to behold. Yonder, day by day, must my *Ka* sit watching my desecrated flesh, torn from the pyramid that, with cost and labour, I raised up to be an eternal house wherein I might hide till the hour of resurrection. Others of us lie in far lands. Thus, as he can tell you, my predecessor, Man-kau-ra, he who built the third of the great pyramids, the Pyramid of Her, sleeps, or rather wakes in a dark city, called London, across the seas, a place of murk where no sun shines. Others have been burnt with fire, others are scattered in small dust. The ornaments that were ours are stole away and sold to the greedy; our sacred writings and our symbols are their jest. Soon there will not be one holy grave in Egypt that remains undefiled."

"That is so," said a voice from the company. "But four months gone the deep, deep pit was opened that I had dug in the shadow of the Pyramid of Cephren, who begat me in the world. There in my chamber I slept alone, two handfuls of white bones, since when I died they did not preserve the body with wrappings and with spices. Now I see those bones of mine, beside which my Double has watched for these five thousand years, hid in the blackness of a great ship and tossing on a sea that is strewn with ice."

"It is so," echoed a hundred other voices.

"Then," went on the young king, turning to Menes, "I ask of your Majesty whether there is no means whereby we may be avenged on those who do us this foul wrong."

"Let him who has wisdom speak," said the old Pharaoh.

A man of middle age, short in stature and of a thoughtful brow, who held in his hand a wand and wore the feathers and insignia of the heir to the throne of Egypt and of a high priest of Amen, moved to the steps. Smith knew him at once from his statues. He was Khaemuas, son of Rameses the Great, the mightiest magician that ever was in Egypt, who of his own will withdrew himself from earth before the time came that he should sit upon the throne.

"I have wisdom, your Majesties, and I will answer," he said. "The time draws on when, in the land of Death which is Life, the land that we call Amenti, it will be given to us to lay our wrongs as to this matter before Those who judge, knowing that they will be avenged. On this night of the year also, when we resume the shapes we were, we have certain powers of vengeance, or rather of executing justice. But our time is short, and there is much to say and do before the sun-god Ra arises and we depart each to his place. Therefore it seems best that we should leave these wicked ones in their wickedness till we meet them face to face beyond the world."

Smith, who had been following the words of Khaemuas with the closest attention and considerable anxiety, breathed again, thanking Heaven that the engagements of these departed monarchs were so numerous and pressing. Still, as a matter of precaution, he drew the cigar-box which contained Ma-Mee's hand from his pocket, and pushed it as far away from him as he could. It was a most unlucky act. Perhaps the cigar-box grated on the floor, or perhaps the fact of his touching the relic put him into psychic communication with all these spirits. At any rate, he became aware that the eyes of that dreadful magician were fixed upon him, and that a bone had a better chance of escaping the search of a Rontgen ray than he of hiding himself from their baleful glare.

"As it happens, however," went on Khaemuas, in a cold voice, "I now perceive that there is hidden in this place, and spying on us, one of the worst of these vile thieves. I say to your Majesties that I see him crouched beneath yonder funeral barge, and that he has with him at this moment the hand of one of your Majesties, stolen by him from her tomb at Thebes.

Now every queen in the company became visibly agitated (Smith, who was watching Ma-Mee, saw her hold up her hands and look at them), while all the Pharaohs pointed with their fingers and exclaimed together, in a voice that rolled round the hall like thunder:

"Let him be brought forth to judgment!"

Khaemuas raised his wand and, holding it towards the boat where Smith was hidden, said:

"Draw near, Vile One, bringing with thee that thou hast stolen."

Smith tried hard to remain where he was. He sat himself down and set his heels against the floor. As the reader knows, he was always shy and retiring by disposition, and never had these weaknesses oppressed him more than they did just then. When a child his favourite nightmare had been that the foreman of a jury was in the act of proclaiming him guilty of some dreadful but unstated crime. Now he understood what that nightmare foreshadowed. He was about to be convicted in a court of which all the kings and queens of Egypt were the jury, Menes was Chief Justice, and the magician Khaemuas played the *role* of Attorney-General.

In vain did he sit down and hold fast. Some power took possession of him which forced him first to stretch out his arm and pick up the cigar-box containing the hand of Ma-Mee, and next drew him from the friendly shelter of the deal boards that were about the boat.

Now he was on his feet and walking down the flight of steps opposite to those on which Menes stood far away. Now he was among all that throng of ghosts, which parted to let him pass, looking at him as he went with cold and wondering eyes. They were very majestic ghosts; the ages that had gone by since they laid down their sceptres had taken nothing from their royal dignity. Moreover, save one, none of them seemed to have any pity for his plight. She was a little princess who stood by her mother, that same little princess whose mummy he had seen and pitied in the Director's room with a lotus flower thrust beneath her bandages. As he passed Smith heard her say:

"This Vile One is frightened. Be brave, Vile One!"

Smith understood, and pride came to his aid. He, a gentleman of the modern world, would not show the white feather before a crowd of ancient Egyptian ghosts. Turning to the child, he smiled at her, then drew himself to his full height and walked on quietly. Here it may be stated that Smith was a tall man, still comparatively young, and very good-looking, straight and spare in frame, with dark, pleasant eyes and a little black beard.

"At least he is a well-favoured thief," said one of the queens to another.

"Yes," answered she who had been addressed. "I wonder that a man with such a noble air should find pleasure in disturbing graves and stealing the offerings of the dead," words that gave Smith much cause for thought. He had never considered the matter in this light.

Now he came to the place where Ma-Mee stood, the black-browed Pharaoh who had been her husband at her side. On his left hand which held the cigar-box was the gold Bes ring, and that box he felt constrained to carry pressed against him just over his heart.

As he went by he turned his head, and his eyes met those of Ma-Mee. She started violently. Then she saw the ring upon his hand and again started still more violently.

"What ails your Majesty?" asked the Pharaoh.

"Oh, naught," she answered. "Yet does this earth-dweller remind you of anyone?"

"Yes, he does," answered the Pharaoh. "He reminds me very much of that accursed sculptor about whom we had words."

"Do you mean a certain Horu, the Court artist; he who worked the image that was buried with me, and whom you sent to carve your statues in the deserts of Kush, until he died of fevers — or was it poison?"

"Aye; Horu and no other, may Set take and keep him!" growled the Pharaoh.

Then Smith passed on and heard no more. Now he stood before the venerable Menes. Some instinct caused him to bow to this Pharaoh, who bowed back to him. Then he turned and bowed to the royal company, and they also bowed back to him, coldly, but very gravely and courteously.

"Dweller on the world where once we had our place, and therefore brother of us, the dead," began Menes, "this divine priest and magician" — and he pointed to Khaemuas —

"declares that you are one of those who foully violate our sepulchres and desecrate our ashes. He declares, moreover, that at this very moment you have with you a portion of the mortal flesh of a certain Majesty whose spirit is present here. Say, now, are these things true?"

To his astonishment Smith found that he had not the slightest difficulty in answering in the same sweet tongue.

"O King, they are true, and not true. Hear me, rulers of Egypt. It is true that I have searched in your graves, because my heart has been drawn towards you, and I would learn all that I could concerning you, for it comes to me now that once I was one of you — no king, indeed, yet perchance of the blood of kings. Also — for I would hide nothing even if I could — I searched for one tomb above all others."

"Why, O man?" asked the Judge.

"Because a face drew me, a lovely face that was cut in stone."

Now all that great audience turned their eyes towards him and listened as though his words moved them.

"Did you find that holy tomb?" asked Menes. "If so, what did you find therein?"

"Aye, Pharaoh, and in it I found these," and he took from the box the withered hand, from his pocket the broken bronze, and from his finger the ring.

"Also I found other things which I delivered to the keeper of this place, articles of jewellery that I seem to see tonight upon one who is present here among you."

"Is the face of this figure the face you sought?" asked the Judge.

"It is the lovely face," he answered.

Menes took the effigy in his hand and read the cartouche that was engraved beneath its breast.

"If there be here among us," he said, presently, "one who long after my day ruled as queen in Egypt, one who was named Ma-Mé, let her draw near."

Now from where she stood glided Ma-Mee and took her place opposite to Smith."Say, O Queen," asked Menes, "do you know aught of this matter?"

"I know that hand; it was my own hand," she answered. "I know that ring; it was my ring. I know that image in bronze; it was my image. Look on me and judge for yourselves whether this be so. A certain sculptor fashioned it, the son of a king's son, who was named Horu, the first of sculptors and the head artist of my Court. There, clad in strange garments, he stands before you. Horu, or the Double of Horu, he who cut the image when I ruled in Egypt, is he who found the image and the man who stands before you; or, mayhap, his Double cast in the same mould."

The Pharaoh Menes turned to the magician Khaemuas and said:—

"Are these things so, O Seer?"

"They are so," answered Khaemuas. "This dweller on the earth is he who, long ago, was the sculptor Horu. But what shall that avail? He, once more a living man, is a violator of the hallowed dead. I say, therefore, that judgment should be executed on his flesh, so that when the light comes here tomorrow he himself will again be gathered to the dead."

Menes bent his head upon his breast and pondered. Smith said nothing. To him the whole play was so curious that he had no wish to interfere with its development. If these ghosts wished to make him of their number, let them do so. He had no ties on earth, and now when he knew full surely that there was a life beyond this of earth he was quite prepared to explore its mysteries. So he folded his arms upon his breast and awaited the sentence.

But Ma-Mee did not wait. She raised her hand so swiftly that the bracelets jingled on her wrists, and spoke out with boldness.

"Royal Khaemuas, prince and magician," she said, "hearken to one who, like you, was Egypt's heir centuries before you were born, one also who ruled over the Two Lands, and not so ill — which, Prince, never was your lot. Answer me! Is all wisdom centred in your breast? Answer me! Do you alone know the mysteries of Life and Death? Answer me! Did your god Amen teach you that vengeance went before mercy? Answer me! Did he teach you that men should be judged unheard? That they should be hurried by violence to Osiris ere their time, and thereby separated from the dead ones whom they loved and forced to return to live again upon this evil Earth?

"Listen: when the last moon was near her full my spirit sat in my tomb in the burying-place of queens. My spirit saw this man enter into my tomb, and what he did there. With bowed head he looked upon my bones that a thief of the priesthood had robbed and burnt within twenty years of their burial, in which he himself had taken part. And what did this man with those bones, he who was once Horu? I tell you that he hid them away there in the tomb where he thought they could not be found again. Who, then, was the thief and the violator? He who robbed and burnt my bones, or he who buried them with reverence? Again, he found the jewels that the priest of your brotherhood had dropped in his flight, when the smoke of the burning flesh and spices over-powered him, and with them the hand which that wicked one had broken off from the body of my Majesty. What did this man then? He took the jewels. Would you have had him leave them to be stolen by some peasant? And the hand? I tell you that he kissed that poor dead hand which once had been part of the body of my Majesty, and that now he treasures it as a holy relic. My spirit saw him do these things and made report thereof to me. I ask you, there-fore, Prince, I ask you all, Royalties of Egypt — whether for such deeds this man should die?"

Now Khaemuas, the advocate of vengeance, shrugged his shoulders and smiled meaningly, but the congregation of kings and queens thundered an an-swer, and it was: "*No!*"

Ma-Mee looked to Menes to give judgment. Before he could speak the dark-browed Pharaoh who had named her wife strode forward and addressed them.

"Her Majesty, Heiress of Egypt, Royal Wife, Lady of the Two Lands, has spoken," he cried. "Now let me speak who was the husband of her Majesty. Whether this man was once Horu the sculptor I know not. If so he was also an evil-doer who, by my decree, died in banishment in the land of Kush. Whatever be the truth as to that matter, he admits that he violated the tomb

of her Majesty and stole what the old thieves had left. Her Majesty says also
— and he does not deny it — that he dared to kiss her hand, and for a man to
kiss the hand of a wedded Queen of Egypt the punishment is death. I claim
that this man should die to the World before his time, that in a day to come
again he may live and suffer in the World. Judge, O Menes."

Menes lifted his head and spoke, saying: —

"Repeat to me the law, O Pharaoh, under which a living man must die for
the kissing of a dead hand. In my day and in that of those who went before
me there was no such law in Egypt. If a living man, who was not her husband,
or of her kin, kissed the living hand of a wedded Queen of Egypt, save in ceremony, then perchance he might be called upon to die. Perchance for such a
reason a certain Horu once was called upon to die. But in the grave there is
no marriage, and therefore even if he had found her alive within the tomb and
kissed her hand, or even her lips, why should he die for the crime of love?

"Hear me, all; this is my judgment in the matter. Let the soul of that priest
who first violated the tomb of the royal Ma-Mee be hunted down and given
to the jaws of the Destroyer, that he may know the last depths of Death, if so
the gods declare. But let this man go from among us unharmed, since what
he did he did in reverent ignorance and because Hathor, Goddess of Love,
guided him from of old. Love rules this world wherein we meet tonight, with
all the worlds whence we have gathered or whither we still must go. Who can
defy its power? Who can refuse its rites? Now hence to Thebes!"

There was a rushing sound as of a thousand wings, and all were gone.

No, not all, since Smith yet stood before the draped colossi and the empty
steps, and beside him, glorious, unearthly, gleamed the vision of Ma-Mee.

"I, too, must away," she whispered; "yet ere I go a word with you who once
were a sculptor in Egypt. You loved me then, and that love cost you your life,
you who once dared to kiss this hand of mine that again you kissed in yonder tomb. For I was Pharaoh's wife in name only; understand me well, in name
only; since that title of Royal Mother which they gave me is but a graven lie.
Horu, I never was a wife, and when you died, swiftly I followed you to the
grave. Oh, you forget, but I remember! I remember many things. You think
that the priestly thief broke this figure of me which you found in the sand outside my tomb. Not so. I broke it, because, daring greatly, you had written
thereon, 'Beloved,' not 'of Horus the God,' as you should have done, but 'of
Horu the Man.' So when I came to be buried, Pharaoh, knowing all, took the
image from my wrappings and hurled it away. I remember, too, the casting
of that image, and how you threw a gold chain I had given you into the cru-
cible with the bronze, saying that gold alone was fit to fashion me. And this
signet that I bear — it was you who cut it. Take it, take it, Horu, and in its place

give me back that which is on your hand, the Bes ring that I also wore. Take it and wear it ever till you die again, and let it go to the grave with you as once it went to the grave with me.

"Now hearken. When Ra the great sun arises again and you awake you will think that you have dreamed a dream. You will think that in this dream you saw and spoke with a lady of Egypt who died more than three thousand years ago, but whose beauty, carved in stone and bronze, has charmed your heart today. So let it be, yet know, O man, who once was named Horu, that such dreams are oft-times a shadow of the truth. Know that this Glory which shines before you is mine indeed in the land that is both far and near, the land wherein I dwell eternally, and that what is mine has been, is, and shall be yours for ever. Gods may change their kingdoms and their names; men may live and die, and live again once more to die; empires may fall and those who ruled them be turned to forgotten dust. Yet true love endures immortal as the souls in which it was conceived, and from it for you and me, the night of woe and separation done, at the daybreak which draws on, there shall be born the splendour and the peace of union. Till that hour foredoomed seek me no more, though I be ever near you, as I have ever been. Till that most blessed hour, Horu, farewell."

She bent towards him; her sweet lips touched his brow; the perfume from her breath and hair beat upon him; the light of her wondrous eyes searched out his very soul, reading the answer that was written there.

He stretched out his arms to clasp her, and lo! she was gone.

It was a very cold and a very stiff Smith who awoke on the following morning, to find himself exactly where he had lain down — namely, on a cement floor beneath the keel of a funeral boat in the central hall of the Cairo Museum. He crept from his shelter shivering, and looked at this hall, to find it quite as empty as it had been on the previous evening. Not a sign or a token was there of Pharaoh Menes and all those kings and queens of whom he had dreamed so vividly.

Reflecting on the strange phantasies that weariness and excited nerves can summon to the mind in sleep, Smith made his way to the great doors and waited in the shadow, praying earnestly that, although it was the Mohammedan Sabbath, someone might visit the Museum to see that all was well.

As a matter of fact, someone did, and before he had been there a minute — a watchman going about his business. He unlocked the place carelessly, looking over his shoulder at a kite fighting with two nesting crows. In an instant Smith, who was not minded to stop and answer questions, had slipped past him and was gliding down the portico, from monument to monument, like a snake between boulders, still keeping in the shadow as he headed for the gates.

The attendant caught sight of him and uttered a yell of fear; then, since it is not good to look upon an *afreet*, appearing from whence no mortal man could be, he turned his head away. When he looked again Smith was through those gates and had mingled with the crowd in the street beyond.

The sunshine was very pleasant to one who was conscious of having contracted a chill of the worst Egyptian order from long contact with a damp stone floor. Smith walked on through it towards his hotel — it was Shepheard's, and more than a mile away—making up a story as he went to tell the hall-porter of how he had gone to dine at Mena House by the Pyramids, missed the last tram, and stopped the night there.

Whilst he was thus engaged his left hand struck somewhat sharply against the corner of the cigar-box in his pocket, that which contained the relic of the queen Ma-Mee. The pain caused him to glance at his fingers to see if they were injured, and to perceive on one of them the ring he wore. Surely, surely it was not the same that the Director-General had given him! *That* ring was engraved with the image of the god Bes. On this was cut the cartouche of her Majesty Ma-mee! And he had dreamed — oh, he had dreamed ——!

To this day Smith is wondering whether, in the hurry of the moment, he made a mistake as to which of those rings the Director-General had given him as part of his share of the spoil of the royal tomb he discovered in the Valley of Queens. Afterwards Smith wrote to ask, but the Director-General could only remember that he gave him one of the two rings, and assured him that that inscribed *"Bes Ank, Ank Bes,"* was with Ma-Mee's other jewels in the Gold Room of the Museum.

Also Smith is wondering whether any other bronze figure of an old Egyptian royalty shows so high a percentage of gold as, on analysis, the broken image of Ma-Mee was proved to do. For had she not seemed to tell him a tale of the melting of a golden chain when that effigy was cast?

Was it all only a dream, or was it — something more — by day and by night he asks of Nothingness?

But, be she near or far, no answer comes from the Queen Ma-Mee, whose proud titles were "Her Majesty the Good God, the justified Dweller in Osiris; Daughter of Amen, Royal Heiress, Royal Sister, Royal Wife, Royal Mother; Lady of the Two Lands; Wearer of the Double Crown; of the White Crown, of the Red Crown; Sweet Flower of Love, Beautiful Eternally."

So, like the rest of us, Smith must wait to learn the truth concerning many things, and more particularly as to which of those two circles of ancient gold the Director-General gave him yonder at Cairo.

It seems but a little matter, yet it is more than all the worlds to him!

To the astonishment of his colleagues in antiquarian research, Smith has never returned to Egypt. He explains to them that his health is quite restored, and that he no longer needs this annual change to a more temperate clime.

Now, *which* of the two royal rings did the Director-General return to Smith on the mummied hand of her late Majesty Ma-Mee?

The Dog-Eared God
by Frank Belknap Long

Frank Belknap Long's "The Dog-Eared God" is both a mummy story and a hallucinatory sojourn into the ancient Egyptian past. Featuring an atypical look-ing mummy, this exquisitely bizarre story first appeared in the November 1926 issue of Weird Tales. *It takes the reader to a time and a place when strange gods roamed the terrestrial moorings we mere mortals call Earth.*

With its explicit textual reference to Edgar Allan Poe, whose humorous "Some Words with a Mummy," appeared earlier in this anthology, Long's eerie story features a fanatical Egyptologist who is doomed by his unceasing desire to both literally and figuratively unwrap the past. It is also, in part, a tongue-in-cheek exploration of the great chasm that exists between the modern, "civilized" world and ancient history.

In "The Dog-Eared God," geographical Egypt is not the setting. Rather, an ancient Egypt of the mind makes its presence known within the confines of a mod-ern New York City brownstone. With its descriptive prose and its evocation of the limits of scientific inquiry, Long's short tale, once read, is not so easily for-gotten. A story of two men coming face-to-face with a strange, grotesque being, it isn't the most literary of works, but nevertheless remains a chilling and im-portant contribution to the development of the ancient Egyptian supernatural tale subgenre.

1

"What do you think of it?" asked Professor Dewey.

The colossal height of the mummy case accentuated my friend's littleness. Somehow (I don't know why the image should have presented itself) I thought of the opium-haunted De Quincey walking wearily about the streets of Lon-don, a grotesque little midget in carpet slippers who carried a world within his head. Professor Dewey bore an amazing resemblance to De Quincey. His forehead was high and shrunken, and covered with wrinkles, and the skin on his lean cheeks was stretched as taut as yellow parchment. His nose could scarcely be described as Roman: it was so excessively Hebraic that a strain of

Jewish blood unquestionably formed a measure of his heritage. His smile, when he did smile, was grim and lifeless; and very few people would have been attracted to him. But beneath his almost repulsive exterior the little chap had a good heart, and I found his companionship delightfully stimulating.

Professor Dewey's hobby was Egyptology, and he imported large quantities of mummies annually, and I am sorry to add, illegally. No prying customs officer ever laid his sternly official hand on one of Professor Dewey's acquisitions. No blue-eyed and impertinent government clerk ever questioned Professor Dewey as to the value of his queer and often repulsive property. The professor had made arrangements with a dozen sly and secretive skippers whose Levantine dealings were seldom above reproach, and as a result of his careful bargaining he never lost a mummy or scarab or precious stone. In the course of a single year eighty-three mummies had been successfully smuggled into his stately brownstone mansion on Riverside Drive.

We stood in Professor Dewey's mummy-room, a great hall carpeted with red velvet and lined with rather sinister black curtains. It seemed ridiculous to me that the professor should furnish this repository with the trappings of occult melodrama, but I have always been singularly incapable of fathoming my friend's amusing whims. Beneath his whimsicality and eccentricity he was reasonably genuine, and it is unfair to expect common sense or restraint from a man of genius.

The mummy before us was unusually tall. It fairly towered in the yellowish gloom of the great room, and it bore unmistakable characteristics of great age. And it was oddly shaped – its breast swelled out curiously and its nose was gigantic. Indeed, the latter member almost protruded through the aromatic and evil-smelling wrappings. "An Egyptian Cyrano," I remarked, and permitted a grin to disturb my usually severe and solemn features (the professor often assured me that my features were severe, and being a very young man I took pardonable pride in the fact!). "How the ladies must have hated him!" I added, seeing my friend scowl.

"This is a serious matter," he said after a pause that seemed interminable. "Nothing like this has ever come out of Egypt. I – do – not – like – it!"

My friend's voice was distressingly hollow. It made me nervous, and I endeavored to quiet him. "There is nothing very unusual about this mummy," I replied. "Some very peculiar types undoubtedly existed among the Egyptians. I daresay they had their sideshows and circuses with the odd assortment of freaks that usually goes with such things. This poor fellow may have been a king's jester – it is really unfair to reproach him with his ugliness after all these years. I am sure his life was a very unhappy one."

The professor's scowl grew in volume. "You must be serious," he retorted. "This mummy is *very* unusual. I am not a sensationalist, my dear boy, but I may say that my enemies would give a great deal to use this thing to discredit me. We must be very wary about publishing the results of our experiments."

"Experiments?" I snatched at the word. I had a boyish and ridiculous eagerness for all varieties of research.

"I have some experiments in mind that will demand a great deal of courage. If you do not feel equal to them I shall want you to tell me so quite frankly. But first I must warn and prepare you, and describe what we have to deal with."

The professor lit an absurdly long panetela and puffed for several moments in silence. The smoke ascended spirally and formed a curious grayish nimbus above the mummy case. The mummy stood out in the depressing gloom like a sinister avenger of the eighty-three defenseless wretches that Professor Dewey had dissected and destroyed.

When my friend spoke again his voice had acquired a small measure of calm. He spoke slowly, punctuating his sentences with an occasional cough. "There are few myths in the treasure-house of mankind that were not originally based upon solid objective facts. I do not believe that the imagination of primitive peoples is capable of creating bogies out of thin air. We are too easily deluded by modern science and altogether too apt to scoff at the legends of gods and goddesses that have come down to us. It is absurd to believe that the Egyptians created their monstrous bestial gods from mere observation of living animals. There is something so immense, so psychically terrible about the Egyptian gods that it is difficult to believe them simply the product of normal human imagination. They are either the imaginings of some dreamer of wild and unheard-of powers, an Edgar Poe among the Egyptians, or –"

Professor Dewey paused without stating his alternative. I presume he wanted his heresy to sink in, for he waited several moments before continuing:

"These crocodile gods, these cat-headed and bat-eared divinities are really more debased than anything to be found anywhere in the modern world. Even your barbarous black fellow in Africa or Australia would be incapable of worshiping anything so vile. And yet if we are to believe historians the Egyptians had a high degree of ethical culture. They would not fashion such horrors willingly. I have often thought –"

Again my friend hesitated, as if ashamed to put his theory into words. My eagerness apparently reassured him.

"*I have often thought that these monsters really existed.* Why should we suppose that men are the only intelligent beings on this planet? There is so much evidence to the contrary, so very much evidence, that I feel justified in my theory. I do not think that I am a fool. My enemies" (I fear my friend suffered from a persecution complex) "would give years of their lives to overhear this conversation. But they shall only hear of the results – *if the results are not too revolting.*"

Professor Dewey sank down on a chair as if exhausted. Beads of sweat stood out horribly on his high yellow forehead. His lips quivered.

"George." he stammered. "We must put it to the test. We must sleep here tonight. Unless, of course, you fear to sleep in the room with *that.*"

"But, what is *that*, really?" I asked, pointing with horror to the colossal mummy.

My friend did not answer me directly, but his words were dreadfully disturbing. "Twenty or thirty thousand years ago the Egyptians buried their first kings. *There were strange kings in the dawn world.*"

2

Professor Dewey was sleeping soundly, but something made me sit up. I am not sure whether I dreamed a sound, or whether a sound had actually come from the corner of the room where the great mummy stood solemnly in its filthy wrappings. But whether the dismal noise had any basis in fact it was a profoundly disturbing thing to hear at 3 o'clock in the morning.

Perhaps you have listened to hounds baying at night across lonely moors, or perhaps you have heard in the tropics the horrid moans of small monkeys when they awake from their mindless sleep and see the stars watching them evilly. If you have heard such sounds you may have a remote idea of how vile these audibly sinister exhibitions of evil and fright seem to a normally constituted man.

The low whining that I heard (and it occasionally seemed to rise to an actual baying) did not frighten me. But had the chair that loomed unpleasantly before me out of the gloom suddenly entered into conversation with the sofa, or had the clock walked across the mantel, I should not have been more horrified.

I sat up and waited. For several moments nothing happened, but then I heard a low scratching and scraping as if something were trying to get out of the closet. Claws of some sort were indubitably at work somewhere.

"Rats!" I reflected, and I clung to the suggestion warmly. Of course there would be rats in a house given over to unhallowed and unsavory practices. "The professor is fortunate to have rats to do the really dirty work," I mused. "They save him the bother of burning the odds and ends. It must be damnably difficult to get rid of fingernails and hair and such things, unless one burns them, and of course the rats would save him that task. The professor is really very fortunate. Dear, jolly rats!"

Then I realized the fatuousness of my reflections and passed my hand rapidly back and forth across my face. My forehead was infernally warm; I was excited, feverish. "It's probably a touch of influenza," I thought. "I should never have slept in this cold room." I recalled that I had been sneezing and coughing most of the previous afternoon. The slightest touch of fever makes me delirious – in that respect I am abnormally favored.

I pulled the blankets about my neck and turned over. I think then that I slept, but I am convinced that what I saw later had some external significance. The thing was more than a mere dream and certainly more than a hallucination. It was, I think, an actual *body of memories* projected across the room. When I saw it I was sitting up, and I heard the clock outside strike 4.

A white immensity spread before me, and for a moment its whiteness blinded me. It was like a series of projections on the silver screen. The white substance was continually changing, now thinning, now thickening, and horrid, distorted forms moved about in it. The forms were amorphous, and I could not at first distinguish them clearly. They were not altogether human. They seemed to have the bodies of men, but *the heads of animals.*

When the vision, or call it what you will, became clearer I saw that the unmentionable creatures had formed into a solid phalanx, and that they were marching solemnly before me. They carried between them some unspeakable object which they made no effort to conceal.

If the forms of the marchers were revolting, the form of the long, distorted *thing* that they carried was infernal. It was covered with hair, but I never had seen anything like it under the stars. It had a sunken bat-like face, and great, dog-shaped ears, and its yellow teeth glittered ominously in the strange, unnatural light. The thing was obviously lifeless, and its cheeks were sunken and hollow.

The watchers carried torches which they waved exultantly as if almost glad that the thing had died. I had a curious sympathy for these others, but heaven knows they were vile enough. The torches gave off a weird blue light and even, I thought, a mephitic smell; and as I watched, new ones were lit and the swaying, blasphemous procession moved forward more rapidly.

And then the chanting and intoning commenced, and the dreadful hymns for the dead swelled and revibrated in the room until I put my hands before my ears to shut out the ancient and obscene chants.

"Our master out of the skies is dead!" they wailed. "Deep, deep in the earth shall we bury our king. Long has he ruled us, and horrible the evil he did to us, but he was our king out of the skies, and we revere his memory. Horrible his black tongue that shot out fire, horrible the maidens he devoured, horrible the blood he drank, but he was a king. In the book of the dead it is written that he shall be judged by gods, by his peers he shall be judged. He shall appear as a snake, as a reptile before his peers, but by his ears they shall know him."

Then the picture cleared terribly, and I saw that the procession trod hot reddish sands, and a great stone effigy loomed up behind them. It was a sphinx, but a more ancient sphinx than the one we know, and its eyes glowed banefully. And in a deep and perfectly round hole dug in the sand at the statue's base they buried their king, and strewed gold dust upon him, and anointed his limbs with oil which they poured from jars of veined porphyry.

Unmentionable were the rites they performed above him, and the last words of their loathsome high priest, *who had the head of a lizard*, were lethal words, and I shivered when I realized at whom they were directed.

"For thirty centuries you shall sleep, but a little shameless creature with no hair to cover him shall drag you forth, because in his time he shall be as a god. But his evil day will not be long under the sun. He too shall return unto dust, and a very thin creature with neither legs nor eyes shall play havoc with his bones. It is written. Rest in peace, and remember us who worshiped you!"

The vision grew vaguer, and the forms seemed to converge and merge into each other. Then gradually the darkness closed in, and I found myself staring with frightened eyes at Professor Dewey's monstrous acquisition. It loomed vaguely out of the blackness, and it seemed to be stirring, and squirming about.

I watched fascinated while the ancient wrappings fell away, and *two long pink hands* fumbled hectically with mildewed cerements. The hands were abnormally emaciated, and covered with thin, reddish hair.

I endeavored to rise, but the eyes of the thing watched me evilly, and ordered me to be silent. It seemed angry that I should question its spiritual supremacy. It had uncovered its eyes, but the great loathsome nose remained mercifully concealed by several layers of disintegrating wrappings. It was frightful to watch the thing's efforts to free itself. It wriggled and squirmed, and in its vileness it resembled a great fleshy worm endeavoring to escape from some deep sewer of earth.

What followed will always remain confused in my memory. I seem to recall Professor Dewey upon his back with closed eyes, and something standing above him in the dim light like an immemorial avenger. I seem to glimpse a supremely ghastly exterior – two great ears protruding from a narrow and greenish skull, and a great nose like an elephant's trunk showing briefly in profile.

Then fire – a deluge of colored fire, which shot out of the creature's nose and mouth, fire from hell, fire from beyond Arcturus. I saw the professor's eyes open, and I saw him stare at the thing for a moment in triumph. The exultation in his face was quickly replaced by agony and despair. He threw out his arms as if endeavoring to ward off an immediate doom, and while I watched, his face shriveled and blackened.

"I was right," he shrieked. "The Egyptians did not worship men. God pity my poor soul!"

I did not stay to comfort my stricken friend. I ran shrieking from the room, and out of the house into the street. I looked up to see thick black smoke pouring from an upper window, but I turned in no alarm. I ran wildly across deserted squares and through winding alleys and finally found my way to a leering subway entrance.

I fled insanely down the stairs, and climbed over the turnstile without depositing a fare. Luckily no one saw me. In a moment I was in a roaring train, my arms flung about a drunken beggar, and into his astonished ears I poured a tale that made him gasp and shake his head.

"You young 'uns allus get it somewhere," he grimaced. "I wish I had your luck."

I have always found newspaper men exceedingly prosaic. The following cutting from a New York paper demonstrates my point:

A fire in the upper West Side caused a great deal of disturbance yesterday morning, when police reserves from three stations fought with firemen to keep excited passers-by from entering the burning building. For two hours thirty or forty hooded men endeavored to rescue the inmates, and caused a great deal of disturbance. The police were unable to explain why utter strangers should take such an interest in one poor perishing wretch, since it was later ascertained that the house was occupied by an eccentric professor and misanthrope who is suspected of bootlegging operations. Patrolman Henley, from the West 93rd Street Station, claims that one of the would-be rescuers removed his hood for a brief moment, and that his face was covered with fur, *and eaten away at the corners.* Luckily for Patrolman Henley's reputation he is known to suffer from migraine, and it is probable that what he imagined he saw had no basis in fact.

The wildly excited attempts of strangers to enter the building completely frustrated operations. For a moment he was seen at the window, and those who were standing on the sidewalk immediately underneath declare that his hair and beard were actually on fire. The upper portion of the building was completely destroyed. A number of curious bones were found in the room, including the skeleton of a gigantic dog. During the past week three previous fires have been reported in the neighborhood, and the police are investigating rumors of a firebug.

Tarbis of the Lake

By E. Hoffmann Price

With its Lourdes, France, setting, E. Hoffmann Price's "Tarbis of the Lake" has an overarching Gothic sensibility to it. Originally published in the February 1934 issue of Weird Tales, *Price's story features a doomed protagonist who, against his better judgment, seeks forbidden knowledge.*

As an uncanny reflection on the power of love and its ability to transcend time and space, "Tarbis of the Lake" takes the reader by the hand and leads him deeper into the shadowy netherworld where the demarcations between reality and illusion gradually dissolve. As a meditation on obsessive love, the story is likewise quite reminiscent of H. Rider Haggard's masterful "Smith and the Pharaohs," also included in this collection.

Written in a style both archaic and modern, Price's story likewise encapsulates the best elements of short story writing. There's a protagonist who deeply wants something and who will do whatever it takes to achieve his objective, rising tension, the foreshadowing of peril, and a climatic ending that resolves the story's most pressing conflict. Indeed, Price's skillful mastery of the short story form is on full display here. Furthermore, as a story in which the familiar trope of a magical past interrupting the calm waters of modernity, "Tarbis of the Lake" remains a valuable, if still little known, contribution to the emergence of a distinct ancient Egyptian supernatural tale subgenre within weird and supernatural fiction.

"My son," said white-haired Father Peytral to his companion, whose steel-grey eyes seemed far older than his rugged, bronzed features, "suppose that you abandon this hypothetical *friend* of yours and tell what is worrying *you*. Never mind what I'll think. Just express yourself."

John Rankin started. His face darkened for an instant; then he smiled as he caught the kindly expression in the old priest's eyes.

"I might have known you'd see through it, Father Peytral. But before I go any further, tell me who – what – well, *was* there ever a woman named Tarbis? I mean, other than –"

Rankin abruptly checked his speech, stared at the earth and at the heels of the unending throng of pilgrims who passed along the Esplanade.

Father Peytral's scrutiny of Rankin became keener at the mention of Tarbis.

"What's that?" he demanded. "*Tarbis?*" The priest frowned as he groped for a moment for a thought that was evading him, then resumed. "There is an old tradition to the effect that Tarbis, Queen of Ethiopia –"

"Ethiopia?" interrupted Rankin. "Why – *she* is as white as I am."

Father Peytral's eyebrows rose. Then, instead of asking the question that was on his lips, he explained, "Ethiopia in those days was the upper kingdom of Egypt. A queen of that country was no more negro than Rameses the Great.

"And Tarbis," he continued, "offered her hand and crown to Moses, who declined both. The pride of the queen and the woman being sorely wounded, she abandoned her throne and set sail, wandering until she reached France. She founded not only the city of Tarbes, which to this day bears her name, but also its neighbor Lapurdum – our modern Lourdes which God has so signally honored in selecting it as the place for the apparition of the Holy Virgin to appear.

"They say that the site of the original Lapurdum was three kilometers from here. Its inhabitants practised black magic. The place became a den of necromancers, an affront to God, man, and nature. But instead of following the Scriptural precedent, and destroying Lapurdum with fire, the Almighty caused a flood to rise out of the earth and overwhelm the city, whence the present lake, not far from the outskirts of the modern city of Lourdes.

"All of which," concluded Father Peytral. "is to be found in the archives of Lourdes."

"Good God!" muttered Rankin. "Worse and worse! You've just succeeded in confirming my outrageous fancy – the thing I've tried to deny... ."

Rankin suddenly sat bolt-upright. His bronzed cheeks had become sickly yellow. His eyes were burning with an unnatural light, and his face was drawn and haggard as he regarded the priest for a moment before continuing, "That Ethiopian queen never died. *She is living in Lourdes, on the street that leads to the chateau.* I knew – I sensed – and now you have confirmed it!"

Father Peytral recognized solemn-voiced knowledge.

"My son," he said in a low, even voice, "that any human being, man or woman, could attain everlasting physical life is denied both by the Church and by science. Whatever the source of your obsession, you must forget such fantastic thoughts!"

"Forget them?" exclaimed Rankin. "I've tried that for several years. You've often tried to get me to open up. I evaded your queries, but my fear finally got the best of me. First it was a lover's fancy, that idea that Tarbis Dulac had in the dim past discovered the secret of eternal youth. That didn't alarm me. It was just a quaint conceit, a whimsical fancy about a girl I think a great deal of. But at last I found that I was telling myself that I didn't believe anything of the kind."

"Which," said the priest, "assured you that you did believe just that, and it frightened you."

Rankin nodded.

"So I left Lourdes. I roamed all over Asia, trying to forget. And when I finally succeeded in driving her antique smile from my conscious memory, and with it the idea that she was someone who had lived for ages, she returned and haunted me in nightmarish dreams. She made statuesque gestures, like – you've seen them, sculptured –"

"*Mais oui,*" agreed Father Peytral. "In the Louvre, for instance."

"She wore a tall, curious head-dress. She murmured words that I could not understand, except in momentary flashes. And what I understood troubled me more than what I didn't. I'm afraid of Tarbis – and I'm in love with her."

He raised his eyes and made a despairing gesture of his hand, then let his head droop wearily. Father Peytral murmured to himself as he contemplated the hopelessly baffled expression of Rankin's rugged features.

"And now you tell me a legend of a Tarbis who was a queen, Lord knows how many centuries ago," muttered Rankin. "And of the lake – her very name today, Dulac... *du Lac*..." Then, jerking himself erect: "What do you say? Am I utterly insane?"

"No," replied the priest as he grasped Rankin by the shoulder. "On the contrary, your doubts prove your sanity. An insane person is assured that everyone but himself is unbalanced. Your denying this delusion is your best assurance."

"Well, what am I to do?" demanded Rankin, taking heart. "I can't stand being near a woman who I *know* is an uncanny creature that should have died ages ago. And neither can I stay away from her. I've tried both!"

For a moment neither spoke. Then Father Peytral's frown of perplexed pondering was replaced by a smile of calm assurance.

"You have unwittingly taken the right course," he said, "in speaking your thought aloud instead of letting it be an inner murmuring that has poisoned your mind. See this Tarbis Dulac, look her in the eye, speak to her and tell her your thought. Never mind what she thinks of your sanity. Face her unflinchingly and express yourself. Ask her solemnly who and what she is, and tell her why you ask. If she cares for you, she will not be harsh in her judgment."

"Father Peytral, I can't do that!" protested Rankin. "She'll think –" He regarded the priest with outraged amazement.

"You seem to forget –"

Father Peytral shook his gray head. His smile was a tale of time-mellowed grief.

"My son," he said in a voice that was none the less authoritative for being low, "I do not forget. I know. If she cares for you, she will not judge harshly. And once you have enunciated this outrageous thought, you will have conquered it. Your fear and your furtive denials have fostered this obsession, even as your speaking boldly will burn it out."

Rankin pondered for a moment. He rose from the stone bench and stood erect. His eyes were less haggard, and his drawn face had relaxed.

"Thank you, Father," he said. "I'll see her tonight, and I'll follow your advice."

Rankin lifted his hat and bowed. Then, to himself, as he strode down the Esplanade, "Fine old man... not a sign of a sermon... seems perfectly natural to call him *Father*...."

Like those pilgrims who flock toward Lourdes, Rankin had crossed land and sea for the good of his soul, even though he had not come to pray, or to drink the water of the spring that had miraculously burst forth from the grotto of the great black rock of Massabielle. But, though Father Peytral's assurance gave Rankin a new grip on himself, and a weapon with which to combat his obsession, the priest's words had at the same time strengthened Rankin's ever-present feeling that he was dealing with one whose name was written on the first pages of the archives of that city which had not always been a holy place, comparable to Rome, Jerusalem, or Mecca.

That evening Rankin sat once more in the luxuriously furnished reception room of that outwardly unprepossessing house which was perched on the steep slope of the hill whose high-walled fortress and square donjon built by the Moslem conquerors commanded the valley of the Gave.

"It is good to see you again, *mon ami*," she said as she regarded Rankin with her smoldering, long-lashed eyes. "Incurable nomad, you tried to forget Tarbis, didn't you?"

"But I couldn't," Rankin admitted somberly. The assurance that he had gained from Father Peytral was slowly melting before the loveliness of Tarbis Dulac. "And I know now that I never shall. You've haunted me. Your memory followed me and made a madness of my dreams. So I've returned."

"I knew that you would, some day," murmured the girl. "I've been expecting you."

She smiled that slow, archaic smile that had haunted Rankin; but her eyes were dolorous and incredibly ancient. They contradicted the youthful freshness of her skin and the gracious contours of her throat and shoulders. Tarbis was uncommonly lovely, and any one but Rankin would have accepted her without undue wonderings and fancies.

Then Rankin nerved himself for the assault.

"I've returned to solve the riddle," said Rankin. "You've evaded me and mocked me with that sphinx smile of yours, and your eyes have laughed at me. I've wondered entirely too long who and what you are. So I've returned to find out, once and for all," he concluded.

The girl's eyebrows rose in Moorish arches, and she made a fleeting gesture of her slender hand. That damnable, haunting gesture! That insidious suggestion of sculptured fingers on the granite of deserted temples and rifled tombs!.

"Insatiable, aren't you?" she chided. "What more do you want? What have I ever denied you?"

Tarbis was right. Any sane man should have been content. Yet there was that same evasion which had always left Rankin baffled. Rankin knew that he had flinched from the assault; that he had failed solemnly to demand who and what she was.

"Tarbis, how old are you?" he asked in blunt-spoken desperation.

"Such a question, *mon ami!*" Her laugh was light. She refused to take him seriously. Then she answered, "I'm ever so much older than you suspect, John. But would I be any more pleasing if you could catalogue me like a piece of antique furniture, a bit of jade, a Persian carpet?"

Rankin had to admit that Tarbis was right. And to consider her as a normal woman was the sane and logical thing; yet there would be no peace until she had answered the solemn adjuration he was to make.

"I wonder," she continued, "if you are sure that you want to know. Did you ever stop to think that you might have long regrets?"

Worse and yet worse! She was hinting at the very thought that he had sought to disown.

"You know," said Tarbis after a long pause during which her lips were alternately smiling and grave, "I could just as well question you, and wonder why you've left me several times, with never a quarrel or any apparent necessity. And I do know that you've always cared for me – a great deal. There is nothing to prevent your staying in Lourdes. You know I'd not seek any claim on you. Yet you've always left."

"Yes, and always returned!" he retorted, stung by the memory of his resolutions to forget her, and his inevitable relapse from his determination. "But this time I'm going to get the answer. You're so much more than you appear to be. You're not one woman but a world of women in one, and you are withholding a hundredfold more than you'll ever reveal."

"Such versatility should be pleasing," suggested Tarbis with lightness that belied her unsmiling eyes.

Rankin decided that she was not mocking him, but he would no longer accept evasion. He rose abruptly and seized her by the wrist.

"Let's not fence any longer! Just because I've not found word to express my-self – "

Rankin stopped short. He had found words, but he dared not use them.

"Then tell me what is on your mind, John," said Tarbis. "Maybe I'll understand."

She spoke very solemnly now. Her voice was grave, and her eyes were unsmiling and age-old. Rankin released her wrist and stared at the golden-olive tint that crept back to erase the white imprint of his grasp. She regarded him intently for a long moment, then spoke again.

"Can't you forget your morbid curiosity?" she pleaded. "Can't you take me for what I am, and without question? Kiss me, and love me for the sake of the evening, and for myself. And if you do care enough to be jealous, stay here in Lourdes, always, and watch me as closely as any Turk ever guarded his harem."

Rankin saw the gleam of tears in her great lustrous eyes. He knew that he was about to weaken as he had so many times before. At the moment, his thoughts seemed outrageous and insane beyond expression. And then he thought of the obsession that had overwhelmed him and affronted every trace of reason. No matter what she thought of his sanity, he had to declare himself. It would be better for her to think him utterly mad than for him to become so in fact. He nerved himself for the final plunge.

"Tarbis, do you know that most of the time I've been resisting the thought that you are not a woman at all, but *something* – "

"Must you know *all* about me?" she interrupted, recoiling from the implication of his last word, and eager to prevent his expressing that which she sensed would follow. "John, can't you take anything for granted? Have I ever –"

"No, I can't," declared Rankin, evading her attempted change of subject. "I've reached the verge of madness, telling myself, arguing with myself to prove that you are not older than any woman has a right to be. In my own mind I've denied breaths of rumors and hints that no rational person would bother to deny."

"Oh, those damnable, meddling priests and villagers!" exclaimed Tarbis with a despairing, impersonal bitterness. "Can't they live and let live? Can't they be content to go their placid, ordained ways and leave me in peace?"

"But they didn't talk about you," protested Rankin.

"No, but they spoke of *her*," countered Tarbis. "John, can't you forget all this? You do care for me, don't you? Or am I just another riddle that your insatiable mind must solve lest it perish of unsatisfied vanity? Must you know everything?"

"Not everything. Tarbis. But this one thing, yes; for the good of my soul and my sanity. Who and what are you?" he demanded desperately, steeling himself to resist the appeal that he read in her eyes.

She was about to yield. He could not now relent.

"Since you insist, I'll tell you," she finally assented. "No, I'll show you, and let you draw your own conclusion. I will let you meet my rival face to face."

"*Your* rival?" gasped Rankin, amazed at that turn. "You mean *my* rival don't you?"

"No, I mean what I said: *my* rival," affirmed Tarbis. "My rival, and my damnation. She will drive you away. She will everlastingly destroy the happiness I have stolen – we have stolen. But since it must be –"

She took Rankin by the hand, and half turned toward the winding stairway. Then she paused and reached for her wine-glass.

"A toast, John," she proposed, with the air of one gallantly drinking to impending doom. "To my rival and to her damnation!"

Rankin drained his glass. Tarbis barely moistened her lips, and set the stemmed glass back on the old lace runner that crossed the table. Then she led the way upstairs.

As Rankin passed the carved newel post and followed her up through the dim light, it seemed that he was marching toward a perilous rendezvous. For a moment he wanted to take the steps three at a bound, seize her and carry her back to the warmth and light of that familiar living-room, to fight those torturing fancies on the level ground of sanity. But Rankin remembered his resolve and stifled the sadness that was mingled with his sense of impending peril.

Tarbis halted at the head of the stairs. Her blue-black hair glistened under the glow of a shaded oil lamp. Queer, how this luxurious house of hers should be so obsolete in some details. The square-cut emerald on her finger was phosphorescent as the eyes of a beast of prey. Rankin knew why he observed and made mental comment on such irrelevancies... once, in crossing a courtyard to face a firing-squad, he had noted the pattern of the tiles and had observed that the color scheme was clashing... .

"She is waiting for us," he heard Tarbis saying. "Here, in my own room."

Rankin fought the raging impulse to retreat and let well enough alone. He followed her into the dimness of that familiar room with its canopied bed and its dressing table. A hand-mirror lay, as always, face down, the twining golden serpents of its handle gleaming in the faint light. Rankin wondered again why that mirror was never face up.

Then, in a niche in the masonry of the wall he saw a mummy-case whose gilded features stared vacantly at him.

"She is here," said Tarbis. "I will leave you with her. Her last words were spoken far back in the first youth of time. Her lips are silent, but she will speak to your mind. And when you know, you may return to the living-room. I'll probably be asleep on the divan."

She paused and regarded him intently for a moment; then she continued, "Perhaps, when she tells you who I am, and how old I am, you'll pass quietly on, without even a word of farewell. But, perhaps – the memories we share – I hope –"

She turned, without expressing her hope. The door closed behind her, leaving Rankin with his strange companion. The loneliness of the room oppressed him. The departure of Tarbis made it appallingly like a tomb.

He felt in his vest pocket for cigarettes, but found none. Well, no matter; although a smoke would be company while be sat there, seeking the point of the tableau she had arranged. Then he saw a silver case among the combs and perfume vials and powder boxes. It was half filled with long, slender cigarettes. He struck light to one. It was ever so faintly scented and had a curious but not un-pleasant aroma. That exotic tobacco was appropriate to Tarbis. Rankin snapped his lighter closed and leaned back in his chair to contemplate the gilded features of the sycamore case and its rows of painted hieroglyphs.

Through the gray wisps of smoke he regarded the gilded mask, at first idly, then with an intentness that he sought to deny himself. Something new was stirring disquietingly in his mind. He forced himself to think of Tarbis whose slender length was now stretched out on the Shemaka rug that covered the divan. Tarbis du Lac... Tarbis of the Lake... asleep or awake, she would be smiling in whimsical mockery of her latest lover.

Even though she had never once hinted that he had any predecessors in her affections, Rankin knew that Tarbis must have had many lovers before him. He knew that she must have learned ever so long ago that illusion is more alluring than candor.

And this thought slowly but certainly brought his consciousness back to the gilded face before him. The convictions that had haunted him so long became stronger than ever before. Had the occupant of that sycamore case lived until today, she too would have learned from experience that no lover cares for candor about his predecessors. *Had she lived –*

Then Rankin surrendered to a new madness which was more perturbing than that which he had sought to conquer that evening. It was terrifying. He shivered and sat erect in his chair. The scented poison of the cigarette curled unheeded around his fingers and stained them.

If the carver had given life and animation to those long almond-shaped eyes, they would be the eyes of Tarbis. The fire of the cigarette ate into his fingers and momentarily broke the spell. He ground the butt into the rug beneath his feet and struck light to another smoke. But the distraction was not enough to stop the surge of surmise that had become knowledge. That curved, antique smile of gilt was Tarbis herself staring at him, mocking the wooden conventions of Egyptian carving and fighting through the gold leaf into faithful portraiture.

He knew now what Tarbis had intended to convey to him. He had been haunted by the outlandish idea that Tarbis, ages ago, had discovered the secret of everlasting youth. Rankin had considered such a fancy outrageous, and any woman who inspired the like, uncanny. But now –

Tarbis had become something infinitely more terrifying: she was not one who had, ages ago, discovered the secret of eternal youth, but rather the product of an Egyptian magic which had enabled dead Tarbis to materialize and present the semblance of a physical woman.

Rankin clutched the arms of his chair. Every memory of Tarbis and her amorous encircling arms denied the conviction carried by that gilded smile; yet as he stared, Rankin began to remember things which he wished that he had never learned. To distract himself from the fancy that Tarbis was age-old, he had listened to adepts in High Asia, who muttered of Tibetan lore, and the lost magic of Egypt, never suspecting that he was acquiring a knowledge that would in the end be more horrible than the whim he sought to cast out.

He wondered when she emerged from the painted case with its painted hieroglyphs. He wondered what she had done with her endless yards of linen bandages, and how she had escaped their firm embrace. Then, bit by bit, there came back to Rankin the words of that slant-eyed adept he had befriended.

"There are nine elements which when fused into a unit make what your eye sees as a single human body: the physical, flesh-and-blood body; the shadow; the double, or astral counterpart called the *ka*; the soul, or *ba*; the heart; a spirit called *khu*; a Power; a Name; and a ninth component which is a motivating force.... And all these, mark you, are used in a mystical, or esoteric sense. Yet this knowledge if truly interpreted and rightly used can serve to work all the wonders of the hidden Egyptian magic that was codified by Thoth...."

The embalmed physical body of Tarbis was in the case before Rankin; and that which had seemed to him to be a living woman was but an aggregation of elements that had joined the *ka*, which lingers near the physical body until it utterly disintegrates.

Every whimsical speech and mannerism of Tarbis came trooping back to confirm Rankin's dismaying conviction. His brain reeled at the recollection of her avoidance of daylight.

"My dear," she had murmured one evening, "you sit up to the most unusual hours making love to me – oh, ever so charmingly! – and then you marvel that I'd rather not spend the following day strolling along the Esplanade, or scaling Pic de Jer. And it's one of my pet vanities, *tu comprends*, this being seen only at my best, at night, by my own lighting...."

It was clear, now. That ancient necromancy had not been able to restore the missing *shadow*, so that Tarbis could not appear by the shadow-casting sun. The Name, the Power, the *ka*... perhaps all but the one missing irreplaceable element were present.

Then Rankin's sanity revolted. He fought the urge to wrench the lid from the sycamore case. He dared not yield to the demand to find out what was behind that gilded, smiling mask. If indeed it was empty, that would mean that that dead, bandage-swathed thing emerged from its cell to offer him the unholy semblance of a living woman.

Rankin shivered as though a breath of the abysmal outer spaces had been exhaled into his veins and was chilling his blood.

"It can't be empty!" his mind screamed to his self. "Good God, if it's empty –!"

He dared not complete the utterance. He refused to think of the slender, shapely arms of Tarbis and her curved, carmine smile.

"But if *it* is in there, then she's an illusion – a shadow from the tomb. That is as bad – or is it worse?"

Rankin forced his brain to cease that insistent surging that would end by cracking his skull. The veins in his temples would in another moment burst like rotted fire-hose.

Then the strokes of the cathedral bell mercifully interrupted the dread that he could neither accept nor deny. And during the moment of respite accorded him by that sound from the outer world, he noted for the first time the possible significance of the peculiar aroma of the cigarettes Tarbis had left in her case. It was reminiscent of something they smoked in Persia and Hindustan.

He smiled at the gilded mask. The last rich note of the cathedral bell reminded him that Lourdes was a holy city. He envied the calm priests and the pious pilgrims, and was glad that they were there, not far from the foot of the hill.

"Tarbis, you devil, and your cigarettes!" he exulted, gratefully ascribing his dreadful fancies to the influence of *charras*, or whatever other like drug they might have contained thus to upset his mind. He sighed with relief and weariness. "But maybe I deserve it."

He rose and found that he still trembled violently. His legs barely supported his weight; but his brain no longer rocked and shivered from clamorings from beyond the Border.

Tarbis would be waiting for him in the living-room. She would see the mark of terror still branding his features. But he forgave her the ghastly jest. He could be generous, now that he had conquered his obsession by expressing it in words. He had asked her: and she had answered by showing him in her oblique way that there were fancies infinitely more disturbing than that of her possessing everlasting youth. Only Tarbis could have devised such an answer: slender, alluring Tarbis curled up on the Shemaka rug.

But as he reached the door, a lurking residue of the evening's horror returned to remind him that his conquest had not been complete. He knew that in the end he would begin to wonder anew whether that case was or was not empty, and whether Tarbis was a revenant imprisoned by day, but loose at night to fascinate him with her archaic, Egyptian smile. And Rankin's dreadful surmise marched once more in a circle that was started afresh by his glance of premature triumph at that gilded mask. That subtle, gild smile! That hint of a hidden jest!

He retraced his steps. With an effort he grasped the cover. And then he slowly withdrew his hands. He knew that his sanity demanded that he refrain from giving any physical expression to the question. But, as he was about to step back, he knew what would become of his regained reason if he retreated without having learned, forever and always, what the case contained, whose names and titles were depicted in painted hieroglyphs upon that carven sycamore.

Rankin thrust the cover aside. And then he tore the crumbling linen bandages that swathed the features of the dead. He had ceased thinking; he had nerved himself to the task and he could not stop. His mind was dead, but his fingers lived. They tore another layer of bandages, and another.

Something forced him to look at that face. A blind instinct and compelling terror urged him to learn the truth, whatever it might be. The dust of centuries mingled with the dust of crumbled linen and pungent spices and choked him. Then he stepped back and regarded the shrunken, hideously life-like features. The gilded mask had been a portrait; *but here he faced Tarbis herself!*

He gasped for breath. He sought to deny his eyes, refute the evidence of his senses, prove that he had not felt the burning ardor of those shriveled lips. This was the supreme horror, the uttermost outrage.

Rankin forced his eyes at last to leave that mockery of the loveliness of Tarbis. He saw what was worse: the final link in the evidence that bound Tarbis to that which had lived and died, ages ago. On the now exposed breast of the mummy he could see a knife scar: that same scar that marred the perfection of the living Tarbis – or the one that he had thought was living.

Rankin was bereft of all sensation but a terrific whirring in his ears and a drumming at his temples. He leaped back and flung open the door of the room. For a moment he thought of flight – flight in any direction whatsoever. Then he knew that he could never escape that which he had seen face to face, never elude the recollection of an Egyptian magic that was based on the re-assembling of the scattered nine elements of a corpse. Rankin had penetrated the veil; he had pried, and loosened upon himself a doom.

He thought for an instant of the day when he met Tarbis, a living, lovely woman. Each move that he had made had taken him farther from the woman he loved; yet the knowledge that there was no refuge from that which stared at him drove him to his final desperate resource.

Rankin snatched the oil lamp from its bracket and unscrewed its top. Then he poured the contents of the bowl over the mummy. He applied the still-burning wick to the linen bandages. That would settle it, once and for all: decide now and forever who and what was waiting for him in that living-room, one flight below, and centuries away.

As the flames enveloped the bandaged figure, he heard the voice of Tarbis screaming from the anguish of the dissolution of the bonds that tied the spiritual essences to the mummified body. He heard that awful cry from the living-room and knew that that fascinating simulacrum was in the agony of a second and final separation from its body. And the horror of having loved a shadow from the tomb was drowned in the greater horror of having caused the everlasting extinction of one who had loved life so well that she had returned from the dead.

Rankin dared not pass through that lower room to escape. And escape he must! Instantly, or never; yet to see beloved Tarbis – beloved though she was but the *khu*, the *ka*, the Name, and the Power assembled by a forgotten necromancer – to see her being consumed by the astral counterpart of the flames which enveloped the linen-bandaged body –

Rankin burst through the window at the head of the stairs. As he leaped, he heard above the crash and tinkle of glass a scream of mortal misery and despair more acute than any flame could wrench from her lips. He heard her very clearly pronounce his name.

She knew. As much of her as still remained knew that no power could ever restore her; that Rankin had destroyed her.

Rankin picked himself from the ground and fled blindly, without thought or sensation, and maddened by that final cry of agony. In his flight down the steep slope of the street leading from the hill of the citadel to the level of the city, Rankin stumbled and pitched headlong in a heap against a wall.

The impact numbed his senses and for the moment dulled the misery of his mind. Then a man's voice pronounced his name, and a firm hand helped him to his feet.

In the moonlight he recognized Father Peytral. The old priest's usually placid features were tense, as with a reflected terror that he read in Rankin's staring eyes.

"My son," said Father Peytral in a low, trembling voice, "I was watching across the street. I heard, and I saw the flames.... You have freed her earthbound soul... no, don't try to explain....

"Little as I know, it is too much. But she is released from an abomination. I understand your grief," the old man continued, as he took Rankin's arm. "Let us pray for her soul, and the healing of yours."

"Too late," muttered Rankin in a strained, hoarse voice. The unutterable grief of Tarbis rang again through his memory. "My soul is damned beyond the redemption of time, or your prayers."

Rankin bowed; and the priest did not seek to detain him as he turned and strode down the slope.

The Soul of Ra-Moses
by John Murray Reynolds

Written in clear, straightforward prose, John Murray Reynolds's "The Soul of Ra-Moses" succeeds admirably in transporting the reader to a very strange place indeed. Harking back to Edgar Allan Poe's "Some Words With a Mummy," Reynolds's work evokes a resplendent sense of wonder with the ancient Egyptian past and its enduring hold on the Anglo-American imagination.

Originally published in the May 1940 issue of Weird Tales, *this story by a prolific pulp writer who also dabbled in science fiction is distinguished in part by being set neither in Egypt nor in the remote past. A Depression-era pawnshop, a small mysterious house positioned among brownstones and apartment buildings, and a museum replace the pyramids along the Nile as the primary locales of some very strange happenings.*

As in many of the other tales assembled in this volume, "The Soul of Ra-Moses" is a story in which an ancient, cryptic past brusquely intrudes upon the modern era. In this tale, a mysterious old stranger with an uncanny knowledge of archaeology briefly enters the life of one Lathrop Wells, a novice collector of antiquities. Who this man really is and what he wants with Mr. Wells make this story a captivating foray into the nebulous borderlands between a seemingly magical bygone past and a gritty urban present.

———🔲———

The little gilt image was in one corner of the pawn-shop window. It caught the eye of Lathrop Wells as he went past. He halted in midstride, and then stood close against the glass to peer in through the dingy pane. The window was filled with the usual assortment of junk found in pawn-shops, but the image stood by itself in one corner.

The thing had the body of a seated woman, and the head of a cat. Around the flat base were Egyptian hieroglyphics. Wells was an amateur archeologist of considerable experience, and he knew that the thing was an image of that sinister goddess known to the folk of the Nile as Bast. Usually they had referred to her as SHE of Babustis — to avoid speaking her name at all. Wells went into the shop.

A bell rang when he opened the door, clanging discordantly in some back recess of the dingy little pawn-shop. An unshaven old man in a black skull-cap came shuffling forward. He took his stand behind the counter and stared at his visitor with watery and rather suspicious eyes.

"Well?" he asked.

An odd sensation came to Lathrop Wells at that moment. He felt a sudden desire to turn around and walk out without saying a word. It was physical rather than mental. His orderly mind told him that the image was something in his line that he would probably want to buy. Yet — he had that feeling that he should leave at once. It seemed to come from somewhere outside himself.

Wells shook his shoulders irritably, and forced himself to speak.

"I'd like to see that little gold figure in the window," he said harshly.

"It ain't gold, Mister." The pawn-broker reached down into the cluttered window for the figurine, and slid it across the counter with the casual unconcern of a merchant for goods he does not greatly value. "Feller that brought it in was fit to be tied when I proved to him that there's only base metal under the gilt."

"I wonder where he got it!" Wells muttered aloud.

The old man's rheumy eyes went dull, as though he had abruptly drawn down some shade between them and the mind behind. The musty air of the pawn-shop became heavy with suspicion. Wells suspected that the figurine had been stolen from some museum, or else from some private collection.

"I wouldn't know, Mister," the old man said. "I never ask no questions of my customers. You want to buy it?"

The thing was about six or seven inches high. It seemed exceptionally heavy for its size, indicating either lead or iron underneath the gilt. When Wells shook it close to his ear he could sense something move inside. It was not a sharp rattle or anything of that sort, such as would have been made by a bit of metal or other hard object. Instead he got the impression that an inner space was partly filled with liquid. The image was cold and heavy in his hand — very heavy, and unnaturally cold.

The pawn-broker was fidgeting restlessly, but Lathrop Wells took his time about examining the gilt figure. It was unquestionably an image of the Goddess Bast, but it was an unusual type. He had never seen one quite like it before.

The thing was almost certainly genuine, of ancient Egyptian workmanship. Either that, or it was the work of a very clever faker. Wells did not think so. An artisan capable of making such a clever and convincing fake would have devoted his talents to something of greater intrinsic value. The hieroglyphics around the base were not one of the conventional groupings from the *Book of the Dead* with which Wells had become familiar, but they seemed genuine.

"What do you want for this?" he asked.

"Two dollars," the pawn-broker said with a shrug of his thin shoulders.

Wells put the image down and reached into his pocket for his wallet. The thing was certainly worth more than that as a curiosity. The wallet stuck in his pocket so that he had trouble pulling it out. The zipper that closed the compartment where he kept his bills was jammed so that he could hardly force it open. Meanwhile, stronger than ever, there came a return of that conviction that he should leave this place at once without having anything more to do with the cat-headed image.

For perhaps half a minute Wells stood there in the dingy little pawn-shop, while his mind served as a battleground for two forces that tried to dominate it. One was his normal conviction that he wanted this little figurine for his modest collection. Of course he did! It was the most natural thing in the world for him to buy it. Yet a secret voice seemed to be whispering a warning into some inner recess of his brain. He looked down at the figurine again, and the face of Bast seemed to have become evil and malevolent. Some trick of the dim light made the cat's-eyes glow with a green fire.

A more superstitious man would have probably given up and walked out of the shop, leaving the gilded image behind him. Lathrop Wells was not superstitious, and he was a very stubborn man. He jerked open his wallet and slammed two one-dollar bills down on the scratched glass counter.

"I'll take it!" he snapped.

The pawn-broker put the money in the till, and slid the image into a brown paper bag before handing it over.

"Here y'are, mister," he said. At that moment the bell jangled loudly and another customer hurried into the shop.

The newcomer was a small, sturdy man in a black suit. He had a Homburg hat set rakishly on one side of his head, and he swung a gold-headed cane. It was hard to tell his age. His lined face and short white beard were those of a very old man, but his step was springy and his black eyes were very bright. They darted briskly from the pawn-broker to Wells and back again. There was, Wells thought, something puckish and satyr-like about the little man. A suggestion of lusty humor.

"Good morning, gentlemen, good morning!" the man said in a brisk and chirpy voice. "Splendid day!" He had an odd and indefinable accent, one that Wells was certain he had never heard before. "Splendid day!" he repeated.

"It's all right," the pawn-broker conceded grudgingly. The old man beamed at him, and rapped briskly on the counter with the tip of his cane.

"Come, come, my good man! You should look at life with brighter eyes. By the time you're my age, you'll shake off that abysmal glum. And now — to business. You have a little gilt image which I would like to buy."

"This gentleman just bought it," the pawn-broker said.

The old man turned and smiled at Wells, leaning on his cane with his legs wide apart. His sharp black eyes seemed to have no division at all between iris and pupil.

"You have the advantage of me, sir," he said. "It is too bad. I had set my heart on that trinket. Would you consider selling it to me?"

Now that secret voice rang in the corridors of Wells's mind with the loud clarity of a trumpet! It was telling him that he should sell the thing to this man and get it off his hands; that he would be well out of the whole affair if the incident ended here! But — Lathrop Wells was a very stubborn man.

"I'm sorry," he said.

The old man frowned, and twirled his cane.

"Come, come, young man!" he said, and though he only came to Wells's shoulder he had adopted a fatherly and condescending attitude. "Be reasonable. The thing has no real value. It's just a bauble. It appeals to me as a collector, and it has a certain sentimental value. You cannot have paid over two or three dollars for it. I will give you ten dollars. Is it agreed?"

"I'm sorry," Wells repeated, "I happen to be a collector myself, in a modest way, and I—"

"Ah — so! You are also a collector. That makes a difference, sir." The old man rocked back and forward two or three times, first back on his heels, then up on his toes. "That does make a difference. Forgive me for having tried to — what is the phrase? — high-pressure you. May I ask your name?"

"Lathrop Wells."

"It is a pleasure to know a fellow collector, sir. My card."

From a leather card-case the old man took out a card which he handed to Wells with a flourish. In plain block letters it bore the name: M. Sunson. The old man clicked his heels together in a sort of military bow.

"Since you are also an antiquarian, Mr. Wells, we have much in common. My house, as it happens, is just a block away. If you will honor me by dropping in for a few minutes, I think you will find many things in my collection to interest you."

"I don't want to bother you," Wells said. Sunson twirled his cane and shifted his black hat to an even jauntier angle.

"Nonsense, sir! It will be a pleasure. I have been somewhat a recluse of late, for reasons that do not concern us now, and it is a long time since I have talked to a fellow Egyptologist. Come along!"

They left the shop and went down the street together. Wells had a long-legged stride, but he had to go at a brisk pace to keep up with his companion, who skipped along with his short legs going like pistons. The metal ferule of his cane beat a brisk tattoo on the pavement. His pointed and highly polished black shoes twinkled in the sunlight. M. Sunson was a very brisk and chipper little man.

They went around the corner and halfway down the next block. Wells was carrying the image of Bast, under his arm, still wrapped in the brown paper bag. All his feeling of disquiet and nervousness had left him.

As they rounded into the next street, Wells noticed that there was a delicatessen on the corner. Half of the block consisted of old-fashioned brownstone-fronts that had been the elegant private residences of an earlier day. The last half of the block was occupied by modern apartment buildings. Sandwiched in between them, occupying a narrow lot between the last of the brownstones and the first of the apartments, was a neat little house of red brick.

"My residence, sir," said Sunson. He bowed slightly, and waved to Wells to precede him up the stoop.

The house was as small and compact and neat as its owner. The brickwork was bright and clean. The wooden trim at the windows was newly painted. There was something painfully precise about the place, something not quite natural. Even the red flowers in the wooden window boxes did not reassure. Wells began to feel a curious disinclination to go in. This was a feeling that came from within himself, not like his earlier urges in connection with the image of Bast.

"Really, I don't want to bother you," he said.

Sunson brushed his objection aside. "Nonsense, sir, nonsense! Come right in."

The door was opened before Sunson had a chance to either ring or knock. A very tall and very black man-servant stepped aside and bowed in silence. Sunson handed him his hat and cane.

"We are going into the library, Menai," Sunson said. "This is Mr. Wells. He will be with us for a little while."

Lathrop Wells began to grow angry with himself. He felt uncomfortable, ill at ease. The sense of disquiet that he had felt when he paused on the street in front of the house was now stronger than ever. He brushed it aside. His nerves must be getting in bad shape, he reflected irritably, to read anything ominous into this visit to the odd house of an eccentric old archeologist. He had even imagined a threat in Sunson's cryptic remark to the servant about the length of his own visit! He shook his shoulders angrily, and followed his host into a large room that opened off the hall to their right.

The room ran across the entire front of the little house. It was dim and quiet, with only a subdued light coming in through the closely drawn blinds. Some shaded lamps burned on the tables for additional light. The air was exceptionally still and quiet, almost lifeless. It was not stale or unpleasant, not even musty, but it was the sort of air that might be encountered in a place that had remained closed for a long time — a very long time.

Another peculiarity of this room was that the noises of the street did not penetrate at all. The usual busy traffic of a thoroughfare in midtown New York went by outside those carefully covered windows, but neither sound of voices nor rumble of autos could be heard inside. The place was absolutely still, so silent that Wells could hear his pulses pounding loudly in his ears.

"Perhaps you would like to look at my curios now," Sunson said gently.

Sunson had called the room his library, but it was really a private museum. All around the walls were glass cases and rows of enclosed shelves. A large and very ancient bronze statue of the Goddess Bast stood between the windows, with a row of alabaster offering-jars on the pedestal before it. A beautifully carved and painted chair of the Third Dynasty period stood by the central table. However, it was the smaller objects in the cases that particularly attracted Wells's attention.

After the first thirty seconds of his stay in the place, Lathrop Wells knew that this quiet room held a greater wealth of treasures of the ancient world than many large museums. Piles of clay tablets bearing the spiny imprint of Babylonian cuneiform lay on the shelves beside stacks of neatly rolled manuscript of Egyptian papyri. Rows of Minoan pottery stood beside Etruscan bronzes. The jeweled necklace of a Delta princess gleamed on a shelf beside the inlaid sword-blade of an ancient Hittite king.

"But — but this is amazing!" Wells said. "I'm only an amateur at this game, but I know that there are things here which no one has believed were still in existence. Why — this papyrus in the glass case bears the cartouche of Cleopatra!"

"Written in her own hand," Sunson said quietly. "That is the original note she sent to Anthony at Actium. Most of the objects in my collection are comparatively small — but very valuable. Come over here."

They moved slowly along the lines of shelves. Sunson opened each case as they came to it, taking some of the things out for Wells to examine at close range. His voice was calm and matter-of-fact.

"These cups were on the table of the last Minos of Crete when the barbarians swept in to burn Broad Knossus and bring the Cretan empire to an end in the bleak autumn of the year 1450 B. C.," Sunson said, handing Wells two delicately carved goblets of pure gold. "They are, I think, even better than the so-called Vaphio Cups which were found by Schliemann. This sword in the next case is the actual blade of Alexander the Great. He carried it at Issus. That jeweled pendant was given by Abraham to a lady who did not happen to be one of his wives — an episode which your Bible tends to ignore. Now let me call your attention to this cup of heavy Cypriote glass..."

The tale went on. Lathrop Wells began to feel dizzy. Perhaps it was the close air in the room; perhaps it was because his mind could not easily grasp the unbelievable assortment of archeological treasures with which he was now surrounded. He would not have believed another man at all, but somehow the words of M. Sunson carried conviction. Wells himself could tell that it was undoubtedly an ancient Macedonian blade. Something made him believe Sunson, believe that it was really the sword carried by that wild young genius out of Macedonia who led his Immortals to conquest of half the world in the days when Rome was only an isolated city and most of Europe was a mass of dense forests roamed by fur-clad barbarians.

"But this is amazing!" Wells repeated again. That word had been constantly coming to his lips. "Only, with a collection of things like these, I cannot see why you were so anxious to get that little gilt image."

"Do you know exactly what it is?" Sunson took the paper bag which Wells had laid on the table, and carefully drew out the figurine. "Many priests of ancient Egypt imprisoned their *ka* or soul in a leaden image of the deity they served. Such images are seldom found, so that you are probably not familiar with the type. Very few men are." Sunson's finger traced the hieroglyphics around the base. "This image holds the soul of a certain Ra-Moses, who was high priest of the Goddess Bast in the reign if Sesostris of the Fourth Dynasty. That was over five thousand years ago!"

Sunson was holding the image in both hands, his fingers moving caressingly over the gilded surface. He nodded toward another case across the room, one that Wells had not noticed before. It held a whole row of gilded figurines of similar type.

"I happen to have made a specialty of collecting these," Sunson said, "so that I am very anxious to add this one to my collection, I will make you a proposition. Give me this, and I will trade you any of the papyri in the second case."

"That seems a fair bargain," Wells said.

He unrolled and glanced at half a dozen of the manuscripts of papyrus paper that were covered with neat lines of hieroglyphics. Probably all of them were hitherto unknown to the world at large! The possession of any one would make him the envy of his fellow collectors. He could imagine the surprise and envy of Paul Roebling, who was curator of Egyptology at the McCosh Museum.

"I'll take this one," he said at last.

Sunson glanced at it.

"You have chosen well, my young friend. That is the only existing version of the amazingly frank autobiography of Hatasu the Sorceress Queen. You have indeed chosen well. Menai will wrap it up for you."

As the dark-skinned servitor wrapped the papyrus in a neat paper bundle, Wells turned to his host.

"It seems a shame that such a remarkable collection of yours should remain practically hidden, sir," he said. "I wish you would let me bring my friend Roebling from the McCosh Museum around some time."

"I already have a slight and rather one-sided acquaintance with Mr. Roebling," Sunson said with an oddly sardonic twitch of his lips, "but I will be glad to have him see me any time he wishes."

As he went down the stoop a few minutes later, Wells found himself blinking in the bright noonday sun after the shaded dimness of Sunson's museum. He turned to the left and started briskly up the street toward home. He was anxious to examine the papyrus at his leisure, to study and brood over it with the enthusiasm of the collector, before he took it to someone better able to translate it from Egyptian hieroglyphics to modern English. He was carrying the package carefully in his left hand, and from time to time he glanced down at it.

When Lathrop Wells reached his apartment he tossed his hat on the nearest chair and hastily cleared off the top of his desk. His head had begun to ache severely a few minutes ago, just after he left Sunson's house, but he hardly noticed it. Then he opened his package. Inside the single sheet of brown wrapping-paper was nothing but a tightly rolled newspaper.

He had been tricked! In some way the eccentric collector or his dark-skinned servant had made a last minute switch and substituted the newspaper for the papyrus.

Wells's mouth became a grim line. No matter who Sunson might be, the man could not get away with this! Wells picked up his hat and went out again. He did not think this would be a matter for the police. At least, not until he had made an attempt to settle the matter himself.

That shabby side street still drowsed in the noonday quiet. Wells went by the delicatessen shop and walked briskly past the long row of brownstone-fronts. Then he came to an abrupt stop. The brownstones had ended, the newer apartments had begun, and the house of M. Sunson was not there.

Wells swore under his breath. It must be that in his anger and impatience he had turned into the wrong street. All these blocks were so much alike that it was easy to be fooled. He had not noticed the street sign at all, simply depending on memory. The next block above must be the one that he wanted. He turned on his heel and strode back the way he had come.

At the corner Wells halted again. This *was* the right street! Now he even remembered the name on the window of the delicatessen, and the unusual way some piles of canned goods were arranged in that window. He had seen it twice before, when he went down with Sunson and when he came back alone, and he did not think he could be mistaken.

Slowly Wells began to retrace his steps once more. As he walked past the row of brownstone houses, he saw and remembered several other little things that he had idly noticed the first time he went by. At one spot there was a crooked slab in the sidewalk. The fourth house was unoccupied, and dingy yellow shades were drawn down behind the dirty window-panes. The front door of another of the houses had been newly painted a bright yellow.

This was the right street, without any doubt. There was no question about it. And yet — there was no little red brick house between the last of the brown-stones and the first of the apartments. The house of M. Sunson had com-pletely vanished! Not only that, there was not even any place where it could have been. The apartment was built squarely against the wall of the last house, with no space at all between them.

Lathrop Wells took off his hat and wiped his forehead. He could feel the short hairs prickling all the way down the back of his neck. There was some-thing macabre here, something grotesque and sinister. He might have thought he was going insane, except that a cold sanity in the back of his mind told him that there was nothing out of adjustment in his mental processes. M. Sunson, his red brick house and his dark-skinned servant, his collection of unbeliev-ably rare and valuable relics of ancient civilizations and long-dead heroes, all had vanished.

A uniformed doorman was idling in front of the first apartment, standing under the canvas of the marquee. Wells walked up to him.

"Did you ever see any small red brick building next to this one?" he asked.

The doorman looked puzzled.

"That old brown house has been there since long before this building was put up," he said. They tore down a lot of them old houses to build this apart-ment."

"Did you notice anything queer going on around here this morning?"

"Not a thing, Mister. This is a quiet street. Nothing ever happens here. What's on your mind?"

"I wish I knew!" Wells said feelingly.

Just to satisfy himself, Wells walked through the blocks above and below the one from which Sunson's house had vanished. They were entirely differ-ent in appearance. There could not possibly be any confusion. What had hap-pened to him that morning had happened here.

On a sudden thought he took a taxi to the McCosh Museum.

The Egyptian wing of the museum had few visitors at this hour of the day, but a number of people were grouped around a glass case in the room where the mummies were kept. As Wells hurried forward he saw that his friend Paul

Roebling was one of the group. The glass case contained a mummy with its painted wooden casing, and Wells bent down to read the printed card that rested against the foot if the case. It announced that the mummy was that of one Ra-Moses, a priest of the Goddess Bast, and was believed to date from either the third or the fourth dynasty.

Nodding hastily to Roebling, Wells peered down through the glass top of the case. The upper half of the painted wooden casing had been removed and rested beside the lower half that held the mummy. Enough of the linen wrappings had been removed to show the dried and sunken face of a rather short and stocky man. His shriveled hands were crossed on his breast. Directly below the crossed hands was a gilt image of the cat-headed goddess Bast!

"That's the image," a uniformed guard was explaining excitedly to Roebling. "That's the one a thief stole from this case that night they broke into the museum some weeks ago. I just noticed that it had come back when I walked by a few minutes ago and glanced down into the case. There it is! I guess the guy who stole it must have decided to bring it back, though it beats me how he managed to get it inside the glass case again. It's a good half-hour's work to take out the screws and get one of those things open."

"There's something queer about that little figurine anyway," Roebling said slowly. He was a big, heavy-set man with close-cropped gray hair. "Several times I've taken it out of the mummy-case and put it on one of those cabinets on the wall. Someone always moves it back again. I could never find out how it's done."

Wells was still staring down at the dried remains of what had once been a priest named Ra-Moses. He knew that the name meant Son of the Sun God. Sunson! He looked at the mummy again. It was hard to tell, in its sere and shrunken condition, but the lines of the face did look a little familiar. Then one of the guards touched Wells on the shoulder.

"These were lying on the floor behind you," Mister," he said, "right there beside the mummy-case. Guess they must have just dropped from your pocket." He held out two crisp, new one-dollar bills.

Paul Roebling was still running one hand over his short gray hair, his heavy eyebrows pulled together in a frown.

"Oh, well — the image is back," he said; "that's the main thing. There's something I don't understand, and I'm not going to try. After this I guess we'll just let the image stay in there with the mummy."

"I think it would be a good idea," Lathrop Wells said quietly, "and you can make that card read more accurately, if you want. Ra-Moses lived in the reign of Sesostris of the Fourth Dynasty."

"How do you know?" Roebling asked.

Wells shrugged. "He told me so."

Part III: The Extraordinary and the Exotic

The Wings of Horus
by Algernon Blackwood

Algernon Blackwood's "The Wings of Horus" (1914), originally published in
Century Magazine, *is both a supernatural tale and an insightful meditation on*
the oft-cited linkage between creativity and madness. The story's protagonist, a
Russian named Binovitch, is so cosmically enthralled with birds, and with Ho-
rus, the ancient Egypt falcon god in particular, that his very physicality ends up
blurring the demarcations between man and bird.

The story of how a visit to Egypt can change a man, "The Wings of Horus"
remains a captivating tale in which dreaming, reality, and imagination collide
with tragic results. Binovitch, a man consumed with his passion for the ancient
Egyptian past, proffers a particularly intriguing theory as to how those great
monuments were constructed. He suggests that those gigantic artifacts from the
past that dot the Egyptian desert landscape were constructed not through nor-
mal human means.

At once a fascinating exploration of creativity and imaginative genius and an
important contribution to the ancient Egyptian supernatural tale subgenre,
"The Wings of Horus" is also an enthralling literary adventure in its own right.

Binovitch had the bird in him somewhere: in his features, certainly, with his
piercing eye and hawk-like nose; in his movements, with his quick way of flitting, hopping, darting; in the way he perched on the edge of a chair; in the
manner he pecked at his food; in his twittering, high-pitched voice as well;
and, above all, in his mind. He skimmed all subjects and picked their heart
out neatly, as a bird skims lawn or air to snatch its prey. He had the bird's-eye
view of everything. He loved birds and understood them instinctively; could
imitate their whistling notes with astonishing accuracy. Their one quality he
had not was poise and balance. He was a nervous little man; he was neurasthenic. And he was in Egypt by doctor's orders.

Such imaginative, unnecessary ideas he had! Such uncommon beliefs!

"The old Egyptians," he said laughingly, yet with a touch of solemn conviction in his manner, "were a great people. Their consciousness was different from ours. The bird idea, for instance, conveyed a sense of deity to

them—of bird deity, that is: they had sacred birds—hawks, ibis, and so forth—and worshipped them." And he put his tongue out as though to say with challenge, "Ha, ha!"

"They also worshipped cats and crocodiles and cows," grinned Palazov. Binovitch seemed to dart across the table at his adversary. His eyes flashed; his nose pecked the air. Almost one could imagine the beating of his angry wings.

"Because everything alive," he half screamed, "was a symbol of some spiritual power to them. Your mind is as literal as a dictionary and as incoherent. Pages of ink without connected meaning! Verb always in the infinitive! If you were an old Egyptian, you—you"—he flashed and spluttered, his tongue shot out again, his keen eyes blazed—"you might take all those words and spin them into a great interpretation of life, a cosmic romance, as they did. Instead, you get the bitter, dead taste of ink in your mouth, and spit it over us like that"—he made a quick movement of his whole body as a bird that shakes itself—"in empty phrases."

Khilkoff ordered another bottle of champagne, while Vera, his sister, said half nervously, "Let's go for a drive; it's moonlight." There was enthusiasm at once. Another of the party called the head waiter and told him to pack food and drink in baskets. It was only eleven o'clock. They would drive out into the desert, have a meal at two in the morning, tell stories, sing, and see the dawn.

It was in one of those cosmopolitan hotels in Egypt which attract the ordinary tourists as well as those who are doing a "cure," and all these Russians were ill with one thing or another. All were ordered out for their health, and all were the despair of their doctors. They were as unmanageable as a bazaar and as incoherent. Excess and bed were their routine. They lived, but none of them got better. Equally, none of them got angry. They talked in this strange personal way without a shred of malice or offence. The English, French, and Germans in the hotel watched them with remote amazement, referring to them as "that Russian lot." Their energy was elemental. They never stopped. They merely disappeared when the pace became too fast, then reappeared again after a day or two, and resumed their "living" as before. Binovitch, despite his neurasthenia, was the life of the party. He was also a special patient of Dr. Plitzinger, the famous psychiatrist, who took a peculiar interest in his case. It was not surprising. Binovitch was a man of unusual ability and of genuine, deep culture. But there was something more about him that stimulated curiosity. There was this striking originality. He said and did surprising things.

"I could fly if I wanted to," he said once when the airmen came to astonish the natives with their biplanes over the desert, "but without all that machinery and noise. It's only a question of believing and understanding——"

"Show us!" they cried. "Let's see you fly!"

"He's got it! He's off again! One of his impossible moments."

These occasions when Binovitch let himself go always proved wildly entertaining. He said monstrously incredible things as though he really did believe them. They loved his madness, for it gave them new sensations.

"It's only levitation, after all, this flying," he exclaimed, shooting out his tongue between the words, as his habit was when excited; "and what is levitation but a power of the air? None of you can hang an orange in space for a second, with all your scientific knowledge; but the moon is always levitated perfectly. And the stars. D'you think they swing on wires? What raised the enormous stones of ancient Egypt? D'you really believe it was heaped-up sand and ropes and clumsy leverage and all our weary and laborious mechanical contrivances? Bah! It was levitation. It was the powers of the air. Believe in those powers, and gravity becomes a mere nursery trick—true where it is, but true nowhere else. To know the fourth dimension is to step out of a locked room and appear instantly on the roof or in another country altogether. To know the powers of the air, similarly, is to annihilate what you call weight—and fly."

"Show us, show us!" they cried, roaring with delighted laughter.

"It's a question of belief," he repeated, his tongue appearing and disappearing like a pointed shadow. "It's in the heart; the power of the air gets into your whole being. Why should I show you? Why should I ask my deity to persuade your scoffing little minds by any miracle? For it is deity, I tell you, and nothing else. I *know* it. Follow one idea like that, as I follow my bird idea—follow it with the impetus and undeviating concentration of a projectile—and you arrive at power. You know deity—the bird idea of deity, that is. *They* knew that. The old Egyptians knew it."

"Oh, show us, show us!" they shouted impatiently, wearied of his nonsense-talk. "Get up and fly! Levitate yourself, as they did! Become a star!"

Binovitch turned suddenly very pale, and an odd light shone in his keen brown eyes. He rose slowly from the edge of the chair where he was perched. Something about him changed. There was silence instantly.

"I *will* show you," he said calmly, to their intense amazement; "not to convince your disbelief, but to prove it to myself. For the powers of the air are with me here. I believe. And Horus, great falcon-headed symbol, is my patron god."

The suppressed energy in his voice and manner was indescribable. There was a sense of lifting, upheaving power about him. He raised his arms; his face turned upward; he inflated his lungs with a deep, long breath, and his voice broke into a kind of singing cry, half prayer, half chant:

"O Horus,
Bright-eyed deity of wind,
Feather my soul *
Though earth's thick air,
To know thy awful swiftness——"
* The Russian is untranslatable. The phrase means, "Give my life wings."

He broke off suddenly. He climbed lightly and swiftly upon the nearest table—it was in a deserted card-room, after a game in which he had lost more pounds than there are days in the year—and leaped into the air. He hovered a second, spread his arms and legs in space, appeared to float a moment, then buckled, rushed down and forward, and dropped in a heap upon the floor, while every one roared with laughter.

But the laughter died out quickly, for there was something in his wild performance that was peculiar and unusual. It was uncanny, not quite natural. His body had seemed, as with Mordkin and Nijinski, literally to hang upon the air a moment. For a second he gave the distressing impression of overcoming gravity. There was a touch in it of that faint horror which appals by its very vagueness. He picked himself up unhurt, and his face was as grave as a portrait in the academy, but with a new expression in it that everybody noticed with this strange, half-shocked amazement. And it was this expression that extinguished the claps of laughter as wind that takes away the sound of bells. Like many ugly men, he was an inimitable actor, and his facial repertory was endless and incredible. But this was neither acting nor clever manipulation of expressive features. There was something in his curious Russian physiognomy that made the heart beat slower. And that was why the laughter died away so suddenly.

"You ought to have flown farther," cried some one. It expressed what all had felt.

"Icarus didn't drink champagne," another replied, with a laugh; but nobody laughed with him.

"You went too near to Vera," said Palazov, "and passion melted the wax." But his face twitched oddly as he said it. There was something he did not understand, and so heartily disliked.

The strange expression on the features deepened. It was arresting in a disagreeable, almost in a horrible, way. The talk stopped dead; all stared; there was a feeling of dismay in everybody's heart, yet unexplained. Some lowered their eyes, or else looked stupidly elsewhere; but the women of the party felt a kind of fascination. Vera, in particular, could not move her sight away. The joking reference to his passionate admiration for her passed unnoticed. There was a general and individual sense of shock. And a chorus of whispers rose instantly:

"Look at Binovitch! What's happened to his face?"

"He's changed—he's changing!"

"God! Why he looks like a—bird!"

But no one laughed. Instead, they chose the names of birds—hawk, eagle, even owl. The figure of a man leaning against the edge of the door, watching them closely, they did not notice. He had been passing down the corridor, had looked in unobserved, and then had paused. He had seen the whole performance. He watched Binovitch narrowly, now with calm, discerning eyes. It was Dr Plitzinger, the great psychiatrist.

For Binovitch had picked himself up from the floor in a way that was oddly self-possessed, and precluded the least possibility of the ludicrous. He looked neither foolish nor abashed. He looked surprised, but also he looked half angry and half frightened. As some one had said, he "ought to have flown farther." That was the incredible impression his acrobatics had produced— incredible, yet somehow actual. This uncanny idea prevailed, as at a séance where nothing genuine is expected to happen, and something genuine, after all, does happen. There was no pretence in this: Binovitch had flown.

And now he stood there, white in the face—with terror and with anger white. He looked extraordinary, this little, neurasthenic Russian, but he looked at the same time half terrific. Another thing, not commonly experienced by men, was in him, breaking out of him, affecting *directly* the minds of his companions. His mouth opened; blood and fury shone in his blazing eyes; his tongue shot out like an ant-eater's, though even in that the comic had no place. His arms were spread like flapping wings, and his voice rose dreadfully:

"He failed me, he failed me!" he tried to bellow. "Horus, my falcon-headed deity, my power of the air, deserted me! Hell take him! Hell burn his wings and blast his piercing sight! Hell scorch him into dust for his false prophecies! I curse him—I curse Horus!"

The voice that should have roared across the silent room emitted, instead, this high-pitched, bird-like scream. The added touch of sound, the reality it lent, was ghastly. Yet it was marvellously done and acted. The entire thing was a bit of instantaneous inspiration—his voice, his words, his gestures, his whole wild appearance. Only—here was the reality that caused the sense of shock—the expression on his altered features was genuine. *That* was not assumed. There was something new and alien in him, something cold and difficult to human life, something alert and swift and cruel, of another element than earth. A strange, rapacious grandeur had leaped upon the struggling features. The face looked hawk-like.

And he came forward suddenly and sharply toward Vera, whose fixed, staring eyes had never once ceased watching him with a kind of anxious and devouring pain in them. She was both drawn and beaten back. Binovitch advanced on tiptoe. No doubt he still was acting, still pretending this mad nonsense that he worshipped Horus, the falcon-headed deity of forgotten days, and that Horus had failed him in his hour of need; but somehow there was just a hint of too much reality in the way he moved and looked. The girl, a little creature, with fluffy golden hair, opened her lips; her cigarette fell to the floor; she shrank back; she looked for a moment like some smaller, coloured bird trying to escape from a great pursuing hawk; she screamed. Binovitch, his arms wide, his bird-like face thrust forward, had swooped upon her. He leaped. Almost he caught her.

No one could say exactly what happened. Play, become suddenly and unexpectedly too real, confuses the emotions. The change of key was swift. From fun to terror is a dislocating jolt upon the mind. Some one—it was Khilkoff, the brother—upset a chair; everybody spoke at once; everybody stood up. An unaccountable feeling of disaster was in the air, as with those drinkers' quarrels that blaze out from nothing, and end in a pistol-shot and death, no one able to explain clearly how it came about. It was the silent, watching figure in the doorway who saved the situation. Before any one had noticed his approach, there he was among the group, laughing, talking, applauding—between Binovitch and Vera. He was vigorously patting his patient on the back, and his voice rose easily above the general clamour. He was a strong, quiet personality; even in his laughter there was authority. And his laughter now was the only sound in the room, as though by his mere presence peace and harmony were restored. Confidence came with him. The noise subsided; Vera was in her chair again. Khilkoff poured out a glass of wine for the great man.

"The Czar!" said Plitzinger, sipping his champagne, while all stood up, delighted with his compliment and tact. "And to your opening night with the Russian ballet," he added quickly a second toast, "or to your first performance at the Moscow Théâtre des Arts!" Smiling significantly, he glanced at Binovitch; he clinked glasses with him. Their arms were already linked, but it was Palazov who noticed that the doctor's fingers seemed rather tight upon the creased black coat. All drank, looking with laughter, yet with a touch of respect, toward Binovitch, who stood there dwarfed beside the stalwart Austrian, and suddenly as meek and subdued as any mole. Apparently the abrupt change of key had taken his mind successfully off something else.

"Of course—'The Fire-Bird,'" exclaimed the little man, mentioning the famous Russian ballet. "The very thing!" he exclaimed. "For *us*," he added, looking with devouring eyes at Vera. He was greatly pleased. He began talking vociferously about dancing and the rationale of dancing. They told him he was an undiscovered master. He was delighted. He winked at Vera and touched her glass again with his. "We'll make our début together," he cried. "We'll begin at Covent Garden, in London. I'll design the dresses and the posters 'The Hawk and the Dove!' *Magnifique!* I in dark grey, and you in blue and gold! Ah, dancing, you know, is sacred. The little self is lost, absorbed. It is ecstasy, it is divine. And dancing in air—the passion of the birds and stars—ah! they are the movements of the gods. You know deity that way— by living it."

He went on and on. His entire being had shifted with a leap upon this new subject. The idea of realising divinity by dancing it absorbed him. The party discussed it with him as though nothing else existed in the world, all sitting now and talking eagerly together. Vera took the cigarette he offered her, lighting it from his own; their fingers touched; he was as harmless and normal as a retired diplomat in a drawing-room. But it was Plitzinger whose subtle maneuvering had accomplished the change so cleverly, and it was Plitzinger who presently suggested a game of billiards, and led him off, full now of a fresh enthusiasm for cannons, balls, and pockets, into another room. They departed arm in arm, laughing and talking together.

Their departure, it seemed, made no great difference at first. Vera's eyes watched him out of sight, then turned to listen to Baron Minski, who was describing with gusto how he caught wolves alive for coursing purposes. The speed and power of the wolf, he said, was impossible to realise; the force of their awful leap, the strength of their teeth, which could bite through metal stirrup-fastenings. He showed a scar on his arm and another on his lip. He was telling truth, and everybody listened with deep interest. The narrative lasted perhaps ten minutes or more, when Minski abruptly stopped. He had come to an end; he looked about him; he saw his glass, and emptied it. There was a general pause. Another subject did not at once present itself. Sighs were heard; several fidgeted; fresh cigarettes were lighted. But there was no sign of boredom, for where one or two Russians are gathered together there is always life. They produce gaiety and enthusiasm as wind produces waves. Like great children, they plunge whole-heartedly into whatever interest presents itself at the moment. There is a kind of uncouth gambolling in their way of taking life. It seems as if they are always fighting that deep, underlying, national sadness which creeps into their very blood.

"Midnight!" then exclaimed Palazov, abruptly, looking at his watch; and the others fell instantly to talking about that watch, admiring it and asking questions. For the moment that very ordinary timepiece became the centre of observation. Palazov mentioned the price. "It never stops," he said proudly, "not even under water." He looked up at everybody, challenging admiration. And he told how, at a country house, he made a bet that he would swim to a certain island in the lake, and won the bet. He and a girl were the winners, but as it was a horse they had bet, he got nothing out of it for himself, giving the horse to her. It was a genuine grievance in him. One felt he could have cried as he spoke of it. "But the watch went all the time," he said delightedly, holding the gun-metal object in his hand to show, "and I was twelve minutes in the water with my clothes on."

Yet this fragmentary talk was nothing but pretence. The sound of clicking billiard-balls was audible from the room at the end of the corridor. There was another pause. The pause, however, was intentional. It was not vacuity of mind or absence of ideas that caused it. There was another subject, an unfinished subject that each member of the group was still considering. Only no one cared to begin about it till at last, unable to resist the strain any longer, Palazov turned to Khilkoff, who was saying he would take a "whisky-soda," as the champagne was too sweet, and whispered something beneath his breath; whereupon Khilkoff, forgetting his drink, glanced at his sister, shrugged his shoulders, and made a curious grimace. "He's all right now"— his reply was just audible—"he's with Plitzinger." He cocked his head sidewise to indicate that the clicking of the billiard-balls still was going on.

The subject was out: all turned their heads; voices hummed and buzzed; questions were asked and answered or half answered; eyebrows were raised, shoulders shrugged, hands spread out expressively. There came into the atmosphere a feeling of presentiment, of mystery, of things half understood; primitive, buried instinct stirred a little, the kind of racial dread of vague emotions that might gain the upper hand if encouraged. They shrank from looking something in the face, while yet this unwelcome influence drew closer round them all. They discussed Binovitch and his astonishing performance. Pretty little Vera listened with large and troubled eyes, though saying nothing. The Arab waiter had put out the lights in the corridor, and only a solitary cluster burned now above their heads, leaving their faces in shadow. In the distance the clicking of the billiard-balls still continued.

"It was not play; it was real," exclaimed Minski vehemently. "I can catch wolves," he blurted; "but birds—ugh!—and human birds!" He was half inarticulate. He had witnessed something he could not understand, and it had touched instinctive terror in him. "It was the way he leaped that put the wolf first into my mind, only it was not a wolf at all." The others agreed and disagreed. "It was play at first, but it was reality at the end," another whispered; "and it was no animal he mimicked, but a bird, and a bird of prey at that!"

Vera thrilled. In the Russian woman hides that touch of savagery which loves to be caught, mastered, swept helplessly away, captured utterly and deliciously by the one strong enough to do it thoroughly. She left her chair and sat down beside an older woman in the party, who took her arm quietly at once. Her little face wore a perplexed expression, mournful, yet somehow wild. It was clear that Binovitch was not indifferent to her.

"It's become an *idée fixe* with him," this older woman said. "The bird idea lives in his mind. He lives it in his imagination. Ever since that time at Edfu, when he pretended to worship the great stone falcons outside the temple— the Horus figures—he's been full of it." She stopped. The way Binovitch had behaved at Edfu was better left unmentioned at the moment, perhaps. A slight shiver ran round the listening group, each one waiting for some one else to focus their emotion, and so explain it by saying the convincing thing. Only no one ventured. Then Vera abruptly gave a little jump.

"Hark!" she exclaimed, in a staccato whisper, speaking for the first time. She sat bolt upright. She was listening. "Hark!" she repeated. "There it is again, but nearer than before. It's coming closer. I hear it." She trembled. Her voice, her manner, above all her great staring eyes, startled everybody. No one spoke for several seconds; all listened. The clicking of the billiard-balls had ceased. The halls and corridors lay in darkness, and gloom was over the big hotel. Everybody was in bed.

"Hear what?" asked the older woman soothingly, yet with a perceptible quaver in her voice, too. She was aware that the girl's arm shook upon her own.

"Do you not hear it, too?" the girl whispered.

All listened without speaking. All watched her paling face. Something wonderful, yet half terrible, seemed in the air about them. There was a dull murmur, audible, faint, remote, its direction hard to tell. It had come suddenly from nowhere. They shivered. That strange racial thrill again passed into the group, unwelcome, unexplained. It was aboriginal; it belonged to the unconscious primitive mind, half childish, half terrifying.

"*What* do you hear?" her brother asked angrily—the irritable anger of nervous fear.

"When he came at me," she answered very low, "I heard it first. I hear it now again. Listen! He's coming."

And at that minute, out of the dark mouth of the corridor, emerged two human figures, Plitzinger and Binovitch. Their game was over: they were going up to bed. They passed the open door of the card-room. But Binovitch was being half dragged, half restrained, for he was apparently attempting to run down the passage with flying, dancing leaps. He bounded. It was like a huge bird trying to rise for flight, while his companion kept him down by force upon the earth. As they entered the strip of light, Plitzinger changed his own position, placing himself swiftly between his companion and the group in the dark corner of the room. He hurried Binovitch along as though he sheltered him from view. They passed into the shadows down the passage. They disappeared. And every one looked significantly, questioningly, at his neighbour, though at first saying no word. It seemed that a curious disturbance of the air had followed them audibly.

Vera was the first to open her lips. "You heard it *then*," she said breathlessly, her face whiter than the ceiling.

"Damn!" exclaimed her brother furiously. "It was wind against the outside walls—wind in the desert. The sand is driving."

Vera looked at him. She shrank closer against the side of the older woman, whose arm was tight about her.

"It was *not* wind," she whispered simply. She paused. All waited uneasily for the completion of her sentence. They stared into her face like peasants who expected a miracle.

"Wings," she whispered. "It was the sound of enormous wings."

And at four o'clock in the morning, when they all returned exhausted from their excursion into the desert, little Binovitch was sleeping soundly and peacefully in his bed. They passed his door on tiptoe. But he did not hear them. He was dreaming. His spirit was at Edfu, experiencing with that ancient deity who was master of all flying life those strange enjoyments upon which his own troubled human heart was passionately set. Safe with that mighty falcon whose powers his lips had scorned a few hours before, his soul, released in vivid dream, went sweetly flying. It was amazing, it was gorgeous. He skimmed the Nile at lightning speed. Dashing down headlong from the height of the great Pyramid, he chased with faultless accuracy a little dove that sought vainly to hide from his terrific pursuit beneath the palm trees. For what he loved must worship where he worshipped, and the majesty of those tremendous effigies had fired his imagination to the creative point where expression was imperative.

Then suddenly, at the very moment of delicious capture, the dream turned horrible, becoming awful with the nightmare touch. The sky lost all its blue and sunshine. Far, far below him the little dove enticed him into nameless depths, so that he flew faster and faster, yet never fast enough to overtake it. Behind him came a great thing down the air, black, hovering, with gigantic wings outstretched. It had terrific eyes, and the beating of its feathers stole his wind away. It followed him, crowding space. He was aware of a colossal beak, curved like a scimitar and pointed wickedly like a tooth of iron. He dropped. He faltered. He tried to scream.

Through empty space he fell, caught by the neck. The huge spectral falcon was upon him. The talons were in his heart. And in sleep he remembered then that he had cursed. He recalled his reckless language. The curse of the ignorant is meaningless; that of the worshipper is real. This attack was on his soul. He had invoked it. He realised next, with a touch of ghastly horror, that the dove he chased was, after all, the bait that had lured him purposely to destruction, and awoke with a suffocating terror upon him, and his entire body bathed in icy perspiration. Outside the open window he heard a sound of wings retreating with powerful strokes into the surrounding darkness of the sky.

The nightmare made its impression upon Binovitch's impressionable and dramatic temperament. It aggravated his tendencies. He related it next day to Mme. de Drühn, the friend of Vera, telling it with that somewhat boisterous laughter some minds use to disguise less kind emotions. But he received no encouragement. The mood of the previous night was not recoverable; it was already ancient history. Russians never make the banal mistake of repeating a sensation till it is exhausted; they hurry on to novelties. Life flashes and rushes with them, never standing still for exposure before the cameras of their minds. Mme. de Drühn, however, took the trouble to mention the matter to Plitzinger, for Plitzinger, like Freud of Vienna, held that dreams revealed subconscious tendencies which sooner or later must betray themselves in action.

"Thank you for telling me," he smiled politely, "but I have already heard it from him." He watched her eyes for a moment, really examining her soul. "Binovitch, you see," he continued, apparently satisfied with what he saw, "I regard as that rare phenomenon—a genius without an outlet. His spirit, intensely creative, finds no adequate expression. His power of production is enormous and prolific; yet he accomplishes nothing." He paused an instant. "Binovitch, therefore, is in danger of poisoning—himself." He looked steadily into her face, as a man who weighs how much he may confide. "Now," he continued, "*if* we can find an outlet for him, a field wherein his bursting imaginative genius can produce results—above all, *visible* results"—he shrugged his shoulders—"the man is saved. Otherwise"—he looked extraordinarily impressive—"there is bound to be sooner or later——"

"Madness?" she asked very quietly.

"An explosion, let us say," he replied gravely. "For instance, take this Horus obsession of his, quite wrong archaeologically though it is. *Au fond* it is megalomania of a most unusual kind. His passionate interest, his love, his worship of birds, wholesome enough in itself, finds no satisfying outlet. A man who *really* loves birds neither keeps them in cages nor shoots them nor stuffs them. What, then, can he do? The commonplace bird-lover observes them through glasses, studies their habits, then writes a book about them. But a man like Binovitch, overflowing with this intense creative power of mind and imagination, is not content with that. He wants to know them from within. He wants to feel what they feel, to live their life. He wants to *become* them. You follow me? Not quite. Well, he seeks to be identified with the object of his sacred, passionate adoration. All genius seeks to know the thing itself from its own point of view. It desires union. That tendency, unrecognised by himself, perhaps, and therefore subconscious, hides in his very soul." He paused a moment. "And the sudden sight of those majestic figures at Edfu— that crystallisation of his *idée fixe* in granite—took hold of this excess in him, so to speak—and is now focusing it toward some definite act. Binovitch sometimes—feels himself a bird! You noticed what occurred last night?"

She nodded; a slight shiver passed over her.

"A most curious performance," she murmured; "an exhibition I never want to see again."

"The most curious part," replied the doctor coolly, "was its truth."

"Its truth!" she exclaimed beneath her breath. She was frightened by something in his voice and by the uncommon gravity in his eyes. It seemed to arrest her intelligence. She felt upon the edge of things beyond her. "You mean that Binovitch did for a moment—hang—in the air?" The other verb, the right one, she could not bring herself to use.

The great man's face was enigmatical. He talked to her sympathy, perhaps, rather than to her mind.

"Real genius," he said smilingly, "is as rare as talent, even great talent, is common. It means that the personality, if only for one second, becomes everything; becomes the universe; becomes the soul of the world. It gets the flash. It is identified with the universal life. Being everything and everywhere, all is possible to it—in that second of vivid realisation. It can brood with the crystal, grow with the plant, leap with the animal, fly with the bird: genius unifies all three. That is the meaning of 'creative.' It is faith. Knowing it, you can pass through fire and not be burned, walk on water and not sink, move a mountain, fly. Because you are fire, water, earth, air. Genius, you see, is madness in the magnificent sense of being superhuman. Binovitch has it."

He broke off abruptly, seeing he was not understood. Some great enthusiasm in him he deliberately suppressed.

"The point is," he resumed, speaking more carefully, "that we must try to lead this passionate constructive genius of the man into some human channel that will absorb it, and therefore render it harmless."

"He loves Vera," the woman said, bewildered, yet seizing this point correctly.

"But would he marry her?" asked Plitzinger at once.

"He is already married."

The doctor looked steadily at her a moment, hesitating whether he should utter all his thought.

"In that case," he said slowly after a pause, "it is better he or she should leave."

His tone and manner were exceedingly impressive.

"You mean there's danger?" she asked.

"I mean, rather," he replied earnestly, "that this great creative flood in him, so curiously focused now upon his Horus-falcon-bird idea, may result in some act of violence——"

"Which would be madness," she said, looking hard at him.

"Which would be disastrous," he corrected her. And then he added slowly: "Because in the mental moment of immense creation he might overlook material laws."

The costume ball two nights later was a great success. Palazov was a Bedouin, and Khilkoff an Apache; Mme. de Drühn wore a national head-dress; Minski looked almost natural as Don Quixote; and the entire Russian "set" was cleverly, if somewhat extravagantly, dressed. But Binovitch and Vera were the most successful of all the two hundred dancers who took part. Another figure, a big man dressed as a Pierrot, also claimed exceptional attention, for though the costume was commonplace enough, there was something of dignity in his appearance that drew the eyes of all upon him. But he wore a mask, and his identity was not discoverable.

It was Binovitch and Vera, however, who must have won the prize, if prize there had been, for they not only looked their parts, but acted them as well. The former in his dark grey feather tunic, and his falcon mask, complete even to the brown hooked beak and tufted talons, looked fierce and splendid. The disguise was so admirable, yet so entirely natural, that it was uncommonly seductive. Vera, in blue and gold, a charming head-dress of a dove upon her loosened hair, and a pair of little dove-pale wings fluttering from her shoulders, her tiny twinkling feet and slender ankles well visible, too, was equally successful and admired. Her large and timid eyes, her flitting movements, her light and dainty way of dancing—all added touches that made the picture perfect.

How Binovitch contrived his dress remained a mystery, for the layers of wings upon his back were real; the large black kites that haunt the Nile, soaring in their hundreds over Cairo and the bleak Mokattam Hills, had furnished them. He had procured them none knew how. They measured four feet across from tip to tip; they swished and rustled as he swept along; they were true falcons' wings. He danced with Nautch-girls and Egyptian princesses and Rumanian Gipsies; he danced well, with beauty, grace, and lightness. But with Vera he did not dance at all; with her he simply flew. A kind of passionate abandon was in him as he skimmed the floor with her in a way that made everybody turn to watch them. They seemed to leave the ground together. It was delightful, an amazing sight; but it was peculiar. The strangeness of it was on many lips. Somehow its queer extravagance communicated itself to the en-

tire ball-room. They became the centre of observation. There were whispers.
"There's that extraordinary bird-man! Look! He goes by like a hawk. And
he's always after that dove-girl. How marvellously he does it! It's rather awful. Who is he? I don't envy *her*."

People stood aside when he rushed past. They got out of his way. He
seemed forever pursuing Vera, even when dancing with another partner.
Word passed from mouth to mouth. A kind of telepathic interest was estab-
lished everywhere. It was a shade too real sometimes, something unduly
earnest in the chasing wildness, something unpleasant. There was even
alarm.

"It's rowdy; I'd rather not see it; it's quite disgraceful," was heard. "*I* think
it's horrible; you can see she's terrified."

And once there was a little scene, trivial enough, yet betraying this reality
that many noticed and disliked. Binovitch came up to claim a dance, pro-
gramme clutched in his great tufted claws, and at the same moment the big
Pierrot appeared abruptly round the corner with a similar claim. Those who
saw it assert he had been waiting, and came on purpose, and that there was
something protective and authoritative in his bearing. The misunderstanding was ordinary enough—both men had written her name against the
dance—but "No. 13, Tango" also included the supper interval, and neither
Hawk nor Pierrot would give way. They were very obstinate. Both men
wanted her. It was awkward.

"The Dove shall decide between us," smiled the Hawk politely, yet his
taloned fingers working nervously. Pierrot, however, more experienced in the
ways of dealing with women, or more bold, said suavely:

"I am ready to abide by her decision"—his voice poorly cloaked this ag-
gravating authority, as though he had the right to her—"only I engaged this
dance before his Majesty Horus appeared upon the scene at all, and therefore
it is clear that Pierrot has the right of way."

At once, with a masterful air, he took her off. There was no withstanding
him. He meant to have her and he got her. She yielded meekly. They vanished
among the maze of coloured dancers, leaving the Hawk, disconsolate and van-
quished, amid the titters of the onlookers. His swiftness, as against this
steady power, was of no avail.

It was then that the singular phenomenon was witnessed first. Those who
saw it affirm that he changed absolutely into the part he played. It was dreadful; it was wicked. A frightened whisper ran about the rooms and corridors:

"An extraordinary thing is in the air!"

Some shrank away, while others flocked to see. There were those who
swore that a curious, rushing sound was audible, the atmosphere visibly
disturbed and shaken; that a shadow fell upon the spot the couple had vacated;

that a cry was heard, a high, wild, searching cry: "Horus! bright deity of wind," it began, then died away. One man was positive that the windows had been opened and that something had flown in. It was the obvious explanation. The thing spread horribly. As in a fire-panic, there was consternation and excitement. Confusion caught the feet of all the dancers. The music fumbled and lost time. The leading pair of tango dancers halted and looked round. It seemed that everybody pressed back, hiding, shuffling, eager to see, yet more eager not to be seen, as though something dangerous, hostile, terrible, had broken loose. In rows against the wall they stood. For a great space had made itself in the middle of the ball-room, and into this empty space appeared suddenly the Pierrot and the Dove.

It was like a challenge. A sound of applause, half voices, half clapping of gloved hands, was heard. The couple danced exquisitely into the arena. All stared. There was an impression that a set piece had been prepared, and that this was its beginning. The music again took heart. Pierrot was strong and dignified, no whit nonplussed by this abrupt publicity. The Dove, though faltering, was deliciously obedient. They danced together like a single outline. She was captured utterly. And to the man who needed her the sight was naturally agonizing—the protective way the Pierrot held her, the right and strength of it, the mastery, the complete possession.

"He's got her!" someone breathed too loud, uttering the thought of all. "Good thing it's not the Hawk!"

And, to the absolute amazement of the throng, this sight was then apparent. A figure dropped through space. That high, shrill cry again was heard:

"Feather my soul ... to know thy awful swiftness!"

Its singing loveliness touched the heart, its appealing, passionate sweetness was marvellous, as from the gallery this figure of a man, dressed as a strong, dark bird, shot down with splendid grace and ease. The feathers swept; the swings spread out as sails that take the wind. Like a hawk that darts with unerring power and aim upon its prey, this thing of mighty wings rushed down into the empty space where the two danced. Observed by all, he entered, swooping beautifully, stretching his wings like any eagle. He dropped. He fixed his point of landing with consummate skill close beside the astonished dancers. He landed.

It happened with such swiftness it brought the dazzle and blindness as when lightning strikes. People in different parts of the room saw different details; a few saw nothing at all after the first startling shock, closing their eyes, or holding their arms before their faces as in self-protection. The touch of panic fear caught the entire room. The nameless thing that all the evening had been vaguely felt was come. It had suddenly materialised.

For this incredible thing occurred in the full blaze of light upon the open floor. Binovitch, grown in some sense formidable, opened his dark, big wings about the girl. The long grey feathers moved, causing powerful draughts of wind that made a rushing sound. An aspect of the terrible was about him, like an emanation. The great beaked head was poised to strike, the tufted claws were raised like fingers that shut and opened, and the whole presentment of his amazing figure focused in an attitude of attack that was magnificent and terrible. No one who saw it doubted. Yet there were those who swore that it was not Binovitch at all, but that another outline, monstrous and shadowy, towered above him, draping his lesser proportions with two colossal wings of darkness. That some touch of strange divinity lay in it may be claimed, however confused the wild descriptions afterward. For many lowered their heads and bowed their shoulders. There was terror. There was also awe. The onlookers swayed as though some power passed over them through the air.

A sound of wings was certainly in the room.

Then someone screamed; a shriek broke high and clear; and emotion, ordinary human emotion, unaccustomed to terrific things, swept loose. The Hawk and Vera flew. Beaten back against the wall as by a stroke of whirlwind, the Pierrot staggered. He watched them go. Out of the lighted room they flew, out of the crowded human atmosphere, out of the heat and artificial light, the walled-in, airless halls that were a cage. All this they left behind. They seemed things of wind and air, made free happily of another element. Earth held them not. Toward the open night they raced with this extraordinary lightness as of birds, down the long corridor and on to the southern terrace, where great coloured curtains were hung suspended from the columns. A moment they were visible. Then the fringe of one huge curtain, lifted by the wind, showed their dark outline for a second against the starry sky. There was a cry, a leap. The curtain flapped again and closed. They vanished. And into the ball-room swept the cold draught of night air from the desert.

But three figures instantly were close upon their heels. The throng of half-dazed, half-stupefied onlookers, it seemed, projected them as though by some explosive force. The general mass held back, but, like projectiles, these three flung themselves after the fugitives down the corridor at high speed— the Apache, Don Quixote, and, last of them, the Pierrot. For Khilkoff, the brother, and Baron Minski, the man who caught wolves alive, had been for some time keenly on the watch, while Dr. Plitzinger, reading the symptoms clearly, never far away, had been faithfully observant of every movement. His mask tossed aside, the great psychiatrist was now recognised by all. They reached the parapet just as the curtain flapped back heavily into place; the next second all three were out of sight behind it. Khilkoff was first, however, urged forward at frantic speed by the warning words the doctor had whispered as they ran. Some thirty yards beyond the terrace was the brink of the crumbling cliff on which the great hotel was built, and there was a drop of sixty feet to the desert floor below. Only a low stone wall marked the edge.

Accounts varied. Khilkoff, it seems, arrived in time—in the nick of time—to seize his sister, virtually hovering on the brink. He heard the loose stones strike the sand below. There was no struggle, though it appears she did not thank him for his interference at first. In a sense she was beside—outside—herself. And he did a characteristic thing: he not only brought her back into the ball-room, but he *danced* her back. It was admirable. Nothing could have calmed the general excitement better. The pair of them danced in together as though nothing was amiss. Accustomed to the strenuous practice of his Cossack regiment, this young cavalry officer's muscles were equal to the semi-dead weight in his arms. At most the onlookers thought her tired, perhaps. Confidence was restored—such is the psychology of a crowd—and in the middle of a thrilling Viennese waltz he easily smuggled her out of the room, administered brandy, and got her up to bed. The absence of the Hawk, meanwhile, was hardly noticed; comments were made and then forgotten; it was Vera in whom the strange, anxious sympathy had centred. And, with her obvious safety, the moment of primitive, childish panic passed away. Don Quixote, too, was presently seen dancing gaily as though nothing untoward had happened; supper intervened; the incident was over; it had melted into the general wildness of the evening's irresponsibility. The fact that Pierrot did not appear again was noticed by no single person.

But Dr. Plitzinger was otherwise engaged, his heart and mind and soul all deeply exercised. A death-certificate is not always made out quite so simply as the public thinks. That Binovitch had died of suffocation in his swift descent through merely sixty feet of air was not conceivable; yet that his body lay so neatly placed upon the desert after such a fall was stranger still. It was not crumpled, it was not torn; no single bone was broken, no muscle wrenched; there was no bruise. There was no indenture in the sand. The figure lay sidewise as though in sleep, no sign of violence visible anywhere, the dark wings folded as a great bird folds them when it creeps away to die in loneliness. Beneath the Horus mask the face was smiling. It seemed he had floated into death upon the element he loved. And only Vera had seen the enormous wings that, hovering invitingly above the dark abyss, bore him so softly into another world. Plitzinger, that is, saw them, too, but he said firmly that they belonged to the big black falcons that haunt the Mokattam Hills and roost upon these ridges, close beside the hotel, at night. Both he and Vera, however, agreed on one thing: the high, sharp cry in the air above them, wild and plaintive, was certainly the black kite's cry—the note of the falcon that passionately seeks its mate. It was the pause of a second, when she stood to listen, that made her rescue possible. A moment later and she, too, would have flown to death with Binovitch.

A Descent Into Egypt
by Algernon Blackwood

Algernon Blackwood's "A Descent into Egypt," the longest story to appear in this volume, encapsulates the mysteries and strangeness of the ancient Egypt supernatural tale at its very best. As a rhapsodic story that is both invigorating and mesmerizing, "A Descent into Egypt" follows a man who becomes literally captivated by, and lost in, the distant Egyptian past. Mike Ashley, in his biography, Algernon Blackwood: An Extraordinary Life *(2001) contends that the final paragraph in the story "is one of the most moving in all of Blackwood's work." Strong words indeed, and something to keep in mind as you, the reader, begin the slow, rapturous descent deep into the mysterious, forbidden, and enchanting ancient Egyptian past through the portal of Blackwood's fiction.*

I

He was an accomplished, versatile man whom some called brilliant. Behind his talents lay a wealth of material that right selection could have lifted into genuine distinction. He did too many things, however, to excel in one, for a restless curiosity kept him ever on the move. George Isley was an able man. His short career in diplomacy proved it; yet, when he abandoned this for travel and exploration, no one thought it a pity. He would do big things in any line. He was merely finding himself.

Among the rolling stones of humanity a few acquire moss of considerable value. They are not necessarily shiftless; they travel light; the comfortable pockets in the game of life that attract the majority are too small to retain them; they are in and out again in a moment. The world says, "What a pity! They stick to nothing!" but the fact is that, like questing wild birds, they seek the nest they need. It is a question of values. They judge swiftly, change their line of flight, are gone, not even hearing the comment that they might have "retired with a pension."

And to this homeless, questing type George Isley certainly belonged. He was by no means shiftless. He merely sought with insatiable yearning that soft particular nest where he could settle down in permanently. And to an accompaniment of sighs and regrets from his friends he found it; he found it, however, not in the present, but by retiring from the world "without a pension," unclothed with honours and distinctions. He withdrew from the present and slipped softly back into a mighty Past where he belonged. Why; how; obeying what strange instincts—this remains unknown, deep secret of an inner life that found no resting-place in modern things. Such instincts are not disclosable in twentieth-century language, nor are the details of such a journey properly describable at all. Except by the few—poets, prophets, psychiatrists and the like—such experiences are dismissed with the neat museum label— "queer."

So, equally, must the recorder of this experience share the honour of that little label—he who by chance witnessed certain external and visible signs of this inner and spiritual journey. There remains, nevertheless, the amazing reality of the experience; and to the recorder alone was some clue of interpretation possible, perhaps, because in himself also lay the lure, though less imperative, of a similar journey. At any rate the interpretation may be offered to the handful who realise that trains and motors are not the only means of travel left to our progressive race.

In his younger days I knew George Isley intimately. I know him now. But the George Isley I knew of old, the arresting personality with whom I travelled, climbed, explored, is no longer with us. He is not here. He disappeared—gradually—into the past. There is no George Isley. And that such an individuality could vanish, while still his outer semblance walks the familiar streets, normal apparently, and not yet fifty in the number of his years, seems a tale, though difficult, well worth the telling. For I witnessed the slow submergence. It was very gradual. I cannot pretend to understand the entire significance of it. There was something questionable and sinister in the business that offered hints of astonishing possibilities. Were there a corps of spiritual police, the matter might be partially cleared up, but since none of the churches have yet organised anything effective of this sort, one can only fall back upon variants of the blessed "Mesopotamia," and whisper of derangement, and the like. Such labels, of course, explain as little as most other *clichés* in life. That well-groomed, soldierly figure strolling down Piccadilly, watching the Races, dining out—there is no derangement there. The face is not melancholy, the eye not wild; the gestures are quiet and the speech controlled. Yet the eye is empty, the face expressionless. Vacancy reigns there, provocative and significant. If not unduly noticeable, it is because the majority in life neither expect, nor offer, more.

At closer quarters you may think questioning things, or you may think— nothing; probably the latter. You may wonder why something continually expected does not make its appearance; and you may watch for the evidence of "personality" the general presentment of the man has led you to expect. Disappointed, therefore, you may certainly be; but I defy you to discover the smallest hint of mental disorder, and of derangement or nervous affliction, absolutely nothing. Before long, perhaps, you may feel you are talking with a dummy, some well-trained automaton, a nonentity devoid of spontaneous life; and afterwards you may find that memory fades rapidly away, as though no impression of any kind has really been made at all. All this, yes; but nothing pathological. A few may be stimulated by this startling discrepancy between promise and performance, but most, accustomed to accept face values, would say, "a pleasant fellow, but nothing in him much ..." and an hour later forget him altogether.

For the truth is as you, perhaps, divined. You have been sitting beside no one, you have been talking to, looking at, listening to—no one. The intercourse has conveyed nothing that can waken human response in you, good, bad or indifferent. There is no George Isley. And the discovery, if you make it, will not even cause you to creep with the uncanniness of the experience, because the exterior is so wholly pleasing. George Isley today is a picture with no meaning in it that charms merely by the harmonious colouring of an inoffensive subject. He moves undiscovered in the little world of society to which he was born, secure in the groove first habit has made comfortably automatic for him. No one guesses; none, that is, but the few who knew him intimately in early life. And his wandering existence has scattered these; they have forgotten what he was. So perfect, indeed, is he in the manners of the commonplace fashionable man, that no woman in his "set" is aware that he differs from the type she is accustomed to. He turns a compliment with the accepted language of her text-book, motors, golfs and gambles in the regulation manner of his particular world. He is an admirable, perfect automaton. He is nothing. He is a human shell.

II

The name of George Isley had been before the public for some years when, after a considerable interval, we met again in a hotel in Egypt, I for my health, he for I knew not what—at first. But I soon discovered: archaeology and excavation had taken hold of him, though he had gone so quietly about it that no one seemed to have heard. I was not sure that he was glad to see me, for he had first withdrawn, annoyed, it seemed, at being discovered, but later, as though after consideration, had made tentative advances. He welcomed me with a curious gesture of the entire body that seemed to shake himself free from something that had made him forget my identity. There was pathos somewhere in his attitude, almost as though he asked for sympathy. "I've been out here, off and on, for the last three years," he told me, after describing something of what he had been doing. "I find it the most repaying hobby in the world. It leads to a reconstruction—an imaginative reconstruction, of course, I mean—of an enormous thing the world had entirely lost. A very gorgeous, stimulating hobby, believe me, and a very entic—" he quickly changed the word— "exacting one indeed."

I remember looking him up and down with astonishment. There was a change in him, a lack; a note was missing in his enthusiasm, a colour in the voice, a quality in his manner. The ingredients were not mixed quite as of old. I did not bother him with questions, but I noted thus at the very first a subtle alteration. Another facet of the man presented itself. Something that had been independent and aggressive was replaced by a certain emptiness that invited sympathy. Even in his physical appearance the change was manifested—this odd suggestion of lessening. I looked again more closely. Lessening was the word. He had somehow dwindled. It was startling, vaguely unpleasant too.

The entire subject, as usual, was at his fingertips; he knew all the important men; and had spent money freely on his hobby. I laughed, reminding him of his remark that Egypt had no attractions for him, owing to the organised advertisement of its somewhat theatrical charms. Admitting his error with a gesture, he brushed the objection easily aside. His manner, and a certain glow that rose about his atmosphere as he answered, increased my first astonishment. His voice was significant and suggestive. "Come out with me," he said in a low tone, "and see how little the tourists matter, how inappreciable the excavation is compared to what remains to be done, how gigantic"—he emphasised the word impressively— "the scope for discovery remains." He made a movement with his head and shoulders that conveyed a sense of the prodigious, for he was of massive build, his cast of features stern, and his eyes, set deep into the face, shone past me with a sombre gleam in them I did not quite account for. It was the voice, however, that brought the mystery in. It vibrated somewhere below the actual sound of it. "Egypt," he continued— and so gravely that at first I made the mistake of thinking he chose the curious words on purpose to produce a theatrical effect— "that has enriched her blood with the pageant of so many civilisations, that has devoured Persians, Greeks and Romans, Saracens and Mamelukes, a dozen conquests and invasions besides,—what can mere tourists or explorers matter to her? The excavators scratch their skin and dig up mummies; and as for tourists!"—he laughed contemptuously— "flies that settle for a moment on her covered face, to vanish at the first signs of heat! Egypt is not even aware of them. The real Egypt lies underground in darkness. Tourists must have light, to be seen as well as to see. And the diggers———!''

He paused, smiling with something between pity and contempt I did not quite appreciate, for, personally, I felt a great respect for the tireless excavators. And then he added, with a touch of feeling in his tone as though he had a grievance against them, and had not also "dug" himself, "Men who uncover the dead, restore the temples, and reconstruct a skeleton, thinking they have read its beating heart...." He shrugged his great shoulders, and the rest of the sentence may have been but the protest of a man in defence of his own hobby, but that there seemed an undue earnestness and gravity about it that made me wonder more than ever. He went on to speak of the strangeness of the land as a mere ribbon of vegetation along the ancient river, the rest all ruins, desert, sun-drenched wilderness of death, yet so breakingly alive with wonder, power and a certain disquieting sense of deathlessness. There seemed, for him, a revelation of unusual spiritual kind in this land where the Past survived so potently. He spoke almost as though it obliterated the Present.

Indeed, the hint of something solemn behind his words made it difficult for me to keep up the conversation, and the pause that presently came I filled in with some word of questioning surprise, which yet, I think, was chiefly in concurrence. I was aware of some big belief in him, some enveloping emotion that escaped my grasp. Yet, though I did not understand, his great mood swept me.... His voice lowered, then, as he went on to mention temples, tombs and deities, details of his own discoveries and of their effect upon him, but to this I listened with half an ear, because in the unusual language he had first made use of I detected this other thing that stirred my curiosity more—stirred it uncomfortably.

"Then the spell," I asked, remembering the effect of Egypt upon myself two years before, "has worked upon you as upon most others, only with greater power?"

He looked hard at me a moment, signs of trouble showing themselves faintly in his rugged, interesting face. I think he wanted to say more than he could bring himself to confess. He hesitated.

"I'm only glad," he replied after a pause, "it didn't get hold of me earlier in life. It would have absorbed me. I should have lost all other interests. Now," —that curious look of helplessness, of asking sympathy, flitted like a shadow through his eyes— "now that I'm on the decline ... it matters less."

On the decline! I cannot imagine by what blundering I missed this chance he never offered again; somehow or other the singular phrase passed unnoticed at the moment, and only came upon me with its full significance later when it was too awkward to refer to it. He tested my readiness to help, to sympathise, to share his inner life. I missed the clue. For, at the moment, a more practical consideration interested me in his language. Being of those who regretted that he had not excelled by devoting his powers to a single object, I shrugged my shoulders. He caught my meaning instantly. Oh, he was glad to talk. He felt the possibility of my sympathy underneath, I think.

"No, no, you take me wrongly there," he said with gravity. "What I mean—and I ought to know if any one does!—is that while most countries give, others take away. Egypt changes you. No one can live here and remain exactly what he was before."

This puzzled me. It startled, too, again. His manner was so earnest. "And Egypt, you mean, is one of the countries that take away?" I asked. The strange idea unsettled my thoughts a little.

"First takes away from you," he replied, "but in the end takes you away. Some lands enrich you," he went on, seeing that I listened, "while others impoverish. From India, Greece, Italy, all ancient lands, you return with memories you can use. From Egypt you return with—nothing. Its splendour stupefies; it's useless. There is a change in your inmost being, an emptiness, an unaccountable yearning, but you find nothing that can fill the lack you're conscious of. Nothing comes to replace what has gone. You have been drained."

I stared; but I nodded a general acquiescence. Of a sensitive, artistic temperament this was certainly true, though by no means the superficial and generally accepted verdict. The majority imagine that Egypt has filled them to the brim. I took his deeper reading of the facts. I was aware of an odd fascination in his idea.

"Modern Egypt," he continued, "is, after all, but a trick of civilisation," and there was a kind of breathlessness in his measured tone, "but ancient Egypt lies waiting, hiding, underneath. Though dead, she is amazingly alive. And you feel her touching you. She takes from you. She enriches herself. You return from Egypt—less than you were before."

What came over my mind is hard to say. Some touch of visionary imagination burned its flaming path across my mind. I thought of some old Grecian hero speaking of his delicious battle with the gods—battle in which he knew he must be worsted, but yet in which he delighted because at death his spirit would join their glorious company beyond this world. I was aware, that is to say, of resignation as well as resistance in him. He already felt the effortless peace which follows upon long, unequal battling, as of a man who has fought the rapids with a strain beyond his strength, then sinks back and goes with the awful mass of water smoothly and indifferently—over the quiet fall.

Yet, it was not so much his words which clothed picturesquely an undeniable truth, as the force of conviction that drove behind them, shrouding my mind with mystery and darkness. His eyes, so steadily holding mine, were lit, I admit, yet they were calm and sane as those of a doctor discussing the symptoms of that daily battle to which we all finally succumb. This analogy occurred to me.

"There *is*"—I stammered a little, faltering in my speech— "an incalculable element in the country ... somewhere, I confess. You put it—rather strongly, though, don't you?"

He answered quietly, moving his eyes from my face towards the window that framed the serene and exquisite sky towards the Nile.

"The real, invisible Egypt," he murmured, "I do find rather—strong. I find it difficult to deal with. You see," and he turned towards me, smiling like a tired child, "I think the truth is that Egypt deals with me."

"It draws——" I began, then started as he interrupted me at once.

"Into the Past." He uttered the little word in a way beyond me to describe. There came a flood of glory with it, a sense of peace and beauty, of battles over and of rest attained. No saint could have brimmed "Heaven" with as much passionately enticing meaning. He went willingly, prolonging the struggle merely to enjoy the greater relief and joy of the consummation.

For again he spoke as though a struggle were in progress in his being. I got the impression that he somewhere wanted help. I understood the pathetic quality I had vaguely discerned already. His character naturally was so strong and independent. It now seemed weaker, as though certain fibres had been drawn out. And I understood then that the spell of Egypt, so lightly chattered about in its sensational aspect, so rarely known in its naked power, the nameless, creeping influence that begins deep below the surface and thence sends delicate tendrils outwards, was in his blood. I, in my untaught ignorance, had felt it too; it is undeniable; one is aware of unaccountable, queer things in Egypt; even the utterly prosaic feel them. Dead Egypt is marvellously alive....

I glanced past him out of the big windows where the desert glimmered in its featureless expanse of yellow leagues, two monstrous pyramids signalling from across the Nile, and for a moment—inexplicably, it seemed to me afterwards—I lost sight of my companion's stalwart figure that was yet so close before my eyes. He had risen from his chair; he was standing near me; yet my sight missed him altogether. Something, dim as a shadow, faint as a breath of air, rose up and bore my thoughts away, obliterating vision too. I forgot for a moment who I was; identity slipped from me. Thought, sight, feeling, all sank away into the emptiness of those sun-baked sands, sank, as it were, into nothingness, caught away from the Present, enticed, absorbed.... And when I looked back again to answer him, or rather to ask what his curious words could mean—he was no longer there. More than surprised—for there was something of shock in the disappearance—I turned to search. I had not seen him go. He had stolen from my side so softly, slipped away silently, mysteriously, and—so easily. I remember that a faint shiver ran down my back as I realised that I was alone.

Was it that, momentarily, I had caught a reflex of his state of mind? Had my sympathy induced in myself an echo of what he experienced in full—a going backwards, a loss of present vigour, the enticing, subtle draw of those immeasurable sands that hide the living dead from the interruptions of the careless living…?

I sat down to reflect and, incidentally, to watch the magnificence of the sunset; and the thing he had said returned upon me with insistent power, ringing like distant bells within my mind. His talk of the tombs and temples passed, but this remained. It stimulated oddly. His talk, I remembered, had always excited curiosity in this way. Some countries give, while others take away. What did he mean precisely? What had Egypt taken away from him? And I realised more definitely that something in him was missing, something he possessed in former years that was now no longer there. He had grown shadowy already in my thoughts. The mind searched keenly, but in vain … and after some time I left my chair and moved over to another window, aware that a vague discomfort stirred within me that involved uneasiness— for him. I felt pity. But behind the pity was an eager, absorbing curiosity as well. He seemed receding curiously into misty distance, and the strong desire leaped in me to overtake, to travel with him into some vanished splendour that he had rediscovered. The feeling was a most remarkable one, for it included yearning—the yearning for some nameless, forgotten loveliness the world has lost. It was in me too.

At the approach of twilight the mind loves to harbour shadows. The room, empty of guests, was dark behind me; darkness, too, was creeping across the desert like a veil, deepening the serenity of its grim, unfeatured face. It turned pale with distance; the whole great sheet of it went rustling into night. The first stars peeped and twinkled, hanging loosely in the air as though they could be plucked like golden berries; and the sun was already below the Libyan horizon, where gold and crimson faded through violet into blue. I stood watching this mysterious Egyptian dusk, while an eerie glamour seemed to bring the incredible within uneasy reach of the half-faltering senses…. And suddenly the truth dropped into me. Over George Isley, over his mind and energies, over his thoughts and over his emotions too, a kind of darkness was also slowly creeping. Something in him had dimmed, yet not with age; it had gone out. Some inner night, stealing over the Present, obliterated it. And yet he looked towards the dawn. Like the Egyptian monuments his eyes turned— eastwards.

And so it came to me that what he had lost was personal ambition. He was glad, he said, that these Egyptian studies had not caught him earlier in life; the language he made use of was peculiar: "Now I am on the decline it matters less." A slight foundation, no doubt, to build conviction on, and yet I felt sure that I was partly right. He was fascinated, but fascinated against his will. The Present in him battled against the Past. Still fighting, he had yet lost hope. The desire not to change was now no longer in him....

I turned away from the window so as not to see that grey, encroaching desert, for the discovery produced a certain agitation in me. Egypt seemed suddenly a living entity of enormous power. She stirred about me. She was stirring now. This flat and motionless land pretending it had no movement, was actually busy with a million gestures that came creeping round the heart. She was reducing him. Already from the complex texture of his personality she had drawn one vital thread that in its relation to the general woof was of central importance—ambition. The mind chose the simile; but in my heart where thought fluttered in singular distress, another suggested itself as truer. "Thread" changed to "artery." I turned quickly and went up to my room where I could be alone. The idea was somewhere ghastly.

III

Yet, while dressing for dinner, the idea exfoliated as only a living thing exfoliates. I saw in George Isley this great question mark that had not been there formerly. All have, of course, some question mark, and carry it about, though with most it rarely becomes visible until the end. With him it was plainly visible in his atmosphere at the hey-day of his life. He wore it like a fine curved scimitar above his head. So full of life, he yet seemed willingly dead. For, though imagination sought every possible explanation, I got no further than the somewhat negative result—that a certain energy, wholly unconnected with mere physical health, had been withdrawn. It was more than ambition, I think, for it included intention, desire, self-confidence as well. It was life itself. He was no longer in the Present. He was no longer *here*.

"Some countries give while others take away.... I find Egypt difficult to deal with. I find it ..." and then that simple, uncomplex adjective— "strong." In memory and experience the entire globe was mapped for him; it remained for Egypt, then, to teach him this marvellous new thing. But not Egypt of to-day; it was vanished Egypt that had robbed him of his strength. He had described it as underground, hidden, waiting.... I was again aware of a faint shuddering—as though something crept secretly from my inmost heart to share the experience with him, and as though my sympathy involved a willing consent that this should be so. With sympathy there must always be a shedding of the personal self; each time I felt this sympathy, it seemed that something left me. I thought in circles, arriving at no definite point where I could rest and say "that's it; I understand." The giving attitude of a country was easily comprehensible; but this idea of robbery, of deprivation baffled me. An obscure alarm took hold of me—for myself as well as for him.

At dinner, where he invited me to his table, the impression passed off a good deal, however, and I convicted myself of a woman's exaggeration; yet, as we talked of many a day's adventure together in other lands, it struck me that we oddly left the present out. We ignored today. His thoughts, as it were, went most easily backwards. And each adventure led, as by its own natural weight and impetus, towards one thing—the enormous glory of a vanished age. Ancient Egypt was "home" in this mysterious game life played with death. The specific gravity of his being, to say nothing for the moment of my own, had shifted lower, farther off, backwards and below, or as he put it—underground. The sinking sensation I experienced was of a literal kind....

And so I found myself wondering what had led him to this particular hotel. I had come out with an affected organ the specialist promised me would heal in the marvellous air of Helouan, but it was queer that my companion also should have chosen it. Its *clientele* was mostly invalid, German and Russian invalid at that. The Management set its face against the lighter, gayer side of life that hotels in Egypt usually encourage eagerly. It was a true rest-house, a place of repose and leisure, a place where one could remain undiscovered and unknown. No English patronised it. One might easily— the idea came unbidden, suddenly—hide in it.

"Then you're doing nothing just now," I asked, "in the way of digging? No big expeditions or excavating at the moment?"

"I'm recuperating," he answered carelessly. "I've have had two years up at the Valley of the Kings, and overdid it rather. But I'm by way of working at a little thing near here across the Nile." And he pointed in the direction of Sakkhara, where the huge Memphian cemetery stretches underground from the Dachur Pyramids to the Gizeh monsters, four miles lower down. "There's a matter of a hundred years in that alone!"

"You must have accumulated a mass of interesting material. I suppose later you'll make use of it—a book or——"

His expression stopped me—that strange look in the eyes that had stirred my first uneasiness. It was as if something struggled up a moment, looked bleakly out upon the present, then sank away again.

"More," he answered listlessly, "than I can ever use. It's much more likely to use me." He said it hurriedly, looking over his shoulder as though some one might be listening, then smiled significantly, bringing his eyes back upon my own again. I told him that he was far too modest. "If all the excavators thought like that," I added, "we ignorant ones should suffer." I laughed, but the laughter was only on my lips.

He shook his head indifferently. "They do their best; they do wonders," he replied, making an indescribable gesture as though he withdrew willingly from the topic altogether, yet could not quite achieve it. "I know their books; I know the writers too—of various nationalities." He paused a moment, and his eyes turned grave. "I cannot understand quite—how they do it," he added half below his breath.

"The labour, you mean? The strain of the climate, and so forth?" I said this purposely, for I knew quite well he meant another thing. The way he looked into my face, however, disturbed me so that I believe I visibly started. Something very deep in me sat up alertly listening, almost on guard.

"I mean," he replied, "that they must have uncommon powers of resistance."

There! He had used the very word that had been hiding in me! "It puzzles me," he went on, "for, with one exception, they are not unusual men. In the way of gifts—oh yes. It's in the way of resistance and protection that I mean. Self-protection," he added with emphasis.

It was the way he said "resistance" and "self-protection" that sent a touch of cold through me. I learned later that he himself had made surprising discoveries in these two years, penetrating closer to the secret life of ancient sacerdotal Egypt than any of his predecessors or co-labourers—then, inexplicably, had ceased. But this was told to me afterwards and by others. At the moment I was only conscious of this odd embarrassment. I did not understand, yet felt that he touched upon something intimately personal to himself. He paused, expecting me to speak.

"Egypt, perhaps, merely pours through them," I ventured. "They give out mechanically, hardly realising how much they give. They report facts devoid of interpretation. Whereas with you it's the actual spirit of the past that is discovered and laid bare. You live it. You feel old Egypt and disclose her. That divining faculty was always yours—uncannily, I used to think."

The flash of his sombre eyes betrayed that my aim was singularly good. It seemed a third had silently joined our little table in the corner. Something intruded, evoked by the power of what our conversation skirted but ever left unmentioned. It was huge and shadowy; it was also watchful. Egypt came gliding, floating up beside us. I saw her reflected in his face and gaze. The desert slipped in through walls and ceiling, rising from beneath our feet, settling about us, listening, peering, waiting. The strange obsession was sudden and complete. The gigantic scale of her swam in among the very pillars, arches, and windows of that modern dining-room. I felt against my skin the touch of chilly air that sunlight never reaches, stealing from beneath the granite monoliths. Behind it came the stifling breath of the heated tombs, of the Serapeum, of the chambers and corridors in the pyramids. There was a rustling as of myriad footsteps far away, and as of sand the busy winds go shifting through the ages. And in startling contrast to this impression of prodigious size, Isley himself wore suddenly an air of strangely dwindling. For a second he shrank visibly before my very eyes. He was receding. His outline seemed to retreat and lessen, as though he stood to the waist in what appeared like flowing mist, only his head and shoulders still above the ground. Far, far away I saw him.

It was a vivid inner picture that I somehow transferred objectively. It was a dramatised sensation, of course. His former phrase "now that I am declining" flashed back upon me with sharp discomfort. Again, perhaps, his state of mind was reflected into me by some emotional telepathy. I waited, conscious of an almost sensible oppression that would not lift. It seemed an age before he spoke, and when he did there was the tremor of feeling in his voice he sought nevertheless to repress. I kept my eyes on the table for some reason. But I listened intently.

"It's you that have the divining faculty, not I," he said, an odd note of distance even in his tone, yet a resonance as though it rose up between reverberating walls. "There is, I believe, something here that resents too close inquiry, or rather that resists discovery—almost—takes offence."

I looked up quickly, then looked down again. It was such a startling thing to hear on the lips of a modern Englishman. He spoke lightly, but the expression of his face belied the careless tone. There was no mockery in those earnest eyes, and in the hushed voice was a little creeping sound that gave me once again the touch of goose-flesh. The only word I can find is "subterranean": all that was mental in him had sunk, so that he seemed speaking underground, head and shoulders alone visible. The effect was almost ghastly.

"Such extraordinary obstacles are put in one's way," he went on, "when the prying gets too close to the—reality; physical, external obstacles, I mean. Either that, or—the mind loses its assimilative faculties. One or other happens—" his voice died down into a whisper— "and discovery ceases of its own accord."

The same minute, then, he suddenly raised himself like a man emerging from a tomb; he leaned across the table; he made an effort of some violent internal kind, on the verge, I fully believe, of a pregnant personal statement. There was confession in his attitude; I think he was about to speak of his work at Thebes and the reason for its abrupt cessation. For I had the feeling of one about to hear a weighty secret, the responsibility unwelcome. This uncomfortable emotion rose in me, as I raised my eyes to his somewhat unwillingly, only to find that I was wholly at fault. It was not me he was looking at. He was staring past me in the direction of the wide, unshuttered windows. The expression of yearning was visible in his eyes again. Something had stopped his utterance.

And instinctively I turned and saw what he saw. So far as external details were concerned, at least, I saw it.

Across the glare and glitter of the uncompromising modern dining-room, past crowded tables, and over the heads of Germans feeding unpicturesquely, I saw—the moon. Her reddish disc, hanging unreal and enormous, lifted the spread sheet of desert till it floated off the surface of the world. The great window faced the east, where the Arabian desert breaks into a ruin of gorges, cliffs, and flat-topped ridges; it looked unfriendly, ominous, with danger in it; unlike the serener sand-dunes of the Libyan desert, there lay both menace and seduction behind its flood of shadows. And the moonlight emphasised this aspect: its ghostly desolation, its cruelty, its bleak hostility, turning it murderous. For no river sweetens this Arabian desert; instead of sandy softness, it has fangs of limestone rock, sharp and aggressive. Across it, just visible in the moonlight as a thread of paler grey, the old camel-trail to Suez beckoned faintly. And it was this that he was looking at so intently.

It was, I know, a theatrical stage-like glimpse, yet in it a seductiveness most potent. "Come out," it seemed to whisper, "and taste my awful beauty. Come out and lose yourself, and die. Come out and follow my moonlit trail into the Past ... where there is peace and immobility and silence. My kingdom is unchanging underground. Come down, come softly, come through sandy corridors below this tinsel of your modern world. Come back, come down into my golden past...."

A poignant desire stole through my heart on moonlit feet; I was personally conscious of a keen yearning to slip away in unresisting obedience. For it was uncommonly impressive, this sudden, haunting glimpse of the world outside. The hairy foreigners, uncouthly garbed, all busily eating in full electric light, provided a sensational contrast of emphatically distressing kind. A touch of what is called unearthly hovered about that distance through the window. There was weirdness in it. Egypt looked in upon us. Egypt watched and listened, beckoning through the moonlit windows of the heart to come and find her. Mind and imagination might flounder as they pleased, but something of this kind happened undeniably, whether expression in language fails to hold the truth or not. And George Isley, aware of being seen, looked straight into the awful visage—fascinated.

Over the bronze of his skin there stole a shade of grey. My own feeling of enticement grew—the desire to go out into the moonlight, to leave my kind and wander blindly through the desert, to see the gorges in their shining silver, and taste the keenness of the cool, sharp air. Further than this with me it did not go, but that my companion felt the bigger, deeper draw behind this surface glamour, I have no reasonable doubt. For a moment, indeed, I thought he meant to leave the table; he had half risen in his chair; it seemed he struggled and resisted—and then his big frame subsided again; he sat back; he looked, in the attitude his body took, less impressive, smaller, actually shrunken into the proportions of some minuter scale. It was as though something in that second had been drawn out of him, decreasing even his physical appearance. The voice, when he spoke presently with a touch of resignation, held a lifeless quality as though deprived of virile timbre.

"It's always there," he whispered, half collapsing back into his chair, "it's always watching, waiting, listening. Almost like a monster of the fables, isn't it? It makes no movement of its own, you see. It's far too strong for that. It just hangs there, half in the air and half upon the earth—a gigantic web. Its prey flies into it. That's Egypt all over. D'you feel like that too, or does it seem to you just imaginative rubbish? To me it seems that she just waits her time; she gets you quicker that way; in the end you're bound to go."

"There's power certainly," I said after a moment's pause to collect my wits, my distress increased by the morbidness of his simile. "For some minds there may be a kind of terror too—for weak temperaments that are all imagination." My thoughts were scattered, and I could not readily find good words. "There is startling grandeur in a sight like that, for instance," and I pointed to the window. "You feel drawn—as if you simply *had* to go." My mind still buzzed with his curious words, "In the end you're bound to go." It betrayed his heart and soul. "I suppose a fly does feel drawn," I added, "or a moth to the destroying flame. Or is it just unconscious on their part?"

He jerked his big head significantly. "Well, well," he answered, "but the fly isn't necessarily weak, or the moth misguided. Over-adventurous, perhaps, yet both obedient to the laws of their respective beings. They get warnings too—only, when the moth wants to know too much, the fire stops it. Both flame and spider enrich themselves by understanding the natures of their prey; and fly and moth return again and again until this is accomplished."

Yet George Isley was as sane as the head waiter who, noticing our interest in the window, came up just then and enquired whether we felt a draught and would prefer it closed. Isley, I realised, was struggling to express a passionate state of soul for which, owing to its rarity, no adequate expression lies at hand. There is a language of the mind, but there is none as yet of the spirit. I felt ill at ease. All this was so foreign to the wholesome, strenuous personality of the man as I remembered it.

"But, my dear fellow," I stammered, "aren't you giving poor old Egypt a bad name she hardly deserves? I feel only the amazing strength and beauty of it; awe, if you like, but none of this resentment you so mysteriously hint at."

"You understand, for all that," he answered quietly; and again he seemed on the verge of some significant confession that might ease his soul. My uncomfortable emotion grew. Certainly he was at high pressure somewhere. "And, if necessary, you could help. Your sympathy, I mean, *is* a help already." He said it half to himself and in a suddenly lowered tone again.

"A help!" I gasped. "My sympathy! Of course, if——"

"A witness," he murmured, not looking at me, "some one who understands, yet does not think me mad."

There was such appeal in his voice that I felt ready and eager to do anything to help him. Our eyes met, and my own tried to express this willingness in me; but what I said I hardly know, for a cloud of confusion was on my mind, and my speech went fumbling like a schoolboy's. I was more than disconcerted. Through this bewilderment, then, I just caught the tail-end of another sentence in which the words "relief it is to have … some one to hold to … when the disappearance comes …" sounded like voices heard in dream. But I missed the complete phrase and shrank from asking him to repeat it.

Some sympathetic answer struggled to my lips, though what it was I know not. The thing I murmured, however, seemed apparently well chosen. He leaned across and laid his big hand a moment on my own with eloquent pressure. It was cold as ice. A look of gratitude passed over his sunburned features. He sighed. And we left the table then and passed into the inner smoking-room for coffee—a room whose windows gave upon columned terraces that allowed no view of the encircling desert. He led the conversation into channels less personal and, thank heaven, less intensely emotional and mysterious. What we talked about I now forget; it was interesting but in another key altogether. His old charm and power worked; the respect I had always felt for his character and gifts returned in force, but it was the pity I now experienced that remained chiefly in my mind. For this change in him became more and more noticeable. He was less impressive, less convincing, less suggestive. His talk, though so knowledgeable, lacked that spiritual quality that drives home. He was uncannily less *real*. And I went up to bed, uneasy and disturbed. "It is not age," I said to myself, "and assuredly it is not death he fears, although he spoke of disappearance. It is mental—in the deepest sense. It is what religious people would call soul. Something is happening to his soul."

IV

And this word "soul" remained with me to the end. Egypt was taking his soul away into the Past. What was of value in *him* went willingly; the rest, some lesser aspect of his mind and character, resisted, holding to the present. A struggle, therefore, was involved. But this was being gradually obliterated too.

How I arrived gaily at this monstrous conclusion seems to me now a mystery; but the truth is that from a conversation one brings away a general idea that is larger than the words actually heard and spoken. I have reported, naturally, but a fragment of what passed between us in language, and of what was suggested—by gesture, expression, silence—merely perhaps a hint. I can only assert that this troubling verdict remained a conviction in my mind. It came upstairs with me; it watched and listened by my side. That mysterious Third evoked in our conversation was bigger than either of us separately; it might be called the spirit of ancient Egypt, or it might be called with equal generalisation, the Past. This Third, at any rate, stood by me, whispering this astounding thing. I went out on to my little balcony to smoke a pipe and enjoy the comforting presence of the stars before turning in. It came out with me. It was everywhere. I heard the barking of dogs, the monotonous beating of a distant drum towards Bedraschien, the sing-song voices of the natives in their booths and down the dim-lit streets. I was aware of this invisible Third behind all these familiar sounds. The enormous night-sky, drowned in stars, conveyed it too. It was in the breath of chilly wind that whispered round the walls, and it brooded everywhere above the sleepless desert. I was alone as little as though George Isley stood beside me in person—and at that moment a moving figure caught my eye below. My window was on the sixth story, but there was no mistaking the tall and soldierly bearing of the man who was strolling past the hotel. George Isley was going slowly out into the desert.

There was actually nothing unusual in the sight. It was only ten o'clock; but for doctor's orders I might have been doing the same myself. Yet, as I leaned over the dizzy ledge and watched him, a chill struck through me, and a feeling nothing could justify, nor pages of writing describe, rose up and mastered me. His words at dinner came back with curious force. Egypt lay round him, motionless, a vast grey web. His feet were caught in it. It quivered. The silvery meshes in the moonlight announced the fact from Memphis up to Thebes, across the Nile, from underground Sakkhara to the Valley of the Kings. A tremor ran over the entire desert, and again, as in the dining-room, the leagues of sand went rustling. It seemed to me that I caught him in the act of disappearing.

I realised in that moment the haunting power of this mysterious still atmosphere which is Egypt, and some magical emanation of its mighty past broke over me suddenly like a wave. Perhaps in that moment I felt what he himself felt; the withdrawing suction of the huge spent wave swept something out of me into the past with it. An indescribable yearning drew something living from my heart, something that longed with a kind of burning, searching sweetness for a glory of spiritual passion that was gone. The pain and happiness of it were more poignant than may be told, and my present personality—

some vital portion of it, at any rate—wilted before the power of its enticement.

I stood there, motionless as stone, and stared. Erect and steady, knowing resistance vain, eager to go yet striving to remain, and half with an air of floating off the ground, he went towards the pale grey thread which was the track to Suez and the far Red Sea. There came upon me this strange, deep sense of pity, pathos, sympathy that was beyond all explanation, and mysterious as a pain in dreams. For a sense of his awful loneliness stole into me, a loneliness nothing on this earth could possibly relieve. Robbed of the Present, he sought this chimera of his soul, an unreal Past. Not even the calm majesty of this exquisite Egyptian night could soothe the dream away; the peace and silence were marvellous, the sweet perfume of the desert air intoxicating; but all these intensified it only.

And though at a loss to explain my own emotion, its poignancy was so real that a sigh escaped me and I felt that tears lay not too far away. I watched him, yet felt I had no right to watch. Softly I drew back from the window with the sensation of eavesdropping upon his privacy; but before I did so I had seen his outline melt away into the dim world of sand that began at the very walls of the hotel. He wore a cloak of green that reached down almost to his heels, and its colour blended with the silvery surface of the desert's dark sea-tint. This sheen first draped and then concealed him. It covered him with a fold of its mysterious garment that, without seam or binding, veiled Egypt for a thousand leagues. The desert took him. Egypt caught him in her web. He was gone.

Sleep for me just then seemed out of the question. The change in him made me feel less sure of myself. To see him thus invertebrate shocked me. I was aware that I had nerves.

For a long time I sat smoking by the window, my body weary, but my imagination irritatingly stimulated. The big sign-lights of the hotel went out; window after window closed below me; the electric standards in the streets were already extinguished; and Helouan looked like a child's white blocks scattered in ruin upon the nursery carpet. It seemed so wee upon the vast expanse. It lay in a twinkling pattern, like a cluster of glow-worms dropped into a negligible crease of the tremendous desert. It peeped up at the stars, a little frightened.

The night was very still. There hung an enormous brooding beauty everywhere, a hint of the sinister in it that only the brilliance of the blazing stars relieved. Nothing really slept. Grouped here and there at intervals about this dun-coloured world stood the everlasting watchers in solemn, tireless guardianship—the soaring Pyramids, the Sphinx, the grim Colossi, the empty temples, the long-deserted tombs. The mind was aware of them, sta-

tioned like sentries through the night. "This is Egypt; you are actually in
Egypt," whispered the silence. "Eight thousand years of history lie fluttering outside your window. She lies there underground, sleepless, mighty,
deathless, not to be trifled with. Beware! Or she will change you too!"

My imagination offered this hint: Egypt is difficult to realise. It remains outside the mind, a fabulous, half-legendary idea. So many enormous elements
together refuse to be assimilated; the heart pauses, asking for time and breath;
the senses reel a little; and in the end a mental torpor akin to stupefaction
creeps upon the brain. With a sigh the struggle is abandoned and the mind
surrenders to Egypt on her own terms. Alone the diggers and archaeologists,
confined to definite facts, offer successful resistance. My friend's use of the
words "resistance" and "protection" became clearer to me. While logic
halted, intuition fluttered round this clue to the solution of the influences at
work. George Isley realised Egypt more than most—but as she had been.

And I recalled its first effect upon myself, and how my mind had been unable to cope with the memory of it afterwards. There had come to its summons
a colossal medley, a gigantic, coloured blur that merely bewildered. Only
lesser points lodged comfortably in the heart. I saw a chaotic vision: sands
drenched in dazzling light, vast granite aisles, stupendous figures that stared
unblinking at the sun, a shining river and a shadowy desert, both endless as
the sky, mountainous pyramids and gigantic monoliths, armies of heads, of
paws, of faces—all set to a scale of size that was prodigious. The items
stunned; the composite effect was too unwieldy to be grasped. Something that
blazed with splendour rolled before the eyes, too close to be seen distinctly—
at the same time very distant—unrealised.

Then, with the passing of the weeks, it slowly stirred to life. It had attacked
unseen; its grip was quite tremendous; yet it could be neither told, nor
painted, nor described. It flamed up unexpectedly—in the foggy London
streets, at the Club, in the theatre. A sound recalled the street-cries of the
Arabs, a breath of scented air brought back the heated sand beyond the
palm groves. Up rose the huge Egyptian glamour, transforming common
things; it had lain buried all this time in deep recesses of the heart that are in-
accessible to ordinary daily life. And there hid in it something of uneasiness
that was inexplicable; awe, a hint of cold eternity, a touch of something unchanging and terrific, something sublime made lovely yet unearthly with
shadowy time and distance. The melancholy of the Nile and the grandeur of
a hundred battered temples dropped some unutterable beauty upon the
heart. Up swept the desert air, the luminous pale shadows, the naked desolation that yet brims with sharp vitality. An Arab on his donkey tripped in
colour across the mind, melting off into tiny perspective, strangely vivid. A
string of camels stood in silhouette against the crimson sky. Great winds, great

blazing spaces, great solemn nights, great days of golden splendour rose from the pavement or the theatre-stall, and London, dim-lit England, the whole of modern life, indeed, seemed suddenly reduced to a paltry insignificance that produced an aching longing for the pageantry of those millions of vanished souls. Egypt rolled through the heart for a moment—and was gone.

I remembered that some such fantastic experience had been mine. Put it as one may, the fact remains that for certain temperaments Egypt can rob the Present of some thread of interest that was formerly there. The memory became for me an integral part of personality; something in me yearned for its curious and awful beauty. He who has drunk of the Nile shall return to drink of it again.... And if for myself this was possible, what might not happen to a character of George Isley's type? Some glimmer of comprehension came to me. The ancient, buried, hidden Egypt had cast her net about his soul. Grown shadowy in the Present, his life was being transferred into some golden, reconstructed Past, where it was real. Some countries give, while others take away. And George Isley was worth robbing....

Disturbed by these singular reflections, I moved away from the open window, closing it. But the closing did not exclude the presence of the Third. The biting night air followed me in. I drew the mosquito curtains round the bed, but the light I left still burning; and, lying there, I jotted down upon a scrap of paper this curious impression as best I could, only to find that it escaped easily between the words. Such visionary and spiritual perceptions are too elusive to be trapped in language. Reading it over after an interval of years, it is difficult to recall with what intense meaning, what uncanny emotion, I wrote those faded lines in pencil. Their rhetoric seems cheap, their content much exaggerated; yet at the time truth burned in every syllable. Egypt, which since time began has suffered robbery with violence at the hands of all the world, now takes her vengeance, choosing her individual prey. Her time has come. Behind a modern mask she lies in wait, intensely active, sure of her hidden power. Prostitute of dead empires, she lies now at peace beneath the same old stars, her loveliness unimpaired, bejewelled with the beaten gold of ages, her breasts uncovered, and her grand limbs flashing in the sun. Her shoulders of alabaster are lifted above the sand-drifts; she surveys the little figures of today. She takes her choice....

That night I did not dream, but neither did the whole of me lie down in sleep. During the long dark hours I was aware of that picture endlessly repeating itself, the picture of George Isley stealing out into the moonlit desert. The night so swiftly dropped her hood about him; so mysteriously he merged into the unchanging thing which cloaks the past. It lifted. Some huge shadowy hand, gloved softly yet of granite, stretched over the leagues to take him. He disappeared.

They say the desert is motionless and has no gestures! That night I saw it moving, hurrying. It went tearing after him. You understand my meaning? No! Well, when excited it produces this strange impression, and the terrible moment is—when you surrender helplessly—you desire it shall swallow you. You let it come. George Isley spoke of a web. It is, at any rate, some central power that conceals itself behind the surface glamour folk call the spell of Egypt. Its home is not apparent. It dwells with ancient Egypt—underground. Behind the stillness of hot windless days, behind the peace of calm, gigantic nights, it lurks unrealised, monstrous and irresistible. My mind grasped it as little as the fact that our solar system with all its retinue of satellites and planets rushes annually many million miles towards a star in Hercules, while yet that constellation appears no closer than it did six thousand years ago. But the clue dropped into me. George Isley, with his entire retinue of thought and life and feeling, was being similarly drawn. And I, a minor satellite, had become aware of the horrifying pull. It was magnificent.... And I fell asleep on the crest of this enormous wave.

V

The next few days passed idly; weeks passed too, I think; hidden away in this cosmopolitan hotel we lived apart, unnoticed. There was the feeling that time went what pace it pleased, now fast, now slow, now standing still. The similarity of the brilliant days, set between wondrous dawns and sunsets, left the impression that it was really one long, endless day without divisions. The mind's machinery of measurement suffered dislocation. Time went backwards; dates were forgotten; the month, the time of year, the century itself went down into undifferentiated life.

The Present certainly slipped away curiously. Newspapers and politics became unimportant, news uninteresting, English life so remote as to be unreal, European affairs shadowy. The stream of life ran in another direction altogether—backwards. The names and faces of friends appeared through mist. People arrived as though dropped from the skies. They suddenly were there; one saw them in the dining-room, as though they had just slipped in from an outer world that once was real—somewhere. Of course, a steamer sailed four times a week, and the journey took five days, but these things were merely known, not realised. The fact that here it was summer, whereas over there winter reigned, helped to make the distance not quite thinkable. We looked at the desert and made plans. "We will do this, we will do that; we must go there, we'll visit such and such a place ..." yet nothing happened. It always was to-morrow or yesterday, and we shared the discovery of Alice that there was no real "to-day." For our thinking made everything happen. That was enough. It *had* happened. It was the reality of dreams. Egypt was a dream-world that made the heart live backwards.

It came about, thus, that for the next few weeks I watched a fading life, myself alert and sympathetic, yet unable somehow to intrude and help. Noticing various little things by which George Isley betrayed the progress of the unequal struggle, I found my assistance negatived by the fact that I was in similar case myself. What he experienced in large and finally, I, too, experienced in little and for the moment. For I seemed also caught upon the fringe of the invisible web. My feelings were entangled sufficiently for me to understand…. And the decline of his being was terrible to watch. His character went with it; I saw his talents fade, his personality dwindle, his very soul dissolve before the insidious and invading influence. He hardly struggled. I thought of those abominable insects that paralyse the motor systems of their victims and then devour them at their leisure—alive. The incredible adventure was literally true, but, being spiritual, may not be told in the terms of a detective story. This version must remain an individual rendering—an aspect of *one* possible version. All who know the real Egypt, that Egypt which has nothing to do with dams and Nationalists and the external welfare of the falaheen, will understand. The pilfering of her ancient dead she suffers still; she, in revenge, preys at her leisure on the living.

The occasions when he betrayed himself were ordinary enough; it was the glimpse they afforded of what was in progress beneath his calm exterior that made them interesting. Once, I remember, we had lunched together at Mena, and, after visiting certain excavations beyond the Gizeh pyramids, we made our way homewards by way of the Sphinx. It was dusk, and the main army of tourists had retired, though some few dozen sight-seers still moved about to the cries of donkey-boys and baksheesh. The vast head and shoulders suddenly emerged, riding undrowned above the sea of sand. Dark and monstrous in the fading light, it loomed, as ever, a being of non-human lineage; no amount of familiarity could depreciate its grandeur, its impressive setting, the lost expression of the countenance that is too huge to focus as a face. A thousand visits leave its power undiminished. It has intruded upon our earth from some uncommon world. George Isley and myself both turned aside to acknowledge the presence of this alien, uncomfortable thing. We did not linger, but we slackened pace. It was the obvious, inevitable thing to do. He pointed then, with a suddenness that made me start. He indicated the tourists standing round.

"See," he said, in a lowered tone, "day and night you'll always find a crowd obedient to that thing. But notice their behaviour. People don't do that before any other ruin in the world I've ever seen." He referred to the attempts of individuals to creep away alone and stare into the stupendous visage by themselves. At different points in the deep sandy basin were men and women, standing solitary, lying, crouching, apart from the main company where the dragomen mouthed their exposition with impertinent glibness.

"The desire to be alone," he went on, half to himself, as we paused a moment, "the sense of worship which insists on privacy."

It was significant, for no amount of advertising could dwarf the impressiveness of the inscrutable visage into whose eyes of stone the silent humans gazed. Not even the red-coat, standing inside one gigantic ear, could introduce the commonplace. But my companion's words let another thing into the spectacle, a less exalted thing, dropping a hint of horror about that sandy cup: It became easy, for a moment, to imagine these tourists worshipping— against their will; to picture the monster noticing that they were there; that it might slowly turn its awful head; that the sand might visibly trickle from a stirring paw; that, in a word, they might be taken—changed.

"Come," he whispered in a dropping tone, interrupting my fancies as though he half divined them, "it is getting late, and to be alone with the thing is intolerable to me just now. But you notice, don't you," he added, as he took my arm to hurry me away, "how little the tourists matter? Instead of injuring the effect, they increase it. It uses *them*."

And again a slight sensation of chill, communicated possibly by his nervous touch, or possibly by his earnest way of saying these curious words, passed through me. Some part of me remained behind in that hollow trough of sand, prostrate before an immensity that symbolised the past. A curious, wild yearning caught me momentarily, an intense desire to understand exactly why that terror stood there, its actual meaning long ago to the hearts that set it waiting for the sun, what definite rôle it played, what souls it stirred and why, in that system of towering belief and faith whose indestructible emblem it still remained. The past stood grouped so solemnly about its menacing presentment. I was distinctly aware of this spiritual suction backwards that my companion yielded to so gladly, yet against his normal, modern self. For it made the past appear magnificently desirable, and loosened all the rivets of the present. It bodied forth three main ingredients of this deep Egyptian spell—size, mystery, and immobility.

Yet, to my relief, the cheaper aspect of this Egyptian glamour left him cold. He remained unmoved by the commonplace mysterious; he told no mummy stories, nor ever hinted at the supernatural quality that leaps to the mind of the majority. There was no play in him. The influence was grave and vital. And, although I knew he held strong views with regard to the impiety of disturbing the dead, he never in my hearing attached any possible revengeful character to the energy of an outraged past. The current tales of this description he ignored; they were for superstitious minds or children; the deities that claimed his soul were of a grander order altogether. He lived, if it may be so expressed, already in a world his heart had reconstructed or remembered; it drew him in another direction altogether; with the modern, sensational view of life his spirit held no traffic any longer; he was living backwards. I saw his figure receding mournfully, yet never sentimentally, into the spacious, golden atmosphere of recaptured days. The enormous soul of buried Egypt drew him down. The dwindling of his physical appearance was, of course, a mental interpretation of my own; but another, stranger interpretation of a spiritual kind moved parallel with it—marvellous and horrible. For, as he diminished outwardly and in his modern, present aspect, he grew within—gigantic. The size of Egypt entered into him. Huge proportions now began to accompany any presentment of his personality to my inner vision. He towered. These two qualities of the land already obsessed him—magnitude and immobility.

And that awe which modern life ignores contemptuously woke in my heart. I almost feared his presence at certain times. For one aspect of the Egyptian spell is explained by sheer size and bulk. Disdainful of mere speed today, the heart is still uncomfortable with magnitude; and in Egypt there is size that may easily appall, for every detail shunts it laboriously upon the mind. It elbows out the present. The desert's vastness is not made comprehensible by mileage, and the sources of the Nile are so distant that they exist less on the map than in the imagination. The effort to realise suffers paralysis; they might equally be in the moon or Saturn. The undecorated magnificence of the desert remains unknown, just as the proportions of pyramid and temple, of pylons and Colossi approach the edge of the mind yet never enter in. All stand outside, clothed in this prodigious measurement of the past. And the old beliefs not only share this titanic effect upon the consciousness, but carry it stages further. The entire scale haunts with uncomfortable immensity, so that the majority run back with relief to the measurable details of a more manageable scale. Express trains, flying machines, Atlantic liners— these produce no unpleasant stretching of the faculties compared to the influence of the Karnak pylons, the pyramids, or the interior of the Serapeum.

Close behind this magnitude, moreover, steps the monstrous. It is revealed not in sand and stone alone, in queer effects of light and shadow, of glittering sunsets and of magical dusks, but in the very aspect of the bird and animal life. The heavy-headed buffaloes betray it equally with the vultures, the myriad kites, the grotesqueness of the mouthing camels. The rude, enormous scenery has it everywhere. There is nothing lyrical in this land of passionate mirages. Uncouth immensity notes the little human flittings. The days roll by in a tide of golden splendour; one goes helplessly with the flood; but it is an irresistible flood that sweeps backwards and below. The silent-footed natives in their coloured robes move before a curtain, and behind that curtain dwells the soul of ancient Egypt—the Reality, as George Isley called it—watching, with sleepless eyes of grey infinity. Then, sometimes the curtain stirs and lifts an edge; an invisible hand creeps forth; the soul is touched. And some one disappears.

VI

The process of disintegration must have been at work a long time before I appeared upon the scene; the changes went forward with such rapidity.

It was his third year in Egypt, two of which had been spent without interruption in company with an Egyptologist named Moleson, in the neighbourhood of Thebes. I soon discovered that this region was for him the centre of attraction, or as he put it, of the web. Not Luxor, of course, nor the images of reconstructed Karnak; but that stretch of grim, forbidding mountains where royalty, earthly and spiritual, sought eternal peace for the physical remains. There, amid surroundings of superb desolation, great priests and mighty kings had thought themselves secure from sacrilegious touch. In caverns underground they kept their faithful tryst with centuries, guarded by the silence of magnificent gloom. There they waited, communing with passing ages in their sleep, till Ra, their glad divinity, should summon them to the fulfilment of their ancient dream. And there, in the Valley of the Tombs of the Kings, their dream was shattered, their lovely prophecies derided, and their glory dimmed by the impious desecration of the curious.

That George Isley and his companion had spent their time, not merely digging and deciphering like their practical *confreres*, but engaged in some strange experiments of recovery and reconstruction, was matter for open comment among the fraternity. That incredible things had happened there was the big story of two Egyptian seasons at least. I heard this later only—tales of utterly incredible kind, that the desolate vale of rock was seen repeopled on moonlit nights, that the smoke of unaccustomed fires rose to cap the flat-topped peaks, that the pageantry of some forgotten worship had been seen to issue from the openings of these hills, and that sounds of chanting, sonorous and marvellously sweet, had been heard to echo from those bleak, repellent precipices. The tales apparently were grossly exaggerated; wandering Bedouins brought them in; the guides and dragomen repeated them with mysterious additions; till they filtered down through the native servants in the hotels and reached the tourists with highly picturesque embroidery. They reached the authorities too. The only accurate fact I gathered at the time, however, was that they had abruptly ceased. George Isley and Moleson, moreover, had parted company. And Moleson, I heard, was the originator of the business. He was, at this time, unknown to me; his arresting book on "A Modern Reconstruction of Sun-worship in Ancient Egypt" being my only link with his unusual mind. Apparently he regarded the sun as the deity of the scientific religion of the future which would replace the various anthropomorphic gods of childish creeds. He discussed the possibility of the zodiacal signs being some kind of Celestial Intelligences. Belief blazed on every page. Men's life is heat, derived solely from the sun, and men were, therefore, part of the sun in the sense that a Christian is part of his personal deity. And absorption was the end. His description of "sun-worship ceremonials" conveyed an amazing reality and beauty. This singular book, however, was all I knew of him until he came to visit us in Helouan, though I easily discerned that his influence somehow was the original cause of the change in my companion.

At Thebes, then, was the active centre of the influence that drew my friend away from modern things. It was there, I easily guessed, that "obstacles" had been placed in the way of these men's too close enquiry. In that haunted and oppressive valley, where profane and reverent come to actual grips, where modern curiosity is most busily organised, and even tourists are aware of a masked hostility that dogs the prying of the least imaginative mind—there, in the neighbourhood of the hundred-gated city, had Egypt set the headquarters of her irreconcilable enmity. And it was there, amid the ruins of her loveliest past, that George Isley had spent his years of magical reconstruction and met the influence that now dominated his entire life.

And though no definite avowal of the struggle betrayed itself in speech between us, I remember fragments of conversation, even at this stage, that proved his willing surrender of the present. We spoke of fear once, though with the indirectness of connection I have mentioned. I urged that the mind, once it is forewarned, can remain master of itself and prevent a thing from happening.

"But that does not make the thing unreal," he objected.

"The mind can deny it," I said. "It then becomes unreal."

He shook his head. "One does not deny an unreality. Denial is a childish act of self-protection against something you expect to happen." He caught my eye a moment. "You deny what you are afraid of," he said. "Fear invites." And he smiled uneasily. "You know it must get you in the end." And, both of us being aware secretly to what our talk referred, it seemed bold-blooded and improper; for actually we discussed the psychology of his disappearance. Yet, while I disliked it, there was a fascination about the subject that compelled attraction…. "Once fear gets in," he added presently, "confidence is undermined, the structure of life is threatened, and you—go gladly. The foundation of everything is belief. A man is what he believes about himself; and in Egypt you can believe things that elsewhere you would not even think about. It attacks the essentials." He sighed, yet with a curious pleasure; and a smile of resignation and relief passed over his rugged features and was gone again. The luxury of abandonment lay already in him.

"But even belief," I protested, "must be founded on some experience or other." It seemed ghastly to speak of his spiritual malady behind the mask of indirect allusion. My excuse was that he so obviously talked willingly.

He agreed instantly. "Experience of one kind or another," he said darkly, "there always is. Talk with the men who live out here; ask any one who thinks, or who has the imagination which divines. You'll get only one reply, phrase it how they may. Even the tourists and the little commonplace officials feel it. And it's not the climate, it's not nerves, it's not any definite tendency that they can name or lay their finger on. Nor is it mere orientalising of the mind. It's something that first takes you from your common life, and that later takes common life from you. You willingly resign an unremunerative Present. There are no half-measures either—once the gates are open."

There was so much undeniable truth in this that I found no corrective by way of strong rejoinder. All my attempts, indeed, were futile in this way. He meant to go; my words could not stop him. He wanted a witness—he dreaded the loneliness of going—but he brooked no interference. The contradictory position involved a perplexing state of heart and mind in both of us. The atmosphere of this majestic land, to-day so trifling, yesterday so immense, most certainly induced a lifting of the spiritual horizon that revealed amazing possibilities.

VII

It was in the windless days of a perfect December that Moleson, the Egyptologist, found us out and paid a flying visit to Helouan. His duties took him up and down the land, but his time seemed largely at his own disposal. He lingered on. His coming introduced a new element I was not quite able to estimate; though, speaking generally, the effect of his presence upon my companion was to emphasise the latter's alteration. It underlined the change, and drew attention to it. The new arrival, I gathered, was not altogether welcome. "I should never have expected to find you *here*," laughed Moleson when they met, and whether he referred to Helouan or to the hotel was not quite clear. I got the impression he meant both; I remembered my fancy that it was a good hotel to hide in. George Isley had betrayed a slight involuntary start when the visiting card was brought to him at tea-time. I think he had wished to escape from his former co-worker. Moleson had found him out. "I heard you had a friend with you and were contemplating further exper—work," he added. He changed the word "experiment" quickly to the other.

"The former, as you see, is true, but not the latter," replied my companion dryly, and in his manner was a touch of opposition that might have been hostility. Their intimacy, I saw, was close and of old standing. In all they said and did and looked, there was an undercurrent of other meaning that just escaped me. They were up to something—they *had* been up to something; but Isley would have withdrawn if he could!

Moleson was an ambitious and energetic personality, absorbed in his profession, alive to the poetical as well as to the practical value of archaeology, and he made at first a wholly delightful impression upon me. An instinctive *flair* for his subject had early in life brought him success and a measure of fame as well. His knowledge was accurate and scholarly, his mind saturated in the lore of a vanished civilisation. Behind an exterior that was quietly careless, I divined a passionate and complex nature, and I watched him with interest as the man for whom the olden sun-worship of unscientific days held some beauty of reality and truth. Much in his strange book that had bewildered me now seemed intelligible when I saw the author. I cannot explain this more closely. Something about him somehow made it possible. Though modern to the finger-tips and thoroughly equipped with all the tendencies of the day, there seemed to hide in him another self that held aloof with a dignified detachment from the interests in which his "educated" mind was centred. He read living secrets beneath museum labels, I might put it. He stepped out of the days of the Pharaohs if ever man did, and I realised early in our acquaintance that this was the man who had exceptional powers of "resistance and self-protection," and was, in his particular branch of work, "unusual." In manner he was light and gay, his sense of humour strong, with a way of treating everything as though laughter was the sanest attitude towards life. There is, however, the laughter that hides—other things. Moleson, as I gathered from many clues of talk and manner and silence, was a deep and singular being. His experiences in Egypt, if any, he had survived admirably. There were at least two Molesons. I felt him more than double——multiple.

In appearance tall, thin, and fleshless, with a dried-up skin and features withered as a mummy's, he said laughingly that Nature had picked him physically for his "job"; and, indeed, one could see him worming his way down narrow tunnels into the sandy tombs, and writhing along sunless passages of suffocating heat without too much personal inconvenience. Something sinuous, almost fluid in his mind expressed itself in his body too. He might go in any direction without causing surprise. He might go backwards or forwards. He might go in two directions at once.

And my first impression of the man deepened before many days were past. There was irresponsibility in him, insincerity somewhere, almost want of heart. His morality was certainly not to-day's, and the mind in him was slippery. I think the modern world, to which he was unattached, confused and irritated him. A sense of insecurity came with him. His interest in George Isley was the interest in a psychological "specimen." I remembered how in his book he described the selection of individuals for certain functions of that marvellous worship, and the odd idea flashed through me—well, that Isley exactly suited some purpose of his re-creating energies. The man was keenly observant from top to toe, but not with his sight alone; he seemed to be aware of motives and emotions before he noticed the acts or gestures that these caused. I felt that he took me in as well. Certainly he eyed me up and down by means of this inner observation that seemed automatic with him.

Moleson was not staying in our hotel; he had chosen one where social life was more abundant; but he came up frequently to lunch and dine, and sometimes spent the evening in Isley's rooms, amusing us with his skill upon the piano, singing Arab songs, and chanting phrases from the ancient Egyptian rituals to rhythms of his own invention. The old Egyptian music, both in harmony and melody, was far more developed than I had realised, the use of sound having been of radical importance in their ceremonies. The chanting in particular he did with extraordinary effect, though whether its success lay in his sonorous voice, his peculiar increasing of the vowel sounds, or in anything deeper, I cannot pretend to say. The result at any rate was of a unique description. It brought buried Egypt to the surface; the gigantic Presence entered sensibly into the room. It came, huge and gorgeous, rolling upon the mind the instant he began, and something in it was both terrible and oppressive. The repose of eternity lay in the sound. Invariably, after a few moments of that transforming music, I saw the Valley of the Kings, the deserted temples, titanic faces of stone, great effigies coifed with zodiacal signs, but above all—the twin Colossi.

I mentioned this latter detail.

"Curious *you* should feel that too—curious you should say it, I mean," Moleson replied, not looking at me, yet with an air as if I had said something he expected. "To me the Memnon figures express Egypt better than all the other monuments put together. Like the desert, they are featureless. They sum her up, as it were, yet leave the message unuttered. For, you see, they cannot." He laughed a little in his throat. "They have neither eyes nor lips nor nose; their features are gone."

"Yet they tell the secret—to those who care to listen," put in Isley in a scarcely noticeable voice. "Just because they have no words. They still sing at dawn," he added in a louder, almost a challenging tone. It startled me.

Moleson turned round at him, opened his lips to speak, hesitated, stopped. He said nothing for a moment. I cannot describe what it was in the lightning glance they exchanged that put me on the alert for something other than was obvious. My nerves quivered suddenly, and a breath of colder air stole in among us. Moleson swung round to me again. "I almost think," he said, laughing when I complimented him upon the music, "that I must have been a priest of Aton-Ra in an earlier existence, for all this comes to my finger-tips as if it were instinctive knowledge. Plotinus, remember, lived a few miles away at Alexandria with his great idea that knowledge is recollection," he said, with a kind of cynical amusement. "In those days, at any rate," he added more significantly, "worship was real and ceremonials actually expressed great ideas and teaching. There was power in them." Two of the Molesons spoke in that contradictory utterance.

I saw that Isley was fidgeting where he sat, betraying by certain gestures that uneasiness was in him. He hid his face a moment in his hands; he sighed; he made a movement—as though to prevent something coming. But Moleson resisted his attempt to change the conversation, though the key shifted a little of its own accord. There were numerous occasions like this when I was aware that both men skirted something that had happened, something that Moleson wished to resume, but that Isley seemed anxious to postpone.

I found myself studying Moleson's personality, yet never getting beyond a certain point. Shrewd, subtle, with an acute rather than a large intelligence, he was cynical as well as insincere, and yet I cannot describe by what means I arrived at two other conclusions as well about him: first, that this insincerity and want of heart had not been so always; and, secondly, that he sought social diversion with deliberate and un-ordinary purpose. I could well believe that the first was Egypt's mark upon him, and the second an effort at resistance and self-protection.

"If it wasn't for the gaiety," he remarked once in a flippant way that thinly hid significance, "a man out here would go under in a year. Social life gets rather reckless—exaggerated—people do things they would never dream of doing at home. Perhaps you've noticed it," he added, looking suddenly at me; "Cairo and the rest—they plunge at it as though driven—a sort of excess about it somewhere." I nodded agreement. The way he said it was unpleasant rather. "It's an antidote," he said, a sub-acid flavour in his tone. "I used to loathe society myself. But now I find gaiety—a certain irresponsible excitement—of importance. Egypt gets on the nerves after a bit. The moral fibre fails. The will grows weak." And he glanced covertly at Isley as with a desire to point his meaning. "It's the clash between the ugly present and the majestic past, perhaps." He smiled.

Isley shrugged his shoulders, making no reply; and the other went on to tell stories of friends and acquaintances whom Egypt had adversely affected: Barton, the Oxford man, school teacher, who had insisted in living in a tent until the Government relieved him of his job. He took to his tent, roamed the desert, drawn irresistibly, practical considerations of the present of no avail. This yearning took him, though he could never define the exact attraction. In the end his mental balance was disturbed. "But now he's all right again; I saw him in London only this year; he can't say what he felt or why he did it. Only—he's different." Of John Lattin, too, he spoke, whom agoraphobia caught so terribly in Upper Egypt; of Malahide, upon whom some fascination of the Nile induced suicidal mania and attempts at drowning; of Jim Moleson, a cousin (who had camped at Thebes with himself and Isley), whom megalomania of a most singular type attacked suddenly in a sandy waste—all radically cured as soon as they left Egypt, yet, one and all, changed and made otherwise in their very souls.

He talked in a loose, disjointed way, and though much he said was fantastic, as if meant to challenge opposition, there was impressiveness about it somewhere, due, I think, to a kind of cumulative emotion he produced.

"The monuments do not impress merely by their bulk, but by their majestic symmetry," I remember him saying. "Look at the choice of form alone—the Pyramids, for instance. No other shape was possible: dome, square, spires, all would have been hideously inadequate. The wedge-shaped mass, immense foundations and pointed apex were the *mot juste* in outline. Do you think people without greatness in themselves chose that form? There was no unbalance in the minds that conceived the harmonious and magnificent structures of the temples. There was stately grandeur in their consciousness that could only be born of truth and knowledge. The power in their images is a direct expression of eternal and essential things they knew."

We listened in silence. He was off upon his hobby. But behind the careless tone and laughing questions there was this lurking passionateness that made me feel uncomfortable. He was edging up, I felt, towards some climax that meant life and death to himself and Isley. I could not fathom it. My sympathy let me in a little, yet not enough to understand completely. Isley, I saw, was also uneasy, though for reasons that equally evaded me.

"One can almost believe," he continued, "that something still hangs about in the atmosphere from those olden times." He half closed his eyes, but I caught the gleam in them. "It affects the mind through the imagination. With some it changes the point of view. It takes the soul back with it to former, quite different, conditions, that must have been almost another kind of consciousness."

He paused an instant and looked up at us. "The *intensity* of belief in those days," he resumed, since neither of us accepted the challenge, "was amazing—something quite unknown anywhere in the world to-day. It was so sure, so positive; no mere speculative theories, I mean; as though something in the climate, the exact position beneath the stars, the 'attitude' of this particular stretch of earth in relation to the sun—thinned the veil between humanity—and other things. Their hierarchies of gods, you know, were not mere idols; animals, birds, monsters, and what-not, all typified spiritual forces and powers that influenced their daily life. But the strong thing is—they knew. People who were scientific as they were did not swallow foolish superstitions. They made colours that could last six thousand years, even in the open air; and without instruments they measured accurately—an enormously difficult and involved calculation—the precession of the equinoxes. You've been to Denderah?"—he suddenly glanced again at me. "No! Well, the minds that realised the zodiacal signs could hardly believe, you know, that Hathor was a cow!"

Isley coughed. He was about to interrupt, but before he could find words, Moleson was off again, some new quality in his tone and manner that was almost aggressive. The hints he offered seemed more than hints. There was a strange conviction in his heart. I think he was skirting a bigger thing that he and his companion knew, yet that his real object was to see in how far I was open to attack—how far my sympathy might be with them. I became aware that he and George Isley shared this bigger thing. It was based, I felt, on some certain knowledge that experiment had brought them.

"Think of the grand teaching of Aknahton, that young Pharaoh who regenerated the entire land and brought it to its immense prosperity. He taught the worship of the sun, but not of the visible sun. The deity had neither form nor shape. The great disk of glory was but the manifestation, each beneficent ray ending in a hand that blessed the world. It was a god of everlasting energy, love and power, yet men could know it at first hand in their daily lives, worshipping it at dawn and sunset with passionate devotion. No anthropomorphic idol masqueraded in *that!*"

An extraordinary glow was about him as he said it. The same minute he lowered his voice, shifting the key perceptibly. He kept looking up at me through half-closed eyelids.

"And another thing they wonderfully knew," he almost whispered, "was that, with the precession of their deity across the equinoctial changes, there came new powers down into the world of men. Each cycle—each zodiacal sign—brought its special powers which they quickly typified in the monstrous effigies we label to-day in our dull museums. Each sign took some two thousand years to traverse. Each sign, moreover, involved a change in human consciousness. There was this relation between the heavens and the human heart. All that they knew. While the sun crawled through the sign of Taurus, it was the Bull they worshipped; with Aries, it was the ram that coifed their granite symbols. Then came, as you remember, with Pisces the great New Arrival, when already they sank from their grand zenith, and the Fish was taken as the emblem of the changing powers which the Christ embodied. For the human soul, they held, echoed the changes in the immense journey of the original deity, who is its source, across the Zodiac, and the truth of "As above, so Below" remains the key to all manifested life. And to-day the sun, just entering Aquarius, new powers are close upon the world. The old—that which has been for two thousand years—again is crumbling, passing, dying. New powers and a new consciousness are knocking at our doors. It is a time of change. It is also"—he leaned forward so that his eyes came close before me— "the time to make the change. The soul can choose its own conditions. It can——"

A sudden crash smothered the rest of the sentence. A chair had fallen with a clatter upon the wooden floor where the carpet left it bare. Whether Isley in rising had stumbled against it, or whether he had purposely knocked it over, I could not say. I only knew that he had abruptly risen and as abruptly sat down again. A curious feeling came to me that the sign was somehow pre-arranged. It was so sudden. His voice, too, was forced, I thought.

"Yes, but we can do without all that, Moleson," he interrupted with acute abruptness. "Suppose we have a tune instead."

VIII

It was after dinner in his private room, and he had sat very silent in his corner until this sudden outburst. Moleson got up quietly without a word and moved over to the piano. I saw—or was it imagination merely?—a new expression slide upon his withered face. He meant mischief somewhere.

From that instant—from the moment he rose and walked over the thick carpet—he fascinated me. The atmosphere his talk and stories had brought remained. His lean fingers ran over the keys, and at first he played fragments from popular musical comedies that were pleasant enough, but made no demand upon the attention. I heard them without listening. I was thinking of another thing—his walk. For the way he moved across those few feet of carpet had power in it. He looked different; he seemed another man; he was changed. I saw him curiously—as I sometimes now saw Isley too—bigger. In some manner that was both enchanting and oppressive, his presence from that moment drew my imagination as by an air of authority it held.

I left my seat in the far corner and dropped into a chair beside the window, nearer to the piano. Isley, I then noticed, had also turned to watch him. But it was George Isley not quite as he was now. I felt rather than saw the change. Both men had subtly altered. They seemed extended, their outlines shadowy.

Isley, alert and anxious, glanced up at the player, his mind of earlier years—for the expression of his face was plain—following the light music, yet with difficulty that involved effort, almost struggle. "Play that again, will you?" I heard him say from time to time. He was trying to take hold of it, to climb back to a condition where that music had linked him to the present, to seize a mental structure that was gone, to grip hold tightly of it—only to find that it was too far forgotten and too fragile. It would not bear him. I am sure of it, and I can swear I divined his mood. He fought to realise himself as he had been, but in vain. In his dim corner opposite I watched him closely. The big black Blüthner blocked itself between us. Above it swayed the outline, lean and half shadowy, of Moleson as he played. A faint whisper floated through the room. "You are in Egypt." Nowhere else could this queer feeling of presentiment, of anticipation, have gained a footing so easily. I was aware of intense emotion in all three of us. The least reminder of To-day seemed ugly. I longed for some ancient forgotten splendour that was lost.

The scene fixed my attention very steadily, for I was aware of something deliberate and calculated on Moleson's part. The thing was well considered in his mind, intention only half concealed. It was Egypt he interpreted by sound, expressing what in him was true, then observing its effect, as he led us cleverly towards—the past. Beginning with the present, he played persuasively, with penetration, with insistent meaning too. He had that touch which conjured up real atmosphere, and, at first, that atmosphere termed modern. He rendered vividly the note of London, passing from the jingles of musical comedy, nervous rag-times and sensuous Tango dances, into the higher strains of concert rooms and "cultured" circles. Yet not too abruptly. Most dexterously he shifted the level, and with it our emotion. I recognised, as in a parody, various ultra-modern thrills: the tumult of Strauss, the pagan sweetness of primitive Debussy, the weirdness and ecstasy of metaphysical Scriabin. The composite note of To-day in both extremes, he brought into this private sitting-room of the desert hotel, while George Isley, listening keenly, fidgeted in his chair.

"'Apres-midi d'un Faune,'" said Moleson dreamily, answering the question as to what he played. "Debussy's, you know. And the thing before it was from 'Til Eulenspiegel'—Strauss, of course."

He drawled, swaying slowly with the rhythm, and leaving pauses between the words. His attention was not wholly on his listener, and in the voice was a quality that increased my uneasy apprehension. I felt distress for Isley somewhere. Something, it seemed, was coming; Moleson brought it. Unconsciously in his walk, it now appeared consciously in his music; and it came from what was underground in him. A charm, a subtle change, stole oddly over the room. It stole over my heart as well. Some power of estimating left me, as though my mind were slipping backwards and losing familiar, common standards.

"The true modern note in it, isn't there?" he drawled; "cleverness, I think—intellectual—surface ingenuity—no depth or permanence—just the sensational brilliance of To-day." He turned and stared at me fixedly an instant. "Nothing *everlasting*," he added impressively. "It tells everything it knows—because it's small enough——"

And the room turned pettier as he said it; another, bigger shadow draped its little walls. Through the open windows came a stealthy gesture of eternity. The atmosphere stretched visibly. Moleson was playing a marvellous fragment from Scriabin's "Prometheus." It sounded thin and shallow. This modern music, all of it, was out of place and trivial. It was almost ridiculous. The scale of our emotion changed insensibly into a deeper thing that has no name in dictionaries, being of another age. And I glanced at the windows where stone columns framed dim sections of great Egypt listening outside. There was no moon; only deep draughts of stars blazed, hanging in the sky. I thought with awe of the mysterious knowledge that vanished people had of these stars, and of the Sun's huge journey through the Zodiac....

And, with astonishing suddenness as of dream, there rose a pictured image against that starlit sky. Lifted into the air, between heaven and earth, I saw float swiftly past a panorama of the stately temples, led by Denderah, Edfu, Abou Simbel. It paused, it hovered, it disappeared. Leaving incalculable solemnity behind it in the air, it vanished, and to see so vast a thing move at that easy yet unhasting speed unhinged some sense of measurement in me. It was, of course, I assured myself, mere memory objectified owing to something that the music summoned, yet the apprehension rose in me that the whole of Egypt presently would stream past in similar fashion—Egypt as she was in the zenith of her unrecoverable past. Behind the tinkling of the modern piano passed the rustling of a multitude, the tramping of countless feet on sand.... It was singularly vivid. It arrested in me something that normally went flowing.... And when I turned my head towards the room to call attention to my strange experience, the eyes of Moleson, I saw, were laid upon my own. He stared at me. The light in them transfixed me, and I understood that the illusion was due in some manner to his evocation. Isley rose at the same moment from his chair. The thing I had vaguely been expecting had shifted closer. And the same moment the musician abruptly changed his key.

"You may like this better," he murmured, half to himself, but in tones he somehow made echoing. "It's more suited to the place." There was a resonance in the voice as though it emerged from hollows underground. "The other seems almost sacrilegious—here." And his voice drawled off in the rhythm of slower modulations that he played. It had grown muffled. There was an impression, too, that he did not strike the piano, but that the music issued from himself.

"Place! What place?" asked Isley quickly. His head turned sharply as he spoke. His tone, in its remoteness, made me tremble.

The musician laughed to himself. "I meant that this hotel seems really an impertinence," he murmured, leaning down upon the notes he played upon so softly and so well; "and that it's but the thinnest kind of pretence—when you come to think of it. We are in the desert really. The Colossi are outside, and all the emptied temples. Or ought to be," he added, raising his tone abruptly with a glance at me.

He straightened up and stared out into the starry sky past George Isley's shoulders.

"That," he exclaimed with betraying vehemence, "is where we are and what we play to!" His voice suddenly increased; there was a roar in it. "That," he repeated, "is the thing that takes our hearts away." The volume of intonation was astonishing.

For the way he uttered the monosyllable suddenly revealed the man beneath the outer sheath of cynicism and laughter, explained his heartlessness, his secret stream of life. He, too, was soul and body in the past. "That" revealed more than pages of descriptive phrases. His heart lived in the temple aisles, his mind unearthed forgotten knowledge; his soul had clothed itself anew in the seductive glory of antiquity: he dwelt with a quickening magic of existence in the reconstructed splendour of what most term only ruins. He and George Isley together had revivified a power that enticed them backwards; but whereas the latter struggled still, the former had already made his permanent home there. The faculty in me that saw the vision of streaming temples saw also this—remorselessly definite. Moleson himself sat naked at that piano. I saw him clearly then. He no longer masqueraded behind his sneers and laughter. He, too, had long ago surrendered, lost himself, gone out, and from the place his soul now dwelt in he watched George Isley sinking down to join him. He lived in ancient, subterranean Egypt. This great hotel stood precariously on the merest upper crust of desert. A thousand tombs, a hundred temples lay outside, within reach almost of our very voices. Moleson was merged with "that."

This intuition flashed upon me like the picture in the sky; and both were true.

And, meanwhile, this other thing he played had a surge of power in it impossible to describe. It was sombre, huge and solemn. It conveyed the power that his walk conveyed. There was distance in it, but a distance not of space alone. A remoteness of time breathed through it with that strange sadness and melancholy yearning that enormous interval brings. It marched, but very far away; it held refrains that assumed the rhythms of a multitude the centuries muted; it sang, but the singing was underground in passages that fine sand muffled. Lost, wandering winds sighed through it, booming. The contrast, after the modern, cheaper music, was dislocating. Yet the change had been quite naturally effected.

"It would sound empty and monotonous elsewhere—in London, for instance," I heard Moleson drawling, as he swayed to and fro, "but here it is big and splendid—true. You hear what I mean," he added gravely. "You understand?"

"What is it?" asked Isley thickly, before I could say a word. "I forget exactly. It has tears in it—more than I can bear." The end of his sentence died away in his throat.

Moleson did not look at him as he answered. He looked at me.

"You surely ought to know," he replied, the voice rising and falling as though the rhythm forced it. "You have heard it all before—that chant from the ritual we——"

Isley sprang up and stopped him. I did not hear the sentence complete. An extraordinary thought blazed into me that the voices of both men were not quite their own. I fancied—wild, impossible as it sounds—that I heard the twin Colossi singing to each other in the dawn. Stupendous ideas sprang past me, leaping. It seemed as though eternal symbols of the cosmos, discovered and worshipped in this ancient land, leaped into awful life. My consciousness became enveloping. I had the distressing feeling that ages slipped out of place and took me with them; they dominated me; they rushed me off my feet like water. I was drawn backwards. I, too, was changing—being changed.

"I remember," said Isley softly, a reverence of worship in his voice. But there was anguish in it too, and pity; he let the present go completely from him; the last strands severed with a wrench of pain. I imagined I heard his soul pass weeping far away—below.

"I'll sing it," murmured Moleson, "for the voice is necessary. The sound and rhythm are utterly divine!"

IX

And forthwith his voice began a series of long-drawn cadences that seemed somehow the root-sounds of every tongue that ever was. A spell came over me I could touch and feel. A web encompassed me; my arms and feet became entangled; a veil of fine threads wove across my eyes. The enthralling power of the rhythm produced some magical movement in the soul. I was aware of life everywhere about me, far and near, in the dwellings of the dead, as also in the corridors of the iron hills. Thebes stood erect, and Memphis teemed upon the river banks. For the modern world fell, swaying, at this sound that restored the past, and in this past both men before me lived and had their being. The storm of present life passed o'er their heads, while they dwelt underground, obliterated, gone. Upon the wave of sound they went down into their recovered kingdom.

I shivered, moved vigorously, half rose up, then instantly sank back again, resigned and helpless. For I entered by their side, it seemed, the conditions of their strange captivity. My thoughts, my feelings, my point of view were transplanted to another centre. Consciousness shifted in me. I saw things from another's point of view—antiquity's.

The present forgotten but the past supreme, I lost Reality. Our room became a pin-point picture seen in a drop of water, while this subterranean world, replacing it, turned immense. My heart took on the gigantic, leisured stride of what had been. Proportions grew; size captured me; and magnitude, turned monstrous, swept mere measurement away. Some hand of golden sunshine picked me up and set me in the quivering web beside those other two. I heard the rustle of the settling threads; I heard the shuffling of the feet in sand; I heard the whispers in the dwellings of the dead. Behind the monotony of this sacerdotal music I heard them in their dim carved chambers. The ancient galleries were awake. The Life of unremembered ages stirred in multitudes about me.

The reality of so incredible an experience evaporates through the stream of language. I can only affirm this singular proof—that the deepest, most satisfying knowledge the Present could offer seemed insignificant beside some stalwart majesty of the Past that utterly usurped it. This modern room, holding a piano and two figures of To-day, appeared as a paltry miniature pinned against a vast transparent curtain, whose foreground was thick with symbols of temple, sphinx and pyramid, but whose background of stupendous hanging grey slid off towards a splendour where the cities of the Dead shook off their sand and thronged space to its ultimate horizons…. The stars, the entire universe, vibrating and alive, became involved in it. Long periods of time slipped past me. I seemed living ages ago…. I was living backwards….

The size and eternity of Egypt took me easily. There was an overwhelming grandeur in it that elbowed out all present standards. The whole place towered and stood up. The desert reared, the very horizons lifted; majestic figures of granite rose above the hotel, great faces hovered and drove past; huge arms reached up to pluck the stars and set them in the ceilings of the labyrinthine tombs. The colossal meaning of the ancient land emerged through all its ruined details ... reconstructed—burningly alive....

It became at length unbearable. I longed for the droning sounds to cease, for the rhythm to lessen its prodigious sweep. My heart cried out for the gold of the sunlight on the desert, for the sweet air by the river's banks, for the violet lights upon the hills at dawn. And I resisted, I made an effort to return.

"Your chant is horrible. For God's sake, let's have an Arab song—or the music of To-day!"

The effort was intense, the result was—nothing. I swear I used these words. I heard the actual sound of my voice, if no one else did, for I remember that it was pitiful in the way great space devoured it, making of its appreciable volume the merest whisper as of some bird or insect cry. But the figure that I took for Moleson, instead of answer or acknowledgment, merely grew and grew as things grow in a fairy tale. I hardly know; I certainly cannot say. That dwindling part of me which offered comments on the entire occurrence noted this extraordinary effect as though it happened naturally—that Moleson himself was marvellously increasing.

The entire spell became operative all at once. I experienced both the delight of complete abandonment and the terror of letting go what *had* seemed real. I understood Moleson's sham laughter, and the subtle resignation of George Isley. And an amazing thought flashed birdlike across my changing consciousness—that this resurrection into the Past, this rebirth of the spirit which they sought, involved taking upon themselves the guise of these ancient symbols each in turn. As the embryo assumes each evolutionary stage below it before the human semblance is attained, so the souls of those two adventurers took upon themselves the various emblems of that intense belief. The devout worshipper takes on the qualities of his deity. They wore the entire series of the old-world gods so potently that I perceived them, and even objectified them by my senses. The present was their pre-natal stage; to enter the past they were being born again.

But it was not Moleson's semblance alone that took on this awful change. Both faces, scaled to the measure of Egypt's outstanding quality of size, became in this little modern room distressingly immense. Distorting mirrors can suggest no simile, for the symmetry of proportion was not injured. I lost their human physiognomies. I saw their thoughts, their feelings, their augmented, altered hearts, the thing that Egypt put there while she stole their love from modern life. There grew an awful stateliness upon them that was huge, mysterious, and motionless as stone.

For Moleson's narrow face at first turned hawk-like in the semblance of the sinister deity, Horus, only stretched to tower above the toy-scaled piano; it was keen and sly and monstrous after prey, while a swiftness of the sunrise leaped from both the brilliant eyes. George Isley, equally immense of outline, was in general presentment more magnificent, a breadth of the Sphinx about his spreading shoulders, and in his countenance an inscrutable power of calm temple images. These were the first signs of obsession; but others followed. In rapid series, like lantern-slides upon a screen, the ancient symbols flashed one after another across these two extended human faces and were gone. Disentanglement became impossible. The successive signatures seemed almost superimposed as in a composite photograph, each appearing and vanished before recognition was even possible, while I interpreted the inner alchemy by means of outer tokens familiar to my senses. Egypt, possessing them, expressed herself thus marvellously in their physical aspect, using the symbols of her intense, regenerative power....

The changes merged with such swiftness into one another that I did not seize the half of them—till, finally, the procession culminated in a single one that remained fixed awfully upon them both. The entire series merged. I was aware of this single masterful image which summed up all the others in sublime repose. The gigantic thing rose up in this incredible statue form. The spirit of Egypt synthesised in this monstrous symbol, obliterated them both. I saw the seated figures of the grim Colossi, dipped in sand, night over them, waiting for the dawn....

X

I made a violent effort, then, at self-assertion—an effort to focus my mind upon the present. And, searching for Moleson and George Isley, its nearest details, I was aware that I could not find them. The familiar figures of my two companions were not discoverable.

I saw it as plainly as I also saw that ludicrous, wee piano—for a moment. But the moment remained; the Eternity of Egypt stayed. For that lonely and terrific pair had stooped their shoulders and bowed their awful heads. They were in the room. They imaged forth the power of the everlasting Past through the little structures of two human worshippers. Room, walls, and ceiling fled away. Sand and the open sky replaced them.

The two of them rose side by side before my bursting eyes. I knew not where to look. Like some child who confronts its giants upon the nursery floor, I turned to stone, unable to think or move. I stared. Sight wrenched itself to find the men familiar to it, but found instead this symbolising vision. I could not see them properly. Their faces were spread with hugeness, their features lost in some uncommon magnitude, their shoulders, necks, and arms grown vast upon the air. As with the desert, there was physiognomy yet no personal expression, the human thing all drowned within the mass of battered stone. I discovered neither cheeks nor mouth nor jaw, but ruined eyes and lips of broken granite. Huge, motionless, mysterious, Egypt informed them and took them to herself. And between us, curiously presented in some false perspective, I saw the little symbol of To-day—the Blüthner piano. It was appalling. I knew a second of majestic horror. I blenched. Hot and cold gushed through me. Strength left me, power of speech and movement too, as in a moment of complete paralysis.

The spell, moreover, was not within the room alone; it was outside and everywhere. The Past stood massed about the very walls of the hotel. Distance, as well as time, stepped nearer. That chanting summoned the gigantic items in all their ancient splendour. The shadowy concourse grouped itself upon the sand about us, and I was aware that the great army shifted noiselessly into place; that pyramids soared and towered; that deities of stone stood by; that temples ranged themselves in reconstructed beauty, grave as the night of time whence they emerged; and that the outline of the Sphinx, motionless but aggressive, piled its dim bulk upon the atmosphere. Immensity answered to immensity.... There were vast intervals of time and there were reaches of enormous distance, yet all happened in a moment, and all happened within a little space. It was now and here. Eternity whispered in every second as in every grain of sand. Yet, while aware of so many stupendous details all at once, I was really aware of one thing only—that the spirit of ancient Egypt faced me in these two terrific figures, and that my consciousness, stretched painfully yet gloriously, included all, as She also unquestionably included them—and me.

For it seemed I shared the likeness of my two companions. Some lesser symbol, though of similar kind, obsessed me too. I tried to move, but my feet were set in stone; my arms lay fixed; my body was embedded in the rock. Sand beat sharply upon my outer surface, urged upwards in little flurries by a chilly wind. There was nothing felt: I *heard* the rattle of the scattering grains against my hardened body....

And we waited for the dawn; for the resurrection of that unchanging deity who was the source and inspiration of all our glorious life.... The air grew keen and fresh. In the distance a line of sky turned from pink to violet and gold; a delicate rose next flushed the desert; a few pale stars hung fainting overhead; and the wind that brought the sunrise was already stirring. The whole land paused upon the coming of its mighty God....

Into the pause there rose a curious sound for which we had been waiting. For it came familiarly, as though expected. I could have sworn at first that it was George Isley who sang, answering his companion. There beat behind its great volume the same note and rhythm, only so prodigiously increased that, while Moleson's chant had waked it, it now was independent and apart. The resonant vibrations of what he sang had reached down into the places where it slept. *They* uttered synchronously. Egypt spoke. There was in it the deep muttering as of a thousand drums, as though the desert uttered in prodigious syllables. I listened while my heart of stone stood still. There were two voices in the sky. *They* spoke tremendously with each other in the dawn:

"So easily we still remain possessors of the land.... While the centuries roar past us and are gone."

Soft with power the syllables rolled forth, yet with a booming depth as though caverns underground produced them.

"Our silence is disturbed. Pass on with the multitude towards the East.... Still in the dawn we sing the old-world wisdom.... They shall hear our speech, yet shall not hear it with their ears of flesh. At dawn our words go forth, searching the distances of sand and time across the sunlight.... At dusk they return, as upon eagles' wings, entering again our lips of stone.... Each century one syllable, yet no sentence yet complete. While our lips are broken with the utterance...."

It seemed that hours and months and years went past me while I listened in my sandy bed. The fragments died far away, then sounded very close again. It was as though mountain peaks sang to one another above clouds. Wind caught the muffled roar away. Wind brought it back.... Then, in a hollow pause that lasted years, conveying marvellously the passage of long periods, I heard the utterance more clearly. The leisured roll of the great voice swept through me like a flood:

"We wait and watch and listen in our loneliness. We do not close our eyes. The moon and stars sail past us, and our river finds the sea. We bring Eternity upon your broken lives.... We see you build your little lines of steel across our territory behind the thin white smoke. We hear the whistle of your messengers of iron through the air.... The nations rise and pass. The empires flutter westwards and are gone.... The sun grows older and the stars turn pale.... Winds shift the line of the horizons, and our River moves its bed. But we, everlasting and unchangeable, remain. Of water, sand and fire is our essential being, yet built within the universal air.... There is no pause in life, there is no break in death. The changes bring no end. The sun returns.... There is eternal resurrection.... But our kingdom is underground in shadow, unrealised of your little day.... Come, come! The temples still are crowded, and our Desert blesses you. Our River takes your feet. Our sand shall purify, and the fire of our God shall burn you sweetly into wisdom.... Come, then, and worship, for the time draws near. It is the dawn...."

The voices died down into depths that the sand of ages muffled, while the flaming dawn of the East rushed up the sky. Sunrise, the great symbol of life's endless resurrection, was at hand. About me, in immense but shadowy array, stood the whole of ancient Egypt, hanging breathlessly upon the moment of adoration. No longer stern and terrible in the splendour of their long neglect, the effigies rose erect with passionate glory, a forest of stately stone. Their granite lips were parted and their ancient eyes were wide. All faced the east. And the sun drew nearer to the rim of the attentive Desert.

XI

Emotion there seemed none, in the sense that *I* knew feeling. I knew, if anything, the ultimate secrets of two primitive sensations—joy and awe.... The dawn grew swiftly brighter. There was gold, as though the sands of Nubia spilt their brilliance on each shining detail; there was glory, as though the retreating tide of stars spilt their light foam upon the world; and there was passion, as though the beliefs of all the ages floated back with abandonment into the—Sun. Ruined Egypt merged into a single temple of elemental vastness whose floor was the empty desert, but whose walls rose to the stars.

Abruptly, then, chanting and rhythm ceased; they dipped below. Sand muffled them. And the Sun looked down upon its ancient world....

A radiant warmth poured through me. I found that I could move my limbs again. A sense of triumphant life ran through my stony frame. For one passing second I heard the shower of gritty particles upon my surface like sand blown upwards by a gust of wind, but this time I could *feel* the sting of it upon my skin. It passed. The drenching heat bathed me from head to foot, while stony insensibility gave place with returning consciousness to flesh and blood. The sun had risen.... I was alive, but I was—changed.

It seemed I opened my eyes. An immense relief was in me. I turned; I drew a deep, refreshing breath; I stretched one leg upon a thick, green carpet. Something had left me; another thing had returned. I sat up, conscious of welcome release, of freedom, of escape.

There was some violent, disorganising break. I found myself; I found Moleson; I found George Isley too. He had got shifted in that room without my being aware of it. Isley had risen. He came upon me like a blow. I saw him move his arms. Fire flashed from below his hands; and I realised then that he was turning on the electric lights. They emerged from different points along the walls, in the alcove, beneath the ceiling, by the writing-table; and one had just that minute blazed into my eyes from a bracket close above me. I was back again in the Present among modern things.

But, while most of the details presented themselves gradually to my recovered senses, Isley returned with this curious effect of speed and distance—like a blow upon the mind. From great height and from prodigious size—he dropped. I seemed to find him rushing at me. Moleson was simply "there"; there was no speed or sudden change in him as with the other. Motionless at the piano, his long thin hands lay down upon the keys yet did not strike them. But Isley came back like lightning into the little room, signs of the monstrous obsession still about his altering features. There was battle and worship mingled in his deep-set eyes. His mouth, though set, was smiling. With a shudder I positively saw the vastness slipping from his face as shadows from a stretch of broken cliff. There was this awful mingling of proportions. The colossal power that had resumed his being drew slowly inwards. There was collapse in him. And upon the sun-burned cheek of his rugged face I saw a tear.

Poignant revulsion caught me then for a moment. The present showed itself in rags. The reduction of scale was painful. I yearned for the splendour that was gone, yet still seemed so hauntingly almost within reach. The cheapness of the hotel room, the glaring ugliness of its tinsel decoration, the baseness of ideals where utility instead of beauty, gain instead of worship, governed life—this, with the dwindled aspect of my companions to the insignificance of marionettes, brought a hungry pain that was at first intolerable. In the glare of light I noticed the small round face of the portable clock upon the mantelpiece, showing half-past eleven. Moleson had been two hours at the piano. And this measuring faculty of my mind completed the disillusionment. I was, indeed, back among present things. The mechanical spirit of To-day imprisoned me again.

For a considerable interval we neither moved nor spoke; the sudden change left the emotions in confusion; we had leaped from a height, from the top of the pyramid, from a star—and the crash of landing scattered thought. I stole a glance at Isley, wondering vaguely why he was there at all; the look of resignation had replaced the power in his face; the tear was brushed away. There was no struggle in him now, no sign of resistance; there was abandonment only; he seemed insignificant. The real George Isley was elsewhere: he himself had not returned.

By jerks, as it were, and by awkward stages, then, we all three came back to common things again. I found that we were talking ordinarily, asking each other questions, answering, lighting cigarettes, and all the rest. Moleson played some commonplace chords upon the piano, while he leaned back listlessly in his chair, putting in sentences now and again and chatting idly to whichever of us would listen. And Isley came slowly across the room towards me, holding out cigarettes. His dark brown face had shadows on it. He looked exhausted, worn, like some soldier broken in the wars.

"You liked it?" I heard his thin voice asking. There was no interest, no expression; it was not the real Isley who spoke; it was the little part of him that had come back. He smiled like a marvellous automaton.

Mechanically I took the cigarette he offered me, thinking confusedly what answer I could make.

"It's irresistible," I murmured; "I understand that it's easier to go."

"Sweeter as well," he whispered with a sigh, "and very wonderful!"

XII

The hand that lit my cigarette, I saw, was trembling. A desire to do something violent woke in me suddenly—to move energetically, to push or drive something away.

"What was it?" I asked abruptly, in a louder, half-challenging voice, intended for the man at the piano. "Such a performance—upon others—without first asking their permission—seems to me unpermissible—it's—"

And it was Moleson who replied. He ignored the end of my sentence as though he had not heard it. He strolled over to our side, taking a cigarette and pressing it carefully into shape between his long thin fingers.

"You may well ask," he answered quietly; "but it's not so easy to tell. We discovered it"—he nodded towards Isley— "two years ago in the 'Valley.' It lay beside a Priest, a very important personage, apparently, and was part of the Ritual he used in the worship of the sun. In the Museum now—you can see it any day at the Boulak—it is simply labelled 'Hymn to Ra.' The period was Aknahton's."

"The words, yes," put in Isley, who was listening closely.

"The words?" repeated Moleson in a curious tone. "There are no words. It's all really a manipulation of the vowel sounds. And the rhythm, or chanting, or whatever you like to call it, I—I invented myself. The Egyptians did not write their music, you see." He suddenly searched my face a moment with questioning eyes. "Any words you heard," he said, "or thought you heard, were merely your own interpretation."

I stared at him, making no rejoinder.

"They made use of what they called a 'root-language' in their rituals," he went on, "and it consisted entirely of vowel sounds. There were no consonants. For vowel sounds, you see, run on for ever without end or beginning, whereas consonants interrupt their flow and break it up and limit it. A consonant has no sound of its own at all. Real language is continuous."

We stood a moment, smoking in silence. I understood then that this thing Moleson had done was based on definite knowledge. He had rendered some fragment of an ancient Ritual he and Isley had unearthed together, and while he knew its effect upon the latter, he chanced it on myself. Not otherwise, I feel, could it have influenced me in the extraordinary way it did. In the faith and poetry of a nation lies its soul-life, and the gigantic faith of Egypt blazed behind the rhythm of that long, monotonous chant. There were blood and heart and nerves in it. Millions had heard it sung; millions had wept and prayed and yearned; it was ensouled by the passion of that marvellous civilisation that loved the godhead of the Sun, and that now hid, waiting but still alive, below the ground. The majestic faith of ancient Egypt poured up with it—that tremendous, burning elaboration of the after-life and of Eternity that was the pivot of those spacious days. For centuries vast multitudes, led by their royal priests, had uttered this very form and ritual—believed it, lived it, felt it. The rising of the sun remained its climax. Its spiritual power still clung to the great ruined symbols. The faith of a buried civilisation had burned back into the present and into our hearts as well.

And a curious respect for the man who was able to produce this effect upon two modern minds crept over me, and mingled with the repulsion that I felt. I looked furtively at his withered, dried-up features. He wore some vague and shadowy impress still of what had just been in him. There was a stony appearance in his shrunken cheeks. He looked smaller. I saw him lessened. I thought of him as he had been so short a time before, imprisoned in his great stone captors that had obsessed him....

"There's tremendous power in it,—an awful power," I stammered, more to break the oppressive pause than for any desire in me to speak with him. "It brings back Egypt in some extraordinary way—ancient Egypt, I mean—brings it close—into the heart." My words ran on of their own accord almost. I spoke with a hush, unwittingly. There was awe in me. Isley had moved away towards the window, leaving me face to face with this strange incarnation of another age.

"It must," he replied, deep light still glowing in his eyes, "for the soul of the old days is in it. No one, I think, can hear it and remain the same. It expresses, you see, the essential passion and beauty of that gorgeous worship, that splendid faith, that reasonable and intelligent worship of the sun, the only scientific belief the world has ever known. Its popular form, of course, was largely superstitious, but the sacerdotal form—the form used by the priests, that is—who understood the relationship between colour, sound and symbol, was——"

He broke off suddenly, as though he had been speaking to himself. We sat down. George Isley leaned out of the window with his back to us, watching the desert in the moonless night.

"You have tried its effect before upon—others?" I asked point-blank.

"Upon myself," he answered shortly.

"Upon others?" I insisted.

He hesitated an instant.

"Upon one other—yes," he admitted.

"Intentionally?" And something quivered in me as I asked it.

He shrugged his shoulders slightly. "I'm merely a speculative archaeologist," he smiled, "and—and an imaginative Egyptologist. My bounden duty is to reconstruct the past so that it lives for others."

An impulse rose in me to take him by the throat.

"You know perfectly well, of course, the magical effect it's sure—likely at least—to have?"

He stared steadily at me through the cigarette smoke. To this day I cannot think exactly what it was in this man that made me shudder.

"I'm sure of nothing," he replied smoothly, "but I consider it quite legitimate to try. Magical—the word you used—has no meaning for me. If such a thing exists, it is merely scientific—undiscovered or forgotten knowledge." An insolent, aggressive light shone in his eyes as he spoke; his manner was almost truculent. "You refer, I take it, to—our friend—rather than to yourself?"

And with difficulty I met his singular stare. From his whole person something still emanated that was forbidding, yet overmasteringly persuasive. It brought back the notion of that invisible Web, that dim gauze curtain, that motionless Influence lying waiting at the centre for its prey, those monstrous and mysterious Items standing, alert and watchful, through the centuries. "You mean," he added lower, "his altered attitude to life—his going?"

To hear him use the words, the very phrase, struck me with sudden chill. Before I could answer, however, and certainly before I could master the touch of horror that rushed over me, I heard him continuing in a whisper. It seemed again that he spoke to himself as much as he spoke to me.

"The soul, I suppose, has the right to choose its own conditions and surroundings. To pass elsewhere involves translation, not extinction." He smoked a moment in silence, then said another curious thing, looking up into my face with an expression of intense earnestness. Something genuine in him again replaced the pose of cynicism. "The soul is eternal and can take its place anywhere, regardless of mere duration. What is there in the vulgar and superficial Present that should hold it so exclusively; and where can it find to-day the belief, the faith, the beauty that are the very essence of its life—where in the rush and scatter of this tawdry age can it make its home? Shall it flutter for ever in a valley of dry bones, when a living Past lies ready and waiting with loveliness, strength, and glory?" He moved closer; he touched my arm; I felt his breath upon my face. "Come with us," he whispered awfully; "come back with us! Withdraw your life from the rubbish of this futile ugliness! Come back and worship with us in the spirit of the Past. Take up the old, old splendour, the glory, the immense conceptions, the wondrous certainty, the

ineffable knowledge of essentials. It all lies about you still; it's calling, ever calling; it's very close; it draws you day and night—calling, calling, calling...."

His voice died off curiously into distance on the word; I can hear it to this
day, and the soft, droning quality in the intense yet fading tone: "Calling, calling, calling." But his eyes turned wicked. I felt the sinister power of the man.
I was aware of madness in his thought and mind. The Past he sought to glo-
rify I saw black, as with the forbidding Egyptian darkness of a plague. It was
not beauty but Death that I heard calling, calling, calling.

"It's real," he went on, hardly aware that I shrank, "and not a dream. These
ruined symbols still remain in touch with that which was. They are potent to-
day as they were six thousand years ago. The amazing life of those days
brims behind them. They are not mere masses of oppressive stone; they express in visible form great powers that still are—knowable." He lowered his
head, peered up into my face, and whispered. Something secret passed into
his eyes.

"I saw you change," came the words below his breath, "as you saw the
change in us. But only worship can produce that change. The soul assumes
the qualities of the deity it worships. The powers of its deity possess it and
transform it into its own likeness. You also felt it. *You* also were possessed. I
saw the stone-faced deity upon your own."

I seemed to shake myself as a dog shakes water from its body. I stood up. I
remember that I stretched my hands out as though to push him from me and
expel some creeping influence from my mind. I remember another thing as
well. But for the reality of the sequel, and but for the matter-of-fact result still
facing me to-day in the disappearance of George Isley—the loss to the present time of all George Isley *was*—I might have found subject for laughter in
what I saw. Comedy was in it certainly. Yet it was both ghastly and terrific.
Deep horror crept below the aspect of the ludicrous, for the apparent mim-
icry cloaked truth. It was appalling because it was real.

In the large mirror that reflected the room behind me I saw myself and
Moleson; I saw Isley too in the background by the open window. And the attitude of all three was the attitude of hieroglyphics come to life. My arms indeed were stretched, but not stretched, as I had thought, in mere self-defence.
They were stretched—unnaturally. The forearms made those strange obtuse
angles that the old carved granite wears, the palms of the hands held upwards,
the heads thrown back, the legs advanced, the bodies stiffened into postures
that expressed forgotten, ancient minds. The physical conformation of all
three was monstrous; and yet reverence and truth dictated even the un-
couthness of the gestures. Something in all three of us inspired the forms our
bodies had assumed. Our attitudes expressed buried yearnings, emotions,
tendencies—whatever they may be termed—that the spirit of the Past evoked.

I saw the reflected picture but for a moment. I dropped my arms, aware of foolishness in my way of standing. Moleson moved forward with his long, significant stride, and at the same instant Isley came up quickly and joined us from his place by the open window. We looked into each other's faces without a word. There was this little pause that lasted perhaps ten seconds. But in that pause I felt the entire world slide past me. I heard the centuries rush by at headlong speed. The present dipped away. Existence was no longer in a line that stretched two ways; it was a circle in which ourselves, together with Past and Future, stood motionless at the centre, all details equally accessible at once. The three of us were falling, falling backwards....

"Come!" said the voice of Moleson solemnly, but with the sweetness as of a child anticipating joy. "Come! Let us go together, for the boat of Ra has crossed the Underworld. The darkness has been conquered. Let us go out together and find the dawn. Listen! It is calling, calling, calling...."

XIII

I was aware of rushing, but it was the soul in me that rushed. It experienced dizzy, unutterable alterations. Thousands of emotions, intense and varied, poured through me at lightning speed, each satisfyingly known, yet gone before its name appeared. The life of many centuries tore headlong back with me, and, as in drowning, this epitome of existence shot in a few seconds the steep slopes the Past had so laboriously built up. The changes flashed and passed. I wept and prayed and worshipped; I loved and suffered; I battled, lost and won. Down the gigantic scale of ages that telescoped thus into a few brief moments, the soul in me went sliding backwards towards a motionless, reposeful Past.

I remember foolish details that interrupted the immense descent—I put on coat and hat; I remember some one's words, strangely sounding as when some bird wakes up and sings at midnight—"We'll take the little door; the front one's locked by now"; and I have a vague recollection of the outline of the great hotel, with its colonnades and terraces, fading behind me through the air. But these details merely flickered and disappeared, as though I fell earthwards from a star and passed feathers or blown leaves upon the way. There was no friction as my soul dropped backwards into time; the flight was easy and silent as a dream. I felt myself sucked down into gulfs whose emptiness offered no resistance ... until at last the appalling speed decreased of its own accord, and the dizzy flight became a kind of gentle floating. It changed imperceptibly into a gliding motion, as though the angle altered. My feet, quite naturally, were on the ground, moving through something soft that clung to them and rustled while it clung.

I looked up and saw the bright armies of the stars. In front of me I recognised the flat-topped, shadowy ridges; on both sides lay the open expanses of familiar wilderness; and beside me, one on either hand, moved two figures who were my companions. We were in the desert, but it was the desert of thousands of years ago. My companions, moreover, though familiar to some part of me, seemed strangers or half known. Their names I strove in vain to capture; Mosely, Ilson, sounded in my head, mingled together falsely. And when I stole a glance at them, I saw dark lines of mannikins unfilled with substance, and was aware of the grotesque gestures of living hieroglyphics. It seemed for an instant that their arms were bound behind their backs impossibly, and that their heads turned sharply across their lineal shoulders.

But for a moment only; for at a second glance I saw them solid and compact; their names came back to me; our arms were linked together as we walked. We had already covered a great distance, for my limbs were aching and my breath was short. The air was cold, the silence absolute. It seemed, in this faint light, that the desert flowed beneath our feet, rather than that we advanced by taking steps. Cliffs with hooded tops moved past us, boulders glided, mounds of sand slid by. And then I heard a voice upon my left that was surely Moleson speaking:

"Towards Enet our feet are set," he half sang, half murmured, "towards Enet-te-ntore. There, in the House of Birth, we shall dedicate our hearts and lives anew."

And the language, no less than the musical intonation of his voice, enraptured me. For I understood he spoke of Denderah, in whose majestic temple recent hands had painted with deathless colours the symbols of our cosmic relationships with the zodiacal signs. And Denderah was our great seat of worship of the goddess Hathor, the Egyptian Aphrodite, bringer of love and joy. The falcon-headed Horus was her husband, from whom, in his home at Edfu, we imbibed swift kinds of power. And—it was the time of the New Year, the great feast when the forces of the living earth turn upwards into happy growth.

We were on foot across the desert towards Denderah, and this sand we trod was the sand of thousands of years ago.

The paralysis of time and distance involved some amazing lightness of the spirit that, I suppose, touched ecstasy. There was intoxication in the soul. I was not divided from the stars, nor separate from this desert that rushed with us. The unhampered wind blew freshly from my nerves and skin, and the Nile, glimmering faintly on our right, lay with its lapping waves in both my hands. I knew the life of Egypt, for it was in me, over me, round me. I was a part of it. We went happily, like birds to meet the sunrise. There were no pits of measured time and interval that could detain us. We flowed, yet were at rest; we were endlessly alive; present and future alike were inconceivable; we were in the Kingdom of the Past.

The Pyramids were just a-building, and the army of Obelisks looked about them, proud of their first balance; Thebes swung her hundred gates upon the world. New, shining Memphis glittered with myriad reflections into waters that the tears of Isis sweetened, and the cliffs of Abou Simbel were still innocent of their gigantic progeny. Alone, the Sphinx, linking timelessness with time, brooded unguessed and underived upon an alien world. We marched within antiquity towards Denderah....

How long we marched, how fast, how far we went, I can remember as little as the marvellous speech that passed across me while my two companions spoke together. I only remember that suddenly a wave of pain disturbed my wondrous happiness and caused my calm, which had seemed beyond all reach of break, to fall away. I heard their voices abruptly with a kind of terror. A sensation of fear, of loss, of nightmare bewilderment came over me like cold wind. What *they* lived naturally, true to their inmost hearts, I lived merely by means of a temperamental sympathy. And the stage had come at which my powers failed. Exhaustion overtook me. I wilted. The strain—the abnormal backwards stretch of consciousness that was put upon me by another—gave way and broke. I heard their voices faint and horrible. My joy was extinguished. A glare of horror fell upon the desert and the stars seemed evil. An anguishing desire for the safe and wholesome Present usurped all this mad yearning to obtain the Past. My feet fell out of step. The rushing of the desert paused. I unlinked my arms. We stopped all three.

The actual spot is to this day well known to me. I found it afterwards, I even photographed it. It lies actually not far from Helouan—a few miles at most beyond the Solitary Palm, where slopes of undulating sand mark the opening of a strange, enticing valley called the Wadi Gerraui. And it is enticing because it beckons and leads on. Here, amid torn gorges of a limestone wilderness, there is suddenly soft yellow sand that flows and draws the feet onward. It slips away with one too easily; always the next ridge and basin must be seen, each time a little farther. It has the quality of decoying. The cliffs say, No; but this streaming sand invites. In its flowing curves of gold there is enchantment.

And it was here upon its very lips we stopped, the rhythm of our steps broken, our hearts no longer one. My temporary rapture vanished. I was aware of fear. For the Present rushed upon me with attack in it, and I felt that my mind was arrested close upon the edge of madness. Something cleared and lifted in my brain.

The soul, indeed, could "choose its dwelling-place"; but to live elsewhere completely was the choice of madness, and to live divorced from all the sweet wholesome business of To-day involved an exile that was worse than madness. It was death. My heart burned for George Isley. I remembered the tear upon his cheek. The agony of his struggle I shared suddenly with him. Yet with him was the reality, with me a sympathetic reflection merely. *He* was already too far gone to fight....

I shall never forget the desolation of that strange scene beneath the morning stars. The desert lay down and watched us. We stood upon the brink of a little broken ridge, looking into the valley of golden sand. This sand gleamed soft and wonderful in the starlight some twenty feet below. The descent was easy—but I would not move. I refused to advance another step. I saw my companions in the mysterious half-light beside me peering over the edge, Moleson in front a little.

And I turned to him, sure of the part I meant to play, yet conscious painfully of my helplessness. My personality seemed a straw in mid-stream that spun in a futile effort to arrest the flood that bore it. There was vivid human conflict in the moment's silence. It was an eddy that paused in the great body of the tide. And then I spoke. Oh, I was ashamed of the insignificance of my voice and the weakness of my little personality.

"Moleson, we go no farther with you. We have already come too far. We now turn back."

Behind my words were a paltry thirty years. His answer drove sixty centuries against me. For his voice was like the wind that passed whispering down the stream of yellow sand below us. He smiled.

"Our feet are set towards Enet-te-ntore. There is no turning back. Listen! It is calling, calling, calling!"

"We will go home," I cried, in a tone I vainly strove to make imperative.

"Our home is there," he sang, pointing with one long thin arm towards the brightening east, "for the Temple calls us and the River takes our feet. We shall be in the House of Birth to meet the sunrise——"

"You lie," I cried again, "you speak the lies of madness, and this Past you seek is the House of Death. It is the kingdom of the underworld."

The words tore wildly, impotently out of me. I seized George Isley's arm.

"Come back with me," I pleaded vehemently, my heart aching with a nameless pain for him. "We'll retrace our steps. Come home with me! Come back! Listen! The Present calls you sweetly!"

His arm slipped horribly out of my grasp that had seemed to hold it so tightly. Moleson, already below us in the yellow sand, looked small with distance. He was gliding rapidly farther with uncanny swiftness. The diminution of his form was ghastly. It was like a doll's. And his voice rose up, faint as with the distance of great gulfs of space.

"Calling ... calling.... You hear it for ever calling ..."

It died away with the wind along that sandy valley, and the Past swept in a flood across the brightening sky. I swayed as though a storm was at my back. I reeled. Almost I went too—over the crumbling edge into the sand.

"Come back with me! Come home!" I cried more faintly. "The Present alone is real. There is work, ambition, duty. There is beauty too—the beauty of good living! And there is love! There is—a woman … calling, calling…!"

That other voice took up the word below me. I heard the faint refrain sing down the sandy walls. The wild, sweet pang in it was marvellous.

"Our feet are set for Enet-te-ntore. It is calling, calling…!"

My voice fell into nothingness. George Isley was below me now, his outline tiny against the sheet of yellow sand. And the sand was moving. The desert rushed again. The human figures receded swiftly into the Past they had reconstructed with the creative yearning of their souls.

I stood alone upon the edge of crumbling limestone, helplessly watching them. It was amazing what I witnessed, while the shafts of crimson dawn rose up the sky. The enormous desert turned alive to the horizon with gold and blue and silver. The purple shadows melted into grey. The flat-topped ridges shone. Huge messengers of light flashed everywhere at once. The radiance of sunrise dazzled my outer sight.

But if my eyes were blinded, my inner sight was focused the more clearly upon what followed. I witnessed the disappearance of George Isley. There was a dreadful magic in the picture. The pair of them, small and distant below me in that little sandy hollow, stood out sharply defined as in a miniature. I saw their outlines neat and terrible like some ghastly inset against the enormous scenery. Though so close to me in actual space, they were centuries away in time. And a dim, vast shadow was about them that was not mere shadow of the ridges. It encompassed them; it moved, crawling over the sand, obliterating them. Within it, like insects lost in amber, they became visibly imprisoned, dwindled in size, borne deep away, absorbed.

And then I recognised the outline. Once more, but this time recumbent and spread flat upon the desert's face, I knew the monstrous shapes of the twin obsessing symbols. The spirit of ancient Egypt lay over all the land, tremendous in the dawn. The sunrise summoned her. She lay prostrate before the deity. The shadows of the towering Colossi lay prostrate too. The little humans, with their worshipping and conquered hearts, lay deep within them.

George Isley I saw clearest. The distinctness, the reality were appalling. He was naked, robbed, undressed. I saw him a skeleton, picked clean to the very bones as by an acid. His life lay hid in the being of that mighty Past. Egypt had absorbed him. He was gone….

I closed my eyes, but I could not keep them closed. They opened of their own accord. The three of us were nearing the great hotel that rose yellow, with shuttered windows, in the early sunshine. A wind blew briskly from the north across the Mokattam Hills. There were soft cannon-ball clouds dotted about the sky, and across the Nile, where the mist lay in a line of white, I saw the tops of the Pyramids gleaming like mountain peaks of gold. A string of camels, laden with white stone, went past us. I heard the crying of the natives in the streets of Helouan, and as we went up the steps the donkeys arrived and camped in the sandy road beside their *bersim* till the tourists claimed them.

"Good morning," cried Abdullah, the man who owned them. "You all go Sakkhâra to-day, or Memphis? Beat'ful day to-day, and vair good donkeys!"

Moleson went up to his room without a word, and Isley did the same. I thought he staggered a moment as he turned the passage corner from my sight. His face wore a look of vacancy that some call peace. There was radiance in it. It made me shudder. Aching in mind and body, and no word spoken, I followed their example. I went upstairs to bed, and slept a dreamless sleep till after sunset....

XIV

And I woke with a lost, unhappy feeling that a withdrawing tide had left me on the shore, alone and desolate. My first instinct was for my friend, George Isley. And I noticed a square, white envelope with my name upon it in his writing.

Before I opened it I knew quite well what words would be inside:

"We are going up to Thebes," the note informed me simply. "We leave by the night train. If you care to——" But the last four words were scratched out again, though not so thickly that I could not read them. Then came the address of the Egyptologist's house and the signature, very firmly traced, "Yours ever, George Isley." I glanced at my watch and saw that it was after seven o'clock. The night train left at half-past six. They had already started....

The pain of feeling forsaken, left behind, was deep and bitter, for myself; but what I felt for him, old friend and comrade, was even more intense, since it was hopeless. Fear and conventional emotion had stopped me at the very gates of an amazing possibility—some state of consciousness that, *realising* the Past, might doff the Present, and by slipping out of Time, experience Eternity. That was the seduction I had escaped by the uninspired resistance of my pettier soul. Yet, he, my friend, yielding in order to conquer, had obtained an awful prize—ah, I understood the picture's other side as well, with an unutterable poignancy of pity—the prize of immobility which is sheer stagnation, the imagined bliss which is a false escape, the dream of finding beauty away from present things. From that dream the awakening must be rude indeed. Clutching at vanished stars, he had clutched the oldest illusion in the world. To me it seemed the negation of life that had betrayed him. The pity of it burned me like a flame.

But I did not "care to follow" him and his companion. I waited at Helouan for his return, filling the empty days with yet emptier explanations. I felt as a man who sees what he loves sinking down into clear, deep water, still within visible reach, yet gone beyond recovery. Moleson had taken him back to Thebes; and Egypt, monstrous effigy of the Past, had caught her prey.

The rest, moreover, is easily told. Moleson I never saw again. To this day I have never seen him, though his subsequent books are known to me, with the banal fact that he is numbered with those energetic and deluded enthusiasts who start a new religion, obtain notoriety, a few hysterical followers and—oblivion.

George Isley, however, returned to Helouan after a fortnight's absence. I saw him, knew him, talked and had my meals with him. We even did slight expeditions together. He was gentle and delightful as a woman who has loved a wonderful ideal and attained to it—in memory. All roughness was gone out of him; he was smooth and polished as a crystal surface that reflects whatever is near enough to ask a picture. Yet his appearance shocked me inexpressibly: there was nothing in him—nothing. It was the representation of George Isley that came back from Thebes; the outer simulacra; the shell that walks the London streets to-day. I met no vestige of the man I used to know. George Isley had disappeared.

With this marvellous automaton I lived another month. The horror of him kept me company in the hotel where he moved among the cosmopolitan humanity as a ghost that visits the sunlight yet has its home elsewhere.

This empty image of George Isley lived with me in our Helouan hotel until the winds of early March informed his physical frame that discomfort was in the air, and that he might as well move elsewhere—elsewhere happening to be northwards.

And he left just as he stayed—automatically. His brain obeyed the conventional stimuli to which his nerves, and consequently his muscles, were accustomed. It sounds so foolish. But he took his ticket automatically; he gave the natural and adequate reasons automatically; he chose his ship and landing-place in the same way that ordinary people chose these things; he said good-bye like any other man who leaves casual acquaintances and "hopes" to meet them again; he lived, that is to say, entirely in his brain. His heart, his emotions, his temperament and personality, that nameless sum-total for which the great sympathetic nervous system is accountable—all this, his soul, had gone elsewhere. This once vigorous, gifted being had become a normal, comfortable man that everybody could understand—a commonplace nonentity. He was precisely what the majority expected him to be—ordinary; a good fellow; a man of the world; he was "delightful." He merely reflected daily life without partaking of it. To the majority it was hardly noticeable; "very pleasant" was a general verdict. His ambition, his restlessness, his zeal had gone; that tireless zest whose driving power is yearning had taken flight, leaving behind it physical energy without spiritual desire. His soul had found its nest and flown to it. He lived in the chimera of the Past, serene, indifferent, detached. I saw him immense, a shadowy, majestic figure, standing—ah, not moving!—in a repose that was satisfying because it *could* not change. The size, the mystery, the immobility that caged him in seemed to me—terrible. For I dared not intrude upon his awful privacy, and intimacy between us there was none. Of his experiences at Thebes I asked no single question—it was somehow not possible or legitimate; he, equally, vouchsafed no word of explanation—it was uncommunicable to a dweller in the Present. Between us was this barrier we both respected. He peered at modern life, incurious, listless, apathetic, through a dim, gauze curtain. He was behind it.

People round us were going to Sakkhâra and the Pyramids, to see the Sphinx by moonlight, to dream at Edfu and at Denderah. Others described their journeys to Assouan, Khartoum and Abou Simbel, and gave details of their encampments in the desert. Wind, wind, wind! The winds of Egypt blew and sang and sighed. From the White Nile came the travellers, and from the Blue Nile, from the Fayum, and from nameless excavations without end. They talked and wrote their books. They had the magpie knowledge of the present. The Egyptologists, big and little, read the writing on the wall and put the hieroglyphs and papyri into modern language. Alone George Isley knew the secret. He lived it.

And the high passionate calm, the lofty beauty, the glamour and enchantment that are the spell of this thrice-haunted land, were in my soul as well—sufficiently for me to interpret his condition. I could not leave, yet having left I could not stay away. I yearned for the Egypt that he knew. No word I uttered; speech could not approach it. We wandered by the Nile together, and through the groves of palms that once were Memphis. The sandy wastes beyond the Pyramids knew our footsteps; the Mokattam Ridges, purple at evening and golden in the dawn, held our passing shadows as we silently went by. At no single dawn or sunset was he to be found indoors, and it became my habit to accompany him—the joy of worship in his soul was marvellous. The great, still skies of Egypt watched us, the hanging stars, the gigantic dome of blue; we felt together that burning southern wind; the golden sweetness of the sun lay in our blood as we saw the great boats take the northern breeze upstream. Immensity was everywhere and this golden magic of the sun....

But it was in the Desert especially, where only sun and wind observe the faint signalling of Time, where space is nothing because it is not divided, and where no detail reminds the heart that the world is called To-Day—it was in the desert this curtain hung most visibly between us, he on that side, I on this. It was transparent. He was with a multitude no man can number. Towering to the moon, yet spreading backwards towards his burning source of life, drawn out by the sun and by the crystal air into some vast interior magnitude, the spirit of George Isley hung beside me, close yet far away, in the haze of olden days.

And, sometimes, he moved. I was aware of gestures. His head was raised to listen. One arm swung shadowy across the sea of broken ridges. From leagues away a line of sand rose slowly. There was a rustling. Another—an enormous—arm emerged to meet his own, and two stupendous figures drew together. Poised above Time, yet throned upon the centuries, They knew eternity. So easily they remained possessors of the land. Facing the east, they waited for the dawn. And their marvellously forgotten singing poured across the world....

The Lost Elixir
by George Griffith

Although not particularly well known today, George Griffith, a late-nineteenth century contemporary of H.G. Wells, was a highly prolific science fiction writer whose works were widely read in his native England. The author of numerous books and stories, including The Mummy and Miss Nitocris: A Phantasy of the Fourth Dimension *(1906), Griffith's left-wing views informed a good deal of his literary output.*

Neither utopian nor socialist politics feature in his "The Lost Elixir," however. Griffith's story is a considerably apolitical contribution to the development of the ancient Egyptian supernatural tale subgenre. Originally published in the October 1903 issue of Pall Mall Magazine, *"The Lost Elixir" is written in a comparably archaic style and in a somewhat awkward story-within-a-story manner.*

That said, the story is at once formulaic and highly inventive, incorporating the familiar plot device wherein an adventurer recounts his uncanny experiences in an exotic land, in this case Egypt. Griffith includes standard tropes of the ancient Egyptian supernatural tale, including how events from centuries ago continue to influence the present. What sets "The Lost Elixir" apart and makes it a valuable edition to this anthology, however, is its subtle reflection on the field of archaeology and the critical role that the translation of ancient texts plays in modern understandings of the long distant past. The story likewise seems to indicate that Griffith, with his depiction of a private social club, was exceedingly familiar with the Edwardian upper class's enduring fascination with the esoteric mysteries of ancient Egypt.

A week after I had passed my examination before the committee of the Narrative Club, which, as you may know, is an assembly into which none are admitted save those who have many wanderings to their account and are able to tell tales about them, I received a notice from the Secretary to the effect that he was in a position to accept my cheque in payment of my entrance fee, and, further, that he would be happy to introduce me to my fellow-wanderers at the usual monthly supper on the following Sunday, at 9pm.

"You are rather in luck as regards your introduction to-night," he said, when we met in his rooms. "According to the strict rules you would have been called upon to justify your calling and election by telling us a story; but it so happens that this evening will be the only one for nearly a year that we can get hold of a man who is, perhaps, our most distinguished member. You know him by name, and you may have run across him in some of your travels – Professor Hessetine."

Of course the world-famed name was familiar to me, as it is to everybody who has read anything outside novels and newspapers; but as I had had the great privilege of sitting at the same table with him a couple of years before on a West Coast boat from Panama to Lima – whither he was going to write a monograph on the prehistoric tombs of the ancient seaboard towns – the freemasonry of travel entitled me to claim acquaintance with him.

"Then that's all right," said the Secretary, himself a noted climber of hills and slayer of retiring beasts which affect the most neck-breaking localities to be found above the snow-line, when I had mentioned this: "he'll be delighted to see you again and have a chat about Inca-land with you. Personally, I am expecting quite a treat, apart from any story he may have to tell us; for he promised me, in his letter accepting the invitation to be the narrator of the evening, that we should be the first to hear of what he has done at Susa. Even before the scientific papers get it, I mean."

"If he does that I don't much care whether he tells us a story or not," I said. "I can hardly imagine any ordinary travel yarn that would be anything like as interesting as Hessetine on Susa."

"That, my dear fellow," he replied, with a smile, "is probably because you have only just become a member of the Tale Club, as some of our irresponsible globe-trotters have christened it. Oh, and, by the way, that reminds me," he went on, turning towards me, "there's just one hint I ought to give you. You'll have to expect some pretty tough-laid yarns at our distinguished symposia, but we have a tacit understanding as to the acceptance of the aphorism that truth is often stranger than fiction, and so we often give truth – and the narrator – the benefit of the doubt."

"That's nothing," I laughed: "I know some myself, perfectly true, which no British jury would believe if I told them on oath in the witness-box."

Now this was a true saying, but – well, if anyone else than a man of European reputation had told Professor Hessetine's story and staked that reputation on its truth I should still have had my doubts as to the complete purity of his facts.

It so happened that during supper – by the way, a supper at the Narrative Club is quite the most delightfully free-and-easy meal in the confines of civilisation – the conversation, led off by a young doctor who had just been making a long study of the so-called miracle-healing practised by the priest-physicians of Corea, turned upon the many well-authenticated traditions which exist among nearly all peoples belonging to the older civilisations as to the possibility of prolonging human life, and even youth, indefinitely by the regular eating of certain combinations of herbs, or the direct mingling of certain animal and vegetable essences with the blood.

I noticed that, although the Professor listened most attentively to the conversation, he only assisted it by an odd remark, always very much to the point, thrown in here and there, and every now and then an approving nod or a dissenting head-shake. When the table was cleared, and the chairman, according to custom, gave up the post of honour to the Narrator of the evening, it was not very long before we discovered that he had a reason for his reticence, for the first words that he spoke after the glasses had been filled and the pipes loaded were:

"Fellow-wanderers by sea and land," – that is the usual form of address – "I daresay you will have noticed that I have been exceedingly interested in the conversation which took place during supper. It is, of course, a most absorbing topic for all students of human things who are able to approach the most impossible-seeming subjects with that perfectly open mind which, as most of us believe, only long study and intensive travel can give. But whether it be what is commonly called a coincidence or not, I may as well preface the story I am going to tell you by saying that it bears with exceeding closeness upon that very subject."

While the Narrator was saying this he seemed to some of us, certainly to myself, to have grown – I was almost saying – centuries younger. That, however, was not quite what I mean. He might himself have been of any age, clime or nationality, and his features and expression had suddenly undergone a subtle change which seemed a reversion to some former state of being. In other words, he appeared to transfer his personality from the present into that remote epoch of which he was going to tell us, an epoch of which he certainly knows more than any man alive – that is, as far as we know, now alive.

"You must not think," he went on, perhaps having noticed a certain involuntary lifting of eyebrows round the table, "that I am going to tell you that since our last meeting I have had the privilege of making the acquaintance of the Flying Dutchman or the Wandering Jew, although I fear I shall have to make an almost equal demand upon your credulity for, gentlemen, I am going to ask you not to disbelieve me when I tell you that I, who am speaking to you tonight with the lips of flesh, only a few weeks ago spoke, also in the flesh, with one who, as I have every reason to believe, lived and toiled, loved and thought in the long-buried city of Susa in the far-off days when Rameses the Great was king."

In any other assembly such a tremendous announcement, coming in all seriousness from the lips of such a man, would have been received with what the reporters, are accustomed to describe parenthetically as "sensation"; but among the Wanderers by Sea and Land not an eye winked. Only a deeper silence fell upon us as we waited for the Professor to continue.

"I may presume," he went on after a little pause, "that you all know I have just returned after some months' work in connection with the excavations at Susa, one of the buried cities of upper Egypt, which appears to have been a sort of pleasure resort on the shores of a now vanished lake, to which the aristocracy of Thebes were accustomed to go as Londoners and Parisians now go to Homburg or Aix. Indeed, as a matter of fact, I am now quite certain that this was so, for I have in my possession an almost unique treasure in the shape of a complete plan of it, illustrated with drawings of its principal buildings, from the hand of one who saw it in all its pride and beauty.

"This is, however, a slight anticipation. I have the plan with me, and you shall see it afterwards. I was engaging my staff of skilled diggers and excavators – quite a different class from the common fellah labourers – at Memphis, as the best men are nearly always to be found there; and one day, when I had almost completed my staff and was thinking of making a start northward, I was taking my usual evening stroll among the ruins to the north of the modern city, when I was considerably startled by hearing a man's voice speaking in strangely musical tones and in a tongue totally foreign to me. It came from the other side of the fallen statue of Rameses, at the back of which I was leaning, smoking a contemplative pipe.

"I say that I was startled, because I think I may affirm without boasting that I am familiar, not only with all the dialects spoken in the Nile Valley, but with most of the languages of the far and the near East. Yet I searched my memory in vain for the recollection of a single syllable or inflection, until I heard him say quite distinctly, and yet with an accent and intonation utterly strange to me, the words, or rather the exclamation, 'O Rameses, Rameses!'

"No one could have pronounced the name with such exquisite purity and such profound depth of feeling – I had almost said sorrow. Gentlemen, I am not ashamed to admit that in that moment a keen thrill of awe passed through my soul, for the accents seemed to awaken some long-stilled echo of a memory belonging to a life that had been lived in other ages, and with it came the thought, I know not whence, that I was listening to a speech that human lips had not uttered for nearly thirty centuries.

"I put out my pipe and went round the base of the statue, and there I found myself face to face with such a man as I had never set eyes on before. He might have stood as model to the sculptor who designed the statue beside which we were standing. There was the broad, square, low forehead, and under it looked out at me the large, level-set eyes that might have belonged to the Great King himself. The straight, massive nose, the full, delicately-curved, sensuous lips, and the firm, commanding chin – I recognised them all, and the whole countenance wore that almost indescribable expression of contemptuous repose which is so inevitably characteristic of the royal race of Old Egypt.

"He did not show the slightest sign of surprise at my appearance. His eyes looked too weary with seeing for that. He returned my salute with a grave dignity that was, even there, in strange contrast to the scanty rags and the frayed and faded cotton shawl which hung from his shoulders. I addressed him in Arabic for somehow the pure and ancient speech of the desert suggested itself as the most fitting medium at my command and asked him if he would do me the favour of telling what language he had been speaking when I had unintentionally overheard him a few moments before. He replied in Arabic which was far more fluent and idiomatic than my own:

"'That, Effendi, was the speech in which my brother Rameses, by whose time-worn effigy we stand, wooed our cousin Nephert-Anat, the star-eyed Lily of the Upper Nile, in the days when the desert that has buried our glories laughed and sang with the joy of its fruitfulness, and Egypt was Queen of the Earth.'

"Now, you are very well aware, gentlemen, that insanity, in its milder and more inoffensive forms, is not regarded in the East as it is here. It is treated with tolerance and by most people with respect as a sign of the special protection of the Deity. You will, I am sure, understand me when I say that my new acquaintance's first utterance inclined me to the belief that he was a scholar whom over-study and under-feeding had made mad. But there was no sign of madness in the calm, luminous eyes which looked so steadily into mine while he was making this extraordinary speech. There was none of the restlessness of the feet and hands, or the sideways movements of the head, which are the almost certain accompaniments of insanity. On the contrary, his attitude was easy and yet full of dignity, and his manner was rather that of a man who is uttering a commonplace which has become wearisome to him.

"I, of course, realised at once that no good end could possibly be served by any show of incredulity, and so I replied just as seriously as he had spoken: 'Truly, then, O brother of the Great King, since thy days have been prolonged on earth so far beyond the common span of mortal life, great must be the blessing or grievous the curse that the High Gods have laid upon thee. Is it permitted that a stranger from a far-off land should ask thee of why the shade of thy mighty brother hath waited so many cycles for thee in the Halls of Amenti?'

"'Ah,' he exclaimed, bending down towards me for, as I have said, he was a man of splendid stature, fully a head taller than I am – and bringing his eyes to a level with mine, 'dost thou believe me, then? or is it only thy charity which thus listens with a show of credulity to what thou, like the others, takest for the idle tale of a madman? Speak truly, Effendi, as thy soul liveth, for on thy faith hangs the fate of one who, in the days that are forgotten, by his own rash and presumptions act, brought upon his soul the anger of the High Gods, and cut himself off from the common lot of man.'

"I confess that I was strangely and deeply moved; and I replied, as though some inner impulse had been prompting me: 'O Egyptian, who am I, the child of yesterday, that I should say what is and is not possible to the might of the Gods? Shall the sand-grain by the seashore say to its fellow, "With thee and me the limits of Ocean end?" I would make no trespass on thy confidence, yet if thou hast the will to tell me, thy story will not fall on idle ears, and when the proof is given, belief shall not be wanting.'

"'It is just,' he said, his lips making the faintest movement of a smile. 'Yet it is well said that trust is twofold. Will the Effendi trust me in a small matter if I will trust him in a great one?'

"It may seem to you like a piece of arrant foolishness in an old traveller, but I positively could not distrust the man, and so I answered: 'So far as it is lawful and fair dealing between man and man, Egyptian, I will trust thee to the half of my goods.'

"'I have no need of thy goods, Effendi,' he replied, with a sigh which was the saddest I have ever heard from a human breast: 'I who have feasted with kings and conquerors and scattered gold and jewels to the four winds of heaven till wealth became as dross in my hands and I had sickened of all that earth could sell – what is thy poor little fortune to me? Yet it is because I am what men call poor in money that I would ask for thy faith and thy help. The matter is in this wise. Thou art going to Susa, the city of my youth and happiness, and the scene of the crime against the High Gods which made the one unfading and destroyed the other forever. At Susa thou wilt seek to clear the dust of ages from the house in which I and mine dwelt, the temples in which we worshipped, and the tombs where the mummies of my dear ones are resting, while I, self-doomed, count on the countless suns of endless days. Now, what I ask is this: that thou shouldst make me one of thy company, the meanest of them if thou wilt, and take me to Susa, and there I will show thy workmen where to dig that they may find that which thou seekest. I will draw thee pictures of the temples and the theatres and the tombs, and mark out the streets and the squares, until all Susa in its ruins shall be as plain to thee as it was in its glory to me.'

"I don't suppose that any archaeologist had ever had such an astoundingly tempting offer made to him, and I candidly admit that I was not only tempted – I fell. But there was still the undeniable fact that, under all known human conditions, such a thing was absolutely impossible. Certain doubts, too, which I will come to shortly, had occured to me while he was making his proposition. Still, all said and done, I stood to risk nothing but his railway fare and keep – I was already risking them and absurdly high wages too for men not half as likely-looking as my strange friend – even if I was only able to use that commanding air of his by making him an overseer, so I held out my hand, and said:

"'It is agreed, Egyptian. Tomorrow we start by the train that leaves at sundown. Come to me after the early coffee, and I will tell the dragoman and the overseer that I have engaged thee. After the paper is signed I will advance money to buy what thou hast need of. Then in thine own time thou shalt make plain those things which are now dark to my eyes.'

"Our hands met. As I believe now, it was a grip which drew two living men together across a gulf of thirty centuries. That strikes you, no doubt, as a somewhat fantastic and farfetched notion, but I am not without hope that your opinion will change when you have heard my reason for believing as I do."

The Professor, who had so far told his extraordinary story in the most commonplace conversational tone, paused and took a draught from a great tankard of lager before him. The silence was so strained that no one seemed to care to break it, even to get a drink. When he put his tankard down and faced us again, some of us began to find a sort of likeness in those symmetrically-cut features of his to others that we had seen on the wall-paintings at Luxor and Karnac and other familiar places on the now, if possible, vulgarised Nile, as well as on the mighty carved monoliths which even now raise their giant bulk above the sands of time, changeless in the midst of change, silently contemptuous of the roar of the noisy centuries and the chatter of their yester-born children.

"During the journey to Thebes," he went on, just as quietly as before, "my friend the Egyptian took his place among the other men in my employment, and scarcely exchanged a score of words with me. This was, of course, perfectly natural. In the East master is master and servant is servant, and there are no board schools. But as soon as we had left the train at Thebes and began to prepare for crossing the fifty-odd miles of desert to the site of what once was the pleasure-city of Susa, a sudden change came over him. Those of you who have seen a man breathing his native air after years of exile will understand what I mean. He began to exert a sort of unofficial authority which not even the dragoman or the overseer tried to resist after the first few hours, during which they somehow learnt that he was at home and they were not.

"We reached the semicircle of granite hills under which the long-dead citizens of Susa once found protection from the worst of the desert winds, during the second march of the third day. We chose our camping-ground and pitched our tents. After supper I took my pipe and went for a stroll round the encampment, to see that everything was shipshape. There was such a moon in the sky as one only sees from the desert; and when my inspection was over I wandered towards the edge of the bay of smooth sand, broken by outcrops of stone which were for vanished Susa what the Monument and Nelson's Column may someday be for London – if they last as long.

"I had not gone far from the camp when I heard close by me the grave, gentle voice of my Egyptian saying, still in the classic Arabic of the Koran:

"'Effendi, thou has kept thy part of that which was agreed between us. This is Susa, and my eyes already see the flood of ages rolled back, the sands swept away, and the likeness of the temples and the palaces once more reflected in the mirror of the lake which washed their everlasting walls. Diana, as I have heard the old Greeks say, is smiling full-eyed on us tonight. Hast thou the leisure and the will to learn why Pent-ar, priest of the Royal Blood in the House of Amen-ra and Writer of the Sacred Records, sought thy help and charity to return to the place of his birth?'

"I confess that I started a little at the mention of that name, so famous to all Egyptian scholars, by the lips of a man who claimed it as his own, but I managed to tell him in my usual tone that if he was prepared to give me his confidence, I was quite ready to receive it; and so I sat down on a huge slab of granite, and he, declining with a graceful gesture my request that he too would be seated, stood before me, a strangely eloquent figure in the bright moonlight, and told me his story with a simple dignity of diction and expression which, translating from his exquisite Arabic as I am, I cannot hope to emulate.

"'My history, Effendi.' he began, after a long look over the wilderness of ruins, 'shall be brief, since no man could tell even in many hours the narrative of the changing ages. And first I will explain what may have seemed strange to thee – that I, who, as I told thee at Memphis, have squandered counted treasures, should be too poor to pay my way here and do the work for myself which I am to do for thee. It comes about in this wise. Not many months ago I learned from such a seeker as thou art for the hidden glories of my people that a certain papyrus had been found at Thebes which was of the time of the Great King and a little after, and signed by one Panit-Ahmes, priest of Sekhet and scribe of the College of Physicians at Thebes. Further, I was told that this papyrus, which is now in your great Museum of London, contained certain passages which, though plain to decipher, had no outward meaning, and contained, moreover, characters which the most learned of those skilled in the writing of the old Egyptians could not make words or phrases of.

"'Now in the days of the Great King this Panit-Ahmes shared with me the fame which in those days was greater than that which men could win with bow and spear, the fame of learning and of the knowledge of hidden things. This of itself, though it might have made us rivals for the favour of the High Gods, would not by necessity have made us enemies; but there was that between us which hath set man's hand against his brother since first the world began – the love of a fair woman. I divined instantly that the passages which your scholars could not read were written in the Hermetic character which was known only to the initiates of the Sacred Mysteries, and that, since this lore has been lost for many ages, there was no other on earth who could read them save myself.

"'That day I sold a few curious jewels, the last of a once great store, to the explorer, bought myself some clothes of the European fashion, and took passage to London. As I can speak your language, as I can all others which I have seen come into being since my nurse taught me the ancient tongue of Khem, I went to the chief keeper of manuscripts in your Museum and offered to translate this papyrus for him, though in doing so I was breaking the oath of my initiation, so strong upon me was the desire to learn what Panit-Ahmes had hidden in the Hermetic passages.

"'He looked on me at first in wonder, as thou didst, Effendi, when we stood that evening by the statue of Rameses; but there was unbelief as well as wonder in his eyes and his speech, so I went to a case in which some papyri of the time of the Second Amen-ho-tep, who took the great city of Ninevah, rested, and these I read off into English as quickly as you, Effendi, would translate from an Arabic writing. Then he believed, but his wonder grew greater; and in the end, after much talk and writing to many people, as is the fashion of the English, the permission I craved was given to me, and in a day I made the translation and a copy of the Hermetic passages for myself. The scholars of the Museum were greatly amazed, and offered me a high stipend to remain and work for them; but how could I, Pent-ar the Initiate, take money for the revealing of the Holy Mysteries to unbelievers? Also, I had deceived them, for the meaning I wrote down of the mystic sentences was not the true one. Had I written them they would have laughed at me, and I should have broken my oath for nothing.

"'Now the meaning of the passages was this – and by it thou shalt learn, ere that many days have passed, whether Pent-ar the Scribe hath told thee the truth or a lie:

"'*O thou who in the days to come shalt be weary of the burden of years: Behold, my hate shall be buried in my tomb, that I may greet thee as friend in the Halls of the Assessor.*

"'*When the High Gods, whose holiness thine impiety hath outraged, shall judge thy cup of penance to be full, it may be that thine eyes shall see this writing, which thou alone of men wilt in those days be able to read with understanding.*

"'*Then shalt thou learn that the flame lit in thy veins by the Elixir of Long-Drawn Days may be quenched only by the dew which thou shalt find even then moist on the waiting lips of Love. It was given to me to learn the secret of the poison which was the antidote to the venom of endless days. Thy mistaken love bound her soul in the flesh-fetters which through ages of weariness thou shalt learn to curse. My love gave her rest.*

"'*From her lips, in the good time of the High Gods, it may be given to thee to drink the Elixir of the Lesser Death. On the green shores of Amenti we wait and pray for thee.*

"'Effendi, thou hast already heard the story of Pent-ar, for beyond the recital of the Passages of Panit-Ahmes – once my rival and enemy, and now my friend and only hope – there is little to tell that thou hast not already guessed.

"'In many climes and ages I have seen men seeking the essence which they in their ignorance called the Elixir of Life. I could have given it to them, as I could give it to thee if I wished to repay thy friendship with a curse; for it was I who, guided by the malice of the Infernal Gods, discovered the reality of which they were seeking the shadow and the manner of finding it was this:

"'When the Great King was building the Hall of Seti at Luxor, many structures were cleared away to make room, and great excavations were necessary for its foundations. In one of these I, when, as Keeper of the Records, examining the ground that no hidden sacred place might be violated by the workmen, found a very ancient temple, so old that it was buried in those days even as Susa is buried in these. By virtue of my office I passed into it alone; – would that my feet had rotted to the ankles before I had crossed that fatal threshold! In the inmost sanctuary, in the place of hiding behind the chief altar, I found a golden casket of scrolls, which, as was my right, I took home with me, that I might if possible discover new secrets amongst their contents. That which I sought I found, and more.

"'Fastened by a blood-red seal to the smallest of the scrolls was a great emerald wrapped in many folds of leaf of gold. The scroll, deciphered after much labour, told me that it was hollow, and that its cavity was filled with the Elixir of Long-Drawn Days. "O thou," ran the scroll, "whose learning shall teach thee the meaning of these words: know that the Elixir of the Emerald is the last of the secrets of the Infernal Gods vouchsafed to man. If thou hast courage, and wouldst outlive the changing ages, thyself unchanged amidst them; if thou wouldst see the generations of men pass away like shadows from the bright morning of thine eternal youth, mingle but a drop of this ichor – which is the tears of Isis – with thy blood, and never shall it be chilled with frosts of age, nor its flow arrested by the hand of Death. Dost thou love? Then shall one drop more in the veins of thy beloved give thee and her the delights of quenchless love and deathless passion as long as the ages last. Immortal –

the Infernal gods greet thee!"

"'Alas! Effendi, I loved, and through my love I was lost. I would fain spare myself and thee, Son of the Younger Days, the story of that which was the same then as it is now, and as it shall be when the last son and daughter of man pledge their troth on the brink of the common grave. Let it therefore suffice to say that Amaris was in my eyes even fairer and more desirable than her sister the lovely Nefert-Anat herself, who was honoured by the love of the Great King. Endless days of fadeless youth with her – what more could the Gods themselves give me? I took the elixir in my satchel one evening when I was to walk with her through our favourite paradise among the palms. I read the scroll to her and showed her the emerald. Then I tempted her as I had been tempted, and because she loved me I won my way with her.

"'Soon afterwards we were married, for I was of the Royal Blood and Panit-Ahmes was not. Moreover Rameses and Nefert were my friends and pleaded my cause well. My rival cloaked his wrath and his hate under a guise of resignation, but the fires burnt still in his breast and well-nigh consumed him.

"'On our marriage night I instilled the elixir into my veins and hers, and we went to rest dreaming that, as long as the sands of time should run, for us all nights would be like this, all mornings like the morrow. The next day, in the boasting pride of my happiness and triumph, I told Panit-Ahmes of what I had done, and then, telling him that I and my Amaris, alone of the sons and daughters of men, should live and love for ever, I flung the emerald and what was left in it of the tears of Isis far out among the brown waves of the Nile.

"'What hidden lore Panit-Ahmes may have known then or discovered later I know not, but he laughed when he saw me throw away what kings would have given their dominions for, and told me that since I had kept part of the curse of the Infernal Gods for myself I was welcome to do what I would with the rest. "As for Amaris thy wife," he said, as he turned away from me, "I have loved her, and I will save her from the doom that thou shalt someday pray the High Gods in vain to take away from thee."

"'For a year, Effendi, I was happy – happy, perchance, as no other wedded lover has been since then, for that year was to me only the first of the countless years which should all be as bright as it was. Then Panit came to me, and told me that he had found in a dream, which was a revelation from the High Gods, the secret of the antidote to the tears of Isis. I laughed him to scorn, so marvellously had the elixir renewed my already fading youth within the short space of a year. I boasted that I would drink a measure of it as I would a draught of the red wine of Cos, but he flung my laugh back at me, saying that since I loved the life of the flesh so well, I should live it. It was not for me, but for Amaris, that she might lay down the burden of living when the Gods pleased or she was weary of carrying it.

"'Then said I, in my pride, "O Panit-Ahmes, Amaris will be singing the songs of youth in the days when thy mummy is dust. Let her drink if she will. She is my most precious gift from the Gods; thou canst not take her from me."

"'Never was vainglorious boast more bitterly requited, never was boaster made more humble than I was. Amaris, full of faith and vivid life as I was, took the hazard of the draught laughingly, and seemingly was none the worse for it. Yet another year had not gone by before she sickened of a fever that followed a low Nile, and died. Mad with grief, I took the fever too, and for many days lay in delirium. When I returned to health and reason, the mummy of Amaris already lay in its place in the City of the Dead, over yonder behind the northern spur of the hills, and Panit-Ahmes too was dead and had taken his secret with him over the River of Darkness into the Land of Shadows.

"'Effendi, my tale is told, nor will I weary thee further by telling thee the awful story of the years that have passed between then and now. I have seen the races of men come and go, and their empires wax and wane. I have seen altars rise and fall, faiths born and die, like shadows drifting over the eternal sea. I have learnt the vanity of human things – the shame of glory and the poverty of wealth and the dream of dominion – and here I stand before thee, poor and lonely, without a friend or a lover among all the myriads of men, weary of living, and asking only of the High Gods and thee to find the tomb of Amaris, that I may lay my lips on hers, and from them receive the sweet summons to join her waiting shade on the green shores of Amenti.'

"Such, gentlemen," continued the Professor, laying down a few slips of paper which he had used every now and then to help his memory, "such was the extraordinary story which I heard under such singular circumstances amidst the ruins of Susa. I will tell you the sequel to it in as few words as possible, for I must confess that my theme has somewhat run away from me. Marvellous as it may seem to you, I must ask you to accept it as I saw it and as I tell it to you. There are some things which do not admit of discussion or explanation, and I think you will agree with me that this is one of them.

"Pent-ar was as good as his word, so far as his knowledge of the locality went. The precision with which he indicated the course of the streets and the positions of the hidden buildings was little short of miraculous. For upwards of a month he possessed his world-weary soul in patience, until he had completed the plan of which I spoke some time ago. When he brought it to me, soon after sunrise one morning, he said, with that strange, joyless smile of his:

"'Effendi, have I kept faith with thee? Have I promised aught that I have not performed? If thou art content with me give me now my freedom, that I may go and seek the tomb of Amaris.'

"My answer was an order to my overseer to move the camp at once under his direction to the City of the Dead. Once there, his whole manner changed.

His eyes burned with the fire of an eager anticipation, and he worked with pick and shovel harder than the best of the labourers. At the end of a week we had laid bare a small pyramid, the apex of which, only showing a couple of feet or so above the sand, he had found with unerring instinct or memory after an hour's survey of the wilderness of ruins amidst which it stood. Just before sunset on the last day he came to me with two lamps in one hand and a powerful crowbar in the other.

"'My friend,' he said, using the term for the first time, 'Pent-ar has come to bid thee farewell. The tomb is found, and Amaris waits for me within. I go to open the way to her. If thou wouldst see with thine own eyes the proof of the things which I have told thee, come with me now to the Gate of Death. But bring all thy courage with thee, for it may be thou wilt need it.'

"'I will come, Pent-ar,' I said. It did not seem a time for more words, so I took one of the lamps and followed him to the tomb in silence. It would have taken my workmen hours to remove the great stone slab which closed the entrance; but he, evidently knowing all the secrets of the lost art, laid the passage open in less than an hour. Still silent, we went in, he leading. After I had counted twenty paces the passage ended in a chamber about twelve feet square and fifteen high. In the middle of it, on a huge cube of polished black marble, lay two splendidly adorned sarcophagi. One was open and empty, the other closed.

"'The resting place of him who died not,' Pent-ar whispered, holding his lamp over it. Then he gave the lamp to me, and set to work with a chisel and mallet, which he had picked up outside the pyramid, on the lid of the other sarcophagus. When he had loosened it I helped him to raise it. A mummy-case lay inside, and this with reverent hands we lifted out and laid across the end of the stone. For a moment Pent-ar stood beside it, with hands raised above his head, and murmured in the ancient tongue what was doubtless a prayer for forgiveness and the favour of his outraged Gods. This finished, he took his knife from his belt and with a few deft silent movements detached and removed the cover of the case.

"'Amaris! Amaris!' he murmured again, falling on his knees beside the case, and saying some more words in his own speech.

"I looked over his shoulders, and to my amazement I saw, not the mummy I had expected to find, but the unswathed, white-robed figure of an exquisitely beautiful girl, who, instead of having lain there hidden from the sight of men for thirty centuries, might have fallen asleep only an hour before.

"'It is time,' said Pent-ar, rising and taking my hands. 'Is she not beautiful, my love, my bride? See, are not her sweet lips moist still with the dew of love, as Panit said? Now farewell, Son of the Younger Days and last of my friends on earth. In a few moments Pent-ar will be walking in the groves of Amenti hand in band with Amaris. Farewell, and let not thy courage fail thee in the presence of Death the Releaser."

"As I pressed his hands and bade him farewell, a flood of memories swept over my soul, I know not whence. Was it possible that I, with other eyes, had once looked with love on that fair face? Who knows? But before I could frame the question I would have asked Pent-ar, he had stretched himself lengthways over the case and pressed his lips to those of his dead love.

"Gentlemen, I hope I may never see such another sight as that which I beheld in the next few moments. No sooner had their lips met than the fair flesh of the mummy grew dark and shrivelled into a thousand wrinkles. The eyes sank back into the sockets, the gloss faded from the gold-brown hair, and the rounded form shrank together under the garments. But even this was as nothing to the awful change which the magic of the Death-kiss had wrought on Pent-ar. He who a moment before had stood with me, a living breathing man, holding my hands and speaking to me in his now familiar voice, became, as it were in an instant, not a corpse, but a skeleton covered with a dry brown skin, through which the grey bones broke their way as they dropped with a gentle rustling sound into the case in which the ashes of the long-parted lovers at length were permitted to mingle.

"In my wonder and horror I dropped the lamps I was holding, and when I had groped my way into the outer air I found it full of flying grains of sand. I fought my way, half choked, back into camp. That night the worst sandstorm I have ever seen raged until morning, and when I was able to go back to the City of the Dead I found nothing but a wide, level plain of driven sand where our excavations had been made. It was the winding-sheet of Pent-ar and Amaris, and beneath it their ashes shall, I trust, rest in peace until the dawn of the day whose sun will never set."

The Cat

by Sax Rohmer

Originally published in The New Magazine *in March 1914, Sax Rohmer's "The Cat" is a subdued jab at late Edwardian upper class social mores. The story's protagonist, one Inez Durward, is the daughter of a British Egyptologist, and she is, shall we say, a little different. Inez not only wears a lapus lazuli cat necklace, but she also seems to be somehow bizarrely connected to a long dead Egyptian priestess. Much as in other ancient Egyptian supernatural tales, the tropes of reincarnation and a mysterious past rudely intruding upon modernity are present in this lesser known Rohmer story.*

Although in some ways "The Cat" feels slightly incomplete, as if it were striving for something it could not quite reach, it nevertheless remains a significant story within the ancient Egyptian supernatural tale subgenre. Indeed, what distinguishes this Sax Rohmer story is that the pivotal character is neither a human nor a mummy. It is, as the title clearly indicates, a cat. And not just any cat, but a feline described as a "monstrous creature" with "moonlike eyes." This surreptitious black cat not only manages to form an unusual bond with the story's main female character, but also engages in activities that have enormous social repercussions for the entire coterie of characters, not all of whom are exactly who they first appear to be.

Altogether, it's a lighthearted story, at least in comparison with some of the truly bizarre and often over the top mummy stories published in pulp magazines decades later. Still, Rohmer's "The Cat" hints at a metaphysical darkness lingering in the civilized world and, while not an oft-reprinted story, it indirectly paved the way for later authors to build upon its mystical elements and to utilize them in their own literary endeavors.

Inez Durward listlessly turned the page of music before her and played on for a few more bars, *diminuendo*; then ceased entirely. With her dark eyes gazing into vacancy she sat, and by the slightly dilated pupils an observer, had there been one, might have divined that her thoughts were in the past – might have divined from the expression upon her face that the past whereof she dreamed was troublous.

A faint creaking of shoes upon the carpet told her that she no longer was alone. She glanced at the framed photograph of her father upon the piano and in it saw the reflection of a man's face – more than ordinarily handsome. The newcomer was bending towards her. She turned, raising her eyes to his.

For a moment they stayed so, he with his fair head inclined to her dark one; she looking up at him with a touch of colour upon her pale cheeks.

"I have waited, as I promised," he said gently. "Your father's goodwill remains unchanged. I have only to ask you for – your final answer."

He touched her hand as it rested upon the piano. She did not withdraw it, and he clasped it in his own. Still she sat looking up at him with her big, mysterious eyes. In them he could read no answer, no invitation, yet no actual rebuff. He had thought to find her in a different mood, but tonight the mystic phase of her nature asserted itself – the phase he did not understand, had never understood.

When Inez Durward looked at him as she was looking at him now, he always found himself likening her pale, cold beauty to that of a Vestal. At such times her red lips were no less inviting than in her softer moods, her charm no less voluptuous; but in those sombre eyes lay a burning rebuke to human passion. It seemed a sacrilege to touch her white fingers.

Sir Marcus Auckland released her hand – and Inez replaced it upon the piano. He drew himself upright, with something like pain upon his handsome face.

"I" – he locked his hands behind him – "I'm sorry."

His voice was unsteady. Still the girl did not speak, but watched him in that oddly impersonal way.

"Perhaps," he continued slowly, "I have adhered too closely to the spirit of our compact. For six months I have been to you no more than an ordinary acquaintance. During that time has – someone else – ?"

Inez seemed to arouse herself; the pupils of her eyes contracted to a more normal size. She stood up.

"Forgive me, Sir Marcus," she said. "I should have answered you before. Surely you know there is not, cannot be anyone else."

He took a step forward.

"No!" she pushed him gently back, "please do not think there is anyone else, nor imagine that I am trifling with you; but I wish – I suppose I am odd and queer – but I wish you to do something for me. Not a great thing, or perhaps you may think it is a great thing."

"Inez! No! I haven't that right! Miss Durward, great or small, if it be possible, you know you have only to ask!"

The girl began to toy with the amulet which hung upon the slender gold chain about her neck. It was the figure of a cat, carved in lapis lazuli. With her eyes lowered she stood, and the light from the rose-shaded standard lamp gleamed softly upon her bare shoulders, with the hint of southern gold warming their whiteness.

"You will not think that I ask it from any vain motive, any womanish foible or desire to – to exact – sacrifices?"

"I know you to be above such motives."

"Then my request is a simple one. You may not, you cannot, understand what prompts it; I scarcely do myself." She glanced up again, almost pathetically. "Do you know, Sir Marcus, I often think I am at least two individuals – that I am ruled by two distinct intelligences – but that is all beside the question. When you asked me to marry you, I asked in return that you should wait for six months. For both our sakes, I wanted to be sure –"

She hesitated.

"Yes?" he prompted gently.

"There are two more days!"

Sir Marcus started.

"Are you sure?"

"Quite sure. You must be angry with me for keeping so careful a record?"

"Not at all," he said, but a trifle ruefully. "I – I am to blame. Truth to tell, I had forgotten the exact date. I hardly thought you meant it in that way – to be observed to the very day, I mean."

"Perhaps I didn't – at the time. But are two days so very long to wait, when one has patiently and loyally waited for six months?"

"No," he replied. "But, Inez" – he rested one knee upon the music chair, leaning suddenly forward, with ardent gaze fixed upon her face – "it is unnecessary for me to tell you what those six months have been. You do not intend it so, I know, but you are torturing me! Tell me, at least, that I may hope, that no one, nothing, has changed you –"

"Of course not," she said, with the calm, spiritual light returning to her eyes. "Nothing ever could change me now."

He mastered the tumult within him – felt ashamed, unworthy, as he always did when that strange, heatless flame burned in her eyes. At such times it seemed that a soul – a soul wise with the wisdom of a thousand ages – looked out from the eyes of Inez Durward.

"Then you wish me to go and to return in two days?"

She laughed, taking his arm almost affectionately. Instantly she was become the Inez he knew, the Inez he understood and dreamed of possessing. Sir Marcus was no student of psychic mysteries, but these abrupt transitions made him wonder if it were within the great scheme of things for a woman's body to be the casket of two souls.

"How absurd!" she said. "Of course I don't want you to go. Whatever would father think?"

But her tone revealed that the subject was closed for two days.

So, chatting lightly of light matters, they returned together to the huge apartment where Professor Durward, amid a museum of Egyptian curiosities, sat reading the correspondence which had come by the last mail. Inez had christened the room "Bubastis"; for the thousand and one relics which littered it had principally been recovered from the ruins of that ancient city. The famous Egyptologist was engaged upon a monumental work dealing with the worship of Bast and Sekhet as they entered.

"I'll wager you a box of cigars, *real* cigars," whispered Inez to Sir Marcus, "against one of gloves, that father's first remark is 'Bubastite'!"

"I accept!" said he.

"Listen to this, Inez," began the Professor, holding a letter in his hand, "it is from Meeson – the dealer in Bloomsbury, you know. I really cannot understand how these valuable finds escape my Fellows. This Meeson has a sarcophagus, which he vaguely refers to as "excavated at Zagazig," and from his description and the photograph enclosed I cannot doubt that it is that of a Bubastite princess of Sekhet!"

Inez burst out laughing, whereat the Professor, adjusting his pince-nez, stared at her amazedly.

"Why do you laugh?"

"Because I have won a box of gloves!" she said, stooping and slipping her graceful arm about his neck, a twinkle in her eyes the while.

"Ah!" cried her father, smiling in turn, "I see, yes, yes; I am obsessed by my subject, I admit! I hope, Auckland" – he turned to the latter – "I don't bore you –"

"Not at all! Though hopelessly ignorant of the subject, I can realise something of its fascination."

"Its fascination, Auckland, is irresistible. Even Inez, though she pretends to laugh at me, has succumbed to it. Her knowledge of ancient Bubastis frequently surprises me."

Inez leant back against the huge table, its green leather hidden beneath rolls of papyrus, busts, statuettes, cases of scarabs, broken utensils, potsherds, and tablets. Her eyes grew dreamy.

"You are joking, father," she said. "My ideas of Bubastis are purely imaginary."

"I envy you your imagination, Inez," replied the Professor. "Do you know, Auckland, when Inez and I visited Bubastis in January, she instinctively located the sites of the principal buildings and by a process of imaginative reasoning enabled me to rectify errors into which Brugsch had fallen. She even convinced me that Flinders Petrie's judgement had been at fault in one solitary instance."

"How remarkable," said Auckland, staring at the girl. "You must have studied deeply."

"On the contrary," answered Inez, "I have never studied the subject in the slightest. Oh, there's nothing very wonderful about it! Plenty of people who visit such old lands as Egypt, Assyria, and Palestine for the first time, experience a sense of familiarity with their surroundings."

Sir Marcus was watching her, a curious expression upon his handsome face.

"You almost tempt me to believe in the reincarnation of souls!" he remarked.

"Tempt you to believe?" she said, turning her sombre eyes upon him. "What, is there anyone today who doubts?"

Auckland looked uncomfortable. The Professor smiled, but shook his head.

"Inez," he said, "how often have I pointed out to you the absurdity of such theories – shown you that they rest upon the unsubstantial reasoning of sensational novelists?"

Inez made no reply.

"And now," continued her father, "before I forget, I shall be leaving town tomorrow by an early train, as you know, and I want you to call at Meeson's and see the sarcophagus. If it is genuine, secure it, of course."

"But, how shall I know if it is genuine?"

"My dear Inez, you are never in error respecting any Bubastic relic!"

Inez glanced across at Auckland.

"Yet I don't know upon what I base my opinions!" she said dreamily. "You are taking risks, father, by trusting to my mysterious instinct!"

"Never mind. You will go?"

"It will have to be in the evening, between six and seven."

"That will do nicely. I will write them a line."

Very shortly afterwards Sir Marcus Auckland took his departure, Inez again exhibiting toward him something so like affection that he flushed deeply, and was only restrained from the protestation that burnt upon his tongue by the cold eyes – which bade him respect his strange bargain.

Professor Durward's sister, who presided over the widower's household, came to Inez's room later. She seated herself beside the girl upon the chesterfield where Inez often sat for hours during her "queer" moods.

"Tell me, child," she said, with her arm around the girl's shoulders, "is all well between you and Marcus Auckland? Your father quite expected to hear that all was settled."

"It will be settled in another two days, dear – on the nineteenth."

"What! You have put him off again! God bless me, he has the patience of Job! It is not every eligible baronet who would have given you six months to make up your mind, Inez. And I so carefully left you alone together after dinner tonight!"

Inez laughed merrily.

"Dear Aunt Alison!" she said, "I know you did! You are a most efficient match-maker!"

Alison Durward shrugged her plump shoulders eloquently.

"Is he not a splendid match, child? He is of a family nearly as old as the Durwards, young, good-looking, and as open as the day. He confessed to me that he had been a fool with his money in the past; therefore he will know how to take care of it in the future – yours as well as his own; for in a modest way you are something of an heiress. You will be mistress of Morton Priory, and although you are rarely seen in Society, will have captured the most desirable bachelor at present upon the matrimonial market!"

"Dear Aunt Alison, you should have been a stockbroker!"

Something in the girl's voice – a faint note of weariness – caused her aunt to stare at her anxiously. She took Inez's hand, holding it in her firm clasp.

"Inez," she said anxiously, "you no longer regret that poor misguided Ralph Heppel?"

"Of course not," replied Inez listlessly.

"In any event it was an impossible match – after it was found that his uncle, Sir Roger, had for some reason left him out of his will! He hadn't a penny, and his crime –"

Inez stood up.

"Don't call it a crime, Aunt Alison."

"Not a crime!" cried her aunt, "not a crime, when he had the ruby in his possession! When it was actually found on him!"

Inez sighed wearily, walking across to the bookcase.

"There is nothing to be gained by re-opening that old discussion, dear," she said, "is there?"

"Yes, Inez," persisted her aunt, "there is. I suspected that you still cared about him."

Inez took a book from the shelf and stood turning the leaves.

"Your father, of course, never suspected, Inez. Mr Heppel was simply a secretary to *him*. I wish you could get to think of him more in that way, too – in the light, I mean, of a – a defaulting cashier!"

"Oh, aunt!"

"Sir Marcus Auckland's attitude was so admirable on that unfortunate occasion. You recall how he tried to shield Mr Heppel? – and his solicitor, Mr Rufus, was most kind, too!"

"Yes," agreed Inez. "I have always respected him from that time."

"Whatever book have you there, child?"

The girl held it, cover forward, towards the speaker.

"*Temples of Bubastis*," read Aunt Alison. "My dear Inez, *one* Egyptian lunatic is sufficient for any family! I should be simply delighted to find you reading a really sloppy novel, dear!"

Inez replaced the book, and kissed her aunt affectionately. But that good lady departed wholly dissatisfied with the girl's frame of mind – dissatisfied with her absorption in obscure studies, and with her regrets for the young secretary who, in a moment of inexplicable weakness, had stolen the great ruby which Professor Durward had found in the tomb of a long-dead queen.

Alison Durward thought of rejoining her brother in the study. Then she reflected that what she had learnt was learnt in confidence, and went to her own room. She sat brushing her abundant brown hair, in which no fleck of grey yet showed, when a sound came which froze her to a sudden stillness. Brush in hand, she sat, transfixed

It was a low cry, yet a cry of acute fear. It fell to a moan, which died into the silence.

She snatched her dressing-gown, threw open the door, and ran along the corridor to Inez's room. Light showed under the door. She entered.

Inez stood before the big mirror, both hands raised to her face. She had not even commenced to undress.

"My dear, my dear! What is it?"

Alison Durward clasped her motherly arms about the girl. Inez turned to her, a vague fear still haunting her big eyes.

"Oh," she said, "it was something impossible. You will say I imagined it. I suppose I must have done. But when I looked in the mirror –"

"Well, child?"

"The reflection – was not mine!"

"Inez, whatever can you mean?"

"I mean that out of the mirror *someone else* was looking at me, someone with wonderful eyes."

"A woman?"

"A woman, yes; and I seemed to know her, oh, so well! She wore –well, dear" – the girl's courage was returning, and she smiled a trifle wanly – "she was hardly quite proper, I fear! She wore very little; but around her neck was a thin gold chain, and upon it hung –"

Inez raised the cat carven in lapis lazuli which was suspended about her own neck.

"My dear child, that conclusively proves that it was your own reflection, and that you were deceived by some odd effect of the light. You see, now, the folly of reading such rubbish as *Temples of Bubastis*! Leave all that to your father, dear."

"Perhaps you are right, aunt. Good night. I am so sorry to have troubled you. I don't know why I cried out; I was not really frightened."

"You are sure you will be all right?"

"Certain. Honestly, I am not nervous in the least."

Josiah Meeson it is unnecessary to describe: Balzac has described him in *The Magic Skin*. He is the curio-dealer from that wonderful book in the flesh. No man had ever seen him otherwise arrayed than in dressing-gown and skull-cap. As for his emporium, that is indescribable.

Inez Durward had visited it before, on more than one occasion; but had never grown accustomed to the place nor to its proprietor. Meeson exhibited no desire to do business.

"Here is the sarcophagus, Miss Durward," he said, in his snuffy, guide-like voice. "It was excavated from a tomb between Tel Bast and Zagazig. The tomb was that of Sekhar, a priestess of Bast or of Sekhet, the sister goddess, wife of Ptah and mother of Im-hotep –"

"The Aesculapius of the Greeks."

"Yes." Meeson stared curiously. "Yes. You are right. That is a very rare amulet you are wearing, very rare. The cat is not met with in Egyptian sculpture, yet that amulet is Egyptian."

"It was worn by a priestess – of Sekhet; and the cat, of course, was sacred to that goddess."

She turned to examine the sarcophagus. It was in a fine state of preservation, and in addition to the usual inscriptions from the Book of the Dead, bore numerous figures of cats, executed with that striking fidelity observable in Egyptian drawings of certain animals, and which is as singular as the ancient craftsmen's ignorance of other creatures, and notably of the human form.

"This is the sarcophagus of a high priestess," she said, as one making an exact statement, and her eyes were sombre and dreamy. "It has been opened and the mummy removed."

"Quite right," said old Meeson respectfully. "The Professor observed this from the photograph?"

"No; he did not say so. Sekhar, the priestess, was very beautiful."

Meeson stared as curiously as he was capable of staring.

"The goddess Sekhet symbolised passion," he said slowly. "Her priestesses were usually women of beauty."

"Will you please remove the lid?"

"Remove it? Why? Ah, I see! You want to look at the interior inscriptions – yes, yes."

In Inez he recognised a connoisseur.

He shuffled into some inside apartment, but shortly returned and set to work to remove the heavy lid. Inez watched him dreamily. She had felt herself compelled, in some strange fashion, to ask that the lid be removed, but she was conscious of no interest in the operation. Her thoughts were of Sir Marcus Auckland and of the answer she must give him so soon, of her father – and of Ralph Heppel.

As the heavy lid began to come away, like a slowly opening door, she was reviewing again the happenings of that dreadful night.

Suddenly the lid fell forward, almost upsetting Meeson. It seemed to the startled girl and to the equally startled man that something had thrust it from within.

Inez uttered a low, frightened cry, and Meeson, with a face of horror, drew back from the sarcophagus.

For it was not empty. There was something within – something *alive*!

Following a moment of breathless suspense, wherein the objects about the shadowy shop seemed to grow sentient – ominous – came a blaze of brilliant eyes from the gloom.

A huge black cat leapt out, clearly seen by both who watched, landed with its lithe spring in silence on the littered floor, leapt again – and was gone!

"My God!" whispered the old dealer. "My God!"

Inez reached out, gropingly, for support. She was sick with sudden, awful terror.

"No cat," continued Meeson dully, "could have lived without food, for all that time – since someone – Arabs – opened the sarcophagus–"

With a great effort the girl controlled herself, choking down the laugh of hysteria that trembled upon her lips.

"Mr Meeson," she said – and her voice was not her own – "my father will take the sarcophagus. Please send it to him. Will you call me a cab?"

Meeson was trembling. Through a tortuous grove of relics he threaded his way to the outer shop, Inez close beside him. An old clerk sat at a desk, upon which burned a dim oil lamp, with a paper shade.

"Baldwin," said Meeson shakily, "did a cat come in here?"

The clerk looked mildly surprised. The emotions of those who remain long in such surroundings become atrophied.

"No, Mr Meeson, I have seen no cat."

"Not a big black cat?"

"No cat."

Some difficulty was experienced in finding a cab; and Inez, who found herself recovering from her fright, and whose mind now discovered several natural explanations of the episode, decided to walk on until she met one. Meeson was peering into the dark corners with dreadful apprehension.

Through the growing dusk she passed. The streets seemed strangely deserted. She was not very familiar with that part of London, and after traversing a number of dingy thoroughfares lying somewhere between New Oxford Street and Drury Lane, it occurred to her that she had taken the wrong turning.

She paused before the entrance to a block of dwellings and looked back. Then, all thought of return was dismissed. She must go on, and quickly, hoping to reach some familiar street.

For lurking in the shadows of the high building some twenty yards behind, was a shape, a lithe shape, of something that pursued!

Inez hurried forward, her heart beating so that its pulsations seemed to choke her. Coming to a narrow court with iron pillars, she turned blindly, and almost ran along it towards the lights of the thoroughfare at the farther end. When within some few yards of the entrance and within touch of the human activity beyond, she ventured to glance back.

A slinking shape passed beneath the light of a gas lamp less than ten paces away – and was lost from sight.

Inez ran forward. A cab appeared; the first she had seen since leaving Meeson's. It was disengaged, and a moment after entering it and giving the man the address, her strength deserted her, and she lay back in the corner in a semi-swoon, from which she only recovered as the cab drew up before the door of the house.

She went straight to her room to dress for dinner. She could not trust herself to think what that pursuing shape might mean; therefore she strove not to think of it at all. Her mirror held terrors for her, but, her aunt entering the room shortly afterwards, she experienced no repetition of the phenomenon of the previous night.

"You look tired, dear," said Alison Durward; "it is hardly fair of the Professor to send you worrying around after his musty relics."

Inez was about to relate the episode at Meeson's when her maid entered. The girl addressed the elder lady.

"Such a lovely black Persian cat," she said, "has just come in through the kitchen window–"

Inez turned suddenly as pale as death and clutched dizzily at her aunt for support. The girl, not noticing, continued:

"She has made herself quite at home and is such a beautiful creature. Do you mind if we keep her?"

Alison Durward looked in alarm at Inez.

"Whatever is the matter?" she said, "you are not afraid of cats?"

"Of course not! You know how fond I am of them."

"Don't you want them to keep it?"

"What an idea! Why, it is unlucky to refuse hospitality to a black cat!"

Inez forced a smile to her lips. She was determined to conquer the mysterious, indefinable dread which threatened to obsess her mind. She saw clearly now, and comforted herself with the reflection, that the cat which had appeared in Meeson's shop was merely some poor, half-starved animal that had entered the sarcophagus for shelter and in some way got fastened in. The neighbourhood through which she had come, too, was one where she might expect to encounter lurking felines; and the advent of this strange Persian could be nothing more than a coincidence. She suddenly determined to relate nothing of the happening at Meeson's.

"I love cats," she said. "I hope it will stay."

Sir Marcus Auckland was come to dine. As the party of three – for Professor Durward was yet away – took their seats, Inez felt a furry body being gently rubbed against her dress. She started, chilled to the heart; then calling up all her courage, stooped and fondled the small shapely head of the magnificent black cat which crouched beside her. As her hand touched the long glossy fur all her dread left her.

"Look, Aunt Alison!" she cried. "Do come and look! Is she not a beauty?"

"I have seen her, dear," was the reply; "she has made herself quite at home, but we shall probably have to return her to her rightful owner. She is the most magnificent creature I have ever set eyes upon. Pussy!" she called. "Pussy, come here. Just look at her, Sir Marcus; she strayed in this evening."

But the great cat, with her gleaming eyes raised to Inez, and purring with contentment, moved not at all.

"You are evidently the favourite, Miss Durward," said Auckland. "Her majesty scorns all others!"

Throughout dinner the cat crouched at the girl's feet. A maid attempted to remove her once, but the great creature stood up, with arched back, resenting approach. She would permit no hand to touch her but that of Inez.

When the three passed out to the drawing-room, the cat walked stately ahead. Auckland, at the door, stooped to caress her – and drew back his hand with a subdued cry of anger.

"Confound the animal!" he added irritably, and raised his wounded finger to his lips.

"Oh, I am so sorry!" cried Inez. "You must bathe it in antiseptic. Is it a very deep scratch?"

"It's nothing at all," was the smiling reply. "I decline, absolutely, to bathe it in antiseptic, though it was very, very kind of you to propose that I should."

"Lawrence," said Inez, to a maid, and the note of regret in her voice was involuntary, "this cat is dangerous, I'm afraid. Take her downstairs."

Gingerly the girl approached. The cat arched its back and fixed such a wicked glare upon her with its brilliant green eyes that she drew back, thoroughly affrighted.

"She seems to have become quite unmanageable," cried Alison Durward. "I thought you had made friends with her downstairs?"

"We had, madam," replied the girl. "She drank some milk which we gave her, but now that I come to think of it, she would not let me touch her, although she didn't act so spiteful as this!"

"Quite a queenly animal," said Auckland "I respect her. May I see what I can do?"

"Be careful, sir!" whispered the servant. "See how she's looking at you!"

Indeed, the black cat was behaving in a singular manner. About the character of stray cats, as a rule, there is nothing assertive. But this great creature was an exception. As Sir Marcus Auckland turned to her the cat advanced to meet him. In the subdued light the animal's eyes looked enormous, abnormal, and their iridescence unlike that of any other animal.

"Merciful heavens!" gasped Alison Durward, "she is going to spring!"

Auckland bit his lip and instinctively raised his arms to guard his face and throat. The cat crouched low, its blazing eyes set upon him, its long, gleaming claws dug deeply into the carpet. It was a scene wildly grotesque, utterly bizarre. No one could predict its termination.

Then Inez stepped quietly forward, stopped, and laid her white hand upon the small, shapely head with its pointed ears flattened back wildly.

She spoke to the animal, in a soft voice, and stepped forward, entering the drawing-room. Meekly the cat followed.

"Inez!" said her aunt excitedly, "shall I send for a veterinary surgeon to destroy the creature? I think it is mad!"

"Oh, aunt!" cried Inez, "how can you be so cruel! I am awfully sorry that she scratched Sir Marcus, but it was only because of her strange affection for me and her resentment at being taken away!"

"But surely," said Auckland, "these are the attributes of a faithful but savage dog? There is something unnatural about a cat that behaves in this way."

"I agree with you!" cried Aunt Alison, "I shall never sleep in peace whilst such a dreadful creature remains in the house!"

"Don't be so absurd, dear," said Inez gently.

She sank on to a settee, and the cat spread its great lithe body at her feet, looking up to her with moonlike eyes. Seen now, in the bright light, it was truly a monstrous creature, black as Erebus, with eyes like liquid fire. Auckland looked at it from the opposite side of the room. He was unable wholly to disguise his growing fear of the cat.

Curiously, Inez was the only one of the party who experienced none.

Auckland, throughout the evening, showed himself oddly ill at ease. Palpably he was anxious for an intimate chat with the girl; but Inez so clearly exhibited to her aunt an equal anxiety to avoid this, that Alison Durward played the part of duenna to Spanish perfection. It was a curious, three-handed game, watched by the green eyes of the cat with what might have been interest.

The house of Professor Durward was an old one, with those unexpected brief flights of stairs and illogical planning of corridors which lead to abrupt turns and singular angles; the type of architecture more common in country mansions than in London houses.

When Auckland, at a late hour, took his leave, Inez and her aunt stood chatting with him in the hall whilst he lighted a cigarette. With a man's characteristic helplessness in such cases, he stood holding the extinguished match in his hand and looking about for some receptacle in which to deposit it. Inez laughed gleefully, and offered no advice.

"You jeopardise your carpet!" Auckland assured her; "for bachelor man is irresponsible where used matches are concerned. But I shall show that he can reform and shall deposit this in the copper urn to fertilise the palm!"

He retraced his steps to the recess near the foot of the stairs, where a large palm stood in half-shadow. His tall figure was lost from view for a moment.

Then came a feline howl of pain – and a sputtering and hissing. A smothered curse – and Auckland reappeared.

"Whatever has happened?" cried Inez.

"A simple thing," replied Auckland; and one might have detected a faint note of satisfaction in his voice. "I trod on your black cat!"

"Poor pussy!"

"Poor me! I was nearly precipitated down the steps into that little room which an insane architect has concealed beneath the staircase!"

Always there was the suggestion of irritable distaste underlying his references to the creature. And when he had made his departure:

"My dear," said Aunt Alison, "when you are Lady Auckland there must be no black cat!"

"Whatever do you mean, aunt?"

"I mean that in the interests of domestic peace your new pet must be left behind when you go to Morton Priory."

"Sir Marcus is naturally annoyed because the cat scratched him. He will have forgotten that tomorrow, though."

"It is a terrible creature!"

"Then, since I am its only friend, it must remain with me." Alison Durward sighed.

"You will think better of that, my child," she said, "when you have been married six months!"

And now arose a new trouble for Inez, but a joy for her aunt. The black cat could not be found! Callings of "Puss, puss" were prolific of no result.

"Never mind," said Aunt Alison, with great philosophy, "these stray cats rarely remain anywhere for long. She has probably jumped out of a window and resumed her wanderings."

"She was not that kind of cat," declared Inez. "She was of the patrician order!"

But the household retired for the night with the conviction that the wanderer, having briefly sampled its hospitality, had indeed resumed her wanderings.

Inez sat brushing her hair before the mirror. Her maid she had sent to bed. With a perplexed little frown upon her white brow, she studied her features. She experienced no fear tonight that they would melt and merge into those other features, so like yet so unlike her own. Something told her that the phenomenon would not be repeated.

She held the little image of lapis lazuli between her fingers, the image that had been worn by the priestess of old. When she had stood before the great sarcophagus in Meeson's shop the knowledge had come to her – unaccountably, as the figure had seemed to come in the mirror – that it was the sarcophagus wherein that fair figure had lain; that the priestess of Sekhet was the woman of the mirror and the former wearer of the cat amulet.

Could she trust this knowledge, which seemingly sprang from her imagination? She did not know; it was all very wonderful. And it seemed to fit into a vast, mystic scheme. From childhood Inez had possessed a quite abnormal power of control over cats, the most intractable of domestic creatures. The cat had been sacred to Bast and Sekhet. Her mystic mind lost itself in this world of strange dreams. Did it all mean anything, or was she the victim of an unhealthy imagination?

Was it her duty to conquer such imaginings, as her father had assured her, or were they the key to that great Riddle which exact science has failed to solve? Sir Marcus Auckland had no sympathy with her mystic moods. As his future wife should she not seek to conquer them? For her common-sense self had already accepted him as husband, whilst her mystic self urged delay. But tomorrow the common-sense Inez, in defiance of the mystic, must say "Yes!"

A sound disturbed her reverie. Somewhere a cat had meowed. Inez stood up, listening. The house was very still. Into that quiet square penetrated only the faintest murmur from the thoroughfare beyond. And the night was far advanced.

Instantly her mind supplied an explanation of the sound. The black cat had not left the house, but had been shut in the little room beneath the stair, which no one had thought of searching. Without hesitation she went out into the corridor and downstairs to the darkened hall. Softly, in order to arouse no one, she opened the little door at the head of the steps down which Sir Marcus had so narrowly escaped falling. Then, for the first time, fear ran through her.

For two blazing green eyes shone up from the gloom. She had anticipated this, but the eyes looked abnormally large. Moreover, they looked, not like the eyes of a cat, but like that rare natural phenomenon – luminous human eyes!

She paused, catching her breath. A soft meow, followed by purring, came to her ears; and the momentary fancy, with its attendant fear, left her.

"Poor pussy," she said. "Did they lock you in?"

The cat continued to purr but did not move. The great eyes looked up to her, unblinkingly.

"Come along, pussy," she coaxed, but the cat did not stir.

Inez felt for, and found, the electric switch, and turned on the lower hall light, which enabled her to see into the little apartment. The huge cat, purring happily, lay stretched upon the floor with its paws resting upon a green leather pocket-case. The case was open; and several letters lay strewn about.

"Why, Sir Marcus must have dropped his case from his pocket when he stumbled over you in the dark, pussy!" said Inez. "Have you lain there in hiding so that I might be privileged to pick it up?"

Inez descended the steps, and the cat rose and rubbed itself affectionately against her. She, stooped for the book, and her gaze quite involuntarily fell upon the opening sentence of a letter which lay open on the floor. It was this:

MY DEAR MARCUS: Unless your engagement to Miss Durward is announced before the 18th inst., the old man insists that he'll be compelled to dispose of Morton Priory –

Something like a dagger-thrust seemed to strike her heart. Then the pain passed, and Inez took up the letter with the rest and returned to the hall, the black cat following. Conscious of no scruple, she stood under the light and read the letter to the end:

I understood, and so did the guv'nor, that the conjuring trick with the Professor's ruby would put the first favourite out of the running. You undertook to marry the girl within six months of that date. Without a scrap of ill-will, dear boy, I must remind you that you haven't stuck to the contract. You know what the old 'un is. I'm helpless. We reach Liverpool per *Mauretania* on the 15th. Sorry, dear boy, but look out for squalls.

Yours as ever,
JAKE RUFUS

The door-bell began to ring, followed by a loud knocking. Very pale, but perfectly composed, Inez drew her dressing-gown closely about her and un-bolted the door. She knew as well as though its solid panels had been of glass who stood outside; and when she opened the door and saw the pale, handsome face of Sir Marcus Auckland she exhibited no trace of surprise. But her eyes told him.

"My God!" he whispered, "you!"

"I have just found your pocket-book," she said quietly, and handed it to him. "This letter had fallen out. Goodbye!"

The pallor of his face changed to a tone of grey.

Inez re-closed and re-bolted the door. She turned to look for the cat. It was not to be seen. Again she was conscious of no surprise; nor did she trouble to look for the creature, but extinguishing the light, went up to her room. No one had been aroused, apparently. Vaguely she wondered why.

As the clock in the hall struck two, she rose from the chesterfield. There came to her ears from the distance the clangour of bells and the beat of gal-loping hooves. A fire engine was passing the entrance to the square.

"You look unwell this morning, Inez," said her aunt at breakfast.

Inez glanced up with a smile.

"I'm rather tired," she replied. "I slept badly; but I am not in the least un-well, dear; in fact, I am better than I have been for a very long time."

"Ah," said her aunt, "people who worry about temples of Bubastis can't ex-pect to sleep the sleep of the just. I suppose you will be off to Bloomsbury im-mediately after breakfast?"

"To Bloomsbury! Why?"

"Because, child, according to the morning paper, Meeson's has been burnt out. Since you had purchased that sarcophagus thing on your father's behalf, I fear your father will be the loser if it is destroyed"

"Oh!" said Inez, scarcely comprehending how much or how little this might portend. "How unfortunate; and how very extraordinary!"

A maid came in.

"Well?" asked Alison Durward, "have you found that dreadful cat?"

"No, madam."

"I think," said Inez slowly, "it went away last night. I will tell you all about it presently. Was anyone hurt at the fire?"

"No," replied her aunt. "There was no one there at the time but an old clerk who was working late. He gave the alarm, I understand. But you haven't read your letters."

Inez turned dully to the letters beside her plate. Then a hot blush spread from her brow to her throat, and faded, leaving her deathly pale. One letter,

bearing an Australian postmark, was addressed in a hand that she knew but
had not expected to see. It was from Ralph Heppel, stating simply that he was
sailing for home, and asked if she would see him, as he had procured information from a discharged employee of Messrs Rufus and Son which led him
to believe that he could at last prove himself to be the victim of a vile conspiracy.

She passed the letter to her aunt and went quietly upstairs to dress.

An hour later she stood with Mr. Meeson – for the first time in her experience arrayed otherwise than in a dressing-gown – before the smouldering
ruins of the famous curiosity shop.

"It was all insured," he informed her. "Yes, yes; except the sarcophagus of
Sekhar. That had only newly arrived."

"How was the fire caused?"

Josiah Meeson took her arm and drew her aside from the group of police,
and others. Then:

"Mind you," said he in his snuffy voice, "this is old Baldwin's story. I
don't answer for it. But he was working late in the office; nearly always does.
There's an oil lamp in there; you've seen it. It's old fashioned – yes. Well, he
was sitting there, when– Remember that cat we saw?"

"Of course I do."

"Well, a black cat – must have been the same – suddenly jumped in through
the window over the desk, upset the lamp (it may be a lie!), and went bounding into the warehouse – where the sarcophagus was."

"Heavens!" whispered Inez; "what does it all mean?"

"It means that everything's been burnt – cat and all, if it didn't come out
again. But it means something else. It means that it's an ill wind –"

"An ill wind?"

"You know the old saying? I had a Sheraton desk there that used to belong
to Sir Roger Heppel."

"Sir Roger – Heppel!"

"Uncle of the gentleman who was the Professor's secretary. The firemen got
a few things out, this desk among them. They broke it in getting it through
the window, though, and a secret drawer – one I hadn't found – dropped out."

"Yes," said Inez in a barely audible voice. "What was in it?"

"Nothing much. The missing codicil of Sir Roger's will. But it means about
ten thousand a year to Mr Ralph Heppel!"

The Whispering Mummy
by Sax Rohmer

In "The Whispering Mummy," Sax Rohmer returns to many of the themes first explored in "The Cat" (1912). Perhaps the most atmospheric tale in this anthology, it features a woman who may be the modern day reincarnation of an ancient Egyptian priestess. Originally published as part of a 1918 collection entitled Tales of Secret Egypt, *this Rohmer tale hints at the powerful, mystical hold that ancient Egypt can have on a seemingly rational, scientific present. There's also, even if briefly, a lean and furtive feline afoot and a villain who is described as moving like a cat.*

There is, of course, a mummy in "The Whispering Mummy." As readers shall soon learn, however, its importance is somewhat secondary to the story's overall theme. In this tale, a French painter is both transfixed by, and out of his depths in, early twentieth-century Cairo. Sax Rohmer skillfully contrasts European modernity and Continental cultural norms with the mores of both modern Egypt and the Egyptian past. Not surprisingly, given that Rohmer created the legendary villain Fu Manchu, there are hints of a secret sect known for treating their enemies harshly. All told, "The Whispering Mummy" remains an enchanting tale, one that takes the reader deep into the mysteries of both time and love.

I

Felix Bréton and I were the only occupants of the raised platform at the end of the hall; and the inartistic performance of the bulky dancer who occupied the stage promised to be interminable. From motives of sheer boredom I studied the details of her dress — a white dress, fitting like a vest from shoulder to hip, and having short, full sleeves under which was a sort of blue gauze. Her hair, wrists, and ankles glittered with barbaric jewelry and strings of little coins.

A deafening orchestra consisting of tambourines, shrieking Arab viols, and the inevitable *darabukeh*, surrounded the performer in a half-circle; and three other large-sized *ghawâzi* mingled their shrill voices with the barbaric discords of the musicians. I yawned.

"As a quest of local color, Bréton," I said, "this evening's expedition can only be voted a dismal failure."

Felix Bréton turned to me, with a smile, resting his elbows upon the dirty little marble-topped table. He looked sufficiently like an artist to have been merely a painter; yet his gruesome picture "Le Roi S'Amuse" had proved the salvation of the previous Salon.

"Have patience," he said; "it is Shejeret ed-Durr (Tree of Pearls) that we have come to see, and she has not yet appeared."

"Unless she appears shortly," I replied, stifling another yawn, "I shall disappear."

But even as I spoke, there arose a hum of excitement throughout the crowded room; the fat dancer, breathless from her unpleasing exertions, resumed her seat; and all the performers turned their heads towards a door at the side of the stage. A veiled figure entered, with slow, lithe step; and her appearance was acclaimed excitedly. Coming to the centre of the stage, she threw off her veil with a swift movement, and confronted the audience, a slim, barbaric figure. I glanced at Felix Bréton. His eyes were glittering with excitement. Here at last was the *ghazîyeh* of romance, the *ghazîyeh* of the Egyptian monuments; a true daughter of that mysterious tribe who, in the remote past of the Nile-land, wove spells of subtle moon-magic before the golden Pharaoh.

A monstrous crash from the musicians opened the music of the dance — the famous Gazelle dance — which commenced to a measure of long, monotonous cadences. Shejeret ed-Durr began slowly to move her arms and body in that indescribable manner which, like the stirring of palm fronds, speaks the veritable language of the voluptuous Orient. The attendant dancers clashing their miniature cymbals, the measure quickened, and swift passion informed the languorous body, which magically became transformed into that of a leaping nymph, a bacchante, a living illustration of Keats' wonder-words:

"Like to a moving vintage, down they came,
Crown'd with green leaves, and faces all aflame;
All madly dancing through the pleasant valley,
To scare thee, Melancholy!"

At the conclusion of her dance, Shejeret ed-Durr, resuming her veil, descended to the floor of the hall and passed from table to table, exchanging light badinage with those patrons known to her.

"Do you think you could induce her to come up here, Kernaby?" said Bréton excitedly; "she is simply the ideal model for my 'Danse Funébre.'"

"Any inducement other than our presence in this select part of the establishment," I replied, offering him a cigarette, "is unnecessary. She will present herself with all reasonable despatch."

Indeed, I had seen the dark eyes glance many times towards us, as we sat there in distinguished isolation; and, even as I spoke, the girl was ascending the steps, from whence she approached our table, smiling in friendly fashion. Bréton's surprise was rather amusing when she confidently seated herself, giving an order to the cross-eyed waiter in close attendance. It would be our privilege, of course, to pay the bill. Of its being a privilege, no one could doubt who had observed the envious glances cast in our direction by less favored patrons.

As Bréton spoke no Arabic, the task of interpreter devolved upon me; and I was carrying on quite mechanically when my attention was drawn to a peculiarly sinister-looking person seated alone at a table close beside the corner of the stage. I remembered having observed him address some remark to Shejeret ed-Durr, and having noted that she seemed to avoid him. Now, he was directing upon us a glare so electrically baleful that when I first detected it I was conscious of a sort of shock. The man was rather oddly dressed, wearing a black turban and a sort of loose robe not unlike the *burnus* of the desert Arabs. I concluded that he belonged to some religious order, and that his bosom was inflamed with a hatred of a most murderous character towards myself, Felix Bréton, and the dancer.

I endeavored, without attracting the girl's notice to indicate to Bréton the presence of the Man of the Glare; but the artist was so engrossed in contemplation of Shejeret ed-Durr and kept me so busy interpreting, that I abandoned the attempt in despair. Having made his wishes evident to her, the girl readily consented to pose for him; and when next I glanced at the table near the stage, the Man of the Glare had disappeared.

What induced me to look towards the rear of the platform upon which we were seated I know not, unless I did so in obedience to a species of hypnotic suggestion; but something prompted me to glance over my shoulder. And, for the second time that night, I encountered the gaze of mysterious eyes. From a little square window these compelling eyes regarded me fixedly, and presently I distinguished the outline of a head surmounted by a white turban.

The second watcher was Abu Tabâh!

What business could have brought the mysterious *imam* to such a place was a problem beyond my powers of conjecture, but that he was silently directing me to depart with all speed I presently made out. Having signified, by a gesture, that I had grasped the purport of his message, I turned again to Bréton, who was struggling to carry on a conversation with Shejeret ed-Durr in his native French.

I experienced some difficulty in inducing him to leave, but my arguments finally prevailed, and we passed out into the dimly lighted street. About us in the darkness pipes wailed, and there was the dim throbbing of the eternal *darabukeh*. We were in that part of El-Wasr adjoining the notorious Square of the Fountain. Discordant woman voices filled the night, and strange figures flitted from the shadows into the light streaming from the open doorways. It was the centre of secret Cairo, the midnight city; and three paces from the door of the dance hall, a slim, black-robed figure suddenly appeared at my elbow, and the musical voice of Abu Tabâh spoke close to my ear:

"Be on the terrace of Shepheard's in half an hour."

The mysterious figure melted again into the shadows about us.

II

On the deserted hotel balcony, Abu Tabâh awaited me.

"It was indeed fortunate, Kernaby Pasha," he said, "that I observed you this evening."

"I am greatly obliged to you," I replied, "for watching over me with such paternal solicitude. May I inquire what danger I have incurred?"

I was angrily conscious of feeling like a schoolboy suffering reproof.

"A very great danger," Abu Tabâh assured me, his gentle, musical voice expressing real concern. "Ahmad es-Kebîr is the lover of the dancer called Shejeret ed-Durr, although she who is of the *ghawâzi* of Keneh does not return his affections."

"Ahmad es-Kebîr? — do you refer to a malignant looking person in a black turban?" I inquired.

Abu Tabâh gravely inclined his head.

"He is one of the *Rifa'iyeh*, the Black *Darwîshes*. They practise strange rites and are by some accredited with supernatural powers. For you the danger is not so great as for your friend, who seemed to be speaking words of love to the *ghazîyeh*."

I laughed shortly.

"You are mistaken, Abu Tabâh," I replied; "his interest was not of the character which you suppose. He is an artist and merely desired the girl to pose for him."

Abu Tabâh shrugged his shoulders.

"She is an unveiled woman," he said contemptuously, "but love in the heart of such a one as Ahmad is a terrible passion, consuming the vitals and rendering whom it afflicts either a partaker of Paradise or as one of the evil *ginn*."

"In the particular case under consideration," I said, "it would seem distinctly to have produced the latter and less agreeable symptoms."

"Let your friend step warily," advised Abu Tabâh; "for some who have aroused the enmity of the Black *Darwîshes* have met with strange ends, nor has it been possible to fix responsibility upon any member of the order."

"You think my poor friend, Felix Bréton, may be discovered some morning in an unpleasantly messy condition?"

"The Black *Darwîshes* do not employ the knife," answered Abu Tabâh; "they employ strange and more subtle weapons."

I stared hard at him in the darkness. I thought I knew my Cairo, but this sounded unpleasantly mysterious. However —

"I am indebted to you, Abu Tabâh," I said, "for your timely warning. As you know, I always personally avoid any possibility of misunderstanding in regard to my relations with Egyptian womenfolk."

"With some rare exceptions," agreed Abu Tabâh, "particulars of which escape my memory at the moment, you have always been a model of discretion, Kernaby Pasha."

"I will warn my friend," I said hastily, "of the view of his conduct mistakenly taken by the gentleman in the black turban."

"It is well," replied Abu Tabâh; "we shall meet again ere long."

With that and the customary dignified salutations he departed, leaving me wondering what hidden significance lay in his words, "we shall meet again ere long."

Experience had taught me that Abu Tabâh's warnings were not to be lightly dismissed, and I knew enough of the fanaticism of those strange Eastern sects whereof the *Rifa'îyeh*, or Black *Darwîshes*, was one, to realize that it would prove an unhealthy amusement to interfere with their domestic affairs. Felix Bréton, who possessed the rare gift of capturing and transferring to canvas the atmosphere of the East with the opulent colorings and vivid contrasts which constitute its charm, had nevertheless but little practical experience of the manners and customs of the golden Orient. He had leased a large studio situated on the roof of a fine old Cairene palace hidden away behind the Street of the Booksellers and almost in the shadow of the Mosque of el-Azhar. His romantic spirit had prompted him after a time to give up his rooms at the Continental and to take up his abode in the apartment adjoining the studio; that is to say, completely to cut himself off from European life and to become an inhabitant of the Oriental city. With his imperfect knowledge of the practical side of native life in the East, I did not envy him; but I was fully alive to his danger, isolated as he was from the European community, indeed from modernity; for out of the boulevards of modern Cairo into the streets of the

Arabian Nights is but a step, yet a step that bridges the gulf of centuries.

As I entered his studio on the following morning, I discovered him at work upon the extraordinary picture "Danse Funébre." Shejeret ed-Durr was posing in the dress of an ancient priestess of Isis. Bréton briefly greeted me, waving his hand towards a cushioned *dîwan* before which stood a little coffee-table bearing decanters, siphons, cigarettes, and other companionable paraphernalia. Making myself comfortable, I studied the picture and the model.

"Danse Funébre" was an extraordinary conception, representing an elaborately furnished modern room, apparently that of an antiquary or Egyptologist; for a multitude of queer relics decorated the walls, cabinets, and the large table at which a man was seated. Boldly represented immediately to the left of his chair stood a mummy in an ornate sarcophagus, and forth from the swathed figure into the light cast downwards from an antique lamp, floated a beautiful spirit shape — that of an Egyptian priestess. Upon her face was an expression of intense anger, as, her fingers crooked in sinister fashion, she bent over the man at the table.

The mummy and sarcophagus depicted on the canvas stood before me against the wall of the studio, the lid resting beside the case. It was moulded, as is sometimes seen, to represent the face and figure of the occupant and was as fine an example of the kind as I had met with. The mummy was that of a priestess and dancer of the Great Temple at Philae, and it had been lent by the museum authorities for the purpose of Bréton's picture.

His enthusiasm at first seeing Shejeret ed-Durr was explainable by the really uncanny resemblance which the girl bore to the modeled figure. Studying her, from my seat on the dîwan, as she posed in that gauzy raiment depicted upon the lid of the sarcophagus, it seemed indeed that the ancient priestess was reborn in the form of Shejeret ed-Durr the *ghazîyeh*. Bréton had evidently tabooed make-up, with the exception of the characteristic black bordering to the eyes (which appeared in the presentment of the servant of Isis); and seen now in its natural coloring the face of the dancing-girl had undoubted beauty.

Presently, whilst the model rested, I informed Bréton of my conversation with Abu Tabâh; but, as I had anticipated, he was skeptical to the point of derision.

"My dear Kernaby," he said, "is it likely that I am going to interrupt my work now that I have found such an inspiring model, because some ridiculous *darwîsh* disapproves?"

"It is highly unlikely," I admitted; "but do not make the mistake of treating the matter lightly. You are right off the map here, and Cairo is not Paris."

"It is a great deal safer!" he cried in his boisterous fashion, "and infinitely more interesting."

But my mind was far from easy; for in the dark eyes of the model, when their glance rested upon Felix Bréton, there was that to have aroused poisonous sentiments in the bosom of the Man of the Glare.

III

During the course of the following month I saw Felix Bréton two or three times, and he was enthusiastic about the progress of his picture and the beauty of his model. The first hint that I received of the strange idea which was to lead to stranger happenings came one afternoon when he had called upon me at Shepheard's.

"Do you believe in reincarnation, Kernaby?" he asked suddenly.

I stared at him in surprise.

"Regardless of my personal views on the matter," I replied, "in what way does the subject interest you?"

Momentarily he hesitated; then —

"The resemblance between Yâsmîna" (this was the real name of Shejeret ed-Durr) "and the priestess of Isis," he said, "appears to me too marked to be explainable by mere coincidence. If the mummy were my personal property I should unwrap it ——"

"Do you seriously desire me to believe that you regard Yâsmîna as a reincarnation of the elder lady?"

"That or a lineal descendant," he answered. "The tribe of the *Ghawâzi* is of unknown antiquity and may very well be descended from those temple dancers of the days of the Pharaohs. If you have studied the ancient wall paintings, you cannot have failed to observe that the dancing girls represented have entirely different forms from those of any other women depicted and from those of the ordinary Egyptian women of to-day."

His enthusiasm was tremendous; he was one of those uncomfortable fanatics who will ride a theory to the death.

"I cannot say that I have noticed it," I replied. "Your knowledge of the female form divine is doubtless more extensive than mine."

"My dear Kernaby," he cried excitedly, "to the trained eye the difference is extraordinary. Until I saw Yâsmîna I had believed the peculiar form to which I refer to be extinct like the blue enamel and the sacred lotus. If it is not reincarnation it is heredity."

I could not help thinking that it more closely resembled insanity than either; but since Bréton had made no reference to the wearer of the black turban, I experienced less anxiety respecting his physical than his mental welfare.

Three days later there was a dramatic development. Drifting idly into Bréton's studio one morning I found him pacing the place in despair and glaring
at his unfinished canvas like a man distraught.

"Where is Shejeret ed-Durr?" I inquired.

"Gone!" he replied. "She disappeared yesterday and I can find no trace of
her."

"Surely the excellent Suleyman, proprietor of the dancing establishment,
can assist you?"

"I tell you," cried Bréton savagely, "that she has disappeared. No one
knows what has become of her."

I looked at him in dismay. He presented a mournful spectacle. He was unshaven and his dark hair was wildly disordered. His despair was more acute
than I should have supposed possible in the circumstances; and I concluded
that his interest in Yâsmîna was deeper than I had assumed or that I was incapable of comprehending the artistic temperament. I suppose the Gallic
blood in him had something to do with it, but I was unspeakably distressed
to observe that the man was on the verge of tears.

Consolation was impossible, and I left him pacing his empty studio distractedly. That night at an unearthly hour, long after I had retired to my own
apartments, he came to Shepheard's. Being shown into my room, and the servant having departed —

"Yâsmîna is dead!" he burst out, standing there, a disheveled figure, just
within the doorway.

"What!" I exclaimed, standing up from the table at which I had been writing and confronting him. "Dead? Do you mean ——"

"He has murdered her!" said Bréton, in a dull monotonous voice—"that
fiend of whom you warned me."

I was appalled; for I had been utterly unprepared for such a tragedy.

"Who discovered her?"

"No one discovered her; she will never be discovered! He has buried her
body in some secret spot in the desert."

My amazement grew with every word that he uttered, and presently —

"Then how in Heaven's name did you learn of her murder?" I asked.

Felix Bréton, who had begun to pace up and down the room, a truly pitiable
figure, paused and looked at me wildly.

"You will think that I am mad, Kernaby," he said; "but I must tell you—I
must tell someone. I could see that you were incredulous when I spoke to you
of reincarnation, but I was right, Kernaby, I was right! Either that or my reason is deserting me."

My opinion inclined distinctly in the direction of the latter theory, but I remained silent, watching Bréton's haggard face.

"Tonight," he continued, "as I sat looking at my unfinished picture and trying to imagine what could have become of Yâsmîna, the mummy — the mummy of the priestess — *spoke to me!*"

I slowly sank back into my chair. I was now assured that Felix Bréton had formed a sudden and intense infatuation for Yâsmîna and that *her* mysterious disappearance had deranged his sensitive mind. Words failed me; I could think of nothing to say; and bending towards me his haggard face —

"It whispered to me," he said, "in *her* voice — in my own language, French, as I have taught it to her; just a few imperfect words, but sufficient to convey to me the story of the tragedy. Kernaby, what does it mean? Is it possible that her spirit, released from the body of Yâsmîna, has returned to that which I firmly believe it formerly inhabited?..."

I had had the misfortune to be a party to some distressing scenes, but few had affected me so unpleasantly as this. That poor Felix Bréton was raving I could not doubt, but having persuaded him to spend the night at Shepheard's and having seen him safely to bed, I returned to my own room to endeavor to work out the problem of what steps I should take regarding him on the morrow.

In the morning, however, he seemed more composed, having shaved and generally rendered himself more presentable; but the wild look still lingered in his eyes and I could see that the strange obsession had secured a firm hold upon him. He discussed the matter quite calmly during breakfast, and invited me to visit the scene of this supernatural happening. I assented, and hailing *arabîyeh* we drove together to the studio.

There was nothing abnormal in the appearance of the place, but I examined the mummy and the mummy case with a new curiosity; for if Felix Bréton was not mad (and this was a point upon which I recognized my incompetence to decide) the phantom voice was clearly the product of some trick. However, I was unable to discover anything to account for it. The sarcophagus stood against the outer wall of the studio and near to a large lattice window before which was draped a heavy tapestry curtain for the purpose of excluding undesirable light upon that side of the model's throne. There was no balcony outside the window, which was fully, thirty feet from the street below; therefore unless someone had been hiding in the window recess beside the sarcophagus, trickery appeared to be out of the question. Turning to Bréton, who was watching me haggardly —

"You searched the recess last night?" I said.

"I did — immediately. There was no one there. There was no one anywhere in the studio; and when I looked out of the open window, the street below was deserted from end to end."

Naturally, I took it for granted that he would avoid the place, at any rate by night; and I said as much, as we passed along the Muski together. I can never forget the wildness in his eyes as he turned to me.

"I *must* go back, Kernaby," he said. "It seems like desertion, base and cowardly."

IV

Bréton did not join me at dinner that evening as we had arranged that he should do, and towards the hour of ten o'clock, growing more and more uneasy on his behalf, I set out for the studio, half hoping that I should meet him. I saw nothing of him, however, as I crossed the Ezbekîyeh Gardens and the Atabet el-Khadrâ into the Muski. From thence onward to the Rondpoint the dark and narrow streets were almost deserted, and from the corner of the Shâria el-Khordâgîya to the Street of the Bookbinders I met with no living thing save a lean and furtive cat.

My footsteps echoed hollowly from wall to wall of the overhanging buildings, as I approached the door giving access to the courtyard from which a stair communicated with the studio above. The moonlight, slanting down into the ancient place, left more than half of it in densest shadow, but just touched the railing of the balcony and the lower part of the *mushrabîyeh* screen masking what once had been the *harem* apartments from the view of one entering the courtyard. Far above me, through an open lattice, a dim light shone out, though vaguely. This part of the house was bathed in the radiance of the moon, which dimmed that of the studio lamp; for the open window was the window of Bréton's studio.

The door at the foot of the stairs was partly open, and I ascended slowly, since the place was quite dark and I was forced to feel my way around the eccentric turnings introduced by an Arab architect to whom simplicity had evidently been an abomination.

A modern door had been fitted to the studio; and although this door was also unfastened, I rapped loudly, but, receiving no answer, entered the studio. It was empty. The lamp was lighted, as I had observed from below, and a faint aroma of Turkish tobacco smoke hung in the air. Clearly, Bréton had left but a few moments earlier; and I judged it probable that he would be returning very shortly, for had he set out for Shepheard's he would not have left his door unlocked, and in any event I should have met him on the way. Therefore, having glanced into the inner room, which, latterly, Bréton had been using as a bedroom, I sat down on the *diwan* and prepared to await his return.

The lamp whose light I had seen shining through the window was that which hung before the model's throne, and the curtain which usually draped the window recess had been partially pulled aside, so that from where I sat I could see part of the centre lattice, which was open. My mind at this time was entirely occupied with uneasy speculations regarding Bréton, and although I had glanced more than once at the large unfinished picture on the easel, from which the face of Shejeret ed-Durr peered out across the shoulder of the seated man, and several times had looked at the mummy set upright in its painted sarcophagus, no sense of the uncanny had touched me or in any way prepared me for the amazing manifestation which I was about to witness.

How long I had sat there I cannot say exactly; possibly for ten minutes or a quarter of an hour: when, suddenly, an eerie whisper crept through the stillness of the big room!

Since I had more than once been temporarily tricked into belief in the supernatural, by means of certain ingenious devices, I did not readily fall a victim to the mysterious nature of the present occurrence. Yet I must confess that my heart gave a great leap and I was forced to exert all my will to control my nerves. I sat quite still, listening intently for a repetition of that evil whisper. Then, in the stillness, it came again.

"Felix," it breathed, "because of you I lie dead in a grave in the desert.... I died for you, Felix, and now I am so lonely...."

The whispering voice offered no clue to the age or the sex of the speaker; for a true whisper is toneless. But the words, as Bréton had declared, were uttered in broken French and spoken with a curious accent.

It ceased, that ghostly whispering; and I realized that my nerves could stand no more of it; for that it came or seemed to come from the mummy of the priestess was a fact as undeniable as it was horrible.

Resorting to action, I sprang up and leaped across the room, grasping first at the curtain draped in the window on the right of the sarcophagus. I jerked it fully aside. The recess was empty. All three lattices were open, on the right, left, and in the centre of the window; but, craning out from the latter, I saw the street below to be vacant from end to end.

Stepping back into the room, and metaphorically clutching my courage with both hands, I approached the sarcophagus, peered behind it, all around it, and, finally, into the swathed face of the mummy itself. Nothing rewarded my search. But the studio of Felix Bréton seemed to have become icily cold; at any rate I found myself to be shivering; and walking deliberately, although it cost me a monstrous effort to do so, I descended the dark winding stairway into the courtyard, and, on regaining the street, discovered to my intense annoyance that my brow was wet with cold perspiration.

I had taken no more than ten paces in the direction of the Suk es-Sudan when I heard the sound of approaching footsteps, and for some reason (I can only suppose as a result of my highly strung condition) I stepped into the shelter of a narrow gateway, where I could see without being seen, and there awaited the appearance of the one who approached.

It was Felix Bréton, his face showing ghastly in the moonlight as he turned the corner. I could not be certain if a mere echo had deceived me, but I thought I could detect faintly the softer footfalls of someone who was following him. From my cover I had an uninterrupted view of the entrance to the house which I had just left; and without showing myself I watched Bréton approach the door. At its threshold he seemed to hesitate; and in that brief hesitancy were illustrated the conflicting emotions driving the man. I recalled the words he had spoken to me that morning. "I must go back, Kernaby; it seems like desertion, base and cowardly." He opened the door and disappeared.

As he did so, a second figure crossed from the shadows on the opposite side of the street — that is, the side upon which I was concealed; and in turn advanced towards the door. As he passed my hiding-place I acted. Without an instant's hesitation I hurled myself upon him.

How he avoided that furious attack — if he did avoid it — or whether in the darkness I miscalculated my spring, I do not know to this day: I only know that I missed my objective, stumbled, recovered myself... and turned with clenched fists to find Abu Tabâh confronting me!

"Kernaby Pasha!" he cried.

"Abu Tabâh!" said I dazedly.

"I perceive that I am not alone in my anxiety for the welfare of M. Felix Bréton."

"But why were you following him? I narrowly missed assaulting you."

"Very narrowly," he agreed in his gentle manner; "but you ask me why I was following M. Bréton. I was following him because I have seen so many of those who have crossed the path of the Black *Darwîshes* meet with violent and inexplicable deaths."

"Murder?" I whispered.

"Not murder — suicide. Therefore, observing, as I had anticipated, a strangeness in your friend's behavior, I have watched him."

"The strangeness of his behavior is easily accounted for," I said. And excitedly, for the horror of the episode in the studio was still strongly upon me, I told him of the whispering mummy.

"These are very dreadful things of which you speak, Kernaby Pasha," he admitted, "but I warned you that it was ill to incur the enmity of the Black *Darwîshes*. That there is a scheme afoot to compass the self-destruction or insanity of your friend is now evident to me; and he has brought this calamity upon himself; for the words which he believed to be spoken by the spirit of the girl Yâsmîna would not have affected him so unpleasantly if his attitude towards her had been marked by proper restraint and the affair confined within suitable limitations."

"Quite so. But although the Black *Darwîshes* may be both malignant and clever, that uncanny whispering is beyond the control of natural forces."

"Such is not my opinion," replied Abu Tabâh. "A spirit does not mistake one person for another; and the whispering voice addressed itself to 'Felix' when Felix was not present. I believe, Kernaby Pasha, that you are the possessor of a pair of excellent opera-glasses? May I suggest that you return to Shepheard's and procure them."

V

The platform of the minaret seemed very cold to the touch of my stockinged feet; for I had left my shoes at the entrance to the mosque below in accordance with custom; and now, from the wooden balcony, I overlooked the neighboring roofs of Cairo, and Abu Tabâh, beside me, pointed to where a vague patch of light broke the darkness beneath us to the left.

"The window of M. Felix Bréton's studio," he said.

Raising the glasses to his eyes, he gazed in that direction, whilst I also peered thither and succeeded in making out the well of the courtyard and the roofs of the buildings to right and left of it. It was not evident to me for what Abu Tabâh was looking, and when presently he lowered the glasses and turned to me I expressed my doubts in words.

"It is surely evident," I said, speaking, as I now almost invariably did to the *imám*, in English, of which he had a perfect mastery, "that we have little chance of discovering anything from here, since nothing was visible from the studio window. Furthermore, who save Yâsmîna could have spoken in the manner which I have related and in broken French?"

"An eavesdropper," he replied, "might have profited by the lessons which Yâsmîna received from M. Bréton; and all vocal characteristics are lost in a whisper. In the second place, Yâsmîna is not dead."

"What!" I cried.

Although, when Bréton had informed me of her death, I myself had doubted him, for some reason the ghostly whisper had convinced me as it had convinced him.

"She has been kept a prisoner during the past week in a house belonging to one of the Black *Darwîshes*," continued Abu Tabâh; "but my agents succeeded in tracing her this morning. By my orders, however, she has not been allowed to return to her home."

"And what was the object of those orders?"

"That I might learn for what purpose she had been made to disappear," replied Abu Tabâh; "and I have learned it tonight."

"Then you think that the whispering mummy——"

He suddenly clutched my arm.

"Quick! raise your glasses!" he said softly. "On the roof of the house to the left of the light. There is the whispering mummy!"

Strung up to a high pitch of excitement, I gazed through the glasses in the direction indicated by my companion. Without difficulty I discerned him — a man wearing a black turban — who crept like some ungainly cat along the flat roof, carrying in his hand what looked like one of those sugar canes which pass for a delicacy among the natives, but which to European eyes appear more suitable for curtain-poles than sweetmeats. Springing perilously across a yawning gulf, the wearer of the black turban gained the roof of the studio, crept along for some little distance further, and then, lying prone, began slowly to lower the bamboo rod in the direction of the lighted window.

I found that unconsciously I had suspended my respiration, and now, breathlessly, as the truth came home to me —

"It is a speaking-tube!" I cried, "I cannot see the end of it, but no doubt it is curved so as to protrude through the side of the lattice window. Do you look, Abu Tabâh: I propose to act."

Thrusting the glasses into the *imam*'s hand, I took my Colt repeater from my pocket, and, having peered for some seconds steadily in the direction of the dimly visible *Darwîsh*, I opened fire! I had fired five shots in the heat of my anger at that sinister crouching figure, ere Abu Tabâh seized my wrist.

"Stop!" he cried; "do you forget where you stand?"

Truly I had forgotten in my indignation, or I should not have outraged his feelings by firing from the minaret of a mosque. But sufficient of my wrath remained to occasion me a thrill of satisfaction, when, peering through the dusk, I saw the *Darwîsh* throw up his arms and disappear from view.

"There is blood in the courtyard," said Abu Tabâh; "but Ahmad es-Kebîr has fled. Therefore he still lives, and his anger will be not the less but the greater. Depart from Cairo, M. Bréton: it is my counsel to you."

"But," cried Felix Bréton, glaring wildly at the big canvas on the easel, "I must finish my picture. As Yâsmîna is alive, she must return, and I must finish my picture!"

"Yâsmîna cannot return," replied Abu Tabâh, fixing his weird eyes upon the speaker. "I have caused her to be banished from Cairo." He raised his hand, checking Bréton's hot words ere they were uttered. "Recriminations are unavailing. Her presence disturbs the peace of the city, and the peace of the city it is my duty to maintain."

THE END

Notes for Further Reading

For those readers interested in discovering additional ancient Egyptian supernatural tales and mummy stories, Brian J. Frost's *The Essential Guide to Mummy Literature* (Scarecrow Press, 2008) is an excellent reference guide to learn about hundreds of short stories and novels. In addition, readers fascinated by the ancient Egyptian past and its enduring hold on modern readers might find much to value in Susan D. Cowie and Tom Johnson's *The Mummy in Fact, Fiction, and Film* (McFarland & Company, 2002) and David Huckvale's *Ancient Egypt in the Popular Imagination: Building a Fantasy in Film, Literature, Music and Art* (McFarland & Company, 2012).

I can also recommend several previously published literary anthologies devoted to mummy stories. These include Bill Pronzini's *Mummy! A Chrestomathy of Cryptology* (1980) and Vic Gidalia's *The Mummy Walks Among Us* (1971). The latter includes Frank Belknap Long's sublimely weird, "A Visitor from Egypt" (1930). Similarly, readers might want to take obtain a copy of John Richard Stephens's *Into the Mummy's Tomb* (2001). Stephens's anthology notably includes Agatha Christie's "The Adventure of the Egyptian Tomb" (1924). Chad Arment's anthology, *Out of the Sand* (Coachwhip, 2008) reprints Sir Arthur Conan Doyle's other ancient Egyptian supernatural tale, "The Ring of Thoth" (1890) as well as Algernon Blackwood's "Sand" (1912).

While by no means an exhaustive list, the aforementioned works are excellent starting points for those readers wanting to descend deeper into works similar to those included in this volume and further appreciate the mysteries of the ancient Egyptian supernatural tale.

Original Dates of Publication

Jane Webb Loudon, *The Mummy: A Tale of the Twenty-Second Century* (1827)

Edgar Allan Poe, "Some Words With a Mummy" *American Whig Review* (1845)

Louisa May Alcott, "Lost in a Pyramid, or the Mummy's Curse" *The New World* (1869)

Arthur Conan Doyle, "Lot No. 249" *Harper's Magazine* (1892)

Bram Stoker, *The Jewel of Seven Stars* (1903)

Tennessee Williams, "The Vengeance of Nitocris" *Weird Tales* (1928)

H. Rider Haggard, "Smith and the Pharaohs" (1921) in *Smith and the Pharaohs and Other Tales*

Frank Belknap Long, "The Dog-Eared God" *Weird Tales* (November 1926)

E. Hoffmann Price, "Tarbis of the Lake" *Weird Tales* (February 1934)

John Murray Reynolds, "Soul of Ra-Moses" *Weird Tales* (May 1940)

Algernon Blackwood, "The Wings of Horus" *Century Magazine* (1914)

Algernon Blackwood, "A Descent Into Egypt" in *Incredible Adventures* (1914)

George Griffith, "The Lost Elixir" *Pall Mall Magazine* (1903)

Sax Rohmer, "The Cat" *The New Magazine* (1914)

Sax Rohmer, "The Whispering Mummy" in *Tales of Secret Egypt* (1918)

Jonathan E. Lewis is an editor and a writer who divides his time between Connecticut and Southern California. After working for many years as a foreign policy analyst in Washington D.C., he has shifted his career focus to supernatural fiction, film history, and popular culture. This is his first book.